A LUKE SANZ NOVEL: BOOK 2

A DANCE
WITH THE
BULLY

SIG. ALEXANDER

ADVANCE READERS COPY

LANSBURG
MEDIA

"Cladhaire," written by Christina L. Pearson © 2024 and used by permission.

Covert Art: https://www.creativindie.com/ Derek Murphy

ISBN-13: 979-8-9886367-3-1 - Paperback
ISBN-13: 979-8-9886367-4-8 – eBook
ISBN-13: 979-8-9886367-5-5 – Hardcover

10 9 8 7 6 5 4 3 2 1
First Edition

For Dona, my wife and partner

For Chloe, Christian, and Jaidyn,
bring your best to every situation

Cladhaire

Born from a line of gravediggers
Buriers of the military's dead
Scoundrels, villains, and rogues
To the spoils of war, they're wed

They took, despised, and destroyed
All that was good in their presence
No one was safe in a wicked world
Evil was the sweat of their essence

So, what chance does a child have
Born into a cruel family, such as this
Beaten, used, punished, and abused
Where does one find his own bliss?

You give what you get, taking control
And all will bow down to you, in fear
With no room for trust or friendships
Only one exception, his sister, dear

Christina L. Pearson
© 07-20-2024

PROLOGUE - August 13, 1990

Jimmy Cladhaire was early to meet with two men at the Campbell Bridge. He typically was late for anything if he decided to show up at all. At six foot three inches in height, he was not necessarily imposing since he was thin and lanky, yet he had sinewy muscles and very little fat, if any. Externally, what was evident about the eighteen-year-old was his scruff and messy red hair, with fades on the side of his head. He kept the top part of his matted hair looking like a mop. Internally, nobody knew that Jimmy had a psychic glimpse into others. Mainly, he could tell whether somebody in his presence was a threat or if they would run off with their tail between their legs in fear. Jimmy's abilities evolved over the years into a type of discernment. He could tell if somebody feared, loathed, or liked him and whether they wanted to run, fight or stay in his presence. He could also sense if somebody planned on attacking him.

He drove to the local burger joint, walked up to the counter, and ordered a bacon cheeseburger with fries and a soda. He paid the cashier and served himself his drink. He heard voices and saw a group of fellow high school students sitting in one of the booths. Todd Ordley waved. Alyssa Mars was sitting with Todd. She leaned in and whispered something to Todd, but Jimmy was too far away to overhear. Two other couples sat with their backs facing Jimmy, but he was unsure who they were. He heard a laugh and thought immediately it had to be that grease monkey, Benji. This would mean it was Birdy or another member of Alyssa's entourage.

The server brought his tray of food to him, so he looked for a seat. Todd waved him over again. He looked at the opposite end of the joint and saw it was crowded. He gave in, walked toward

1

Todd, and immediately sensed that Alyssa and Benji wanted to leave. He did not sense that reaction from Birdy, which made him feel good since he had a crush on her since he saw her in elementary school many years before. He chose an empty table adjacent to Todd.

"Hey, Jimmy, how are you?" Birdy asked.

"Doing well, Birdy. It's good to see you." He stuffed some fries into his mouth nervously and started chewing. "What's cooking, Todd?"

"Just thought I would get something to eat before practicing this afternoon. Looking forward to senior year. How about you?" Todd asked.

"I have to meet some dudes for my dad." Jimmy sensed that Todd was annoyed at him and realized Todd meant something else. "Oh yeah, we'll have a pretty good year." Jimmy could sometimes use his abilities to help him deal with conversations. He just tended to direct everything to the dark part of humanity. He started eating his hamburger, realizing he would have to leave in a few minutes. He ate silently, aware that neither Benji nor Alyssa had acknowledged his existence, which satisfied him morbidly. "What's up, grease monkey?" Jimmy asked as he reached over and slapped Benji's shoulder. *That feeling again of running off*, he sensed.

"Why are you such an ass?" Benji asked slowly.

Jimmy kept eating and, instead of answering, looked at Birdy, who smiled and winked at him. He couldn't sense if she liked him, but she did not fear or dislike him. He took a drink from his soda and swallowed his last bite. He looked at his watch and realized he was kind of late. "Nothing personal, monkey boy. You know you're my favorite, don't you." He stood up and started eating the last of his fries.

"Jimmy, there's no need to be rude. We invited you over," Todd said.

"We, ha?"

"Jimmy, just get out of here. All of us have tried to get on your good side for years, but you just crap over us instead," Alyssa said, finally speaking.

"So eloquent, Alyssa. Yet your first thought when you saw me was to run out of here."

Alyssa appeared stunned and turned her attention to her food.

"Jimmy, we all have known each other since we were born. My mom told me we shared cribs when we were toddlers. Just sit down, and we can talk it out." Birdy continued to look at him and smiled.

What he wanted to do was to sit and have a conversation with her. He needed the time to tell her that he had loved her for years and was always impressed by how she reacted to his presence. Once, when they were kids, she saw him crying after hurting his arm playing on the swing at their school. Birdy sat with him, caressed his arm, and sang a song. It was *Down in the Valley* by Bert Berns and Solomon Burke. Since then, he had pined about being a part of Birdy's life. The trouble was that she was a big flirt and received attention from many young men, not just from Benji, who happened to be just another suitor. What he yearned for most in life and envied in others was what these four had—the ability to have relationships with others that were not caustic. He wanted at least a friendship with Birdy, not necessarily a romantic one. He never had a girlfriend and never thought of it.

"I'm sorry, guys ... I have a chore to attend to." Jimmy began to walk away and turned around. "Thanks for inviting me over, Todd. See you in a couple of hours." He walked out of the restaurant, jumped into his red 1969 Pontiac *Firebird*, and shot out of the parking lot carelessly, almost causing a car accident. Within five minutes, he arrived at Campbell Bridge on Red Hill Road and parked in the easement near the bridge's south entrance. He grabbed a sealed manila envelope, which his father said had $10,000 in cash. He stepped out of the vehicle and saw a black car at the north entrance to the bridge. He walked to the middle of the bridge and saw two men begin to walk toward him. They were dressed in black and appeared to be two hardened-looking men. *I'm going to stab this guy and take his money,* he sensed coming from one of the men. *I'll toss his body over the side,* he sensed from the other man. He winced as if he was in pain and looked back toward his car. It was too far away. The men were getting closer. Their thoughts were full of violence, and they wanted the envelope in Jimmy's hand as much as they wanted him to bleed.

Just then, a car parked on the north end of the bridge. The men turned around and looked at the car, which flashed its headlights. The car looked familiar, but Jimmy could not place it from this distance. The men turned back and commenced walking toward him. He put the envelope in his pocket. He sensed the men were alarmed, but it was too late. He pushed forward and closed the distance with the first man, who was now trying to grab for the knife. Jimmy struck the man's chest violently, and when the man doubled over, he picked him up and threw him over the bridge. *Run, run,* he sensed. Jimmy sprinted toward the man and kicked his left leg. The man fell and struck his head on the pavement as he descended. Jimmy walked up and stomped on the man's torso. The sound of broken ribs resonated in the air. He leaned down, picked up the man, brought him to the bridge's guardrail, and leaned the man on it. Just then, he heard a siren. He turned and saw a police car.

"Let go of that man, Jimmy."

It was a local police officer he knew from prior encounters. He released the man and put his hands up.

"Turn around and put your hands behind your back, Jimmy."

He followed the officers' orders and turned around. The car on the other side of the bridge turned around and left the area. It was his father's work car. *I'm blind to my father's intentions,* he thought. Jimmy was cognizant that he could not sense what his father had planned for him.

The officer placed him in handcuffs, searched him, and took

out the envelope from his pocket. The officer then put him in the cage of the patrol car in the back seat and opened the front door.

Jimmy heard but could not see the officer tear open the envelope and then grunt and toss the open envelope on the front seat before running off to check on the man lying on the ground. Jimmy looked into the front seat and saw the envelope was full of newspaper cut in the shape of currency. The realization came to him immediately that his father had tried to have him killed. It didn't surprise him at all since his father beat him within an inch of death on many occasions. What he missed most in life was what Todd and the others had—the ability to hang out and be with friends. A loving relationship was absent in his life and foreign to him. He only loved his sister, Karen, but they couldn't even have a normal conversation after she was injured several years ago. He thought of telling the officer about the man he threw over the bridge but decided that doing so was not in his interest.

CHAPTER ONE

First Day as a Senior at the LC - August 19, 1991

My boss refused to approve my leave. I only hoped that my dreams would be just that, dreams. In truth, I was a failure and a shell of what I once was. I allowed the fear and threat of losing my safe government job to control my failure to prevent my very reason for being. I knew better but let the concern and the nightmares pass. I was set in life and comfortable where I was. I found myself at home staring at a screen on my wall again. I banged on my desk as priests, bishops, and cardinals were being drug out of buildings on the Vatican compounds. A pile of dead holy men grew in the middle of the square as hoodlums beat and cut the throats of the men.

I was supposed to prevent this day; instead, I sat safely in the comfort of my home in Palmer, Alaska. I was a failure and amounted to nothing, just like my father inferred I would. I grabbed my gun from my desk and removed the magazine and emptied it and removed the round from the chamber. I added one round to the magazine and returned it to the gun and pulled the slide back. I put the gun in my mouth and pulled
...

Luke woke up with the inside of his mouth on fire. The back of his head felt like gooey mush where his skull and hair should be. He jumped off the bed, ran to the bathroom to look in the mirror. He was fine. The gore was gone, and he was intact. He realized he was supposed to remember something. It was pandemonium. He recalled the mountain of priests in black clothing and red sashes. On top of the mound was a man in white clothing with dark stains of blood, but he progressively forgot what led to him placing a firearm in his mouth and taking the easy way out.

A severe void remained in his thoughts, and he could not place it. Instead of dwelling on the echo of the dream and the emptiness, he decided to shower. He turned on the water and took the cold water full on. He wanted to jump out but instead, took the cold for a minute or two until it grew warm and then scalding hot. This gave him something else to think of.

Once dressed, he lay back on his bed and closed his eyes. His alarm clock activated, causing him to dart back into his bed. He reached over to shut it off.

"First day of school … are you ready for it?" Sebastian asked, showing himself.

"What did I dream?" Luke asked.

"A battle of some type at the Vatican. It's not a new dream, but I cannot remember much. It may be why I'm here. I don't know when it will happen, but it's in the future," Sebastian said.

"How can I prevent a calamity if I cannot see it?" Luke asked.

"You will, Luke. We will not fail. You are the protector, and I am your guardian." Sebastian said, slamming his halberd staff down on the carpet. It somehow did not have the effect it did on a hard surface.

The year before, Sebastian, Luke, Father D, and Father Robert defeated the demon Avandeil, preventing him from destroying Luke's home and family. Luke's growth led to the realization that he was destined to protect the Catholic church in the future from some unknown event or catastrophe. Something he did not feel prepared for. Luke received visions in the form of dreams, and when he touched a person, he saw something that could be used to help the person or a situation he was facing.

Luke rose and walked downstairs into the empty kitchen.

Once Daniel left the home, his mother no longer woke to make them breakfast. Standing before the refrigerator, he read the note in thick black marker. *LUKE, THINK CAREER!* His father had been at him all summer to work and find a career. He spent the summer helping his friend Benji at his auto shop near the center of Lansburg, Laio's Customs. It wasn't enough for his father, who wanted him to attend college and have a career.

He quickly whipped six eggs into a froth and added some cooked bacon from the fridge. After slicing some potatoes, he cooked them in a frying pan. He made mixed eggs, or revoltillo, with bacon and some diced green pepper.

"Smells great," Junior said, walking into the kitchen. "Tell me you made some home fries."

Luke served his younger brother breakfast. "Sure did ... just for you." He avoided carbohydrates because he gained weight so quickly.

"Thanks, bro. Is this like our last meal before going back to the electric chair at the LC?" Junior asked.

Junior was in the eleventh grade at Lansburg Center High School. Everyone called the school the LC. They lived in the city of Lansburg within the county of Loudon in Virginia. Luke was a senior. Something he should have been proud of but regretted having to spend another year at the school. His girlfriend, Alyssa, and best friend, Benji, were seniors at the LC. Luke felt closed in and constrained by the school's walls. In truth, he just wanted to start his life, but college and a career were not in his thoughts. He had no master plan other than working out in his home gym or running in the woods.

Luke laughed before joining his younger brother at the table. "I thought we would appreciate some protein before returning to the torture chamber."

Junior laughed, and they both pumped their fists together. "I could smell the eggs cooking, and I expected mom to be here."

"You're funny, Junior. Did you forget that Daniel lives with Joyce and our grandparents," Luke said.

Junior appeared somber and pensive. "Do you mean mom only made us breakfast because Daniel lived here and was going to school?"

Luke shrugged and let a tear drop from his face. He turned and wiped it away with his shirt, hoping his younger brother did not notice. Junior and Luke loved their parents but also came to terms with the fact that they were secondary to their older brother, Daniel, who shined in their parents' and grandparents' eyes. "Finish up ... I want to get there early and meet up with Alyssa before class."

Junior approached the sink and rinsed his plate before placing it in the dishwasher. Afterward, he walked to the refrigerator and took the letter his father left for him. "Think career. You don't want to hear this, but Dad is right. You need to consider what you want to do for a career."

Luke stood up, grabbed the paper from his brother's hand, folded it, and placed it in his backpack. "I know, even if I don't want to know." He smiled at Junior and motioned for him to follow.

On the drive to school, the brothers sat in silence. The year before, Luke considered joining the Army as soon as possible. He had seen himself as an Army Ranger in one of his dreams, but a summer of working and horsing around with Benji in his garage showed him that any place was better than school. He tried to convince himself that he no longer needed to run into the Army. However, this was likely the natural laziness built into a teenager's persona. At times, he was content to sit around doing nothing. He typically had to fight a mental battle before he convinced himself to run to his Fortress of Calmness—his gym in the garage.

Benji's pearl white four-door sedan, a 1980 Plymouth *Gran Fury*, was parked in the middle of the parking lot. Luke parked his two-door coupe, a 1987 Buick Grand National, next to Benji's car. Luke stepped out to say hello to his buddy, but Benji hugged him ... *I fell backward into darkness and now sat inside a car's front driver's seat. I heard a girl moaning behind me. I turned around and saw Benji lying between Birdy's open legs. Alyssa's best friend and Benji's love interest. I looked away, shocked at the sight* ... he pushed Benji back and moved his hands away from his buddy.

"What did you see? Was I with Birdy?" Benji asked with a huge smile.

"Yes ... I am too young to see such things," Luke said, laughing, walking toward the school entrance near the cafeteria.

Benji laughed and jumped in place like a kernel on a hot plate. "It's my year. I can see it."

"Yes, you're going to be a teenage daddy this year if you don't go buy condoms, like real soon," Luke said.

"What's a condom, Luke?" Junior asked, laughing.

"I think you know what a condom is, Junior. It's what our brother Daniel failed to use when he was hanging with Joyce," Luke said, joking. Still, he was happy that Joyce had a one-month-old son named Tristan.

They walked across the tarmac from where the buses were dropping off students. In the distance, he could see Alyssa waving at him by the entrance. She was not alone. Her friends, Birdy, Linnet, and Sandy were with her.

Luke and Alyssa spent much of their free time together during the summer. They meshed exceptionally well, having endured when Avandeil locked her away in the portal in his house last May. Avandeil released her from that supernatural prison as it returned to its ethereal form.

They hugged as if they had not spent the prior afternoon together. Fortunately, when Luke touched Alyssa lately, he rarely saw a vision or the accompanying disorientation.

"Are you ready to start our last year here together?" Alyssa asked.

"Nope ... but with you, it will be tolerable," he responded.

They all walked up the stairs together. Junior walked off into the 3rd-floor corridor toward the eleventh-grade homerooms. The brothers waved at one another as they parted.

Luke noticed a commotion near a locker as he walked toward his homeroom. A tall man with disheveled hair and wearing a leather jacket, who seemed obviously out of place, pinned one kid's head against the lockers while kicking at another student. Before the student ran off, Luke saw the man whisper something in the kid's ear. Luke and the man stared at one another. *That guy worries me*, he thought. It was the Bully Cladhair. He saw the man in a vision last year while preparing to battle Avandeil.

During lunch, Luke and Benji sat at the same round table as Alyssa and her friends in the Beaver Lounge's senior cafeteria. The LC has four lunchrooms. Each one is separated between grades nine to twelve. Luke played with the food in front of him: hamburger patties and bacon. Benji reached and grabbed one of the patties and slapped it on his bread. Luke was so consumed by finding a career that he reacted slowly. Instead of speaking, he folded one of the remaining two patties and shoved as much as possible into his mouth.

"You do that again, and I'll take a bite of your finger," Luke said, still chewing the patties.

"I believe he would, Benji … cut it out," Alyssa said, sitting with her three friends on the other side of the table. Last year, Alyssa made it a point to always sit with her friends at lunch, but she invited Benji and Luke to their table this year.

Luke chewed and then swallowed what he had in his mouth. "How is this Mr. Villanueva with this career development class?"

"He's a busy man and pretty lenient as long as you do what he says," Benji responded before eating his burger.

"I don't know why it bothers me so much, but I feel like we are at that point where we can no longer act like we are just kids without responsibilities," Luke said before eating the rest of the food in front of him.

Benji laughed and slapped his fist on the table. He leaned in toward Luke. "That surprises me, coming from you after what you did with Avandeil."

"That was different. It was my responsibility," he said,

pushing his empty tray toward the center of the table. "At least that's how I felt." Luke reached into his backpack and handed a folded piece of paper to his friend.

"Think career ... is this from your father?" Benji asked.

Luke shook his head affirmatively. "I'm not sure why it bothered me. Can I work at your shop for the career development class?"

"I don't think so, Luke. It's like a three-man shop, and I don't think Villanueva will let two of us work there. You'll find something," Benji said, handing him back his father's note.

Suddenly, Jimmy entered the lunchroom from the outdoor quad. This older guy walked to different tables and grabbed food or drinks from other trays. His hair was unique as it was matted and disheveled unconventionally. The man's haircut was unkept but looked like it was styled that way on purpose.

"My amigo, Jimmy Cladhaire or, as we call him, 'The Bully Cladhair.' His hair is always clad up like that. He's a violent bully." Benji has a disgusted look on his face. "Stay clear from Jimmy."

"I know who he is. I saw him in a vision last year when I touched you," Luke said.

"Why didn't you say anything?" Benji asked.

"It was when Alyssa was missing ... this morning I saw him beating a couple of guys his size. Why don't the teachers stop him? He's stealing food in front of everybody."

"They protect him," Benji said.

Alyssa looked at him and then at Jimmy Cladhaire. "Don't even think of interacting with that guy, Luke," Alyssa said.

"Wasn't planning on it, but he's going to be important this year. How old is he?" Luke asked.

"At least twenty ... can you imagine putting thirteen and fourteen-year-olds in the same school as that monster?" Sandy asked.

"We could say the same thing about you, Lin," Benji said, laughing.

12

"Make fun of my friends, and I won't go to the movies with you this weekend," Birdy said.

"Are you going on another date with him?" Sandy asked, moving her index finger toward her open mouth.

"Well, maybe it's not a date, right Benji," Birdy said, squinting with her left eye. "Maybe the rest of the crew wants to join us."

Benji stood up, walked up to Birdy, knelt beside her, and grabbed her hands.

"It's a little early in the process to propose," Linnet said.

"I'm sorry, baby. I cannot keep my mouth shut at times," Benji said.

"First of all, don't call me baby, and second of all ..." she leaned over and bit Benji's ear lobe.

Benji winced but kept his mouth shut. He kissed her hands. "Sorry, Birdy ... I'll control myself."

"You two make a great couple," Luke said, still looking toward Jimmy, who stared back before raising his chin upward to him in acknowledgment. Luke returned the gesture. He got a gnawing feeling that that gesture affirmed some future conflict.

Luke and Benji walked outside to the other end of the school and stepped into the wing where the music classes were. They entered the classroom together.

"Mr. Waters, this is Luke. He plays the guitar."

The teacher was a hip-looking, twenty-something-year-old guy with a coiffed designer haircut.

"Hey, Luke. Welcome to your class. I'm looking forward to hearing you play. Did you bring your axe?" Mr. Rogers asked.

"It's in the trunk of my car. Should I get it?" Luke asked.

"Today will be a lecture, and the students will list all the instruments they play. Bring your daily guitar tomorrow. Go ahead and take a seat."

While they talked, most of the students came in and took their seats. When he moved to an empty desk, he noticed Alyssa was already in class. They both smiled at one another as he sat beside her. Unlike other classrooms, this class had about ten seats arranged in a curve surrounding the lectern in front of a small teacher's desk.

"Did you know that Mr. Waters is a songwriter?" Alyssa asked.

"I think you or Benji mentioned something like that. Have you heard him sing?"

He looked toward Benji, who was talking with Mr. Waters, still at the head of the class.

"No, but I'm hoping to hear one of his songs. I heard he sang one to last year's class."

"Well, now I'm looking forward to it." She leaned in and caressed his arm ... *everything blinked into darkness until I was hit with a spotlight. I played my guitar, suspended up in the air, and almost lost my balance. I kept playing the guitar* ... he was back in the classroom staring into Alyssa's eyes.

"What are you two up to?" Benji asked as he sat down.

"Stuff," he said quickly and smiled at Alyssa.

"Everyone, this is the senior class for *Music Theory and Practice.* The goal of the course is to learn music theory regarding instruments. We will practice what we learn, prepare, and perform a recital toward the end of the course." Mr. Waters looked at what appeared to be a calendar. "At this time, it will be late April or the beginning of May. The music we'll play will depend on what we have regarding instruments and input from each of you."

Mr. Waters grabbed a stack of papers, walked toward each student, and handed each a form. "Please complete the questionnaire during the remainder of the class and hand it in before you take off. I need to know the instruments you play, whether you want to try vocals, and what type of music you like."

He began to fill out the questionnaire by placing his name. The first question was about musical instruments, and he entered all the string instruments he could play. Under vocal ability, he wrote AWFUL. Under music preference, he wrote Rock and Blues like *Pink Floyd, Led Zeppelin, Eric Clapton,* and *Steve Winwood,* under hobbies: playing guitar and working out. The first bell rang. All students, including himself, placed their completed forms in the basket. With that, he headed to his career development class with Benji after waving goodbye to Alyssa.

Luke and Benji entered the class. The teacher was dressed in business attire, including well-ironed black dress pants, a heavily starched shirt, and a black tie.

"Mr. Villanueva, this is Luke Sanz," Benji said.

"Nice to meet you, Luke … go ahead and take a seat, boys," Mr. Villanueva said, removing items from his briefcase and placing them on the desk.

When Luke took his seat, he quickly realized that Mr. Villanueva had not appeared to work at the school all day. He was working out of his briefcase.

Before the second bell chimed, only ten students were in the classroom, which had seating for twenty-two. Luke sat and counted all the seats while waiting for the class to begin.

"I am Mr. Villanueva, and this is the senior Career Development course. If you are supposed to be in the shop class, that's on the other side of the school."

Benji made to leave the class but sat back down. Students in the class laughed, including Luke.

"Funny, Benji … this packet I'm passing out is the syllabus for the course. It includes the schedule and progression of the course throughout your senior year. The next several months will be lectures and practical exercises. The remaining time will comprise internships or employment. We will meet monthly afterward one-on-one." Mr. Villanueva finished handing out the syllabus and sat at his desk. "The syllabus's final pages list all participating employers, internships, and positions. Some of these positions are paid, and most, if not all, internships are unpaid. Some of you may be able to obtain employment elsewhere, but it must be approved as part of the career development plan. The first page of the syllabus has what looks like an employment application. We'll complete this in class, which will be part of your application for any internship."

With that, Mr. Villanueva launched into his lecture. The class did not have a textbook. The first bell rang, and all the students stood up and spread out to their seventh-period class. Benji motioned him over to Mr. Villanueva's desk.

"Mr. Villanueva, Luke wanted to know whether or not he could work at my father's auto shop?" Benji asked.

Mr. Villanueva shook his head from side to side. "Benji, you're planning on being a mechanic and taking over for your father. It was natural for your internship to be at the shop. Luke, do you plan on being a mechanic?" The teacher was packing up his briefcase while responding to them.

"No, Mr. Villanueva … I'm unsure what to do for my career. I'm thinking of going into the Army," Luke said.

"Read the syllabus and look at the list of internships I have arranged. Check and see what interests you. You still have several months to come up with something," Mr. Villanueva said before putting on his suit coat. "I'll see you both tomorrow … get to your next class." With that, the teacher left the room rapidly.

"He must be in a hurry, too," Benji said.

"I guess we better head to study hall," Luke said.

They walked down to the Beaver Lounge, which doubled as the study hall.

They walked up to the table with one of the gym teachers, who sat reading a book and facing the tables near the serving line.

"Sit wherever you want to. You cannot talk, but you can read or do homework or whatever," the teacher said, speaking as if prerecorded.

"Is there a sign-in sheet?" Luke asked.

"Not for seniors … in a few months, you do not even need to report."

Luke peered at Benji, who was smiling, and motioned him toward the empty table by one of the exits. His dreams of not going to school were coming closer to reality. They sat quietly as the second bell rang.

"I'm going to head to work in a few minutes," Benji said.

"Didn't you hear the gym teacher? He said we don't have to show up after a few months," Luke said.

"Take a look around. The second bell rang, and there are ten students in here," Benji said.

"I can't leave yet. I have to drive Junior home."

"Well, I can see my car and a way out, so I'm taking it. See you later." Benji waved at the gym teacher, who waved back.

Luke took out a book from his backpack and started to read. The thought that he had one year to run around the school perturbed him. After a few minutes, he saw movement through the window into the quad with all the benches outside. Jimmy Cladhaire was outside smoking a cigarette. He focused back on his book and kept reading. After a few minutes, he felt he was being watched and looked out the window. Jimmy stood outside the closest window, staring at him, and motioned him outside. *This reminds me of the television series Salem's Lot with the vampires floating outside the window*, he thought. He placed a book marker, saving his page, and stepped outside.

They stared at one another for a bit, but then Jimmy offered him his hand, which Luke shook ... nothing happened, which shocked him into silence. He squeezed Jimmy's hand but did not release it, trying to induce a vision.

Jimmy grabbed Luke's wrist and moved his hand away. "What's your story, Sasquatch?"

"Sorry about that ... my name is Luke."

"I think Sasquatch suits you fine. I saw you hanging around Benji ... weird kid," Jimmy said. "Where you from?"

"Puerto Rico most recently, but I was born in Australia," Luke responded.

"A foreigner, it figures. Why are you sitting in there?"

"I have homework to do ... might as well get it done."

"Homework, it's the first day. You're not fooling me. You're different somehow, and I find you interesting," Jimmy said.

Luke surmised that it was a threat or possibly an attempt to intimidate him. He realized immediately that Jimmy could hide his thoughts from him. That had happened before, and Luke typically welcomed it. Now, he was not so sure.

"You're just going to stand there? It's like you're thinking of whether you want to fight me or walk away like the pussy Sasquatch you are."

"What are you even talking about, Jimmy?"

"So, you know my name … interesting, interesting how you accepted your new nickname like the pussy I see you are."

"I'm not a pussy, and I haven't accepted anything Bully," Luke said, trying to push Jimmy's buttons.

Jimmy walked up close to Luke, who was almost at eye level with him. "Don't call me that. I wouldn't say I like it … I'm not sure where you stand, Sasquatch. I'll tell you this. Don't get in my way, and we'll get along just fine."

Luke stood silently. *I feel like I'm being managed somehow*, he thought. "I'm just here to finish my school year, Jimmy."

"Good policy, for sure. I didn't want to waste my time here, but my father pressured me to finish my last year," Jimmy said.

"Where were you last year?" Luke asked.

"Jail," Jimmy dropped the butt of his cigarette at Luke's feet and lit a new one. "See you around, Sasquatch … this year is going to be fun with you around." With that, the Bully Cladhair strolled away proudly to the senior parking lot. Luke watched the man until he got into a red Pontiac *Firebird* and drove away in smoke.

Luke felt an emptiness inside as the Bully seemed to get one over on him by giving him a nickname and forcing him to swallow it. Not being able to see a vision when Jimmy touched him was concerning. Something about the man bothered him; he did not need to see a vision to know they were currently directed to some future confrontation. He felt corralled and weak, like an animal being forced into a pen for slaughter.

CHAPTER TWO

First Day at the LC — The Bully Cladhair Perspective

James Robert Cladhaire II went by the name Jimmy. Peers called him the Bully Cladhair, but rarely to his face. He was awakened with an ice-cold cup of water from his mother, Maeve Cladhaire, to the face. The task typically fell upon his father, James Robert Cladhaire who everyone called the LT, because he ran the county drug task force.

Shocked by the freezing water, he opened his eyes and looked at the alarm clock. It was 7:00 a.m., and he realized he was running late for his first day back to school. After having spent most of his senior year in jail for assault and battery charges.

He stared menacingly at his mother, a haggard-looking woman who chain smoked cigarettes, and drank Vodka with her lunch for years. Jimmy could sense his mother would have preferred to bludgeon him to death but waking him with a glass of cold water was a great start.

"Thanks, Mom, I needed that."

"Get up ... waste of space."

"I love you too, Mom." Jimmy was content to be out of jail but was wrangled into going back to school by his probation officer, who happened to be friends with his father.

He refused to go by the name of James because it belonged to what he believed was a hateful man. He considered changing his name but had yet to settle on one. He loved the movie *Goodfellas* and considered changing his name to *Henry* or *Ray*, but that was a year ago. In truth, he loved older films and novels and tended to memorize quotes that influenced him.

He slowly got up and began to get ready for his day. Standing before the mess of his closet was disconcerting. Some of his clean clothes were on hangers, but most were on the closet floor straight from the drier. He picked up a gray flannel shirt, placed it over his sullied T-shirt, and buttoned it up. He stumbled to the hallway bathroom and pissed before grabbing a bottle of mouthwash. He took a swig and gurgled before swallowing. He rinsed his face with soap and water and ran his wet fingers through his matted hair. Not thoroughly, though, because he needed help getting through the tangled, clumped hair. He looked into the mirror and smiled. "Ready to make my rounds, Sir." He made a comical salute while snapping his heels together and walking into the kitchen.

"Your father told me to remind you about your chores at school."

"That's a funny way to call it, Ma. You all rely way too much on humble little me," Jimmy said.

"Watch your filthy disrespectful whorish mouth. We have your sister to take care of." His older sister, Karen, was disabled, and her medical costs exceeded his father's health insurance.

"Thanks for the reminder, Ma." He returned to his room and moved his soiled clothes out of the way. He opened a hidden floor panel, removed a pouch with a shoulder strap, and placed it around his neck, tucking it under his T-shirt. Jimmy stood in front of the mirror, lifted his T-shirt, and grabbed the pouch in one quick, fluid motion. This mimicked the motion he would make selling drugs at school. He moved the pouch to him and peered at each of the divided flaps within the pouch. One section had marijuana dime bags, another had little baggies holding cocaine, and yet another had numerous little, red-topped vials with crack rocks. The pouch had two side pockets with assorted pills and one final hidden flap with some cash that faced his chest. He removed the money he earned from street sales before restocking the pouch from a brown bag his father left on top of his dresser.

His parents preferred Jimmy to sell during school because the target audience was all in one building. In truth, so did he because he did not have to drive throughout town or sit in a parking lot waiting for others to seek him out. The fight he got into last year was with a dealer from the District of Columbia who was planning on ripping or killing him off on his father's orders.

He grabbed the keys to his red *Firebird* and headed out, neglecting to shut the door behind him. He does not have a backpack or even a pencil.

"I'll get the door, Jackass," his mother said before slamming the door shut.

The engine roared to life. He stomped on the pedal, popped the clutch, and burned rubber out of the driveway, launching into the road. An unseen driver braked hard to avoid striking the *Firebird*. Jimmy blew his horn at the other driver and smiled.

He parked in the senior parking lot and right away saw an infraction by an underclassman to his rules. A young punk kid walked away from a car in the senior lot. "Who do you think you are? You little stink nugget."

The boy tried to hand Jimmy a letter.

Jimmy almost punched the boy in the face but opted to grab the note and read.

Dear Jimmy,

This is my brother Kevin Ordley. Stay away from him please or my parents will kill me.

Thanks,

Your quarterback, Todd.

"Kevin Ordley. What's shaking?" Jimmy offered his hand to Kevin.

Reluctantly, Kevin took Jimmy's hand and shook it.

"I know you're scared shitless but I'm not going to hurt you today. Tomorrow, park where you're supposed to. Do you understand?"

Kevin shook his head up and down and walked quickly towards the school building.

Jimmy followed the underclassmen into the school and walked through the first floor hallway, where the freshmen were. He walked toward a couple of them hanging out near the entrance to a classroom and shoved them into the room violently. "Take a seat, children."

He walked up the stairs to the fourth floor, where the senior homerooms were located, and came to his homeroom door. The area was crowded with students trying to get to their seats. He pushed through them as if they were overgrown branches.

He went from class to class throughout the day. However, he primarily used the classrooms as a place to sleep and rest. In between periods, he frequented the restroom to sell whatever drugs he had in his pouch.

He saw what looked like a freshman entering the fourth-floor restroom and he felt joy at the possibility of being able to correct the kid. He quickly grabbed him with his large hand and pushed the scared boy into the wall, trying to squash his head.

"Jimmy, it's me, Jack." The boy handed him a twenty-dollar bill.

He released his hold on Jack and handed him one of the vials with the red cap. "Beat it, Jack." He kicked Jack's backside, which propelled him on his way. He had over six hundred dollars in his jacket by lunchtime and headed into the cafeteria. Jimmy saw a teacher standing over a table, talking with some students, but he paid little attention to anything else. A small rectangular pizza sat on a tray in front of a kid who was turned in his seat. He took the pizza slice with him outside the senior hang-out area. The area included many tables and chairs secured to a concrete pad, covered by a large rectangular ramada to block the typical northern Virginia rain. He sat at one of the tables as he ate the confiscated pizza.

An underclassman walked toward him with a tray from the cafeteria. He pointed his hand at the sky and slammed the tray to the ground, spraying some food on the kid and some on his pants.

Jimmy looked at the food on his pants and looked up to catch a glance at the underclassmen who had food sprayed on his shirt. Jimmy's anger built up, causing him to grab the back of the kid's belt and the top of his shirt collar. "Now I have to wash my favorite jeans." He launched the kid over a planter headfirst. Then, he walked to the bathroom to clean up without worry.

He returned to the senior hang-out area and grabbed a carton of milk from a table and another slice of pizza. The kid he threw over the planter was no longer there. The first bell chime rang out to signal the end of lunch. He felt he was being watched and looked toward two students walking from the cafeteria. One was Benji Laio, the grease monkey; the other was a giant kid with long hair who looked like he belonged as the frontman of a heavy metal band. The sasquatch-looking kid wore black utility work pants and a gray long-sleeve shirt. He's built like an athlete and looked hardened. "That is a dangerous man," he said with hope, nodding his chin upward to the kid in acknowledgment.

Jimmy had a seventh-period study hall, which meant he could go home or wherever he wanted. He headed home and sat on his bed and began reading his book.

I walked outside the study hall and looked into the cafeteria, seeing it was mostly empty. The coach sat at the head of the class, reading a book. I noticed the Sasquatch kid looking toward me. I walked over to the closest window and stared at the kid, trying to figure him out.

I closed my eyes, trying to evoke an emotion or thought from the kid. Nothing ... I could not feel anything from this kid. It aggravated me.

The kid stepped outside and introduced himself. The kid was named Luke, but he would always be Sasquatch to me.

"I don't feel anything when I touch you," I said, trying to pull my hand away from Luke, who had not released my hand. I head-butted Luke

and took my hand back. I punched Luke's chest, but it was blocked. I was incensed and tried to punch again, but my arm was broken at the wrist and was useless. I kicked Luke's leg, but Luke blocked it and countered with a punch to my face, busting my nose and cheekbone open causing searing pain …

"Wake up, dumb ass," his father said, shaking Jimmy.

It was good that he did because his wrist and face were on fire. He looked at his wrist, and it hung loosely. He could barely see his fist through his blood-filled eyes. "I'm awake," Jimmy said, shooting up quickly in bed, grabbing his broken wrist that had miraculously healed.

"Did you meet up with the nasal twins?" his father feigned, snorting through one nostril.

"No, we were supposed to meet at five," he said, looking for his alarm clock, which he recalls unplugging before falling asleep. He hoped he would sleep away in the afternoon and evening.

"Jimmy, wise up, it's six. Get your ass up and meet the twins at the convenience store … you have responsibilities as I do," his father said, closing the door but pausing. "Stop beating up underclassmen. I had to clean up for you again. Are you already trying to get suspended on the first day of school?" his father asked, slamming the door behind him.

Jimmy walked to the bathroom and splashed water on his face. He retrieved the pouch and checked his pockets for his keys. Jimmy had everything he needed. He headed out to his car, lit it up, launched out of the driveway, and almost caused another accident. "This land is meant for you and me, not," Jimmy said, laughing at himself.

He drove to the local convenience store, where two police cars were parked on the side of the building. He walked toward the store and nodded at one of the officers. He grabbed a soda, two packs of peanut butter cups, and a box of powdered donuts. He opened the box of donuts before stepping out of the store and placed a bag containing about an ounce of cocaine and ten crack vials in a sealed bag. He reached for the cash compartment and found only four five-dollar bills, realizing his father must have collected his earnings while he was sleeping. He was so annoyed that he almost left without paying but decided to pay when he caught the cashier staring at him and the police outside. He walked out of the store and approached the patrol car. "What's shaking, officers?"

"Seriously, Bully. You're almost two hours late, and we have overtime tonight." Officer Velasquez said.

The other officer, Leroy Washington, gave him the finger.

"Don't call me that. I don't like it." He handed the box of donuts to Officer Velasquez, who gave him some cash.

"After what you pulled today, you should be paying me. So, this is light," Officer Velasquez said, laughing like the fiend he was.

"Understandable, but I did not do anything wrong. That little shit had it coming and more." Jimmy walked off, got into his car, and launched it home. *These freaking degenerate cops*, he thought.

He visited his sister, who was watching television in her recliner. "Hey Karen, how was your day?" he asked, handing her one of the packs of peanut butter cups. He would save the other for a different day.

"Jimmy. My little Jimbo, be a good boy," Karen said wide-eyed while trying to take the wrapper off the peanut butter cups.

He grabbed the candy and removed the wrapper. "There you go, sis, your Jimmy is a good boy." He reached over and kissed his sister with tears in his eyes. "I love you, sis."

Karen is almost six years older than Jimmy. When she was eighteen and he was twelve, Karen left the house late at night to visit her boyfriend. After midnight, for some reason—only a tyrannical God could explain—she crashed her car into a culvert near the family house. She was found by a passerby wandering on the road with blood pouring from her head. She had a traumatic brain injury. She survived the accident but had undergone many surgeries ever since. Karen was his champion, while his parents naturally neglected and mistreated him. The hate he had in his heart stemmed from the day he realized the loving sister he had was gone.

CHAPTER THREE

Don't Believe Your Lying Eyes

I walked past a red bricked cathedral in Lansburg, down a path adjacent to the parking lot, and down the crest of the hill that decreased in elevation, arriving at a large open iron gate with a sign, Lansburg Memorial Cemetery. I walked into the cemetery, passing granite headstones. I arrived at a mid-sized upright headstone that read Dwayne "Father D" Freeman, date of birth, date of death. A valued friend and mentor. Saved countless families throughout the world in their time of need.

I sat down on a bench near the grave, bowing my head. A small metal plate donated by the Sanz family was affixed to the bench's backrest.

"Thank your father for the donation. My older parishioners do appreciate it, son," Father D said as he sat beside me.

"I'm dreaming, aren't I?" I whispered, the reality of Father D's absence hitting me like a wave of anxiety. Something I rarely felt as I did in the past.

"Yes, as promised, I can speak with you when necessary."

I stayed silent; the priest's passing had affected me immensely. "Where are you when you are not visiting me in my dreams?" I asked.

"I'm mostly with family, but I spend much of my days with my mentor and teacher, William. He's jealous that I could spend time with

a protector," Father D said.

I looked toward the spirit of Father D, who appeared younger. His health no longer affected him. In truth, he looked like the virile, muscular man I saw in a vision pounding on a heavy bag a year ago. "I met a boy who worries me. We touched each other, but I did not see a vision. I feel ..." I stopped and shook my head in disbelief. "I feel powerless over him."

"You are right to feel fear. Jimmy Cladhaire is on the precipice of becoming an extremely violent man like his father. Unlike his father, he can be persuaded to use his gifts for good."

"What gifts?"

"This young man can discern whether somebody in his presence has or will commit violence against others. With that, he knows when to protect himself. With his evolving, he can use it instead to victimize others he knows will not fight back."

I needed help comprehending what Father D explained. "Maybe when I wake up, I will remember this conversation." I held onto my buzzing head, and my ears burned.

"I'll be back again. Be careful with Jimmy. You are in for another trial in life. Be strong and be mindful that you will encounter those in authority who are evil and cannot be trusted," Father D said. The buzzing sound was louder.

"I don't understand, Father ... who will I encounter?" I asked but everything faded.

Luke opened his eyes. The buzzing was his alarm clock. It was 6:10 a.m., which meant his alarm had been on for ten minutes. Tony sat next to him, staring as if worried. "I'm getting up, Ton."

"Luke?" Sebastian asked while Luke showered.

Luke jumped in the shower and almost slipped. "What are you doing? I'm showering, give me some privacy will ya," Luke yelled.

"I need to remind you of something."

"If you must, but you could just wait, buddy." Sebastian did not appear to have materialized in the bathroom, which at least made him feel somewhat unconcerned.

"I showed you the day of my death, but not sure if you recall the whole thing."

Luke thought and was pretty sure he didn't recall the whole dream. "What did I miss?"

"I was killed by a Cladhaire. Jimmy's ancestor."

Luke shut off the shower, stepped out of the stall and grabbed a towel. "What does this mean?"

"I don't know. Our families are intertwined. Just keep that in mind, Luke."

"I will, Sebastian."

He got ready for school and drove in with Junior, who already had his license, but he rarely let him drive the *Grand National*.

"When are you going to let me drive your car?" Junior asked.

Luke laughed, maneuvering toward the school past Joshua Avenue. "Once I start working, I will leave school early every day. You will need to drive the *Taurus* by yourself."

"Seems like a waste of gas … I just want to drive your car."

He looked at Junior and smiled. "I'll let you drive home today."

This made his brother smile. "Cool," Junior said, caressing the dashboard.

"Once you start taking your vocation classes, you'll need your own ride," Luke said.

Junior's face soured, and he crossed his arms. "I don't like driving alone… it gets me nervous."

"Me too, Junes … just push past it, play music, or squeeze one of these hand grip strengtheners," he said, handing his brother an extra one he kept in his center console. "Keep that one."

"Ah, thanks," Junior said, staring oddly at the grip before pressing the exercise tool together. "I understand. It keeps your mind engaged."

Luke pulled into the senior parking lot and parked the car. He saw Jimmy Cladhaire, pushing past some underclassmen talking in a group. "Do you see that guy with the leather jacket, Junes?"

"Yeah, who is he?"

"Jimmy Cladhaire, they call him the Bully Cladhair, without

an *E* at the end. It has to do with his matted hair … look he's dangerous. You see him, you walk the other way, understand?"

"I understand. I saw him push a freshman into a classroom."

"In front of the teachers?" Luke asked.

"Yes, and I saw one teacher laughing," Junior said.

Luke shook his head in disbelief when he realized that something was off in school now compared to their first year at the LC. Jimmy's release from jail to attend his senior year at their school agitated the calm that existed previously.

During lunch, he ate with Benji in the quad area that was meant for juniors and seniors but at times underclassmen made their way outdoors. It was against school rules, but it was up to the teachers to enforce them and not the Bully Cladhair. Jimmy was messing with some underclassmen who happened to wander into the upper classmen area. The smaller underclassman hunched over and turned away, defeated. Jimmy kicked their rear ends as they walked away. Fortunately, neither said anything, so they walked off unscathed. Jimmy would have pounced if they even looked in his direction.

"He should have been a senior last year but was in jail. All I know is that he attacked two grown men and threw one from the Campbell Bridge into the water, and he was arrested. One of them drowned but was revived," Benji said.

"I don't understand. Why is Jimmy still here? How old is he?" Luke asked, rapidly confused.

"Nineteen or twenty, I think. Jimmy plays football, and that helps him get away with everything. His father is also a boss in some drug task force."

The Bully Cladhair walked up to two students, grabbed one of the hamburgers in a tray, and took a bite. "Do you object?" Jimmy asked loud enough for them to overhear.

The student lifted his hands in defeat. "Help yourself, Jimmy."

"I don't mind if I do." Jimmy finished the burger in a couple of bites.

The Bully must see them looking at him because he sauntered over.

"What's up, grease monkey? How are you, Sasquatch?"

"Jimmy, this is Luke."

"We met. You are seniors, but I'm not sure you all belong here. Especially you, monkey boy."

He stared at the Bully Cladhair, and there was an uncomfortable silence for both of them.

Jimmy motioned toward him. "It figures a grease monkey would hang out with a Sasquatch. I'm great at picking nicknames."

Luke stood up reflexively and did not move out of Jimmy's way. and stared at Jimmy but did not speak.

"Easy, big guy. I know you're a senior. I'm just making my rounds. Resign or be prosecuted, any way you want it."

"Raw Deal ... am I correct, Jimmy?" Luke asked.

"You sure are, Sasquatch."

Benji walked up to Luke and grabbed his arm. "Let's go to class, Luke. Grab your bag." Benji guided Luke toward their music class.

His mouth was frozen even though his body was moving. They walked in silence for a couple of minutes. "I will always regret not speaking up for myself. Somebody needs to stand up to him. I can take care of myself, but I choke when I speak up. It doesn't help that my parents browbeat us about fighting at school."

Benji placed his hand on Luke's shoulder. "Jimmy does not face the consequences for anything he does, so you're not on equal footing."

After lunch, he saw Jimmy walking toward a random vehicle, kicking in its fender and spitting on the hood. Then, Jimmy walked toward a red Pontiac *Firebird*, opened the driver's side door, and jumped inside. The engine roared to life. Jimmy smoked the car's tires as it propelled toward the exit.

"Nice car, big asshole." He was pissed that somebody like

Jimmy would have such a nice car.

After his music theory class, he walked toward his career development class, which he shared with Benji. They took a shortcut through an infrequently traveled hallway meant for use by performers behind the school auditorium. Their next class was beyond some exit doors into another school wing. As they passed the entrance, Luke smelled cigarette smoke, stopped walking, and placed his arm out against Benji's chest.

"Why are you stopping?" Benji asked.

"Listen ... someone is up ahead smoking," Luke whispered, hearing voices for the first time. He moved up against the wall slowly, motioning for Benji to follow. As he approached a T-intersection, the voices grew louder to the point that he could understand words.

"Twice in one day. Congratulations, you're developing an expensive habit," one voice said.

"Keep your voice down, Jimmy ... I'll pay you for the extras, but you owe us for what we did."

Luke peered around the corner and saw Jimmy Cladhaire standing alongside Vice Principal Shipmen. He couldn't believe his eyes as Jimmy grabbed under his shirt, produced a small cellophane bag, handed it to the Vice Principal, and grabbed a wad of cash from the teacher.

"Go ahead, get out of here, Jimmy, and keep your mouth shut."

Jimmy threw his cigarette on the floor toward the teacher's feet. "Sure, I'm not the one with the problem, Sir." He turned and walked back toward the hallway and Luke.

He quickly grabbed Benji and moved to the alcove of double doors leading into another classroom. Jimmy ran toward the exit and left the building. Luke and Benji walked back down the hallway toward the same exit doors and saw the vice principal standing in the same spot, staring at the floor.

"Hello, Mr. Shipmen," Benji said while they walked past.

The man recoiled and stared at them. He was stunned into

silence.

Luke waved at the man, and they kept walking toward the exit and into the open air. They walked silently between some trees and onto some grass until they came to the entrance of the other wing. The janitor was mowing the grass with a large red contraption of a lawnmower. A breeze of wind brought the scent of the fresh-cut grass along.

"What the hell did we just witness?" Benji asked.

Luke shook his head in disbelief. "Nothing … it was nothing."

"It looked like a drug deal, Luke."

"With a teacher, the vice-principal. Cast it from your thoughts, Benji. That wouldn't make any sense." Luke felt something inside reminiscent of his bouts of anxiety coupled with the dread that comes with the loss of a loved one.

"Yeah, maybe he was just counseling him, and Jimmy will stop bullying the underclassmen."

"Now, don't go too far, Benji." They laughed as they entered the school wing, heading toward their career development class. They both cast the event they had witnessed from their thoughts as they entered the threshold of the double doors.

CHAPTER FOUR

Cladhair Defied

Jimmy woke up after being shaken by his father, James Cladhaire, the LT, as his friends called him. Jimmy rolled onto his left side and drifted back into a slumber. The LT punched Jimmy's right thigh.

"Jimmy, wake up. I don't have time for this shit."

Jimmy groaned. "I'm awake. Get away from me, man." He grabbed his thigh and tried to rub the spasm away, running his hand through the muscle. He stared at the red mark where his father struck him and knew it would soon bruise.

"Wake up and take a shower now. I need to get to the office. I left you something new to sell in this bag over here. It's heroin and not for everybody. Twenty for each hit. The smack is already prepackaged." The LT propped Jimmy up in bed like a doll.

"How am I supposed to sell that at the school? What's with the mouse?"

"You'll find buyers. Don't you remember that mouse from that amusement park? Take a shower. You stink, and your mother is complaining."

Jimmy took a hot shower. He even washed his hair with shampoo and conditioner and tried to untangle it. He dressed, assembled his drug pouch, and hid it in his usual spot. He walked to the kitchen and saw his haggard mother smoking a cigarette. "Morning, Ma, I showered as ordered."

"What an accomplishment. Some of us do this all on our own. Did you forget to brush your hair?"

Jimmy ran his fingers through his hair. "I don't have a brush."

"What are you doing sitting there?" His mother, Maeve, said while making breakfast.

"Waiting for breakfast, what else, Ma."

"This is for your sister and not for the likes of you."

"Likes of me. I'm your son, Ma."

"Pretty sure you were switched at the hospital. Get out of here, get to school, and make sure you sell all that smack. We have a large medical bill for your sister."

Jimmy shook his head in disbelief. "See you later, Ma."

His mother motioned with her hand to Jimmy as if pushing away an annoying fly. "Off with you. You disgust me."

Jimmy was used to being treated as trash and had long stopped feeling depressed over living in an environment where he was the trash. He only knew the love of his sister; without her, he would have struck out on his own. He went to his sister's bedroom. "Hello, sis. At least you love Jimmy, right."

"Jimmy is a good boy," Karen said.

"Well, Jimmy is trash to hear our Ma. Take care, sis."

He fired up his *Firebird* and raced off toward school but checked his gas gauge and noticed he was nearly empty. He stopped at the local gas station and grabbed for his right rear pocket where his wallet should be, but it wasn't there. He slammed on his steering wheel, angered that his father sidetracked him with the whole taking a shower demand. It caused him to slip and forget his wallet. He hesitated before grabbing the hidden pouch under his shirt and took out four five-dollar bills. He glanced at the gas pump, $1.13 a gallon. *What a rip-off*, he thought.

When he entered the small store, the cashier stared at him oddly. He grew angry and wanted to slap the fat, bearded young man around. He poured a coffee, took a Danish, impulsively took a bite, and walked up to the cashier defiantly. "Put the rest on the pump out there," he said.

The cashier recoiled and stepped back in fear. "Hey Jimmy, are you still at the LC?"

He knew the guy. It came to him when he saw snot on the guy's nose. "Hey, Booger. So, no college for you, ha?"

"Na, I made it one semester and blew my knee. It hurts almost constantly."

If he recalled correctly, Booger liked experimenting with different drug types. "I have something that may help you. It's twenty for a taste."

"I don't have it, man. I have two jobs to pay for a crappy room I'm renting in Leesburg."

He grabbed under his shirt, pulled out a baggie with the Mickey emblem, and swapped it out with the bills he gave Booger earlier. "Put ten on the pump and find me when you need more." He grabbed some more items off the shelves and left the store.

Later, at school, he got annoyed walking down a hallway crowded with underclassmen blocking the stairs. Jimmy grabbed the strap on a student's backpack and pulled the kid out of the way into other students.

"Hey, what the hell, man? Who do you think you are?" the underclassmen asked.

Jimmy turned around and stared at the student—a tall black kid who quickly realized he was mouthing off to the wrong person.

"Sorry." The kid tried to apologize, but it was too late.

Jimmy interrupted the apology with a punch to the kid's chest, launching him into a group of other students who collapsed into a heap. He leaned forward, laughing while repeatedly slapping his knee. *That was a work of art*, he mused.

He walked up the stairs to his homeroom classroom and sat. A student handed Jimmy some folded cash.

"Rock." This kid was looking to buy crack cocaine.

He handed him a small, sealed bag with crystal fragments and motioned the young man to lean toward him. "I have some H, not much more of that crank around. Put it out there, twenty a hit." The young man nodded at him. The first bell rang, and all the students left the classroom.

After the first period, he headed to his favorite restroom as students lined up. He started selling from his pouch and sold off a couple of hits of the smack. By lunchtime, he sold off another six hits of heroin. He went to the lunchroom and recalled he did not have his wallet and would need to dip into his pouch for cash. Some juniors and underclassmen were headed outside with their food trays. He followed them purposely and grabbed the tray off the biggest kid. "Get your own food." The student did not say a word and instead headed back inside.

He sat at a table and began eating what looked like a Salisbury steak lunch. He was almost finished eating when he saw a large shadow standing over him. A large black teenager stood behind him with clenched fists. "What's up, Stan?"

"Why did you punch my brother in the chest?"

"That was your brother? He was being disrespectful."

"You can't be doing that, man. He's a good kid. He's still in the nurse's office when he should be at a hospital."

"Not my problem, Stan. You should teach your brother manners," Jimmy said, putting a forkful of the ground steak into his mouth. He saw red and immediately knew that Stan was planning on hitting him.

"Seriously," Stan said, on impulse, punched Jimmy on the back before pulling him off the table forcibly turning him around. "You've had this coming for some time, Jimmy." Stan hit Jimmy several times and managed to split his lip.

Jimmy spat blood and meat onto the table and laughed. He then threw a combination punch to Stan's midsection and face when Stan doubled over in pain. The abdominal strikes caused Stan to fall to one knee.

"I give up," Stan said, pleading.

"Give up? We are just getting started." He grabbed Stan's head and gave him a knee to his face. "Learn how to fight, brother." Stan was taller than him and an athletic young man who played basketball on the school team. He also sensed that Stan could outdo him with stamina but was not a fighter by any means and to top it off, he was scared. His size and athleticism did not matter when fighting a young man beaten by his father since he was a toddler and whose aggressiveness had no bounds.

A group of students gathered at a discrete distance and surrounded the fighters. Luke and Benji were outside eating at a bench and approached them.

"Jimmy, leave him alone. You're killing him," Benji yelled at him.

Jimmy stood up, grabbed Benji by his shirt collar, and threw him to the ground. Then, he moved toward Benji, but Luke stood before him. Jimmy punched at him, but Luke used Jimmy's momentum and sent him flying toward the ground.

Luke expected to see something when he touched Jimmy, but instead, he saw darkness as if he wore something over his eyes. "Jimmy, it's over, man. The teachers are coming out, and Stan is out cold. I cannot let you hurt Benji."

Jimmy rose. "Sasquatch, how's it going?" He spit more blood on the ground. "What I did to Stan is nothing compared to what you'll get."

Several teachers and the school security guard ran out of the cafeteria.

Luke pointed at the security guard and teachers. "They will care, Jimmy. It would be best if you ran," he said, pointing toward the school staff.

"This isn't over, Sasquatch. Watch yourself." Jimmy wanted to kick Stan once more but noticed the basketball player was unconscious, and his face was bloodied. He turned and ran off toward the front entrance of the school. *He needed to put a stop to that meddlesome Benji and Luke duo*, he thought.

Wards

Principal Matias Devry sat with his head lying in his arms on his desk. He had been trying to sleep it off for the past hour and almost fell asleep a few times. He had a terrible hangover from drinking the prior night. He knew he should limit the drinking to the weekend, but Wednesday nights were his weakness. He had a pill securely tucked into his hand. It was some type of amphetamine he only knew as an upper. He tried to avoid taking it because it made his thoughts race, and he sweated through his clothing. The odor escaping his pores was even noticeable to him. He told his secretary earlier not to interrupt him under any circumstances, but his phone rang. He grabbed the receiver quickly, trying to keep the ringtone from reverberating around his skull.

"I thought I told you not to interrupt me."

"Matias, he did it again. Come to my office now," Nurse Radner ordered, then hung up the phone.

"A please and thank you would have been nice," he said while hanging up the receiver. He opened his fist, stared at the pill, and shrugged his shoulders before popping it into his mouth. He reached for his water bottle, but it was empty, so he went into one of his drawers and grabbed a metal flask. He drank a mouthful and swallowed the pill. The flavor of the bourbon brought a smile to his face. He went to return the flask to his drawer but impulsively took another pull before replacing it.

Matias met with the school nurse, Marie Radner, near her desk and spoke quietly. The upper was kicking in, and he was a bit giddy. He had his hand on her thigh, which she gave up pushing after three tries.

"Matias, please behave … the Johnson brothers are in the room," Marie said, pointing toward a closed door. "That monstrosity of a boy attacked two brothers today already, and the day is only half over."

"How bad is it?" he asked, finally concerned—not for the kids but for himself.

"It's bad enough that we should call the police and the paramedics and let them sort it out."

Matias shook his head in defiance. Thoughts raced fiercely through his mind. He realized that Stan Johnson had much to lose as well.

The hulking basketball player stepped out of the patient room with an ice pack on his face. He stooped down to avoid hitting the top of the door frame.

"Can we go? I want to take my brother out of this shithole."

"You can leave with your brother. It would be best if you got your head examined by a psychologist. You attacked another student without provocation. I should call the police on you," Matias said.

"Wait a minute, Mr. Devry, that animal attacked my brother. Jimmy had that coming, and you know it," Stan said.

"Now your basketball career is over, Mr. Johnson."

"Seriously, you would kick me from the team in my senior year. I'm being scouted, Mr. Devry."

"Not anymore. I'm about to get on the phone and talk to your coach. Your prospects are over."

Stan sat down in a chair and cried. He took the ice pack from his face and placed his head in both hands. His face below the left eye was swollen and purple.

Mr. Devry winced when he saw the boy's face, but any sense of empathy diminished quickly. "What you decide right now, Mr. Johnson will determine your future."

"What do you need me to do?" Stan appeared stoic with his head held high.

"You and your brother, go home. I don't want to hear about this later and I don't want a call from your parents. Go home and take the rest of the week off if necessary."

"Fine." Stan entered the patient room, where his brother

waited. "Come on, Ron, let's get out of this shithole," Stan said before turning to Nurse Radner. "You good with this? That cat will kill one of us, and you will fall with this one." Stan pointed at Mr. Devry. Stan did not wait for a response from Marie Radner, who winced as if stung by a bee.

"Just go, Stan ... remember, take the week off if you need to, but if I get a call," Matias said before running his hand across his throat. "You're cut from the team and suspended."

Stan shook his head in disgust while he helped his brother out of the nurse's office. His brother Ron still held onto his chest where Jimmy had hit him. Stan turned as if to speak but shook his head once again and let the door slam shut behind him.

"He's right, Matias. We need to stop the Bully Cladhair from hurting the kids. They are our responsibility."

He stood up, stumbled a bit, and held his head low in defeat and embarrassment. "He has us by the balls, Marie. We need to tread lightly here."

Marie stared off into the wall while a tear ran down her face. "We're damned then. Why did we let this happen?"

Matias grabbed a seat on the side of her desk and fell into it. "I try not to think of it. We have to deal with the aftermath." He looked toward the open door to the patient room and could see the bed. "Want to go for a round?" he asked, pointing at the bed.

She crossed her arms and made a disgusted look. "You've been drinking, and you stink."

The sweat from the uppers was giving him that melting feeling, but he also had a bulge building in his pants. "Come on, Marie. It will take your problems away for a spell."

She stood up and glared at him before locking the door to her office. She approached, grabbed his hand, and led him into the room.

Matias smiled the whole time, but it turned into a frown when he thought of Stan and Ron's injuries and his duty to protect the children. *We may very well be damned*, he thought.

CHAPTER FIVE

Night of the Overdoses

The LT was at the Lansburg Memorial Hospital with several of his detectives and task force officers assigned to the Loudon County Metro Drug Task Force (LCMDTF). He was an imposing man at six foot five inches tall and over two hundred fifty pounds. At forty-eight, he looked older than his age because of twenty years of heavy drinking in his younger years. His mostly red hair was sprinkled with gray. He had a scarred face with broken blood vessels, especially his nose. The members of his task force had been huddled together in one of the waiting rooms at the hospital since Friday evening after interviewing all the family members of the five overdose victims attending Lansburg Center High School and two more from elsewhere in the community. They did not have any leads yet to determine where the kids bought the drugs, and he tried to ensure it stayed that way.

Only one of the survivors was coherent enough to speak with them. This guy wasn't a student in high school. He worked at a gas station between LT's house and the high school. He recognized the kid as a former football player at the school and sometimes a friend of his son Jimmy, who always called the kid Booger for some reason. He stayed in the room during the interview and looked intently at him without saying a word. That scared Booger sufficiently to shut his trap. Before he left, he tapped Booger's foot and gave him a thumbs up. Booger almost crawled backward into the wall as he retracted from the LT's touch.

"We recovered eight small, sealed bags with mouse stamps on each one," Officer Jose Velasquez said.

"What happened to the other two baggies?" DEA Special Agent (SA) Todd Robert asked.

"Two of the kids were sharing," Officer Velasquez said.

"I missed that. This smack likely came from that DC pusher who goes by Mickey."

"I agree, one Thomas Michael Howard from Arlington. I think Mickey has ties to that Chinese crew in Portsmouth that Terry is looking at." The LT was adept at memorizing what all the detectives and agents were working on within his task force. "Do we have anybody into Mickey?" He knew they did, and when in cleanup mode, he typically mapped out each conversation as if it were a script from a play.

"Dwayne has two buys into him." Detective Juan Bello looked at his watch. "It's four o'clock in the morning. We can set up a buy tonight." Detective Juan Bello is parroting a previously agreed-upon plan. Dwayne Dwight was a patrol officer with the Lovettsville PD, and was also known as DD.

"Cut everyone, and make sure they get some rest before we set up for the buy tonight," he said.

"Do you want Leroy and me there?" Officer Velasquez loved overtime because it fed his habit.

"Yes, but not in uniform. It's all plain clothes tonight. Grab one of the pool vehicles at the office. Finish your shift and meet us in Arlington at eight tonight." His plan did not involve police markings, uniforms, or marked police vehicles.

Jose and Leroy took off, and only three of them remained. Earlier in the day, Juan and James met to arrange how they would add Mickey as a target. In truth they knew it came from one of Mickey's couriers. The task force comprised fifteen officers and agents, including a US Customs special agent and two DEA special agents. The rest were local police officers from the different jurisdictions in the Loudon County area. Juan, Jose, Leroy, and he were involved in a corrupt venture that included seizing the narcotics and separating some of the bulk higher purity powder drugs to keep for themselves. They cut the remainder with laxatives, caffeine, or whatever worked best and then held that as evidence—just enough to get a positive test.

One of the senior detectives was Alexei Morozov or Alex for short. Alex was a senior officer and the office's evidence custodian. He was one of the first officers the LT corrupted when he took over the task force. Alex was central to how they divided the drug seizures by cutting the drugs or not weighing them correctly.

Todd stared at the evidence bag containing the baggies. "I need to head to the DEA office in Arlington and meet with some intelligence analysts. I will try to get these samples sent to the lab."

"I will take that, Todd. Alex is waiting for those to get to the state lab."

Todd looked a bit baffled. "I could rush this, James. Why would you want Alex to handle this?"

"Because we planned it already. Alex is driving the evidence to the state lab and meeting us in Arlington tonight. He will meet with chemists and the state intel analysts to get us more targets for the rest of the week. Mickey could be a wash."

"Got it ... I'll be back tonight." Todd seemed unconvinced that the state lab was the correct lab to analyze the evidence. Todd walked off, letting out a sigh.

Todd would likely meet with his Group Supervisor, or GS, in Arlington. "Watch that guy, Juan. We will be burned tonight if he steps out of line." The LT was concerned, as always, unless he had complete control over all the task force members.

"I can assign him and the others to the outer perimeter of the surveillance," Juan said.

"Write up an operational plan and game it out." He prided himself in controlling every detail of all events that he had an interest in.

"Do you want Leroy?"

"Yes, get him or Jose. Whoever is cleaner to ride with you," he said.

"Copy that. How much do you want DD to buy?"

"Let's make it three kilograms and hope he has more on him. I can justify that. Get going. Let's meet up in Arlington at seven o'clock."

"On my way." Juan walked off but stopped, paused, and turned around. "Everything must be done perfectly. Dwayne already has doubts because he bought from Mickey, and I messed up the weight."

"Hmm … well, we could switch the meet so it's in our jurisdiction. Work it out in your head. It will throw off these make-believe-fed cops. Let's meet at the office before the briefing and solidify this plan."

DD was a certified undercover officer with drug buys into Mickey. The LT knew that DD was by the book on everything and was undergoing the hiring process with the US Customs Service. The kid was focused on building his career, and in the LT's mind, that gave the man a divided loyalty. The LT needed to plan every detail of the operation so as not to cause doubts in Dwayne or the others. He would succeed if he kept Todd and the other feds at bay.

Later in the day, at about seven that night, Juan Bello held a briefing for the drug enforcement operation. He passed a biographical sheet of the targets out to the detectives and officers in the room. "Thank you all for coming this evening. We are conducting a buy-arrest against one, Thomas Michael Howard, also known as Mickey, in the parking lot of the local hotel in Lansburg. Our undercover will be DD, whom you all know. DD, please stand up. As you can see, DD is boldly wearing white jeans, a purple top, and a white hat. Stylish, I may add." Everyone laughed. "DD is already two buys into Mickey. The last one was supposed to be a kilo, but he ripped us off." Juan was the one who ripped them off by taking almost half a kilogram off the key and only repackaging it where the weight amounted to three-quarters of a kilogram.

"Should I bring a scale this time?" DD laughed, oblivious that his bosses were corrupt.

The officers laughed because they were not in on the quip and others, because they were and benefited from the theft.

"As you all know, the buy will take place at the hotel in Lansburg off the parkway. We wanted the buy to occur in the city where the high school kids overdosed. So far, the total number of deaths in Loudon is five, and two of the users are comatose … now Mickey mentioned to DD that he has other sales in the area, so we expect drugs to be hidden in the car. Now, we want you all doubled up, and if you look at the map, you can see where you will be. Once the buy is complete, DD will take off his hat and drive off."

"When do we approach? Some of us in the outer perimeter will have trouble getting to you all," Todd said.

"Todd, we are concerned that Mickey may have somebody prepared to follow DD, so we have you and the protection team set up to follow him. The inner perimeter team will respond and watch for a rip. The outer perimeter will follow DD behind the protection team."

"That makes no sense. DD already has a protection team. Why aren't we doing this in one of the hotel rooms?" Todd appeared defiant on purpose and may suspect the operation was a cover for something else.

"Todd, Mickey wouldn't have it. He is paranoid about being taped and recorded in a room. He mentioned Delorean as an example," DD said.

Todd seemed unhappy and looked at his DEA partner, David Narvaez, who nodded at him, and then at the Customs agent Terry Garcia, who also nodded. The LT noticed and tried to contain his happiness by having neutered the Feds. "We are running out of time, team. Let Juan wrap this up so we can all get into position." The LT was calm yet assertive.

"We need to be doubled up to limit the number of cars around the hotel. Due to prior commitments, we don't have air. I will be paired up with Jose, and Leroy will be paired up with the LT. Make sure you're all on the tactical talk-around channel. We will listen on DD's mic."

"Before we take off, I want DD to meet up with his four-man protection team, who will be on the scene in the *Suburban*. I want everybody set up in thirty minutes and monitor your radios for changes." He stared at Todd with a scowl. "The most important part. We want DD to drive away from the area, and we'll approach when Mickey drives off to keep them from driving away. Understood?" The LT made a point of getting a nod or a verbal affirmation from every participant. He stared at Todd until he averted his eyes and stepped out of the room. *So far, so good,* he thought.

† † †

Doubts

After the operational briefing, Agent Todd Robert felt as if the back of his neck had a chained plate from his gym pulling his head toward the floor. Alarm bells rang so loudly within his skull that he seriously worried his eardrums would be damaged. David and Terry kept glancing at him, realizing they all needed to find a private place to speak candidly. He pointed to the doors leading to the parking lot. They stepped out together, and as he closed the door behind him, he saw the LT and Juan leering at them.

"Can one of you tell me why the LT needs us to follow DD's car once he leaves? He will already have his protection team with four officers." Todd had doubts about the LT since their first enforcement operation over a year ago.

"The LT has something planned, Todd. He is closing a loop on something again. What did our GS say?" David asked.

"He wants to wait and see what happens and wants us to document the event. He does not want the OIG involved yet." Todd preferred that the inspector general was already involved and knew he could have just called them, but he respected his supervisor, who used to be a prior agent with the Bureau of Narcotics and Dangerous Drugs, or the BNDD.

"Maybe we are being paranoid, Todd. The LT could be getting pressure from the board of supervisors and the mayor's office," Terry said, then paused and twisted her lips. But why keep us so far from the buy itself?" Terry Garcia was an impressive woman. She was five foot ten inches tall and weighed at least 160 pounds, much of which was muscle. She had tanned skin that glowed.

"Ter, can you get the Customs Air unit up to record the buy?"

"Sure, Todd. The guys in Dulles may be on call for another operation. I will contact them as soon as I step away," Terry said.

"Did you talk with DD and try to get him to get Mickey to say where the stuff was imported through?" David was the co-case agent on Terry's Chinese Drug Smuggling ring investigation.

"Yes, he promised to find out. DD knows my interest is how they bring their drugs into the US."

"Terry, you and DD are close. Can you tell him to trust his instincts and be careful?" David asked hesitantly.

Terry stared at David intensely, which caused him to take a step back. "Close, ha?"

"Don't take offense, Terry. We know you're good friends with DD and are mentoring him. Nothing more," Todd said cautiously, realizing David had outed private conversations concerning Terry and DD as possibly dating.

"No offense taken. Look, I'm worried about DD, too. I better take off and make some calls." Terry turned and walked quickly toward her brown Ford *Taurus*. Her government ride or as agents called G-ride. She drove off, spinning her front tires out of the parking lot.

Todd shook his head back and forth at David.

"What did I say?"

"Just get in. We need to get in position, and I want to grab a soda and some beef jerky."

CHAPTER SIX

Closing the Loop

By 7:40 p.m., all team members reported they were in place. DD told the surveillance team over the hidden microphone in his shirt that Mickey would be in a red Cadillac sedan but was running late. Mickey will also be accompanied by his right-hand man, Rocky, a former boxer and Mickey's enforcer. DD backed his blue Dodge *Durango* into a parking spot. The LT sat in his car alongside Leroy, and Juan was partnered with Jose in a parked car nearby. They both knew their respective roles in this buy-*kill* operation. The protection team sat in a connected parking lot of a fast-food hamburger joint within a large Chevrolet *Suburban*.

At about 8:15 p.m., a red 1990 Cadillac *Deville* entered the parking lot and drove around the hotel. Two black males dressed in black were visible in the car.

"Surveillance units, DD has reported that this is Mickey's Caddy. Mickey is the passenger, and Rocky is driving ... heads up, Rocky is an enforcer and always armed." As previously arranged, Juan ensured everyone knew Rocky was a safety concern. This warning will appear in officer reports afterward and help them during any subsequent investigation.

Rocky backed the Cadillac up near the *Durango* but at an angle facing DD. Mickey opened the passenger door and stepped out of the Cadillac. He was a large man, easily over three hundred pounds, who wore large gold chains around his neck and many gold rings on his fingers. Mickey appeared muscular under all that fat. Rocky opened the driver's side door and stepped out of the car. The enforcer wore a black tank top, showing off his bulging muscles.

The LT raised the volume on his radio. Both he and Leroy watched the meeting through binoculars. They were far enough away that the targets could not see them clearly, but they were within walking distance of the exchange.

"The *meet* is taking place. Rocky has a gun in his waistband," Juan said over the radio.

"What up, dawg?" DD's scratchy voice could be heard over the radio as his wire was being monitored. Mickey and DD gave one another a quick bro hug.

"Living the life there, DD. Why do you bring us so far out here?" Mickey asked with a noticeable look even through binos.

"I live in this town, and my whip is acting up," DD said, motioning toward the *Durango*.

"No worries, man, we can make this a regular thing. My man over here does some regular re-ups on this route." Mickey motioned toward Rocky.

"I have the cash over in my duffle." DD grabbed his bag and handed it over to Mickey.

Mickey opened the bag quickly and then tossed it over to his enforcer. "Grab the box."

The LT saw Rocky leaning into the vehicle's passenger side and appeared to press the trunk release button in the glove box because the trunk popped open. Rocky kept fumbling with the dashboard before heading to the back of the car. He returned with a shoe box. Rocky and Mickey met halfway. Mickey took the box and walked back toward DD.

"The hand-off has taken place. The outer perimeter team must be ready to follow DD's *Durango* out of the area. Prepare for an approach," the LT called out. With one hand on the mic and the other on the door handle, a rush of adrenalin flowed through his body.

"Put those binos down and make sure you have a round in the chamber," the LT said.

"I have a revolver," Leroy said.

"You need to start carrying a .45 … get ready. This is about to go down."

The LT dropped the mic and looked once again in his binoculars. DD was in the passenger side of his car. Mickey waited near the front of the *Durango,* with Rocky back in front of the Caddy. "Five small bricks, guys, and the weight seems right. The packages looked like they had some age and were not re-cut."

DD walked towards Mickey. "Looks good, bruh. Those packages look a bit old. The stamps look Chinese."

"China White, right off the boat," Mickey said proudly.

"Not re-cut by your crew?" DD asked.

"I don't play that way. I get a large shipment, I cut my stuff for the street, but my quantity customers get the pure shit."

"Miami?"

"Nah, I have a door over in Portsmouth with some Chinese cats. Works out great for all of us."

Mickey walked off toward Rocky. "Put the bag in the trap."

The LT barely heard that last statement but soon realized that the Cadillac must have a hidden compartment in the trunk. This was working out better than he planned.

Rocky returned to the trunk and placed the bag close to the back seat.

DD was back in the Durango and drove up toward the front of the Caddy. "A'ight Mickey, take it easy. Peace, Rocky." DD took off his hat and pointed at Rocky before driving away.

The protection team followed DD's Durango out of the parking lot. The driver of the Tahoe did his best to follow DD outside of Mickey's sight.

"All units, I have eyes on a gold sedan with heavily tinted windows pulling out behind DD. I'm following it out," Todd said over the radio. Unbeknownst to Todd, the driver of that sedan was a CI, who also happened to be one of the LT's girlfriends.

"I'm following behind you." David pulled out of the parking lot.

The LT flashed his lights. He signaled to Jose and Juan to approach, which they did. He nodded at Leroy, and they stepped out of the car. The LT held his Colt *1911* at his side. Jose placed his Beretta *92FS* on his chest, ready to shoot. The LT called out on the radio. At the last moment, he grabbed his Motorola HT-90 radio and depressed the transmit button. "Everyone go, go, go. Begin your approach. Inner perimeter team can move in now." None of them had police markings or their badges on display.

Mickey saw the two men walking toward him and tapped on their car's hood alerting Rocky who immediately stepped out from behind the vehicle's passenger side door for cover and reached for his gun. "Rocky, it's a rip!" Mickey ran to the driver's side, possibly seeking cover from the approaching men.

Juan saw that Rocky had drawn his gun. He walked quickly toward the enforcer, who took the first shot wildly and hit Juan's ankle, which caused him to fall to the ground. The LT saw Rocky had moved behind the passenger side door of the Caddy while shooting at them. Jose fired twice at Mickey through the windshield, and shards of glass sprayed all over the drug dealer, with one bullet striking his chest and one in the face. Mickey grabbed his face in a panic, then jumped out of the car onto the ground with a thud.

The LT hid behind a car when Rocky started shooting toward him. Glass sprayed down on him. He went behind the engine for cover and then tried to get into position to trade shots with Rocky.

Rocky was shooting through the Caddy's windshield, kneeling behind the passenger door pillar. Jose took a hit to his shoulder, causing him to spin like a top before falling to the ground.

The LT returned to his car and grabbed a shotgun loaded with slugs. Rocky must have shot toward him because several rounds went through his windshield. He turned and ran toward the Caddy while shooting into the passenger side door toward Rocky, who tried to fire back, but the third slug went through the door and into Rocky's chest. This knocked the enforcer away from the protection of the car with a geyser of blood spraying out of his back.

"Shots fired, shots fired. Put it out to patrol," he yelled over his hand-held radio.

The perimeter team arrived at the parking lot and exited their cars smoothly as if practiced. They ran toward the carnage, but the shooting was over.

The LT pulled his badge from his neck chain and onto his shirt. He ran toward Juan and told him in a low voice. "Pull your badge." Juan pulled his badge out of his shirt and onto his chest. Juan's ankle was shattered, and his foot was bent awkwardly. The LT looked for Detective Steve Grant, the unit's medic, and motioned him over. "Go get your kit and start working. Juan and Jose are hit." Steve nodded and ran back to his car. He walked back toward Jose and saw that Detective Beers was treating him. Other detectives were checking on Mickey. "Go help Doug with Jose and Juan." Once alone, he checked Mickey for a pulse and surprisingly found one. Mickey opened his eyes, startling him.

"Who the fuck are you?" Mickey was spurting up blood with each breath.

"The Police, Mickey, you fucked up. You're dying, big man," he said with a smile.

"You're a piece of shit. You did not yell, police … I thought it was a rip." Mickey sprayed more blood all over the LT's trousers.

He pulled a gun from his ankle and threw it into the driver's seat. "You should not try to go for a gun when officers are approaching."

"I thought you were ripping me off, man. Get me an ambulance, you piece of shit."

He placed his knee on Mickey's throat to cut off his airway. Mickey tried to move the LT's knee from his neck. The LT pushed harder into Mickey, which caused the man to cough up blood all over the LT's pants. It did not take long before Mickey passed out and expired. He checked for a pulse and did not find one. He stood up, walked toward other officers, and said, "Mickey's gone. What a shame."

"Found a trap, LT. Look at this!" Detective Beers raised a sealed bag containing hundreds of small cellophane bags with the Mickey stamp.

"That closes that." He was filled with pride at another successful plan.

Todd walked up to the LT. "What the hell happened here, LT?"

"Rocky started shooting at Juan during the approach ... is DD all right?"

"Yes, the car that followed them out turned off. DD is with the protection team back at our debriefing area." Todd looked at the whole scene and shook his head in disbelief.

Confirmed Doubts

Once the homicide detectives arrived, most of the team that was not involved in the shooting, were ushered away. Todd, David, and Terry met later in the local mall's parking lot. Terry was on her Motorola radio but put it away into her vest carrier. Todd had never been as angry as he was at this very moment. He knew the LT was planning something, and the man may have succeeded in burying what he wanted to.

"Terry, did air capture any of this on video?" Todd asked.

"The observer caught most of it from different angles while circling. My buddy in the helicopter said it looked like the guy on the passenger side started shooting on approach."

"Great, we provided proof it was a good shoot." Todd slammed his fist on the car before kicking at one of the back tires.

"Something else happened here, Todd. I will set up a time to view the video."

"Todd, whatever happened here is another of LT's cover-ups. He shut the door on something, and unless someone comes forward, this book is closed." David tossed his ball cap against the vehicle's rear window.

Todd was now sure that the LT was an evil man who would do anything to further his bad deeds. He had to be stopped, but it wasn't the job of the DEA to deal with the corrupt commander in a drug task force. He had only been an agent for five years, and James Cladhaire had been a law enforcement officer for almost thirty years.

"Let's just go to our GS and get the OIG to open a case," David said.

Todd shook his head, thinking it would be a waste of time.

"They may just remove us from the task force. There's not enough evidence to prove what we think is going on," Terry said.

"We're done, guys. I need a drink," Todd said. "You guys coming?"

They all nodded their heads and jumped into their cars. When Todd got into his G-ride, he went to slam his fist on the steering wheel but instead grabbed onto it and screamed. He shook his head and turned the key to the car ignition before driving off.

CHAPTER SEVEN

Awakening

I moved quickly in and out of traffic. The needle on the speedometer was pegged at 125. I was being chased by someone who wanted to kill me. I saw traffic building ahead of me, so I slowed down, and the red smoky car approached quickly. I was almost at an exit and took it quickly. I made the first right and drove quickly through a crowded shopping mall parking lot. The red car was still following and appeared to be closing in. I looked ahead and saw a pedestrian in a crosswalk. I hit the brakes and came to a skidding halt buried in smoke. I placed my hand out the window and motioned for the elderly man to move out of the way, but the man gave me the middle finger. I heard what sounded like a gunshot, and my driver's side window shattered, embedding pieces of glass into my face as my hand popped like a massive geyser, spraying blood throughout the car, including the windshield, which I could no longer see through. I slammed the brakes of the car and came to a stop. All the bones in my left hand were poking out of my skin. I took my workout shirt from my passenger seat and tried to wrap my hand. The Bully Cladhair walked up to my window, and he raised a gun to my face.

"Thanks for making it easy for me, Sasquatch ...

Luke screamed as he grabbed onto his face and began to pull the shards of glass from it. Blood spurted from his face wound onto his left hand each time his heart pumped. He jumped out of bed and into the bathroom, blood spraying on the floor. He stepped into the shower and doused himself with cold water. The white base of the shower was now dark red swirling down the drain. He closed his eyes and let the freezing water draw him from the dream. It worked. He opened his eyes, and the shower pan was white again. He switched the knob to heat. The warm water calmed him even more and helped as he massaged his hand in the hot water. His hand was intact but still ached horribly. *I have been here before*, he thought. Several times before, he had taken a cold shower to awaken himself from a horrible dream. In truth, it was a warning of what was to come.

After stepping out of the shower, he prepared quickly for school. He walked downstairs and noticed something was off. Nobody else was awake. He looked at the clock in the kitchen and saw that it was 6:00 in the morning. He left the front door and saw his father's Monte Carlo was. It came to him. It was the weekend.

"Great, I woke up early, and it's Sunday." He lay on the sofa with his backpack on, promptly falling asleep. He was being shaken, causing him to open his eyes. His father was looking down on him.

"Son, why are you all dressed for school? Did you go to sleep like this?"

He sat up groggily. "I had a bad dream, woke up, and got ready for school. I forgot it was Sunday."

"I give you points for trying, at least. It's better than waking up late on a school day," his father said. "I was going to the mall but forgot my wallet … come to breakfast in town with me."

"I'm starving, Dad, and I am all dressed up with nothing to do." He removed his backpack and followed his father out the front door while he rubbed the sleep from his eyes.

"Luke, grab the Sunday paper, please."

He brought the paper to his father's car and read the headline *Five Students at Lansburg High Overdose Overnight*. The article did not have much information other than explaining that two people were in a coma and not expected to survive. Three underage students passed away, and one was being held for observation in the critical care unit. Several people in town also overdosed.

"Dad looks like some kids from my school overdosed on Friday night on a bad mixture of heroin and what they believe to be something called fentanyl. The article said something like this happened in New York City in the 1970s."

"That's terrible. Do you know any of the kids?"

"No names, Dad. Something about the students being minors. There was a police-involved shooting Saturday night at a hotel. According to a source, it was related to the overdoses."

"Let's stop by Benji's shop and see if he knows anything?"

"Sure, Dad. Pull into the back when you get there."

They arrived at Laio's Customs—Benji waved at them from one of the bays.

"Hello, Mr. Sanz. Finally! Do you need me to repaint your car or give the engine some pep? Hey Luke, what's shaking?"

"No, Benji, we needed to talk to you about something. Show him the paper."

Benji read the headline of the paper. "I saw it this morning and made some calls. Most of these kids are seniors, but one was a sophomore. The younger brother of Steve Rustova from art class, who has an addiction problem." Benji knew most of the local kids at the high school.

"Is there Anybody else we should know?" He was worried that one of his acquaintances in his art or music class had passed away.

"One other, yes, maybe Daniel knows him. Oscar Leon is on the baseball team and is not expected to make it. I don't know the others yet, but they were all boys, no girls."

"Where do you think they bought the drugs, Benji?" His father asked with a cop's curiosity.

"Mr. Sanz, I would not know, but if I were to guess, I would say the Bully Cladhair."

"Cladhaire, James Cladhaire's son? He runs the local drug task force. How surprising … the son of the drug task force commander is a pusher."

"Been one for years as far as I know. Where are you headed?"

"To breakfast, Benji. Want to come?"

"No, I need to prep this '66 *Nova* for painting. Leave Luke with me, and I will show him the trade." Benji smiled deviously while he rubbed both hands together.

"Do you want to stay?"

"After breakfast, Dad."

"I'll bring him back in about an hour, Benji."

"Bring your car in for me to check the throttle and exhaust. It sounds like it's lagging." Benji tapped on the hood as he walked away.

"It's been lagging. Luke, I may drive back home after breakfast, and you can bring my car in for Benji to check out."

"Sure, Dad. It's been a long time since I drove the Intimidator." His father told him last year when they gifted him the *Grand National* that Luke should name his car like his father had.

"Have you named your car yet?"

"Not yet, Dad. Still thinking about it." In truth, he hadn't given it much thought. He loved his car but not enough to name the thing.

Jackie Chan

Mr. Waters just finished giving the semester's final lecture. Luke, Benji and Alyssa anticipated this since this they wanted to start the practical aspects of the class.

"Now that we have finalized the lecture and foundational material part of this course, we will move on to practice and implementation. I have reviewed your initial questionnaire responses from the first day of class. I will name each student, and we will establish where we are." Mr. Waters stepped away from his podium with a business portfolio, dragging a chair behind him to the front of the class. "Before I proceed, does anybody have questions?"

None of the students raised their hands. He looked throughout the classroom with concern. Luke was mainly worried that he might be asked to do vocals.

"Nothing ... let's get this started." Mr. Waters opened his portfolio. "Benji will be drums. George will be on percussion and drums backup. Alyssa will be playing the piano. Sally will play the flute and vocals. Luke is on electric and acoustic guitar. Kevin is on trumpet and synthesizer. Ace is bass guitar, double bass, and rhythm guitar. Greta will be playing the violin and vocals. Juana on clarinet and vocals. Lastly, we have Randy on Saxophone." The teacher closed the portfolio. "We will play different numbers and build on what songs we will focus on for the recital in May."

The first bell rang, and he grabbed his backpack from the floor.

Alyssa walked up to him before he left. "I figured you were going to do vocals."

"I'm too shy for that. I would embarrass myself and everybody else when I freeze on stage," Luke said shyly.

"Can you sing at all?" Alyssa asked

"I know the words to my favorite songs, but if I see somebody looking at me, I will freeze. I'm not a true performer."

They walked together in the hallway. He was still shy with Alyssa but comforted by her presence. She grabbed his arm and looked into his eyes ... *I sat in the back seats of the Grand National with Alyssa. Her shirt was open, and her bra was visible. I grabbed at her and stared into her eyes, and we kissed. Her tongue made way into my mouth. My whole body shivered ...* Luke was brought back to the present. He leaned in toward Alyssa and kissed her.

She kissed him back and moved him forward. "Wait a minute. I was about to tell you that you can sing to me, and then you steal a kiss," Alyssa said.

"Exactly ... well, no, I saw something when you touched me and couldn't help myself."

"What did you see?" Alyssa asked as they began to walk down the hallway.

"Something I've seen before, but it hasn't happened yet. We are in the back seat of my car making out, and I think we are about to, well, you know."

She slapped his arm. "Please don't tell me I'm going to lose my virginity in the back of your car." Alyssa covered her face, embarrassed.

"You're not going to lose your virginity in the back of just any car, Alyssa."

She slapped his arm again. "I better get going." She walked away, and he stood still, forgetting what class he had next. She looked at him as if she hoped he was watching her walk away. She wore a skirt today, and he had difficulty not staring at her legs. He just remembered he had his career development class. He turned and saw that Benji had not waited for him, so he darted down the hallway quickly and happened upon Jimmy pushing David Villa, Junior's friend.

"Jimmy, what are you doing? Leave him alone." Luke placed himself between David and Jimmy. "You outweigh him by a hundred pounds."

"This runt told me to leave his food alone during lunch today and then ran off like a punk. Give him to me. He's mine." Jimmy tried to kick David's leg.

Luke blocked Jimmy's kick, which caused him to lose his balance and fall to the floor.

"That one earned you a demerit, Luke." Jimmy shot toward Luke's legs, attempting to take him to the ground. Jimmy crashed into the wall instead as Luke shuffled away quickly. "Sasquatch, take what is due to you, or else."

Jimmy moved toward him and began punching, but Luke blocked each punch by striking at known pressure points on Jimmy's forearms, which caused enough pain to stop the assault.

"Run, David, go to class." He tried to position himself to keep Jimmy from running after David. Jimmy launched himself toward Luke, who rolled away on the floor.

"How can such a big guy be a regular Jackie Chan?" Jimmy asked, still trying to find an opening to attack.

"I'm trying not to hurt you, Jimmy," he responded.

"You don't get it. You lost already. You need to be aggressive, or I win before we start." Jimmy jumped toward Luke, who moved out of the way but struck his head against the wall. Jimmy landed a jab on his face, forcing him to his knees.

"You two cut it out now!" The school security officer yelled from down the hall as Jimmy was about to hammer down on Luke.

Jimmy looked at him. "If it were a teacher, I would have finished you. Don't mess with me when I'm disciplining my vassals." Jimmy ran out of the school toward the senior parking lot.

The out-of-shape security officer came waddling down toward him and helped him up. "Are you okay? Was that the Bully Cladhair?"

"Yes, it was, but I'm fine. I need some ice." Luke's eyes were spinning as if from a long night of drinking.

"I'll tell you what … the principal lets that guy get away with murder. If I tell Mr. Devry, you will get suspended for fighting," the guard said before stepping away.

"I need to get to my career development class anyway," Luke said, dizzy.

"I will bring you some ice. Wait in front of your classroom." The security guard walked away.

I need to fight Jimmy, he thought. He was burning inside, along with the feeling of nearly getting his bell rung. Luke realized he must fight Jimmy before he lashed out against one of Luke's friends or family. However, his mother always told him he must avoid fighting because it proved that you had devolved. His father was different. He made sure they all knew how to fight, but also told him that fighting at school was forbidden. *What's a vassal anyway?* he asked himself, shaking his head, confused and unsteady.

CHAPTER EIGHT

Surveillance

Luke followed Jimmy Cladhaire for a few hours. Sebastian told him it would be worth following Jimmy if he wanted to know what the man was truly up to. He drove the Ford *Taurus* because he worried the *Grand National* would be too easy to spot. He followed Jimmy to a house that Luke presumed was his home. He sat there for an hour or so and almost drove away. Suddenly, the *Firebird* darted out of the driveway into the road carelessly. He looked at his watch, and it was about 5:00 p.m., so he wrote this down on his notes, which looked more like illegible scratches.

Jimmy did not appear to be looking for a tail or have any concern that he was being watched. Sebastian had insisted that Jimmy's actions would be eye-opening. So far, it has been mostly dull, and he considered driving home for the second time after seeing Jimmy enter the local convenience store.

"Wait for it, Luke ... be patient," Sebastian said, pointing to the side of the store where two police cruisers were parked side by side in the parking lot.

He saw Jimmy through the window. He had picked up some items, including a white box and a six-pack of beer, before heading to the cashier to pay but then returned to the coffee counter. His view was obstructed, so he raised his father's binoculars and focused. Jimmy opened the white box and appeared to place something within it. He switched to his father's camera with a zoom lens and began taking pictures.

Jimmy exited the store and placed a bag in his car through an open window. He then walked toward the police cars with the white box, which he handed to one of the officers. The officer handed Jimmy something before returning to his car and driving off. The officers then drove away together.

"Follow the police cars," Sebastian ordered.

He hesitantly followed the patrol cars from a distance. "Why am I following police officers?" he asked. "These officers will be able to pick up on being followed." Luckily, they pulled into a restaurant parking lot. He found an inconspicuous spot near a hotel dumpster across from the restaurant. He grabbed the binoculars, looked around, and saw a streetlamp flicker where one of the police cars was now parked. The dome light turned on when one officer moved to the other's car. Both officers were visible in one of the patrol units. One was a white male, and the other was a black male.

As the streetlight flickered off, he saw the spark of a lighter, and both officers were smoking something. They placed a substance in a glass pipe and lit it. The cops were pounding on each other's chests.

"Murderous fiendish scumbags," a large black man standing next to the dumpster said, pointing at the officer's patrol units.

This startled him enough to drop the binoculars. Something was not right with the man. "Why is that?" Luke asked.

The man looked towards Luke; blood ran down the man's black shirt. His face appeared shades of purple, with his eyes bulging out of his face unnaturally.

"My God ... what happened to you?" he asked.

"Follow them, pigs. Don't let them get away with what they did to Rock and me." The apparition dissipated into the air.

His mouth hung open; he covered it with his hand. His heart was pounding as if he were on one of his runs. The other officer walked back to his patrol car, so Luke attempted to follow both vehicles from a distance. He was buried in thought about what he had just seen and was concerned that the officers would spot him tailing them.

"Luke, they are bad men. Follow them and see," Sebastian said, placing a gloved hand on his shoulder.

"It's not my first ghost, but that one was full of bullet holes."

"I told you that you would do and see things that would harden you. Keep moving, or you will lose them. Turn into this clearing and watch."

He turned where Sebastian indicated into a large parking lot near the mall. He reached for his binos. "This is a mall parking lot, not a clearing."

Sebastian moved his head back and forth, looking at the near-empty parking lot. "It's also a clearing."

He watched the patrol cars join up with people placing vests of varying colors over their shoulders. With his father's binos, he saw the backs of the raid vests with writing. *POLICE, DEA, SHERIFF,* and *US CUSTOMS.* The person wearing the US Customs vest was a woman. He moved the binos around and saw that she had a stunning shape. She was tall with black hair in a ponytail. Her skin tone was something out of a sun tanning lotion commercial.

"Pay attention to all of them, not just the girl," Sebastian ordered.

He broke the view from the binoculars and saw the two uniformed officers had joined the group.

They all drove off in different directions. "Who do I follow? They scattered." He set the binoculars aside and put the car into gear.

"Follow the blue wagon to the right," Sebastian said.

"It looks like a Dodge *Durango.* What am I seeing here?"

"I'm not really sure, but I know you need to see this."

"They seem too busy to notice that I'm following them," he said, reluctantly driving out of the parking lot. After several miles, they entered the opposite side of the mall.

"Park here and watch what happens."

They were on the east side of the Lansburg Shopping Mall, which was relatively small compared to other malls. The *Durango* parked near a pick-up truck. The driver stepped out of the vehicle. He wore a purple shirt and white pants. Two black men approached one another and snapped their hands together. They spoke before, one handed the other a box and the other a paper bag. Then, they walked back to their cars. The man wearing purple removed his hat and got in his vehicle.

"Follow the one with the cart in the back," Sebastian said.

"It's called a pick-up truck."

"Trust me, follow him and watch what happens."

"I trust you, Sebastian." He drove off and followed the pick-up from a few car lengths away. The pick-up passed one of the police cars at an intersection. He was caught at a red light while the pickup proceeded forward. The police car turned to follow the pick-up.

"Watch," Sebastian said.

The police car moved behind the pick-up, and he lost sight of both vehicles as they proceeded. "I lost them."

"Keep going, and you will see."

"The signal flashed green. He pulled forward and drove briefly until he saw flashing lights ahead. The police car had pulled over the pick-up truck. He passed the stopped vehicles and saw the white officer who he saw smoking drugs earlier walk up to the pick-up. He approached another intersection and continued watching via his rearview mirrors. He saw another patrol car waiting at the same red light facing the opposite direction. As the light turned green, he proceeded forward. It was the same black officer from before and the man stared at him as they passed one another.

"Make this left here and park for a few minutes," Sebastian said.

"What happened here?"

"The man in the parking lot sells what you call drugs, and the soldiers are trying to stop him. Most of these men and women are good. Not the people you're after. They are bad men."

"How do you know this?"

"I'm not always with you. I can look at everything else affecting your life and help you when possible. As you know, if I push myself too hard, my energy and manna get used up, making it difficult for me to be with you."

"Can I send you to other places to spy for me, too?" he asked.

"Yes ... turn back on the path here and pass by again."

"It's called a road or highway," he corrected Sebastian.

"Take this road here and drive past them."

He followed Sebastian's instructions. He observed that they had a man on the sidewalk in handcuffs, two boxes, and several brown bags on the patrol car's trunk.

"You saw what you needed to see. Drive back home and go to sleep."

He stopped at a red light at the following intersection. "You're bossy, Sebastian," he said.

"You're the boss, Luke." Sebastian stared out the window past him to Luke's left. "It would be best if we don't have conversations so openly in front of others. People will think you're going crazy."

He was so animated that he yelled out that last part. "We've been with one another long enough that I know when we can talk together. Luke noticed a kid pointing at him from the car to his right just then.

"That kid over there is talking to himself." He overheard through his open windows before driving through the green light.

"Great, now other people know I'm nuts."

"I tried to warn you, Luke."

Luke angrily looked toward Sebastian, letting out a psst sound. "Why did you show me this?"

"You wanted to follow Jimmy around. You needed to see this

because it ties directly to Jimmy. Some of those soldiers are protecting him."

Luke laughed and slapped his thigh. "They aren't soldiers. They are the police. They arrest people who are violating our laws."

"Do you understand what I'm saying? Those two uniformed men protect Jimmy. It could be even more than that."

Luke shook his head with a forceful uncertainty. "I have no idea what to do."

"Neither do I, Luke ... what happens to the people they arrest?"

"Oh, well, the officer presents the case to an attorney for the state or government, and then a judge and jury of their peers come to a decision at trial. It could take months or years to resolve."

"That sounds like a waste of time. If one of my soldiers violated a law, I decided on whether I should whip him or hang him."

"Brutal, Sebastian. Times have changed over the past three hundred years."

"For the better? Why would your society need months or years to resolve what just happened?" Sebastian asked, perplexed.

Luke took a deep breath realizing he just didn't have a correct response. Being just a kid himself, he did not have any strong beliefs concerning the criminal justice system itself. He needed to become more worldly. "I don't have an answer for you. We are just more civilized now."

"Civilized? If you just let that man who sold drugs back into society tomorrow what would he do?"

"He would sell drugs again, because he wasn't punished."

"Exactly. If you gave him six lashes, he would think twice about violating your laws," Sebastian said proudly.

He just arrived home and parked the car next to the *Grand National*. He sat in thought for several seconds. "Maybe, but that's not our way." However, his thoughts betrayed his words. *What is my way?*

He let himself into the house and saw his parents and Junior in the living room watching the television. He closed the door quietly and walked down the stairs.

"Where have you been?" his mother asked. "Why didn't you take your car?"

Luke had thought about how to respond but his mind went blank. He didn't want to lie but he did have Benji change the oil on the Taurus after school. "I was with Benji earlier ... he changed the car oil."

"Well, Father Robert called. He wants you to call him back."

Luke moved quickly toward the phone in the kitchen. "I'll call Robert back before it gets any later."

"That's Father to you, kiddo," his father said.

"Sure, Dad." Luke walked toward his father and grabbed his shoulder ... *my father knows I was being deceptive but is not concerned* ... he kept walking to the kitchen and called Robert.

He dialed the shared phone number to the clergy house. The tone kept on for several minutes.

"Hello?" Robert asked.

"Robert, is that you?" Luke asked.

"It's me. I've been waiting for a couple of hours but couldn't fall asleep until we spoke."

"What's up? Is everything okay?" Luke asked with concern.

"Yes, but I need you to come to church this Sunday. I will be giving my first solo service."

"Of course, Robert. I'll be there with the family. I'm looking forward to it."

Robert let out a deep breath. "Thanks, I could really use a real friend in the audience."

"Of course, I cannot wait ... you can go to sleep now," he said.

"My eyes are closing already. Goodnight, buddy."

The line disconnected and Luke hung up the phone. He looked inside the fridge and closed it quickly realizing he wasn't hungry. He walked back into the living room, and the television was off, and everyone was upstairs except for Tony who stared at him and whined.

"Come on Ton, let's go work out."

CHAPTER NINE

Ostrich

Luke concentrated on grilling the meat for their mother's barbecue. His parents and their family friends were at a table on the opposite side of the deck, closest to the house's living room. Directly behind him was a round table occupied by his brother Daniel, his wife Joyce, and their son Tristan. Junior sat with his friend David Villa. His best friend Benji sat with Birdy, holding hands, partaking in an intimate conversation. He had Benji's burger off to one side, because his friend wanted his meat rare.

Alyssa stood beside him after he had taken his first round of steaks and burgers to the table where his parents sat. She had grown comfortable and friendly with his parents, especially his mother, Helen.

Jorge Valenzuela and his wife, Emily, were at the adult table. Wildomar Rivera sat near his godmother, Kamila Poder. His mother had tried several times over the past year to set those two up romantically, and it finally appeared to be working.

"Are you almost done with this batch, Luke?" Alyssa asked while caressing his arm.

Her touch stirred him inside, keeping him from answering her. He looked into her eyes, taking her in before nodding in the affirmative. He turned off the burners and placed the burgers and hot dogs on the tray she held before him. After placing Benji's burger on the tray, he leaned in and stole a quick kiss that she quickly turned into something more intense

"Get a room, guys. I don't think I can handle the smooching over my burger," Benji said before slapping his thigh.

Luke turned and stared at Benji menacingly but quickly smiled. He realized he could look intimidating and did not want his friend to perceive that he was angry at him.

Alyssa took the tray to the table, and they all served themselves. "Be nice, Benji," she said before leaning in and kissing his cheek.

"That's my man, Alyssa." Birdy grabbed Benji by the ears and kissed him.

"There's enough to go around, girls."

Luke brought Benji's beef patty over to him on a plate. "Here you go, buddy." He leaned in as if to kiss Benji's cheek but instead twisted his buddy's ear.

"That hurt, but it's better than getting a kiss from you." Benji laughed while he prepared his burger with tons of bacon.

Luke sat next to Benji, grabbed two patties without buns, and began eating.

"Are you still looking for a job?" Benji asked.

"Not yet," he said before taking a mouthful of beef. Luke grabbed a couple of hot dogs and began eating one without a bun. He settled with the thought that he would end up working at something he was not interested in.

"You could work in the guitar store in Leesburg, or how about a gym," Alyssa said.

"I tried the guitar shop. It's family-owned and operated. The gym is a good idea. I would get to work out for free." He was happy with his Fortress of Calmness in the garage and did not want to spend his time in a gym close to others who may end up touching him. *I may have to drop the class*, he thought.

"Luke, David is telling me that the Bully Cladhair keeps pestering him," Junior said, changing the conversation.

David lived a few houses down. Like Junior, he was in the eleventh grade and had been friends with Luke's brother since they moved into the neighborhood. Like his brother Daniel, he was a baseball player and an athletic kid. However, Jimmy had an edge over most as a nearly twenty-year-old man who was a football player and had been to jail.

"What does he want, David?" Luke asked before finishing his hot dog.

"My lunch, money, obedience ... I don't know, he's nuts or something. He keeps saying he's making his rounds and doesn't want me outside during lunch," David said.

"Stay clear from that guy, both of you ... nobody seems to want to deal with him," he said. That included him. He did not know how to deal with Jimmy.

"Use all those muscles and kick his ass, Luke," Junior said.

He sighed and shook his head angrily as he touched the bruise on his face. "I already told you I tried, Junes."

"Did you really? You gave it your all?"

Luke folded his hands and developed a frown. "Mom and Dad don't want us fighting in school. Dad let us take boxing as long as we promised that we stuck with it and didn't fight at school ... well, that last part was mom and grandma." He sat silently, with a bit of embarrassment.

"I've heard stories from Todd about Jimmy, Luke. He was a terror when he played football against the other team and his own. He's unreasonable and volatile. I heard he pushed a coach once," Daniel said.

"I saw him push the coach, and Principal Devry didn't kick him off the team or give him detention." Alyssa laid her head on Luke's shoulder, placed her arm around him, and squeezed. "He doesn't have a filter. He doesn't see the consequences of his actions."

He knew her to be correct, but something kept leading him to think that everybody had to have some goodness in them somewhere. "I think you're all taking this too seriously. There must be something he cares about—his car or a dog or something."

"You sound like Dad was last year with Avandeil—your head is in the sand," Junior said, quickly putting his hand over his mouth in regret.

"Ouch, that was pretty harsh, Junior," Daniel said.

Luke placed his head in his hands. A rush of adrenalin ran through him and brought a red tinge to his body and sweat to his brow. Not since his bouts with anxiety had he felt so overwhelmed.

Sebastian appeared beside him and placed a hand on Luke's head. "Luke, you don't need to protect the dignity of a man who treats others so poorly and who is protected by others that fail to protect all who are under their care."

Luke peered at his guardian and smiled. "You're right, guys … I'll work on it, okay?"

"Hey, Luke, how's it going?" Wildomar Rivera stood by their table, holding a beer.

"Oh, Hello, Mr. Rivera … ah, we're fine. Just talking about school," he responded.

"Interesting … it's Wil, Luke, never mind that. I heard from your parents and Jorge that you are taking a career development class."

"Yes, Mr. Rivera, I mean Wil … but why do you ask?"

Wil motioned him towards the corner of the deck and away from the youngster's table.

"This will be fortuitous, Luke. A door is being opened for you." Sebastian stepped aside and floated over the edge of the deck.

Luke followed Wil and all his tension was gone, but he felt odd speaking with the man in semi-privacy.

"Do you know what I do?" Wil asked.

"You're a special agent like my father but with the US Customs Service?"

"I'm the resident agent in charge or RAC of the Customs

76

office covering this area of Loudon County. I started in Puerto Rico as a line agent."

"What's a RAC?" Luke asked.

"Well, it just means I run the office here. I have fifteen other agents, including a group supervisor and some support staff, who help run the office."

"What does a customs agent do?"

"Before I answer that, I wanted to know whether you would be interested in working for me as a Customs Intern. How old are you?"

Luke was speechless, his mind racing. He looked at Sebastian, who gave him the thumbs up. *You don't even know what an intern is*, he thought. "What does an intern do? I'm seventeen but will be eighteen soon."

"In all honesty, you'll be manning our front door, getting the mail, answering phones, washing our cars ... but if you befriend the agents, they will mentor you and show you how to work on cases and more. Some interns don't do anything but the minimum, but if you work hard and volunteer to help, they will teach you. Deep down, agents want to impart what they know on new blood."

"I don't know what to say ... where do I sign up?" Luke asked, with enthusiasm.

"First, I needed to know if you were interested because it's unpaid. You have to be eighteen and technically need to be in college, but I'll figure that one out with my ASAC."

He knew what this one meant from his father. An ASAC was an assistant special agent in charge. "Do I need to fill out an application?"

"Do you have a resume?" Wil asked.

"We are working on that in class, but it's not very impressive. I'm just a high school student ... as you well know, but I'll work very hard."

Wil laughed, walked toward him and slapped him on his back ... *I moved backward into darkness and landed on a seat at a table*

77

in a very damp room. The weather reminded me of Puerto Rico. I looked out of the window and saw a palm tree in between another building with a rusty facade. Suddenly, I heard a moan and looked to a corner of the room where I saw a man crouched inside of a wooden cage made from the branches of trees. There was a stink in the room that reminded me of an outhouse I once pissed in at a construction yard. I stood and walked up to the cage. I recognized the man. It was Wil ... the motion forward brought on a bout of nausea, but he did his best to wave it away.

"I need to speak with your teacher. Did you know that he's Jorge's cousin?"

"No, I didn't know that."

"Small world, but they both are from this area and are very tight," Wil said.

Luke nodded at Wil but did not know what else to say. He noticed that his brother Daniel and Joyce went back into the house.

"I'll let you get back to your friends." With that, Wil returned to the table with all the adults.

His brother Junior soon took off to the side of the house with David Villa who waved at him, which he returned.

He walked back to the table, sat down quietly and looked toward his father who appeared to salute him by raising his beer.

"What was that about?" Benji asked.

"He offered me an internship."

"Are you going to turn their targets while they shoot?" Luke and Benji laughed.

"I hope not ... no, it's to man their front desk, but it will be unpaid."

"Don't look so worried. It's probably the best internship any of us will be doing." Benji leaned in towards Birdy and placed his head in the crook of her neck. "Can we go make out now?"

"Sshh, you little fiend ... give me ten minutes to freshen up," Birdy stood up and ran into the house.

Benji waved to Luke and Alyssa before waving to his parents. He quickly realized that Benji and Birdy would have kids together, and maybe he should warn them to be safe, but instead, he leaned onto Alyssa. "Do you want to go make out?"

Alyssa slapped his shoulder softly. "I promised your mom I would help clean up."

He looked down and appeared devastated but shot up in his seat. "We can always come back … it looks like they will be at it for another hour or two."

She smiled at him, grabbed his hand, and pulled him toward the side of the house toward his car.

His insides stirred as she led him closer to his car. Just then, he recalled the conversation about Jimmy. A fleeting thought remained that it was up to him to find the one thing the Bully cared about, and he could change the man into someone worth keeping in society regardless of what anyone said.

CHAPTER TEN

New Beginnings

Luke and his family arrived at the Lansburg Catholic church off Main Street and Joshua. It felt odd for him, but Luke dressed more formally as if it were Easter Sunday. He wore a gray dress shirt with a thin black tie under a leather jacket his parents bought him last Christmas. His mother looked at him oddly as he left the house earlier.

"I'm trying to place it, but the way you're dressed looks familiar … like from a movie," Junior said, holding his chin while they walked toward the church entrance. "Don't tell me, I'll get it."

"It's not a secret, I'll tell you."

Junior placed his hand up, deep in thought. "It will come to me."

He saw that his brother Daniel and his wife Joyce were waiting at the front of the church. His nephew Tristan was in the stroller, waving at them.

His parents rushed to their grandson and knelt on either side of the stroller.

"How's the most beautiful grandchild in the world?" his mother asked.

His father tickled Tristan, beaming proudly at his grandson

and Luke who stood near the entrance of the church. Tristan stared at Luke and waved animatedly at him.

"I'm thinking *Ren McCormack* from *Footloose*, right?" Daniel said, reaching toward him and slapping his shoulder … *Daniel wore an untucked New York Yankees jersey standing on first base. I stood near the pitcher's mound, watching. A player working the short-stop position tossed a ball at Daniel at full speed, who caught it effortlessly. I looked at my surroundings and couldn't tell which baseball park we were in. Staring toward home plate, I looked up toward a sign that said, "Welcome to Oriole Park at Camden Yards." I was witnessing how Daniel will become an Oriole. I shifted my view and saw Junior standing next to a large man in an Army uniform and a black beret. On the soldier's shoulder was a single chevron with an arc. I walked toward Junior and noticed he looked slightly older and taller than he looked now. The soldier stared at me as if he could see me. He appeared sad and broken somehow. Not hardened, as I had seen him before. It was me …* Daniel looked at Luke and then at Tristan. His brother placed a hand on his chest and shook, motioning with his head up and down. A tear flowed freely from Daniel.

"Dad, can we sit as far up as possible?" Luke asked.

"Sure, son … you choose, just close to the side exit," his father said.

He nodded in the affirmative, confidently led the way into the church's nave, and sat on the left side near the *ambo* or lectern. He saw Robert seated near the altar in the presider's chair, wearing an ornate chasuble. He looked older than his twenty-six years with a worrisome countenance. Robert looked up, and their eyes met, causing Robert to smile. He stood up quickly and walked toward him. Luke felt awkward but stood up and met Robert near the lectern.

"Thanks for coming, Luke … I was worried you wouldn't make it," Robert said.

"I wouldn't have missed it. Thanks for the invite, Robert."

The priest smiled and placed a hand over his heart. He then waved toward Luke's family, and they waved back at the priest before he walked quickly back toward the altar.

Luke turned around and watched as other congregants entered the large church and began to sit. Something caught his eye, and he thought he saw a man sitting on top of another man's shoulders. A woman sat in a wheelchair near the man. He rubbed his eyes and looked again. A tall, red-haired man sat beside a woman with a flushed red face. Next to him sat Jimmy Cladhaire, and beside him was the woman in a wheelchair. Nothing was on any of their shoulders.

"Sit down, Luke. They are about to begin," his mother said.

He sat down as Robert stood behind the ambo and began to speak. He missed the introduction with all the thoughts racing through his mind. *I have never seen Jimmy in church*, he thought.

"It has been six months since my mentor and friend, Father Dwayne Freeman, passed away doing the right thing as he always set off to do. Father D brought me into the clergy after surviving an attack from rival gang members in Cleveland. I was raised in the streets and joined a gang when I was twelve years old. Tragic as it sounds, I still went to school and even graduated from high school. I was never arrested for what I did, but I have plenty of regrets. On my graduation day, I was driving a stolen car with the leader of our gang in my passenger seat. He was shot and killed. One of the bullets went through my leader and hit me here." Robert motioned to the left side of his chest and took a deep breath. "I met Father D as he gave me my last rites at the hospital." Father Robert paused for effect while the members of the congregation gasped.

Luke had heard a variation of this story. Robert passed away and claimed to have met with Father D's mentor, Father William, at the end of a well-lit corridor. The priest told Robert that his journey was only beginning and that he should turn around and take his place next to Father Dwayne.

"I lived, and when I was released from the hospital, I came to live in this clergy house as a helper until I attended seminary. I thought that the church covered the costs ... I only learned recently that Father D paid for my education," Robert said, his voice cracking.

Members of the congregation, including Luke and his family, appeared intrigued. *Robert never told me that part*, he thought.

"Father D left us all early, but he told me many times that he was grooming me to take his place. I thought it would be ten years from now," Robert said as he peered to his right and wiped the tears from his face. "Because of you, I feel prepared to move forward."

Luke looked toward the sacristy, where Robert's gaze led him. Father D was indeed standing there listening to his mentee speak.

Robert looked back toward the congregation. "I want to read a verse from Isaiah. *Forget the former things; do not dwell on the past. See, I am doing a new thing!* I could never forget my mentor, and I will always remember that he lost his life, saving a family from torment. I can only hope to be worthy to stand here today and preach the Gospels."

After the service, Luke attempted to reach Jimmy and his family. He hoped to bring their adversarial relationship to a close. However, all he managed to do was jump into a log jam of other congregants he tried to avoid touching to avert being invaded by unwelcomed visions. He saw an exit and took it. He positioned himself outside to monitor the parking lot. He stood by himself, having now misplaced his family. *I feel like an abandoned child*, he mused. A stroller was pushed out of the doorway from the church's nave. His family poured out behind the stroller, which held a grinning Tristan, pointing a finger at his uncle Luke, who smiled.

He caught a glimpse of a wheelchair headed toward the parking lot. Jimmy was pushing the woman. He waved at his parents and held up a hand, hoping they understood to give him five minutes. He darted off toward Jimmy. "Hey, can I talk to you?"

Jimmy turned around with the wheelchair to face Luke.

"Jimmy is a good boy," the woman in the wheelchair said.

He got a good look at the woman. She was in her mid-twenties, and one side of her face drooped as if she had a stroke at some point.

"What do you want, Sasquatch," Jimmy said sarcastically.

"I wanted to try and resolve things, Jimmy." He looked toward the church and motioned toward it. "Thinking this is the right place and time … I have nothing against you."

Jimmy peered awkwardly at him. "Are you sure about that?"

"Why not? I don't want any problems."

Jimmy peered behind him and then turned back, staring into Luke's soul. "Turn and walk away the next time I'm disciplining the underclassmen."

Luke was shocked. *What's wrong with this guy?* "Jimmy, you know I can't do that. Do you need to rule over everybody?"

"Stop being an idiot and bring Karen over to us. She needs to get something to eat." The woman with flushed red skin, presumably Jimmy's mother, croaked out.

Luke looked at the woman and waved. She sighed and turned in annoyance, shuffling toward the parking lot past a large man with a horrifyingly creepy vulture perched on his shoulders. Its razor-sharp talons seemed to be embedded into the man's flesh. Almost as if melded. The emaciated body of the creature was covered in greenish-brown scales. It had a big Buddha belly along with dusky-gray wings with weathered holes. *It must be a demon, what else could it be?*

"Jimmy, bring your sister now," the man said, pointing toward the car with his left hand. A badge and gun were visible on the man's left side. The abomination on the man's shoulders opened its wings and pointed a clawed finger toward the car as if commanding.

"Walk away, Sasquatch … the two of us will have our talk when the time comes, and you will lose," Jimmy said, waving a fist at him.

With that, Jimmy turned and pushed Karen behind their

parents. The vulture was gone. That slimy creature was melded into the shoulders of Jimmy's father. It had to be a demon feeding off the man's soul. What struck him most was that the demon appeared to be part of the man, as if it had found *its* home long ago. He failed at resolving his issues with the Bully but hoped him to start a conversation. He rejected that demon on the back of Jimmy's father as a mere inconvenience, as if it was unrelated to the negative behavior that Jimmy exuded.

"A boy raised in the home with a demonic possessed man. What sort of man will such a boy become?" Sebastian asked, materializing beside him.

"I figured it was a demon of some type, but it looks like it's growing into him."

"That man gave into that evil spirit years ago. You are one of the few that could discern between the two."

"Luke, are you okay? Why were you talking with the Bully Cladhair?" Junior asked.

He shook his head back and forth, confused and trying to wipe away the thought of what he faced with Jimmy—a man raised in darkness who was keeping the school's students in bondage. "I'm trying to resolve our differences ..." He trailed off into thought, realizing the differences remained.

"Did it work?"

Luke peeked at Sebastian, who shook his head from left to right in the negative. "I hope so," he said, placing a hand on Junior's shoulder ... *darkness and screams filled my ears* ... he was back in the present. The vision did not help his cause at all. Tough times were approaching, and darkness waited patiently because something evil expected to triumph.

CHAPTER ELEVEN

RAC Leesburg

Luke left the school grounds along with Benji. He was a bit nervous because he was heading to the US Customs Service office to meet with Wil to discuss the internship. Now that he was eighteen, he had completed the lecture portion of his career development class with every other classmate. He was ready to start his internship. The possibility of becoming like his father scared him as much as it comforted him. He loved his father deeply and would love to be respected as much as he was.

"You're worrying me. You look a little nervous, Luke," Benji said, standing beside him with their cars parked side by side.

"I have never had a job, and now I'm going to intern in an office with a bunch of guys like my father."

"Get used to it. It sounds like Wil wants you to do this for a living."

"I don't mind learning how to do this, but my father seems to be getting pulled in twenty different directions. Not sure I want that for myself."

"Sounds better than working in the same shop for your whole life," Benji said, sighing. "Great, now I feel depressed because I will work in the same shop my whole life."

This comforted him. Benji's sense of humor was infectious.

"Thanks for the talk, Benji. I'll see you later."

"Stop by the shop on the way home," Benji said.

"Will do," Luke said.

They raced out of the parking lot together but headed separate ways. He drove out of town, passed a strip mall, and saw a US flag and a sign that said *Armed Forces Career Center*. Later, he arrived at Wil's office. As he left his car, a beautiful young woman in a pantsuit approached him. She looked familiar, but he could not place her.

"Nice car. Are you lost?" the young woman asked.

"No, I don't think so ... I'm here to meet with Wil Rivera," Luke said hesitantly.

"Are you his informant or something?" The pushy, attractive, unnamed woman asked.

"Informant? No. Mr. Rivera offered me a customs internship for my career development class at school."

"High School? How old are you?"

"I'm eighteen. My name is Luke Sanz."

"Little young for an internship, but it's nice to meet you, Luke. I'm Terry Garcia. I'm one of Wil's agents," Terry said, offering her hand.

"Nice to meet you, Miss Garcia."

"It's Terry. What's this, Miss shit? I lost my virginity long ago." Terry chuckled a bit. "Go through that door over there. I need to get to the courthouse. Nice meeting you, Luke."

He watched her walk toward her vehicle. Terry was athletic and looked great in her pantsuit with that large handgun on her hip. He smiled, looking at her ample behind, neglecting to watch her face that turned toward him, smiling. *Do all women want you to watch them walking away, or what?*

Nobody was at the front desk, but there was a doorbell, and he pressed it. A few minutes passed before the door opened, and a woman with curly gray hair popped her head through the opening.

"Can I help you?"

"Yes, my name is Luke. I'm here to speak with Wil Rivera."

"Take a seat, and I'll go get him, but I think he's in a meeting."

He took a seat and grabbed a car magazine from the table. He browsed through the whole magazine before looking at his watch. He had been sitting for half an hour. It was 2:30 p.m., and nobody had come in or left the office. He waited for another half-hour, and the front door opened. Several men walked in together. One of them looked at him. "Is that your *Grand National* up front?"

"Yes, it is."

"Sweet ride, man. I always wanted one of those … are you being helped?"

"I'm supposed to meet with Wil Rivera concerning a customs internship position."

"Ah, man, follow me. I'm Carlos Tirado, one of the other supervisors here."

"Nice to meet you, Carlos. I'm Luke Sanz." They shook hands, and Carlos motioned for Luke to follow him.

"Do you know an Angel Sanz?" Carlos asked without turning around.

"Yes, that's my father."

"Seriously? Your father is something else. I almost went to work for him in his new task force, but my wife didn't want me traveling all over the Caribbean."

"I couldn't imagine working for my father … maybe I could, but reasonably sure I would not like that." They made turns through a labyrinth of cubicles. He was sure he could not find his way back to the front door alone. Carlos arrived at the office and saw the name tag, which said, *WILDOMAR RIVERA - RESIDENT AGENT IN CHARGE*. Carlos knocked on the door and opened it.

He overheard Wil, "Carlitos, give me ten minutes."

"Why do you make an appointment when you're going to leave him hanging? Oh, sorry for interrupting." Carlos stepped back with a scared look on his face.

"Is Luke here?" Wil asked.

"Yes, he's been waiting for hours, brother," Carlos said, winking at Luke.

"No, he hasn't. Let him in."

He walked into the room nervously. His father was sitting with Wil in his office, which made Luke nervous, and adrenaline rushed through him. The self-confidence he had built to make it through the door eroded instantly. His father pointed at the seat and downward.

"Hello W ... I mean, Mr. Rivera." He looked at his father. "I wasn't complaining, Dad."

"I know we gave you at least an hour to see if you would complain," Wil said. "Your father told me he took you to an informant meeting once and left you in the car for hours, and you never complained."

"Son, I would never do that again," his father said. Both Wil and Angel laughed.

"Part of being an agent is being patient and sitting for hours in one position. Your father wanted to be here while we explained your limitations while you're an intern."

He looked at his father and was not sure what to say. So, he nodded nervously.

"You'll be manning the front desk, helping with visitors, phone calls, and mail delivery. Agents and analysts in the office will show you different aspects of their duties. The more you help, the more they will trust, teach, mentor, and train you." Wil spoke with him but looked toward his father as if testing boundaries.

"No high-risk stuff. No ride-a-longs, no raids, no enforcement operations." His father glared menacingly at Wil. "Qualification day is fine if your best agent teaches him how to shoot. Nothing high-risk that I need to explain and beg his mother for forgiveness later."

"By the time he's done here, he'll be able to put together and research a case folder like a seasoned investigator." Wil tapped on what looked like a case folder on his desk.

"Are you going to get him a security clearance?"

"Yes, here's a blank SF-86. Once you complete it, I will have one of our investigators review it."

"I'll start this at my office, Luke. We can fill out the rest when I get home."

"I'll have Carlos, and his agents knock it out in a week."

"He was born in Australia, so it will not be that simple. Luke, be respectful and do nothing high-risk. I'm serious. I don't care if you're eighteen."

"Yes, Dad."

His father left the room, taking Luke's tension with him. Wil leaned back in his chair. "Let me give you a tour of the office. Stay away from the younger women, and you will survive." Wil raised his eyebrows and laughed. "Come on. We have a search warrant in an hour. You can sit in on the briefing, but then you need to go home and wait for the background investigation to be finalized."

He looked at Wil, confused. *I don't think Wil heard my father,* he thought.

"It's just a briefing, Luke. We are still following your father's advice."

"Advice ... if you say so, Mr. Rivera."

Wil raised his hands in the air. "It's Wil, Luke. Wil. You make me feel older than I am. Come on, let's meet the screaming squirrels."

He followed his new boss down the blue hallway, wondering why it was painted such a dark shade of blue. Whenever he saw Wil, he was dressed in a dark blue or black suit with various dress shirts and ties. Wil was as tall as him but had a serious, edgy look about him. Wil entered the conference room. An audible, palpable drone of voices emanated from the room. It was immediately overwhelming. He took a deep breath and stepped through the threshold of the doorway.

Sebastian appeared before him and placed his hand on Luke's shoulder, calming him quickly. "Pay attention to the room. Do you understand?" Sebastian asked in Spanish.

He shook his head in the affirmative and scanned the room. He immediately saw Jimmy's father sitting at the head of the conference table at the end of the room. A vulture melded to the man's shoulders and snarled at him. He broke his gaze and kept scanning the room. Terry stood at a lectern, now wearing jeans and a long-sleeved shirt. Wil walked toward her and motioned for Luke to follow him, taking him to the center of the room.

"Terry, this is Luke. He's our new intern," Wil said.

"We met already, boss … we're long-lost friends," Terry said, reaching her hand out to him.

He gladly reached for her hand, which was more like a vise … *I fell backward quickly into darkness and fell hard onto my back. A dense mass was pushing me down deftly. It was Terry dressed in tight shorts. Her whole body felt like it was made of muscle. Suddenly, my arm was pushed outward in a manner where my elbow felt like it was ready to pop.*

"Tap, or I'll break your arm," Terry said.

I was staring at her ample rump and tapped on it. Turned quickly and rolled away.

"That's called an arm bar. Come on let's go again."

I stood up and looked at the woman I outweighed and thought earlier I could crumple easily. I reached toward her, thinking that I was outmatched … he returned to the present and was hit with nausea. He fell slightly forward onto Terry. Her perfume smelled like walking into a bakery.

"Easy, Luke … we'll get closer later."

Wil motioned for him and then leaned in. "I told you to watch out for the younger ones." Wil then faced the rest of the group surrounding the table, who were all still deep into conversation. "All, this is our new intern, Luke Sanz. He'll be manning our front desk and helping here and there. That big redhead over at the end is LT. He runs the local drug task force. Next to him is the task force sergeant, Juan Bello. Terry is about to brief one of her cases she has with the task force. We are supporting with some of our agents."

He waved at both men. The vulture was gone from the LT's shoulder, and the man was not looking toward him. Instead, he was leaning in close to Juan as if whispering.

Two men walked into the room, one with long brown hair and a beard and the other with scruffy black hair and a handlebar mustache. They both walked toward Terry. The one with black hair handed her a manila folder.

"Terry, that's the workup you requested," black mustache said.

"That over there with the unwashed hair is David Narvaez. The clean-cut one is Todd Roberts. They are both with the DEA. All this is Luke Sanz, our new intern."

David waved at him while he stood near Terry. They both chatted behind the podium.

Todd walked up to him and offered his hand, which Luke leaned in and grabbed … *I stood in a room with depressing white walls and a door with a window with a view of another nearby building. Todd stood before the desk of a man wearing an old, out-of-style brown suit with a tie that belonged in the 1970s. The man had a lit cigarette in his mouth down to the nub and a pack of cigarettes in his hand. The man did not look healthy.*

"You bring me crap, and you think you have something … you're old boss warned me about you," the cigarette fiend said, before spitting his butt on this desk and lighting a fresh one quickly.

"Boss, they executed those two men to cover something up. That lieutenant is corrupt and a murderer," Todd said, leaning onto the desk.

"Drug dealers, Todd. He took down two of the worst in this area." The man behind the desk waved Todd toward the door. "Come back when you have evidence … I don't care fuck all about your suspicions."

Todd raised his fist and appeared to want to say something to his boss, but he turned, opened the door, and stepped out.

"Shut the door, genius."

Todd slammed the door shut … Luke let go of Todd's hand and nodded at him. "Nice to meet you, Agent Roberts."

"It's Todd, kid."

"Luke, go take a seat on the opposite side of the table. Terry and David need to brief the case."

Luke sat down. He felt uncomfortable and out of place. Half of these men were old; in their forties type old. Terry and David were in their twenties or so, but Todd had to be in his thirties. He felt uneasy again and looked toward the LT and Juan. They both stared at him while Terry and Todd briefed their case and operation. Luke's unease was well placed. Both men were interested in him, and he surmised it had something to do with Jimmy.

CHAPTER TWELVE

The Shack

Luke and Alyssa stood outside the doorway of the classroom. He had his English class next on the fourth floor, but his prior class was near this one. Every day, he stopped by to steal a kiss midway through the day since they only saw each other during art, lunch and then music class. They agreed early on that he would spend his lunch with Benji, and she would spend time with her friends. Since Benji was dating Birdy, they had all eaten together. Sandy and Linnet were not always happy about that but tolerated it because Luke had helped their friend Claire ascend to heaven and also saved Alyssa when the demon abducted her the year prior.

He held onto her tightly and kissed her softly. Her teacher had warned them not to get carried away outside the classroom. When he touched her, he saw something, but he wanted her to ask him a question.

"Do you have something to ask me?" he asked, knowing she already wanted him to come to her house.

"My parents have been pressuring me, and I wanted you to come over tonight to meet my parents?" Alyssa asked.

"Of course, but you're the one that preferred me not to come over. I know you live over by Campbell Farms, past the gate."

"My parents live in a large house, and I don't want you to feel overwhelmed, or I would have invited you over sooner."

"Bigger than my house? Bigger than my grandparent's house?" Luke asked, now concerned. *I cannot see her house when we touch,* he thought. He noticed she had something to tell him, but it wasn't a complete vision.

"A bit, yes ... we have our staff, and my father has a helicopter."

He was stunned. "Are you serious? Why aren't you going to a private school?"

"It is newer wealth, sort of. My father comes from a wealthy family, but they had a falling out. He began a financial management company ten years ago and a few years later, he created the Mars Fund, which blew up for him. I'm not comfortable with it, and neither is my mother. I always went to public school in Lansburg and wanted to finish up there."

"I should have known since you drive a BMW, but ..."

"What's wrong, Luke?" she asked, bringing him closer.

"I rarely see visions of you anymore," Luke whispered.

"That's Good. I would hate to think you could see whatever you wanted when we touched."

"True." He also considered that there was stuff he really didn't need to see. Some stuff was best kept private. Seeing her venting to her friends angrily would not be something he should see.

"We can practice afterward."

"Of course, I'll bring my guitar."

"My parents live in another world, but I think it's time to do this. They have been looking forward to meeting you."

"Of course. You always preferred to come to my house or hang out elsewhere. I understand, but I am glad we are taking this step."

Alyssa looked into his eyes and grabbed his hands. "Do you know why I haven't had you over?" she touched his face ... *I was in the back seat of a helicopter over the Hudson River in New York City.*

The World Trade Center and the New York skyline surrounded me. I was flying the helicopter with Alyssa sitting beside me ... he came out of this short vision and felt out of place. "It was so odd. I was flying a helicopter over New York City, and you were with me. What does it mean?"

"I'm not sure, but I think it means you'll get along with my father."

He smiled and shook his head in disbelief. Her family was wealthy, and she was embarrassed. The helicopter was probably the beginning. He reluctantly released her hands and walked toward the stairway; his eyes still glued to her. He waved goodbye, turned, and ran up to his English class.

After school he completed a workout in the garage and the necessary shower, he headed back toward Campbell Farms but turned right into Campbell Estates Road. He came up on a left turn lane but saw a small building, a guard shack between the entrance and exit to the gated community. A black two-door Ford *Bronco* with a light bar on the roof was parked near the entrance. There was an obvious entry and exit to the gated community. He drove up to the guard shack. A security officer stepped out of the booth. He looked like a fit, dark-haired young man in his late 20s. His uniform appeared to be a black battle dress uniform with patches that said Campbell Security and a name tag with the name *MILLER*.

"Can I help you?" Officer Miller asked, stepping out of his booth. He had a sidearm on his duty belt.

"I'm here to see Alyssa Mars at 114 Campbell Estates Road."

"Your name?"

"Luke Sanz."

The guard handed him a pass. "It's the fifth estate on your left-hand side. Look for the numbers on the block wall fencing." The guard walked back into the building and hit a button. The gate opened inward.

"Thanks." He drove through the gate and began counting estates. Some have small guard shacks with the same, black-uniformed guards. He passed another black Ford *Bronco* with a seal of the same patch on Officer Miller's uniform. All the estates he passed had long driveways leading to a large building in the distance. "This is something out of a movie set."

"What movies have huge estates like this?" Sebastian asked from the back seat, leaning forward to look through the door windows.

Luke was startled and swerved toward the black patrol unit but pulled away from it quickly. "Do you need to pop out like a jack-in-the-box anytime you want? You startled me, and I almost hit that car."

"I thought you could use my help … keep heading down this path. You seek the villa on the east side, past this hill."

"Use left and right, Sebastian. It makes it easier for me." Luke came up to another gate; the sign said *114*. "This is it." He came up to the gate, and there was a stone structure with some buttons on it, and one of them said, *call*. He pushed the button and waited but hit it again after a few minutes.

"Can I help you?"

"Yes, Luke Sanz, to see Alyssa Mars."

"Come in. Miss Mars will be waiting for you under the portico."

The gate opened, and he drove through the gate along the driveway. "What's a portico?"

"It's a cover over the front of a residence that keeps the elements from people coming in and out," Sebastian said helpfully.

"My grandparent's house has something like that." He saw the house in the distance, which looked more like a mansion. He passed a helicopter on a pad to his left. "There's the helicopter, unbelievable." He knew it was the helicopter from his dream.

"What is that thing? It looks like a large insect." Sebastian asked in awe.

"It's a helicopter, Sebastian. A motorized carriage that flies in the air like a bird without wings."

"I don't understand. How can it fly without wings?" Sebastian kept staring at the helicopter and dissipated.

Alyssa was waving near a black Rolls Royce and Alyssa's BMW. She motioned for him where to park. One could easily fit twenty cars under this entrance and still be able to drive vehicles in and out.

He stepped out of the car and hugged Alyssa. "Your warning was a bit downplayed."

"I'm so embarrassed about this. My father was raised wealthy and is used to a lavish lifestyle, but when I was a young kid, my parents lived modestly. He just invested smartly."

"Invested smart … how many families live here, Alyssa?" Sebastian stood naturally near both, expecting an answer.

He shook his head at Sebastian because he seemed to forget he was a spirit.

"Oh, sorry, Luke. I was caught up in the moment." Sebastian shrugged.

"Come on, don't forget your guitar," Alyssa said, pointing back at the car.

He opened the trunk and grabbed the case with his acoustic Fender guitar.

"Follow me. First, it will be the obligatory meeting of the parents."

"Lead the way. I can see why you didn't invite me over sooner."

"Look around. If the helicopter didn't scare you away, maybe the Rolls Royce, with a chauffeur, would have." Alyssa walked toward a large double door, which opened as they approached.

Luke stood staring at the bottom of the portico and the path leading to the double doors, which seemed like triple doors because of their size. He closed his eyes and waited for an image he hoped would give him strength … *I moved into my past self and found I was holding my father's hand. I stood at the entrance of my grandparents' vast estate in Sydney.*

"They are not better than you, and they are not better than me. They

are your people, and because I am you, they are my people, too," my
father said, looking down at me authoritatively.

Meeting the In-Laws

The vision from Luke's past with his father comforted him as he stood proudly before the door that would place him before people who would be part of his future. He was in the correct place and at the correct time and realized this was one of those critical and life-changing moments in his life.

"Miss Mars, your parents are waiting for you in the salon."

"Thanks, Norman. This is my boyfriend, Luke."

"I see that he is a boy and your friend. Welcome to the Mars residence, Mr. Sanz," Norman said while bowing his head.

"Thanks, Sir." He noticed that Norman was not what he thought a butler would look like. Norman's comportment reminded him of Wil, Jorge, or his father.

Norman winked at him, possibly to ease Luke's tension.

Alyssa followed Norman through a vestibule into a sizable three-story lobby, past an imperial staircase, and into the salon. "This is larger than a lobby at a hotel, and the butler already knows my last name. He carries himself like a cop."

She squeezed his arm. "Norman is a retired police detective who pretends to be a butler. You only have to do this once, Luke," Alyssa said prophetically while protectively moving him into the salon. Her parents were sitting on a fancy settee drinking tea from fancy China and were being served by a woman in a fancy maid's uniform.

Alyssa walked toward her parents, and she was about to speak but was interrupted by Norman.

"Mr. Mars, if I may interrupt. Luke Sanz accompanied by Miss Mars," Norman said, cutting off Alyssa, whose mouth remained open. He must be overemphasizing his role as a glorified butler.

The screw you look on Norman's face was a clue.

"Norman, I'll make it up to you later." Lee Mars stood up, looking Luke up and down. "Alice, stand up."

Norman must be pretending to be a butler as a façade to help Lee somehow, he thought. Lee walked toward him and put his hand out.

Luke reluctantly grabbed Lee's hand ... *I felt like I was dissipating in a way I suspected Sebastian felt as he vanished. I reappeared in a large room in a tall office building, staring out a window that covered the whole wall.*

"You will move to our home in Staten Island and take up residence. You will travel to our office building on Wall Street daily and attend to our family's interests. There will be no discussion."

I turned around and saw a gray-haired, wrinkled man sitting at a large wooden dark mahogany desk with his hands steepled. The man looked haggard but not very old, just worn.

"My wife does not want to leave Virginia. I don't want to leave Virginia. I want my own path, Father," a young Lee Mars said, almost supplicating.

"You will take residence in Staten Island as you're told."

"Father, please hear me out."

"I have important matters to deal with. You will follow my direction, or I will sign this document and disinherit you."

"Father, I love you. I love my mother, God rest her soul, but I must follow my wife. Please, Father, let me live in Lansburg, where our family started," Lee walked toward his father's desk and knelt before him.

The man snorted, took his pen to the paper, and signed. He then hit a button on his desk. A group of rough-looking men walked in ... he returned to the mansion at Campbell Estates with the sound of a paint sprayer creating his very being. The nausea was there, but he remained steady.

"Nice to meet you, Luke. We've tried to get Alyssa to bring you over for months."

"Nice to meet you, Mr. and Mrs. Mars." Lee was as tall as him, physically fit, and impeccably dressed, which was a little intimidating. Luckily, Lee had a welcoming nature.

"Lee and Alice will suit us fine. Don't let the staff scare you off," Lee said with a welcoming smile.

Alice walked over and hugged him ... *I tried to recoil from her, but instead, I felt like I was falling backward and landed in what appeared to be a hotel room.*

"What do you mean, you told your father to screw himself?"

Lee stood next to Alice, who was sitting on a bed holding a young girl, presumably Alyssa. "He was trying to map out our lives, Alice. I want to make my own path ... he wants to control everything, don't you see?"

"Lee, he only wants what's best for Alyssa."

Lee shook his head, shoulder, and arms energetically. "You don't know him like I do. Don't worry. I have money saved up and own a home in Lansburg, which my grandfather left me. We'll be fine, I promise."

"Mom, I'm scared," a young Alyssa said, buried in her mother's arms ... he was back in the present as Alice let him go.

"Alyssa, you did not tell us he was so tall," Alice said.

"He's imposing, Mom, but he's a real softy with me."

"Ma'am, will there be anything else?"

"No, Mary, that will be all. Thanks for bringing everything together," Alice said.

"Luke, would you like any tea?" Alice asked, motioning to the tea service. "Get comfortable. I want you to feel at home." Alice then gestured toward the sofa in front of the tea service.

He put down his guitar case. "I've not done teatime in a bit. That Lamington has been screaming at me since it caught my eye."

"Which one is the Lamington? I must confess our chef and Mary, our housekeeper, decided what to present," Alice said, pointing at the departing maid.

"This little beauty over here is the Lamington. I must have that carrot cake, too." He served two cups of tea and pastry plates and handed Alyssa her portion.

"Have you done this before, Luke? You seem accustomed to taking tea," Lee laughed at his take on English culture.

He had a drink of his tea. "Nice cuppa. I grew up in Australia, and my mother took tea daily. She was raised in a large house like this. My grandparents on my mother's side are landowners in and around Sydney."

"I thought you were raised in Puerto Rico," Alice said.

He felt Alyssa staring at him but continued. "My youngest brother and I were born in Australia. My oldest brother was born in New York. My father was working at the embassy in Sydney when he met my mother at a party. They dated, married, and relocated to New York, where my brother, Daniel, was born. Then, they moved back to Sydney for about ten years, and then to Puerto Rico."

"What does your father do for a living? Government? Why so much moving?" Lee asked worriedly, eyeing and nodding at his wife.

"He's a special agent with the Department of State. He protects mostly US employees and dignitaries. What my father says is … let me get this correct 'for the needs of the service.' That's what they need from him. He runs a unit that currently responds to emergencies throughout Latin America."

"Are you following your father into this lifestyle, Luke?" Alice asked, with apparent concern as she looked at her husband.

"I'm not planning on it. I'm a new US Customs intern and thinking of becoming a special agent, but I have not decided yet."

Lee and Alice looked at each another. Appearing alarmed. "Luke, that is commendable at your age. The prospect of Alyssa getting moved worldwide scares us," Lee said bluntly.

He choked a bit on his Lamington, spilling the tea on himself.

"Dad, we are dating, and you already have me married off and pregnant!" Alyssa almost threw her cup on the coffee table before her.

"Lee, please, not now," Alice said.

"I'm sorry, Luke. I got ahead of myself. You all go practice for your recital. It was great meeting you. You're a remarkable young man, and honestly, I would love to see you as part of the family."

"Dad, please, you're scaring him." Alyssa pulled him toward her forcibly ... *I was staring into a window at a room full of infants swaddled tightly in blankets* ... he mimicked Alyssa and placed his teacup on the table, coughing as he choked a bit on the pastry. He stood up, took a deep breath, and tried to compose himself. "It was nice meeting you both—my compliments to the chef and Mary. The tea was spot on, and the Lamington was mastery," he said with an accent.

Alyssa escorted him out of the salon and down a long hallway. "So now we are married with kids and traveling worldwide. Do you see why it took me so long to bring you here?" They stepped out of the main house and walked down a covered path, heading toward a pond in the distance.

Luke did not know how to respond. He felt comfortable around her parents and knew from his visions that marriage and children was one path on which they were traveling. "Where are you taking me?"

"My music room overlooks the water. I want you to see everything," Alyssa said, beaming.

They walked for about five minutes and came across another part of the home. They entered a door, passed what looked like a gym on one side, and then a windowed room with a piano in the center and art supplies on the other side of the room.

"This is our music hall and art studio. My mother plays, too."

"It's beautiful, Alyssa. I'm impressed and inspired. Let's get started."

Mary entered the room with a tray filled with tea and pastries, including more Lamington. "Alyssa, your parents thought you would benefit from tea and pastries while you practice."

"Thanks, Mary," Alyssa said.

"You're welcome. Please call if you need anything else." Mary was about thirty years old and attractive. He thought it odd that she acted as if she were an older woman of sixty with her mannerisms.

They practiced for the next few hours, intending to solidify their musical instrument number for the recital. "How comfortable do you feel now?" he asked, obviously conflicted.

"I'm getting used to it, but I'm still worried about performing in front of the whole school."

He stood near a bay window and looked toward the pond and the setting sun's reflection. "It's so beautiful out here."

She placed her arms around him. "It sure is. I should have asked you to come to sit on the deck and watch the sunset." She looked up at him with her huge eyes longingly.

Luke looked into Alyssa's eyes, then at her plump lips, and bent down to kiss her. She held onto him firmly and thrust her tongue into his mouth. He tried to pull away, but she held him tight. This was not their first kiss, but he was agitated because he was a guest at her parents' house, and he had a growing yearning inside himself that made him ferociously impulsive. He was finally able to pull away from her. "I need to go, or I'll eat you."

"You promise?" she asked provocatively, pulling at his arm and walking back toward the main house. "This time, I felt like stealing a kiss."

Alyssa led him out to the entrance and his car. He opened his trunk and placed the guitar case inside.

"Are you okay?"

"Yes, I'm fine." He hugged her, and this time, he stole a kiss.

"Come see me tomorrow, please, and let's hang out? I want to spend time with you."

"We can pick this up again tomorrow," he said, with a yearning.

He drove off down the long driveway, past the helicopter again. He shook his head with concern.

"You may be this wealthy one day, Luke," Sebastian said.

"I was thinking, why would anybody want to be that wealthy."

"Maybe it's that helicoopta that worries you."

"Hel·li·cop·ter Sebastian ... will I need a helicopter to please Alyssa?"

"She's not that kind of girl, and you know it too."

"You're right, but wouldn't it be something to be this rich?" Luke asked, imagining what it would be like.

Sebastian turned and looked at the whole landscape of the Mars estate. "My father owned a fleet of ships and villas in three countries. Sorry four countries, and he was, he was ... well, he was an ass."

Luke laughed and started to slap his steering wheel softly. He left the gate of the Mars estate and could not stop laughing. It was odd, and he knew it, but he considered that anybody living in extreme wealth could not understand what it was like to be poor or desperate to push your family ahead. In truth, neither did he. His parents were doing well, financially, but if his father lost his job they would need to move in with their grandparents. He stopped, stepped out of the vehicle, and stared at the security gate that protected the Mars family. He recalled his vision of Lee and then Alice, of that moment of their lives, which was their pinnacle, an inflection point. He thought of the word strife and how it could propel somebody forward into their future.

CHAPTER THIRTEEN

Peanut

Luke sat quietly at the front desk of the RAC Leesburg office. He found out that Wil had created the intern position to cover the front desk so that Marge, the Mission Support Specialist, would have some free time in the afternoon to handle her other office tasks without the interruptions that came with manning the door. In truth, they rarely had visitors, but all the agents expected to be buzzed into the front door instead of using the annoying cipher lock. He typically arrived at the office when all the agents were out for lunch, which meant that once he got settled in, he opened the door for the next hour as the agents trickled back into the office. He concentrated on reading the Customs Special Agent Handbook, which contained all the rules and procedures that dictated how agents performed their jobs.

He felt as if he was being watched and looked up into the bulletproof window at his desk. One of the agents stood outside staring daggers at him. He reached over and hit the buzzer, which unlocked the door.

The agent, his name was Max, walked past the reception area, mumbling something under his breath. "Waste of space … freaking cronyism in this place." Max was as tall or taller than Luke, but the man was almost as wide. He belonged in a biker bar. A tattoo protruded onto the behemoth's neck from both shoulders.

"At least I'm not rude, crude, and tattooed," Luke said.

"What did you say to me?" Max asked, rushing into Luke's space. The man hulked over him as he sat calmly.

Luke stood up and faced Max. "I was reading the manual and didn't see you at the door … you have the access code." Luke tried to be diplomatic and thought Max could squash him like a bug if he happened to fall onto him.

"You may be family friends with the RAC, but from what I can see, you're just another spoiled brat."

"I may have grown up a bit privileged, but nobody has ever spoiled me," Luke said, staring at Max menacingly. This was bound to happen with Max. He was the most standoffish agent and always appeared to be in a bad mood. Terry had told him once to ignore the man because wolves raised him. Max was a special agent and was a designated technical agent. He was the go-to agent for anything related to surveillance and technical equipment. Terry told him it was because Max was a good investigator but foundered when placed in a position to communicate with others.

Max's frown turned into a smile. He extended his hand, offering it in friendship to Luke. "I'm Maxwell Quigley, but you can call me Peanut."

Luke stood dumbstruck at the mention of the man's nickname. If anything, it should be Grizzly, considering the man had brown hair and a fluffy beard and outweighed most men, including him. He reached out for Peanut's hand, *which enveloped his ... I fell backward and landed on the dirty hardwood floor of a darkened room that smelled of beer, sweat, and worse. It was a confusing scene. Men with long hair wore black vests, jeans, and boots, and they were on their knees between a large wooden bar and pool tables. Standing before them were men wearing blue windbreakers with various acronyms, including DEA and ATF, but some said US Customs.*

"Down on your knees, big guy," One of the men wearing a DEA jacket said, pointing his gun at Peanut.

"I would, but it would take too many weaklings to get me back up."

The agent walked over to Peanut and pushed him toward the exit. Peanut snarled, his hands still raised toward the sky.

"Easy, no need for violence, Peanut. Nobody needs to be broken in half today," an agent wearing a balaclava said. Peanut walked toward the exit door.

"Where are you taking Peanut, Fed?" one of the bikers asked.

"Forget it, man. It was a setup. He's a Fed too, don't you get it?" another man asked.

"Are you serious, Carl? Peanut's a Fed?" the man asked, lowering his hands.

"Put your hands back up." One of the ATF agents yelled, pointing his Colt M4 menacingly as he moved forward.

"Do you know why we call him Peanut? He has a small dick. His old lady said so," Carl said, then lowered his hand and placed it in his boot.

The ATF agent pointed his M4 at Carl's center mass.

"Carl, don't do it!" Peanut yelled back at the group.

Carl did not listen and brought a small handgun out of his boot and shot the DEA agent in the stomach. The ATF agent shot the man twice quickly with his M4 ... Luke pried his hand from Peanut's grasp as if it was glued. He moved forward into Peanut unintentionally.

"You okay, Luke?"

"Yes, just slipped a bit ... I guess I'm just happy to be introduced to you," Luke said, at a loss for words.

"I'm sure you are. Come with me. I want to show you something." With that, Peanut walked to the back of the building, and he followed. They exited a door he had never been through before. It was a garage that held a white conversion van with a ladder on top. Peanut unlocked the side door and stepped into the vehicle.

Luke followed the man and felt instant claustrophobia, which worsened when Peanut shut the door behind him. The whole interior fabric of the van was black, including the removable fabric windows. Peanut sat in one of three chairs, facing numerous screens.

"This is a surveillance van. I helped assemble this baby along with Alan. He's an agent who has a background in information technology and surveillance platforms," Peanut said, pointing at a symbol of a Spartan helmet with the initials AS below. "I'll introduce you to him later.

"Why are you showing me this?" Luke asked.

Peanut shrugged his shoulders. "Why not? Do you want to be an agent someday?"

He had been confused since Peanut had behaved as if he were a worthless, spoiled waste of time a few minutes earlier. "I'm a little young, but I think so."

"Well, we are going to have a surveillance soon, and I prefer to have you here helping me out. Deal?"

"Yes, Peanut. Thanks for the invite." Things were looking up indeed. Earlier, he thought he would get into a wrestling match with this bear of a man, and instead, he would learn one more aspect of being an investigator.

When he returned to his desk after using the restroom, he found a stack of case folders along with a little note affixed to the top.

Luke,

Take a stab at fixing these case folders. Follow the case folder guide and Customs handbook you have on your desk. Let me know if you need any help.

See you later, Peanut.

Over the past month, he had dealt with other cases, but it was mostly to check on the Public Access to Court Electronic Records, also known as PACER, for grand jury indictments and judgment and commitment records to close out a case. These case folders were unlike any of the others he dealt with. He immediately opened the top one and noticed it was full of loose forms, notes, pictures, and manila envelopes. Nothing was filed as was proper within each dividing folder. He had to dig in because his shift had only an hour left.

"The RAC is looking for you. He's in his office," Marge said.

"I'll be right there." He walked over to Wil's office and knocked on the door. "Mister ..."

"What did I tell you about that? Close the door and sit down."

Luke wondered what this could be about. Over the past month, he thought he was getting a grasp of what was expected of him. "Is everything okay, Wil ..."

Wil raised his hand and motioned for him to sit down. "How are you fitting in? What do you think of the office?"

"I think I'm getting a handle on what is expected of me. Peanut just dropped a bunch of case folders on my desk. It's kind of a shit show."

"Max is a good agent but not good at casework. I think it's good that he trusts you with his cases, though," Wil said.

Trust me, he just dumped his crap on me, he thought. "I'll take a stab at them. I'm looking forward to learning at least."

Wil stood up and looked heavy-hearted. "Look, I need your help with an investigation. We have been teaching you how to do basic investigator stuff for a reason. I need you to help with one of Terry's investigations."

"Sure, Wil. I'm here to learn and help."

Wil pushed a blue sealed envelope to him. "Open that up."

The envelope contained two identity documents: a Social Security card and a Virginia driver's license. The name on the identity documents was Luke Walker. "Luke Walker. Are you sending me into a battle with *Darth Vader*?"

"Our undercover coordinator has a sense of humor. What can I say?" Wil grabbed another manila envelope and handed it to him.

The large manila envelope contained a file folder, a license plate, a vehicle registration, a set of keys, and a brick of a portable phone. "You're giving me a car?"

"After school, you'll drive here and park your car in the secured lot. I cannot have you driving that car of yours where I need you. Instead, you will use a white Oldsmobile parked in the back and head to this warehouse near the rail yard." Wil reached out to the file folder and opened it. "This folder has all the target information you need for the investigation. This panel had the warehouse information and address. These other tabs have the target list." Wil tossed the folder back to him. "Study the folder at the front desk over the next week or two."

"What am I going to be doing?"

"Sorry, I was going to get into that. The company's owner has complained that some employees work after hours and appear to steal merchandise from some trucks. We think it's a Customs trade money laundering thing. In short, a European company sends merchandise in bulk to the US, but it brings in more than is manifested. The extra merchandise is going to an Italian mob ring out of New York. You don't need to know the specifics."

"Okay, what do I need to know?" He should have pushed everything back to Wil, but he knew he had to try.

"The company owner will explain what is expected of you work-wise. We have two cars and people you must watch out for when you are ready to shut down for the night. There are two dock workers you also need to watch. When you see them with either of the two targets, you call the case agent or me on this phone."

"It seems easy enough."

"You will not be getting your hands dirty. Peanut will sit with you and teach you how to behave. He worked as an undercover agent infiltrating motorcycle clubs for years."

"I know … ahh, I'm a little nervous but looking forward to it."

"One other thing. Don't tell your parents yet. Your father will blow this out of proportion. It's not high-risk, so it still meets his rules."

"I understand, but I don't lie to my parents."

"I'm not asking you to lie to them. You work for the US Customs Service and are doing your job. The job also pays ten dollars an hour for a twenty-hour week."

"I get to keep the money?"

"Kind of, but the checks would be printed to Luke Walker, so the owner plans on paying you in cash. Go ahead, get out of here, and study that file. Terry and Peanut will run you through a mini academy tomorrow."

"Thanks, Mister … I mean Wil."

"You're almost there, Mr. Walker." Wil waved him off but smiled at him.

While sitting at the front desk, he looked through the case folder between answering phone calls, letting visitors in the building, and signing for packages from shipping companies. Before he knew it, it was 6 p.m., and agents began leaving the office. Peanut set up a day to teach him the basics, including how to drive defensively and tell if he was being followed, something called counter-surveillance. Whatever he was getting into seemed more like a dream, but he felt fortunate that what he was genuinely doing was learning a trade. It bothered him, though, not telling his father about the undercover operation Wil had planned.

CHAPTER FOURTEEN

Training Day

Luke was working at the front desk of the US Customs Service office. At 1500 hours, he had an appointment with Terry to learn about the loss prevention job and what was expected of him. A large, overweight man entered the front door and approached the window.

"Can I help you?"

"Yes, I'm John Robertson. I'm here to see Wil Rivera." The man held a binder that said *Robertson and Son Logistics - Loss Prevention Program.*

"Come right in, Mr. Robertson. You're expected." He hit a switch that unlocked the door. He dialed Wil's desk phone. "Mr. Robertson is here, Wil."

"Bring him to the conference room."

"Mr. Robertson, can you come with me, please?"

"Lead the way, young man." John followed behind him for a bit. "You're a big guy, but your hair makes you look stuck in the '80s."

"I'm from the 1980s but was surprised by the '90s when I wasn't looking!"

"I'm not complaining. I experienced the 80s and enjoyed them thoroughly," John said, tapping his ample belly. "You look out of

113

place like you should be working on an oil rig."

He opened the door and saw Wil and Terry in the conference room. Terry looked excellent, as always. He let Mr. Robertson into the room.

"Thanks for coming over, Mr. Robertson." Terry stood and shook Mr. Robertson's hand. She motioned toward him. "What do you think?"

"Is this your man?" John asked with a smile on his face.

Wil stood up to shake John's hand. "Luke Walker here is going to be our inside man. Teach him all he needs to know," Wil said while patting Luke on the shoulder. "I have another meeting to get to. Terry here will stick around and firm the plan up." Wil walked out of the conference room.

John walked over to him and put his hand out. "Nice to meet you, Luke. You can call me John. Thanks for helping."

"I'm looking forward to it."

"Luke Walker ... interesting name, son."

Terry laughed. "Let's get started on this. He needs to know what's expected of him at the warehouse so he can come off as just another worker."

"I brought this training manual, which includes all the required tasks during the shift," John said.

"Luke, open your intelligence folder and go to the targets tab. As you know, two warehouse employees, Jose and Francisco, are suspected of allowing two other targets access to the remaining trailers after hours." Terry explained while pointing at the case folder.

"Then we have two other guys. One drives a red Pontiac *Fiero*, and the other comes in later with a white Chevrolet commercial van. Fictitious plates, but they were identified in traffic stops as George Rossi and Tony Moretti out of New York."

"Exactly, Luke. You don't need to worry about identifying any of the players. Unless they introduce new ones. Still, we need you to let us know who's playing and observe their actions while in the warehouse and, at some point, what trailers they seem interested in," Terry said.

"You have cameras on all the docks … according to these reports, the trailers are not being broken into."

"Luke, we are missing something. It's frustrating." John slammed his fist on the table. "I know they're up to something. I need somebody I can trust in the building to watch them. The way Terry explained it made complete sense to me."

"Train me up, John. Let's see where this goes."

Terry smiled and stood up. "I will give you all an hour, and then we will meet again for a plan."

John shoved the binder over to him. "Open the binder. The envelope has your entry gate pass and a lanyard you must wear while in the lot."

"How do Rossi and Moretti get into the lot?" Luke asked.

"The guard is bought and paid for. I prefer he goes to prison than fire his ass. You can read the rest later. It's mostly employee policy stuff. The rest is your job responsibilities and hourly tasks before the warehouse closes at 5:30 p.m. This map is of the whole lot, property, and facility." John pointed out the entrance, warehouse, areas of concern, and parking lot.

He looked at that map and saw train tracks running on the facility's north end. "What is this? On the north end of the lot."

"That's the rail entry for our Customs bonded items from the seaport. You don't need to worry about that. Let's keep moving on. Your first day is tomorrow."

Luke's thoughts drifted to the railroad yard, which made concentrating on John's briefing difficult to listen to. Regardless, he needed to push through his hesitation about working in an undercover role and whether his father would approve.

The Warehouse

This was his third week at the warehouse, and Luke had learned all his duties but little else. Truthfully, he enjoyed doing the job but looking out for anything illegal seemed futile. Nothing appeared to be happening. Luke finished all his tasks fifteen minutes before closing. He placed locks on all the remaining trailers that hadn't been unloaded. The loss-prevention officer's duties are simple if he doesn't deviate from the task checklist. The primary responsibility was to monitor merchandise movements from secured areas via the warehouses and outgoing sections. He brought value to Terry by letting her know when various subjects arrived at the warehouse, any license plate numbers, and, most importantly, to see who remained after the warehouse had shut down for the night. Previously, Wil provided a Nokia 101 analog phone so he could communicate with Terry whenever a specific target remained at the warehouse. The Customs technology officer received some of these phones to test in the field.

So far that afternoon was different. It is almost as if the workers had prepared for weeks for this day. The red Pontiac *Fiero* was in the employee parking lot, and a white panel van pulled in through the front gate, moving to the north end of the lot toward the rail yard. These vehicles belonged to Terry's targets. It was the first time they had shown up. At the outbound section of the dock, Rossi was talking with Jose and Francisco. They should be packing up for the night, but they showed Rossi some paperwork instead. Francisco looked up from the clipboard and said something to Rossi before looking toward him. He waved at them and kept walking out the door onto the dock. All the other trailers had gone outbound, so Luke had no trailers to lock up. He pushed the button gate controller, and the sectional door rolled down. All the keys are kept in the security booth. The loss prevention manager and the owner of the warehouse kept the duplicates. He dialed Terry's number, and she answered him on the second ring.

"What's up?"

"Rossi is here with Jose and Francisco. They are looking at some of the clipboards. Not sure if they are for the inbound trailers."

"Thanks, they must have something planned tonight. I will put it out to the surveillance team," Terry said.

"One other thing. How about the rail yard?"

"Railyard? What about it?"

"I'm sure I saw Moretti in the white Chevy van heading north toward the rail yard. None of my duties include monitoring that area. Only a thought."

"Oh my God, you're right. The train hoppers and containers? They're unloaded in the morning … I'm calling out air."

He packed all his stuff, including his homework, that he had a chance to work on. He walked toward the exit again, and all three targets entered the restroom. They must hide in the warehouse restroom to access the yard after hours. The manager will end up locking them in for the night. They must have a copy of the key or another way out of the warehouse. He walked around the north end of the parking lot to his white Olds sedan. He saw the white van parked near a line of containers on the rail, and John and the office manager were parked near the entrance/exit gate. The procedure for closing included the security guard acknowledging that everyone had left the lot, and the office manager and owner were the last two people out of the yard at 6:00 p.m. thereabouts.

John walked up to his car door. "Are the two fuckups in there?"

"Rossi is here in the *Fiero*, and the white panel van is parked by the train rail lines."

"The yard. What are they doing back there?"

"It may be where they are moving something tonight. What are in those containers?"

"Those come in throughout the afternoon and are cut into the yard. The railroad crews make the cuts and move the containers and hoppers into our yard and unload in the morning," John responded.

"What are in those?"

"It could be anything. Mostly fabricated parts are headed to Detroit from abroad, but the containers could also be chemicals. It's not a big part of our business. It's everything from South America, Europe, Asia, and Africa. It depends on the ship the containers came in, but truthfully, they could even be from Mexico." John placed his fist on his chin as if confused. "Let's leave and let Terry handle it." John tapped the roof of the Olds and walked away.

He left the gate and headed toward the Customs office but missed something important. Whatever they are doing in the yard may be done before Terry's surveillance team arrives.

"Go down this path here," Sebastian said, making him swerve on the road.

"Geez, Sebastian, you almost made my heart stop!" he said, stopping the car before the gravel road. "What are you talking about?"

"Make this right turn now, and you will see."

He drove down the gravel road northwest of the rail yard and Robertson's lot.

"Park here and walk through the trees."

He parked and grabbed his pack, which contained his surveillance gear. He walked for several minutes until he reached the crest of a small berm. He removed his binoculars and positioned them until he saw the white van. "I have a good view, Sebastian."

"Give it some time so you can see what they do."

"Have you seen them do this before?"

"Yes, but I don't know why they are doing it. Do you see the black container in between the two red ones?"

"I see it."

"Do you have a good view of the bottom of the container?"

"Yes, I can also see the wheels and the tracks."

"That is where they will be working and taking out bricks." Sebastian used the best description of what to expect.

He saw movement coming from the warehouse. The red Fiero

was headed toward the white van, followed by a dark-colored pickup truck.

"The sun is going down, Luke. They are about to begin."

He grabbed the phone and called Terry.

"Luke, is this important? We are trying to get an eye on the area. Air is not here."

"I have an eye on the rail yard and can see what they're doing."

"You were supposed to be headed to the office … ah, forget it; tell me what you see."

"Moretti moved the white van next to a black container between two red containers. They are in a fenced-in area of the rail yard northwest of the Robertson warehouse. The red Fiero and a black pickup are joining him now."

"Can you take pictures?"

He switched to his Canon *EOS Rebel SLR* camera with a telephoto lens and zoomed into them. "Yes, I have a good view, but it's low light. They pointed the headlights at the container. Maybe that will help me as much as it helps them."

"Take pictures and tell me when something changes. I will stay on the phone."

He took pictures of every player and car in the area, including a nice group photo.

"Surveillance units, we have an eye on the area with our man on the inside. Standby for any movement." Terry's voice was loud enough for Luke to hear from the phone's speaker.

"They are starting, Luke," Sebastian said, sounding anxious. The white van moved closer to the container but did not block his view.

He saw Moretti and Rossi under the container, working on something. Jose was walking back and forth in the area, appearing to watch for any surveillance. He continued to take photos but was mindful that he needed to keep enough film for whatever they pulled from the container. *What could they be doing?*

"Pay attention to how they do this."

119

He used the camera zoom to look closer at Moretti, who was pulling on something. He must have gotten it loose because packages began to fall. Moretti continued to pull, and more packages fell. Rossi, Francisco, and Jose formed a line from Moretti to the van, throwing large bricks at one another and into the truck. They continued this for some time. Moretti pulled again, and many more packages fell. He captured all of this perfectly with the camera.

"Luke, can you hear me? Luke."

"Yes, Terry. They are pulling packages from the bottom of the container. They undid an access panel and took packages tied to a rope."

"Great news, hold on. They opened a trap in the container and removed the packages. It looks like a dope load. Standby. Luke, keep watching and let me know when they move out."

"I will, Terry."

"They're done. Watch what these men do," Sebastian said.

One of them grabbed a panel and placed it back on the underside of the container. The men then ran back to their vehicles.

"Terry, they're getting ready to take off. All the packages are in the white Chevy van."

"Copy, Luke …. the surveillance teams are getting ready for movement. The white Chevy van is the target. Don't lose that van. Follow it until it lands somewhere. The rest, follow the *Fiero* and pickup."

"Terry, they are all out of the yard. I'm heading out." That was cool, but he was still perplexed about what happened.

"Copy Luke, and thanks. Head back to the office and wait there. Seriously, Wil is going to kill me!"

"Yes, on my way, Terry. Good luck."

He ran back toward his car and headed toward the office, passing the *Armed Forces Career Center* sign shining brightly like a beacon calling him across a foggy waterway. He stopped at the corner convenience store and grabbed coffee and a sandwich.

When he arrived at the office, he jumped into his car, turned it on, and placed the heater on full blast. He ate his sandwich and coffee, unaware of how often he would do this for many of his meals. He took half the bread off, not wanting to indulge in too many carbs.

Luke completed the remaining homework until he heard the gate open. The white Chevy van pulled into their secured lot, followed by the *Fiero* and black pickup truck. He dropped his textbook and felt an adrenaline rush.

"Don't worry, Luke. It's your soldiers," Sebastian said, realizing his anxiety was building up.

"They're not soldiers and not mine. I work for them."

"Sorry, Luke. You did well."

As ten more cars entered the parking lot, he stepped out of his vehicle. The cars included a Sheriff's marked car and two Chevy *Suburban* sport utility vehicles (SUV) with heavy window tint. Eight agents poured out of these two vehicles wearing balaclavas (dark blue battle dress uniforms) vests and holding submachine guns. They all walked toward him. His nervousness increased, but the agents took turns patting him on the back or shoulder, heading to the white van. Terry came out to him, and she was beaming yet still punched him hard on the arm.

"This was supposed to be a months-long operation, and you did it on the fifteenth day!"

"Sorry, Terry, I did not mean to cock things up."

"What does that mean? Come over here." Terry pulled at his shirt, and he followed her to the white van. The whole back of the van is full of packages that look like giant bricks to build a fence.

"What's that?"

"It's called heroin, Luke. I'm guessing it's about five hundred pounds of heroin."

"Drugs? Great, my father said no drugs."

"This heroin is worth millions—more than I saw in Arizona. I got to run. I'm buying the beer and pizza!" Terry ran off and high-fived Wil, who walked towards them.

"My boy, nicely done. I know talent when I see it." Wil walked to him and hugged him. "Two weeks, and you take down a smuggling ring." Wil held up two fingers and laughed. Did you get good pictures?"

"Yes, I did."

"Take them to Terry and stick around for pizza, but no beer. Your mother called me like ten times already."

"Oh no, what do I tell my parents?"

Wil's smile left his face, and he began to pace back and forth. "Tell them you worked late and nothing else. I will meet up with your parents sometime this week, hopefully. Maybe we can push it for a month or more." Wil placed his arm around him. "Good job, son. Grab your gear and take it to Terry".

He ran off, grabbed his bag, and headed back inside. He walked past Jose and Francisco, who were being fingerprinted. Jose saw him and whistled toward Francisco, then pointed his head at him. "See that, Poncho. The new guy burned us, Jose said in Spanish."

"He's one of us, you jokers." An agent wearing a balaclava said sternly in Spanish.

He kept walking and found Terry and another man in the conference room filling out paperwork. He handed her the roll of film. "I have that film for you. Sorry to say, you are going to need it processed first."

"Thanks, Luke. We will get it done. Thanks for your hard work tonight ... Luke, you remember Detective Juan Bello. He's second in command of the metro taskforce. Juan loaned us a couple of guys, including himself, to help today."

"Good job today. This is the biggest bust in this area I've ever seen."

He noticed that Juan was wearing some prosthetic boot on his foot. "Thanks, Detective Bello." For some reason, he felt a burning sensation on the back of his neck. *I think that Juan Bello is a bad person*, he mused.

"He's a bad man, Luke. Don't ever trust him," Sebastian said.

Terry winked at Luke and gave him a friendly smile.

He took off for the night and rushed home. What he felt leaving the gate that evening was that he wanted to do this as a career.

"That Bello guy was one of the detectives in that drug bust you showed me," Luke said.

"Yes, some of those guys have the devil on their side."

"Terry is part of that group, and she's a good person."

"Yes, but not that guy. Trust my instincts," Sebastian said, self-assured.

Luke knew that Sebastian was correct but still wondered how a co-worker of Terry's could sit so close to her and yet have a different plan than the rest of them.

CHAPTER FIFTEEN

Weirdo

Jimmy's father walked into his room and pulled an uncapped bottle of bourbon from a seemingly unconscious Jimmy's arms. In truth, he lay in bed trying to sleep through the pounding headache he had. He peeked at his father through his mostly closed eyes and saw him smell the open bottle. Instead of taking a drink, the man grabbed the cap from the nightstand and screwed it back on before he slammed the bottle down.

Jimmy opened his eyes but didn't flinch. "Hey, Dad. What's up?"

"What time did you roll in last night?" the LT asked.

"I don't know. I drank most of that bottle before I got home."

"You going to school?"

"I need to take a day. I'm still a little drunk."

"Take a shower and drink some coffee. You need to go to school and put in some work. Those overdoses months ago made us light this month, and we owe a large medical bill." The LT hovered over Jimmy.

"Wasn't my fault. Who did you get that shit from?" Jimmy asked, but he didn't really care.

"One of my detectives took it off some courier working for a pusher in DC who didn't know how much he carried. It looks like they cut it with something bad."

"Is that the dude your boys smoked a while back?"

"The distributor, yes, but don't talk about this stuff to anybody. Get your ass in gear. I woke you early enough to get cleaned up. That bag has what I want you to push before winter break. Wake up and get going, or I will punch you awake."

Sleep avoided him for the past hour or so, but after speaking to his father he felt sleep coming back to him. Jimmy began to nod off. The LT pounded Jimmy in the diaphragm hard enough to wake him and knocked all the air out of his lungs. Jimmy jumped out of bed, trying and failing to catch his breath. He kept struggling for almost a minute, then finally was able to take a breath and vomited all over himself and the bed.

"You awake now?" the LT asked, smiling at his creation.

"More like dying." Jimmy wiped his face with his sheet.

"Clean yourself up, Jimmy, and wash this up tonight or sleep in it for all I care. Get your worthless ass out of here in thirty minutes, or else."

"I will. I will." Jimmy removed his clothes and sheets from his bed before tossing them on the floor with his other filth. He downed the rest of the bottle of bourbon before taking a shower. He walked to his sister's room, handed her a pack of peanut butter cookies, and kissed her cheek.

"You stink, Jimmy boy, you stink."

"Have a good day."

"You be a good boy, you stinker." Karen held her nose with one hand and the cookies with the other.

He drove off to school like a madman. His first few periods were a blur because he slept in each classroom. The teachers didn't seem to mind because he was not disruptive or launching kids into orbit while he slept. He walked to his favorite senior restroom during lunch and took a piss in the urinal. Some students followed him into the bathroom.

"Jimmy, do you have any weed?" Joseph Trent asked as one of Jimmy's top marijuana clients.

"How much?"

"A lid if you got it."

"100."

"Come on, Jimmy. I have 80."

Jimmy stared at Joe pensively. "Going to Joe for 80 bucks." They made the exchange quickly.

"See you later, Jimmy."

Jimmy began selling to a line of students waiting. Five minutes later, if he did the math correctly, he had almost $1,000 in his pouch. He left the restroom and bumped into a kid he had been looking for. "Hey, what's up, Weirdo? Where have you been?" Tim Hall, also known as Weirdo, owed Jimmy money from a prior cocaine sale.

"Around Jimmy. I was sick, and my parents would not let me come to school." Weirdo played with his nose ring and licked his fingers in a disgusting, nervous habit.

"Did you tell them you owed good-natured Jimmy a hundred bucks for some blow?"

"No, Jimmy, I did not tell them that." Weirdo tried to laugh, but it came out as a snort. "That's probably what got me sick."

"I got you sick. That is interesting. So, this is a complaint about bad service. I can forgive that C-note you owe because you caught diarrhea." He poked Weirdo forcefully with two fingers to the soft boy's chest.

"I'm not complaining. I don't have it, Jimmy. I can get it to you in a couple of weeks."

"Did I wait for a month to get you the coke?"

"No, Jimmy, please give me some time. I had to help my mom with groceries."

Jimmy jabbed Weirdo's chest with two stiff fingers from his left hand while he reared his right arm backward and struck the boy's face. The hit forced Weirdo's head into the wall, and an unconscious boy slid down onto the floor.

"What was that sound?" Mrs. Johnson asked as she walked into the restroom. "Jimmy, what did you do now?"

Jimmy looked around the mostly clear hallway and appeared to be considering his options. "He tripped into the wall, Mrs. Johnson."

"Bullshit, Jimmy, go to the office now."

Jimmy took a step toward the teacher menacingly but then walked in the direction of the principal's office. He turned around and saw that the teacher had returned to the bathroom. He ran down the hallway toward the closest stairwell. Jimmy almost reached his car, but the security guard rushed to him in his golf cart. He was tempted to attack the out-of-shape guard when he sensed fear in the man.

Matias Devry and the vice principal, John Shipmen, rushed out of the building and joined them next to Jimmy's *Firebird*.

"Go ahead, Ernie, I got this," Matias told the security officer.

The guard looked at Jimmy and then Matias, and a disgusted look developed over his face. He walked away without saying a word.

"Jimmy, this kid is in bad shape." Matias hesitated and motioned toward Jimmy's car as if hoping he had already driven away.

"He stole from me, Matias. My father would kick my ass if I let that happen."

"I'm not sure if I can cover this one up. Let's see what your father's boy says." Matias motioned, pointing toward Leroy's patrol car, which was pulling into the area. Matias waved him over. Officer Leroy Washington parked as close to them as possible without entering the Senior parking lot. Leroy stepped out of his vehicle, walked towards them, and shook hands with Matias and John.

"John, can you check with Marie for the kid's status," Matias ordered.

"Yes, Matias." John walked off.

"Look, Jimmy, your father has some pull around here, but something like this can knock us all down. Leroy here may need to take you in." Matias said, motioning toward the officer.

"Do what you jokers need to do. Be prepared to answer to my father."

"Jimmy, follow me to the station. Hide your stash in your car first." Leroy was pretending to be a law enforcement officer but doing the opposite of what a real one would do.

"I'll hide it in my trap." Jimmy unhooked his stash pouch. He grabbed some crack vials and handed some to Matias and the rest to Leroy. "This should keep you two on my side for longer." He opened the trap's access panel on his car's center console and placed his stash within it. He closed it up and started the *Firebird*. He reversed from the parking spot, lit up his tires, and followed Leroy to the police station. *What a bunch of buffoons thinking they can stop me*, he thought.

✝ ✝ ✝

Mop-Up

Officer Leroy Washington and his partner in crime, Jose Velasquez, were told by Sergeant Juan Bello to come to the drug task force. They sat in an interview room awkwardly because they were locked in.

"What did you do now, Leroy?" Jose asked, grabbing onto the locked doorknob. Sweat instantly formed on his brow.

"Nothing, I swear … all I did was escort Jimmy to the station after he almost killed another kid. I don't know how many that makes this year."

Jose stared at the camera and pumped his palm downward trying to get his partner to realize they were being watched.

Leroy received the message and stopped speaking.

The door opened, and the LT entered the interview room with Juan and leaned menacingly on the table. "Sit down, jokers."

"What did I do? I was on patrol, I swear," Jose said.

"Maybe you should have been. This idiot took my son to the station, and Leroy's sergeant forced him to roll Jimmy and hold him pending an investigation."

Juan put two envelopes on the table in front of Leroy and Jose. "Open them."

They both opened the envelopes and pulled out a wad of cash.

"That was supposed to be your cut of last month's haul," the LT said before Juan grabbed the envelopes from their hands and replaced them with a little baggy full of white powder.

"The two of you are going to fix this. Interview the victim at the hospital and get this cleared up tonight," the LT said as he stood up.

Leroy looked at the camera and saw the red light was no longer on. The LT was screwing with his head again. He grabbed the hit of cocaine and put it in his top shirt pocket. He stood up and motioned for Jose to follow him.

"Leroy, clean this up and get your Sergeant to back off tonight. I want Jimmy out of custody before midnight strikes … tell me you understand." The LT blocked the door, keeping the officers from leaving the room.

"We understand, LT. I'll clear this up right quick," Leroy said with a bowed head.

"Let them go, LT. They know what they need to do," Juan said.

The LT moved away from the door and opened it for the two officers. "I don't want you around here if you fail us."

The officers left the room with their heads bowed in contrition. They drove in separate patrol cars to the Lansburg Memorial Hospital, ER waiting room together. "I'm looking for Tim Hall's parents," Leroy said loud enough for everyone to hear.

A lone woman stood up wearing a restaurant uniform. "I'm Tim's mother, officer."

"Mrs. Hall, please step into the chapel with me momentarily for privacy." Leroy and Jose agreed earlier to interview the mother in the chapel, which they thought would be intimidating.

"Yes, officer."

She followed them into the empty chapel. They left the door open.

Leroy removed his memo pad from his pocket. "Mrs. Hall, have you heard how Tim is doing?"

"He was conscious, but he has a broken cheekbone." She began to cry while covering her face with her hands.

He doesn't have the patience to deal with a blubbering woman. "I need to interview Tim to find out his point of view on what happened."

"What does the other boy say?" Mrs. Hall asked.

"The other kid claims that Tim stole from him and then ran into the wall trying to run off."

She coughed in her hand. "Tim has been stealing, but he has a class ring mark on his face like from a football player's ring." She appeared concerned. "What did Tim steal from this kid?"

"That needs to be followed up on. The other boy is on the football team. The other boy will not say what he stole and told me to ask Tim." Leroy had trouble looking at Mrs. Hall directly into her eyes.

"That looks like the doctor, Officer." Mrs. Hall stood up and left the chapel. "Doctor, how's Tim?"

"Mrs. Hall, Tim is in recovery and was moved to room 430. The procedure was successful, and he's recuperating."

"Thanks, Doctor. I will head to his room now."

"Officer Washington, did you need to speak with me?"

"Yes, Doctor Jabir. I have a quick question. I heard that Tim was suffering from meningitis. Does that have anything to do with his current condition?"

Dr. Jabir looked at Leroy oddly. "Officer, Tim was punched into a wall and had a broken zygomatic arch facial bone caused by blunt force trauma on the other side of his head. Tim has a mark on his head resembling an outline of a class ring." The doctor emphasized his own LC class ring. "Who are you trying to protect here?" The doctor looked at him with disgust.

Leroy looked at Jose for help because, thus far, he had not said a word. "I'm looking at all angles."

"Whatever, Officer, I need to return to my patients." The doctor looked as disgusted as he felt.

They took the elevator to the fourth floor and found room number 430. He walked in and found Mrs. Hall whispering to Tim.

"Mrs. Hall, Tim, may I have a few minutes?"

"Sure, officer, ask him the questions if you must."

"Tim, I'm Officer Washington. I need to find out what happened." He opened his notepad.

"I bumped into Jimmy, and he wanted the money I owed him. I didn't have the money, and he was angry. The last thing I remember is a fist with his ring headed to my face, and then I woke up at the hospital."

"Jimmy claims you stole something from him and for me to ask you what you stole. He claimed you refused to pay him back. What did you steal from him?"

Tim did not say anything and turned away from Officer Washington. "I don't want to talk anymore."

Officer Leroy motioned to Mrs. Hall to follow him out of the room. "Mrs. Hall, the other boy doesn't want to file theft charges. If your son refuses to explain, I have no choice but to drop the whole matter."

"Arrest my son then, but why drop the whole matter? That man, not a boy, put my son in the hospital. You said the kid plays football. Look at the ring mark on his face. Are you a police officer or not?"

"I am a police officer!" Leroy said, his voice cracking. "We are police officers. If your son wants to cooperate, he can call the station. I'm wasting my time talking with you."

"You're protecting your boss and his son. You should be ashamed of yourself."

"Ma'am, I'm going to make this your decision. If you press this, I'm going to handcuff your son to his bed, and you will not be able to speak to him until after he is booked into juvenile hall,"

Jose said, finally speaking.

She held her hand to her face, and a tear ran down her cheek. "Fine, just leave. Just get away from my son."

Leroy stared at Mrs. Hall, turned around without saying a word, and left the room, followed closely by Jose. They took the elevator in silence and left the hospital. Leroy got into his patrol car, threw his memo pad at his reflection in the rearview mirror, and yelled, "How did I turn into the crap?" Leroy began to slam his fist repeatedly on his dashboard. A pouch with his gear fell onto his weathered floor mat from its *hide* near the glove box. He never thought it would get so bad. When he became a police officer, he would deride other officers caught in scandals and corruption. Look at him now. He reached for his pouch and opened it. He drove the car behind the hospital. The urge, the chase of his last high, was overwhelming, and he succumbed.

CHAPTER SIXTEEN

The Setup

Luke sat down in art class by himself. Alyssa had not arrived yet, and they had a group project to complete together. Benji's seat was empty, yet he knew that Benji was at the school because he passed his friend's car in the parking lot. Something screamed at him that Benji needed help. He stared at the door, waiting for either Alyssa or Benji to enter, but it was just his other classmates each time.

Finally, Alyssa walked into the room, and his rapidly beating heart skipped.

"What's wrong, Luke?" Alyssa asked as she stood next to him.

"It's Benji. He is not at his desk."

"I just saw him running down the hallway. He was talking crazy about Jimmy and his car. I hugged him to calm him down. He was so out of breath."

Luke reached up and grabbed both of Alyssa's shoulders and hugged her ... *I was propelled backward and landed in Benji's homeroom, hovering over his desk. He appeared to be studying for a math test. Benji stood up suddenly and walked toward the window. I followed his gaze and saw that the door to his passenger side car was open, with somebody inside. Benji darted over to his homeroom teacher.*

"Mrs. Moore, can I be excused early to my next class?"

"Benji, you know I cannot do that. What's wrong?"

"Come look. Somebody is in my car." Mrs. Moore walked with Benji, who pointed out the window. "Do you see the car with the door open over there? That's my car." At that moment, the person wearing a gray hoodie walked away from the car toward the school.

"Do you recognize the person in your car?" Mrs. Moore asked.

"It's the Bully Cladhair." Benji ran up to his desk, gathered his things, and was the first out the door as the first bell rang. I followed him as he ran down the stairs to the first floor, looking toward the cafeteria—the man wearing the gray hoodie headed up a different stairwell. Benji ran towards Jimmy, accidentally bumping into some underclassmen.

"Oh, excuse my presence." Uttered one student.

I followed Benji up the stairwell but didn't see Jimmy. I saw the gray hoodie heading toward the third floor. As Benji chased after Jimmy, he bumped into Alyssa. "You okay, Benji?" Alyssa asked with concern. I saw Steve Rostova enter the bathroom down the hallway and followed. Benji wiped the sweat off his forehead with his sleeve and breathed deeply.

"You okay, Benji?" Alyssa asked, holding onto Benji.

I saw another boy enter the bathroom, followed by Jimmy, wearing his gray zipped-up hoodie.

Benji took a deep breath but was unable to respond yet. "Trying to catch my breath." He tried to take another gulp of air, steadying himself. "Tell Luke that we need to talk." Benji broke away from Alyssa's hug ... he steadied himself after letting go of Alyssa.

Steve walked into the classroom and over to Mr. Aames, and they had a short conversation, which caused the teacher to walk to the door. "Everyone, continue working on your projects. I will be right back. Nobody leaves this classroom," Mr. Aames said, pointing toward the floor sharply.

Steve sat down at his desk. The students next to Steve stood up and spoke together. He rushed over to Steve's table and placed a hand on the boy's back ... *I stood in a bathroom stall with Steve, who sat on the toilet. I could hear other voices but couldn't see anything over the stall. Steve pulled his pants up and then sat on the toilet with his feet on the seat cover, trying to keep from being seen by those outside the stall. I flowed outside of the bathroom stall and could see Jimmy leaning against a wall and dealing drugs with a line of four students. Benji stood near the exit.*

"Jimmy, what were you doing in my car?" Benji asked.

Jimmy lowered his hoodie and glared at Benji. "What's it to you? It's your turn for what you did." Jimmy waved off his customers. The second bell rang, and the rest of the students left the restroom. "You lost me some sales," Jimmy said, walking toward him menacingly.

"What do you mean, my turn? I was only trying to keep you from killing Stan—we all went to elementary school together, Jimmy."

Jimmy looked down at him and into his eyes. "You and your Sasquatch of a friend are constantly in my way. This is my world, and your life is about to change." Jimmy turned to walk out of the restroom.

Benji placed a hand on Jimmy's hoodie sleeve. "Jimmy, this isn't necessary. Let's resolve this now."

Jimmy turned, stared at Benji with an evil look, and punched him square in the chest. "Resolved."

Benji collapsed, striking his face on the floor loudly. Jimmy stepped on Benji's right hand, and the sound of broken bones filled the air. I screamed out and tried to punch Jimmy, but I went right through him and collapsed to the floor. Jimmy walked out of the restroom with a pompous gait.

Steve stepped out of the restroom stall and went to his fallen friend. "Benji, are you okay?"

Benji mumbled but did not respond. His hands were up to his chest, trying to massage the pain away.

"Somebody, help ... please help me!" Steve yelled.

Mrs. Johnson, who had a class close to this restroom, entered and knelt over Benji, shaking him. "Benji, wake up. Are you okay?"

"I'm passing out, Mrs. Johnson. It was Jimmy. He planted

135

something in my car."

"Hang in there, Benji, don't fall asleep."

"I can't keep my eyes open," Benji said before rolling his eyes backward, exposing the whites of them.

"Steve, watch him while I call for help," Mrs. Johnson said before running out of the classroom, not waiting for Steve's response.

"Hang in there, Benji," Steve said, holding onto Benji's hand ... he fell slightly forward onto Steve's back.

"Sorry, Steve." He ran toward Alyssa but was confronted by Sebastian.

"Jimmy attacked Benji, Luke." Sebastian seemed unusually frazzled after appearing in front of him.

"Where is he?" Luke asked out loud, carelessly.

"The paramedics are putting him on a litter."

He walked briskly over to Alyssa. "Benji's hurt. I'm going to go check on him." He ran out of the classroom, with Alyssa following close behind. He found Mr. Aames standing in the hallway, speaking to the officers. Paramedics were moving Benji on a gurney toward the only school elevator. There was an oxygen mask on Benji's face, and his hand was taped up on a board.

Mr. Aames walked toward them with a concerned expression. "Why did you leave the classroom? You don't need to see this."

"Benji is my best friend, Mr. Aames. I must be here."

"The paramedics had to resuscitate him. Let's go back to the classroom." Mr. Aames said flustered, ushering both of them away.

"Follow your friend. It would be best if you saw what is going on outside," Sebastian said urgently.

Mr. Aames was walking ahead of them now. He grabbed Alyssa's arm. "Go back to class and cover for me. I will be right there."

"Sure, Luke, I'll think of something."

He rushed in a panic downstairs and made his way outside. He arrived in time to see Benji being loaded into the ambulance.

"Why do I need to see this?"

"Walk to the parking lot," Sebastian said, pointing.

He walked around the ambulance and saw several police cars in the senior parking lot and a tow truck pulling Benji's white *Gran Fury* onto the trailer bed. "Why are they towing Benji's car?"

"Look at who the officers are. It's what you call a setup. Do you see that teacher with the red dress?" Sebastian pointed at the woman with his halberd.

It was Mrs. Moore, Benji's homeroom teacher. He walked up to her. "Ma'am, do you know why the police are towing Benji's car?"

"I'm so confused. Benji and I saw somebody messing with his car from the classroom window. I was waiting to speak with those officers."

"Don't bother. Those cops are in on it."

"Your name's Luke, right? What do you mean?" Mrs. Moore asked with curiosity.

"Yes, ma'am. I'm Luke. They are in on it. Those officers are corrupt, and they are helping to sell out Benji."

"What are you talking about? Shouldn't you be in class?"

"I know it's hard to understand. Please do yourself a favor and don't speak with those officers. They will try to jam you up, too. I promise I will get the right people to speak with you." He thought he should call Terry but didn't know what he would tell her.

"I know you're Benji's friend, and Mr. Devry lets Jimmy get away with murder, so I'll wait. I need to get to my class anyway."

Luke returned to class and patiently waited for his day to end. During music class, he stared at the empty drum set and played poorly with all the distracting thoughts. Mr. Waters told him to step into the hallway and gather his thoughts a few times. Once class was over, he gave Alyssa a firm hug and left the school. It didn't matter anyway because he could not see his friend. Police officers were at the ER. Two of them were the officers he saw doing drugs. Jimmy committed a violent act, and these goons showed up to make sure he would get away with it. It seemed relatively futile to try to stop Jimmy when the people who were supposed to protect the innocent students were the ones serving up the kids to Jimmy like a meal.

CHAPTER SEVENTEEN

Problem Revealed

Luke finished all his classes for the day. It's been a week since Jimmy attacked Benji. He walked past the teacher's lounge and saw Mr. Conway sitting alone, papers scattered on the table like a puzzle. Mr. Conway motioned for him to come over. He walked to the lounge and stood at the doorway.

"Come in, Luke. I want to speak with you."

He looked around and saw a sign that said, *NO STUDENTS ALLOWED.* He remained immobilized at the doorway.

"Don't mind that, Luke. Come in and sit over here with me."

He entered the lounge and sat down, hanging his head. He felt out of place and worried that other teachers might enter the lounge at any moment and see him trespass into their space.

"How's Benji?"

"He's still in the hospital? At least Jimmy was suspended this time, but I feel he will get away with it again."

"It's hard for me to say, but I'm hearing that Jimmy may be back in a week," Mr. Conway said hesitantly.

"Jimmy beat up Benji and framed him for drug possession." It sounded outlandish to hear him speak those words out loud. "Benji is handcuffed to his bed."

"Jimmy has a dark heart. The ones protecting him are not any better."

"He has brought darkness to this school like a demon would. Believe me, I would know," Luke said, wiping a tear from his face.

"I went to see Benji at the hospital. Seeing an officer at the door and one arm secured to the bed was hard to bear, and his other hand in a cast was disheartening." Luke took a deep breath. "Jimmy has the underclassmen enslaved through violence and drugs. Why doesn't somebody stand up to him? Why haven't I stood up to him?" he asked, placing his hands on his opposite shoulders as if trying to comfort himself.

Mr. Conway stood up and sat in the chair beside him. "You're a good kid, Luke, but something is wrong here with this situation. You have an inherent right to defend yourself, and that includes speaking up for yourself. I know you're not perverse or feel pleasure from hurting others, like Jimmy does."

"What do you mean?" he asked, more composed.

"Do you think I could take another's life?"

"I could not see you doing something like that, Mr. Conway."

"You're a large and imposing guy but also quiet and humble."

"I don't think I can hurt somebody," Luke said plainly.

"As you know, I was in the Army during Vietnam. I spent several years in battle. I killed enemies from a distance and some up close. I don't know how many people I killed in battle, but I know I have at least a hundred spirits visiting me at night."

He sat up, looked at Mr. Conway, and was unsure what to say. He feared that he would disrespect him. "I'm not sure how to respond, Mr. Conway."

"I did what I did to protect us from the enemy. They were not evil people but were led by men with evil ideologies. One needs to be physically prepared to take another life, Luke. I hope you never have to."

"I understand, Mr. Conway."

"Evil lurks around every corner and is prepared to strike without remorse or concern. People exist that receive pleasure from hurting and killing others. You need to be prepared to protect yourself and those you love from these people. If you hurt someone or take a life by protecting yourself or others, it will still cause pain, but you would be in the right."

"Is the Bully Cladhair one of those people?"

"I don't think he ever killed another person. However, he does what he does because it makes him feel good to hurt others and cause distress in the life of others," Mr. Conway said.

"Are you saying that I should kill Jimmy?" Luke asked, confused.

"Not at all. I'm saying you always stand up for yourself at the time. The truth is that all the teachers, administrators, and local police are failing the whole community by not confronting him."

"I confronted him sort of. I believe I would be more aggressive if I had the opportunity again. My parents don't want me to fight in school."

"I know that's a rule, but nobody should tell you not to protect yourself or others. I know you are a religious young man. God never meant for us to allow evil to overcome us or force us to bow down to a victimizer. Stand up for what is right … whatever the consequences. Don't bow down to evil or the evil actions of others."

"Does fighting back always involve or need violence?"

"Not always, Luke. Consider that a homicide detective seeks to discover who committed the crime by establishing facts, collecting evidence, and performing interviews. When they find out who committed the murder, they get a warrant from a judge and try to arrest the murderer by force if necessary. However, the officers don't set out to kill a suspect. They aim to arrest a person so the prosecutor can resolve the murder with a trial."

"I understand, Mr. Conway. Jimmy must be confronted and held accountable for his actions and not be allowed to victimize others with impunity."

"Luke, keep your chin up. One day, your strength and courage will tower over your size."

"I hope so." Luke liked what Mr. Conway just said. He was a big kid, but the thought of his courage being more prominent than himself comforted him.

"I know so, Luke. I hope to see you soon."

He left the school and got into his car, still mulling over his conversation with Mr. Conway. The motion in his sideview mirror caught his attention. A man walked up to his driver's side door and pressed a blunt object on his temple.

"I could have killed you, and maybe I should. You keep messing with this bull, and you'll get my horns," Jimmy said.

"You think you are the devil, don't you? What's wrong with you, Jimmy? I saw that you could be a better person. Why would you hurt Benji like that?"

"I can kick your ass or plant drugs in your mother's car, next. You have nothing on me, Luke. You're a lightweight and don't have what it takes to stop me."

He grabbed Jimmy's hand and placed it in a wrist lock while twisting it, causing Jimmy to cry in pain. He was not gifted with the vision he sought to let him know what Jimmy was planning. The object held to his head, a banana, dropped onto Luke's thighs. He grabbed it and peeled it before taking one bite. "Little ripe for my taste. I got your message, but I need to get to work." He burned rubber out of the parking space, shoving Jimmy to the ground with the fender of his car. He left Jimmy with a plume of smoke and his horrible thoughts. Unfortunately for Jimmy, he did not get the message that Luke was not an easy target to stop. Luke did not comprehend that Jimmy would not respond well to defiance and did not mind dying while trying to gain dominance over another person. They were on a path to a violent confrontation.

Sebastian appeared beside Luke, shaking his head. "I'm sorry. I was elsewhere when I saw what was happening."

"Why are we not seeing him coming?" Luke asked, slapping his dashboard. "What good is having the ability to see the future if everything surrounding my enemy is blank?"

"Father D, told you ..."

"I know what he said," Luke yelled, staring at his guardian. He's winning, and I have no idea why. He runs this school and has us all inside his ant farm."

"Ants?" Sebastian looked at his hands and at the floorboard of the car.

"We are his pieces on a chess board, waiting for his next move."

"Yes, yes. I understand," Sebastian said in Spanish. "As long as he has this power over us, we must settle on being reactive to Jimmy."

"You need to go speak with Father Robert."

Luke realized his guardian was correct again. He must seek guidance from his friend, the priest. He parked his car at the Customs office and took his seat at the front desk. He reviewed some case training folders provided by the office's field training officer and browsed through some closed-case folders.

"What are you up to?" Terry asked while standing at the counter. She was wearing workout clothes.

"Working on Peanut's old cases."

"Did you bring your workout gear?"

"Yes, in my bag," he said, pointing at his backpack.

"Come on. I need a sparring partner." Terry walked off toward the gym. She was wearing tights.

He shook his head while he checked out Terry's tight rear end. He headed for the restroom to change before grabbing his bag and gloves and walking out to the gym. Terry was on the mat stretching. Some agents were on the treadmills, and one worked out with free weights. He was a little worried that he might hurt Terry. He trained in the foundations of boxing, wrestling, and Judo. He also took some aikido, but all he ever practiced was boxing. He sat and stretched on the mat, unsure about what to expect. Two sets of headgear and gloves were on the floor near Terry. "Terry, what are you thinking of doing?"

"Do you know how to box? I see you brought some bag

gloves."

"Yes, I learned as a kid."

"Have you heard of mixed martial arts?" Terry asked, bouncing in place.

"No, what's that?" he asked. "It sounds like a mix of boxing, wrestling, jujitsu, or kickboxing."

"It's a mix of stand-up and ground fighting. Want to try it?"

"The truth is, Terry, I'm bigger than you and worried I may hurt you."

Terry laughed. "You are bigger than me, but I want the challenge. I promise to take it easy on you. Twenty percent of normal strength." Terry grabbed the headgear and the gloves and tossed them at him. "Use these."

He puts on the equipment anxiously. Terry reached for a box and pushed a button. The light on top turned on.

"What's that?"

"A gym timer. We fight on green and yellow. We stop on red. Got it?" The light turned green.

As Terry came toward him, ready to lunge, it caused Luke to back off of the mat. She seemed like a little bull trying to run him down.

"Stay on the mat, Luke."

"Sorry, you surprised me."

Terry returned to the timer and reset it. "Don't get nervous. It's just a workout."

The light turned green, and Terry approached him slowly. She jabbed at him, and he jabbed back which struck her head. "Sorry."

She kicked his thigh and then quickly pushed on his shoulder with her other foot. "Don't apologize. Fight."

That kick to the thigh stung, turning it red instantly. That woke Luke up and he began to focus on the sparring session. He hit Terry with a combination of strikes to her abdomen. Terry fell forward toward him as if injured, but she grabbed his legs, and he lost his footing and fell. Then she was on top of him, holding his arm in an unnatural position.

"Tap before I break your arm," Terry said.

He tried to get his arm back but could not flex it the way she controlled it using both of her arms, hips, legs, and feet. He stared at her butt and was tempted to tap her bottom. It was all familiar to him from a prior vision. He tapped her foot instead, and she let go and knelt before him. *I don't have the technique down, but I should be able to use my weight against her*, he thought.

"That's an arm bar. Did you think you hurt me with that punch?"

He shook his head. "Yes, I sure did."

She laughed and stood up. The boxing timer rang, and the light turned yellow. "You took me out in a minute!" he was astonished that a woman he outweighed could quickly submit him.

"Wait for it to go green again. Stop messing around and make it harder for me."

"Sure, Terry, I strive to be the hardest punching bag ever."

Terry laughed and completed several burpees once the light turned red and kept going until the light turned green, launching at him like a lion attacking its prey.

As she approached him, he sprawled and landed on top of her with her face planted into the mat. He immediately felt regret and thought he had killed Terry, who grunted, and his weight forced her to exhale. He lifted himself from her, and she reached in and grabbed his foot. She spun from underneath him, and a second later, he felt as if his ankle was being spun off, and reflexively, he turned himself and tried to pull her off. Whatever way he moved; his ankle felt like it was about to get removed from his leg. He saw Terry's butt before him and spanked it on purpose this time.

She let him go and smiled. "Have I been a bad girl?" she asked as she knelt beside him.

"More like a little terror," he said, smiling and slowly standing up.

The tone rang on the timer. She stood up and pointed toward

the floor, indicating he needed to get into position. The light on the machine turned green, and she moved toward him again. This time, she kicked his side, and he gasped.

Luke survived the sparring session with Terry. He lucked out once, used her motion against her, and sent her flying with an aikido move. Regardless of his pride, he nursed his side on his drive home. It was on fire from several kicks that Terry landed on him. He took a shower in the gym but was still sweating from all the exertion.

CHAPTER EIGHTEEN

Truth

After his sparring session with Terry, he felt confident enough to write notes on everything he knew about Jimmy Cladhaire. He fell asleep jotting them down. The following day, he continued to spend some of his free time writing down, firming up everything he knew about the Bully Cladhair and all those surrounding him. After school, he headed to the Customs office and sought out Terry. He found her in her cubicle, buried in paperwork.

"Can we talk, Terry?"

"I'm swamped, Luke, but anything for you. What's up?"

"Can we go someplace private?"

"Sure, let's go to the gym." She didn't appear interested in what he might say. They walked toward the gym, and luckily, it was empty. "What is it, Luke?"

"I need to speak with you about something at the school. Drug dealing, and this bully named Jimmy Cladhaire, a dealer who almost killed my friend at school."

"Cladhaire? You met the LT a few weeks back. I heard his son is a piece of work."

"That and more. I think a bunch of the officers in your task force are corrupt, and Jimmy sells drugs that his father's officers steal on traffic stops." *I should tell her about the vulture creature on the man's back*, he thought.

"Get the hell out of here. How would you know that?" Terry asked, holding a hand to her face.

"Do you know a guy named Mickey and another named Rocky?"

"How could you know those names? Don't answer. I'll get some guys I trust here. Go to the conference room and wait inside. If you have evidence, bring it there."

He walked over to the conference room and tossed the envelope onto the table. It contained his notes, logs, and pictures. He grabbed the VHS tape from the inside of his jacket and placed it on the table. He felt claustrophobic and decided to take off his jacket and toss it on a seat. He paced nervously in the room, thinking he had overstepped somehow. He recalled that the gym was on the opposite side of the conference room. Luke left the confined room and entered the gym's double doors. *I jumped the gun*, he thought. His gravitated toward the circuit training equipment and quickly began to do a workout. Thirty minutes later, Terry entered the gym. His clothes were now sweaty, and he felt immediately self-conscious.

"We're waiting for you … I figured you would be in here," Terry said.

Luke grabbed a towel from a rack and wiped himself down. He returned to the conference room to find David, Wil, and Todd looking at the contents of his envelope scattered throughout the table. He walked toward the television and VHS machine and waited patiently. Terry walked over to him.

"I'm confused, so how did you know about Mickey and Rocky?" Terry asked.

"I saw it in the paper. A couple of days after the overdoses." He had no choice but to lie or at least muddy his response.

"Seriously, Luke. You added that together."

Luke turned away and looked at Sebastian, who had materialized beside him. "You can't tell her."

"I just figured it out somehow, Terry. The paper said a source within the task force said the deceased dealers provided the drugs that led to the overdose."

"Yes, it said that indeed," Terry said.

Wil walked up to him looking pissed off. He was not his usual good-natured self. "I'm impressed with your logs and notes, but you did all these surveillances yourself. Some of it with our equipment?"

"Yes, Wil … I had no choice. Somebody had to do it to get to the bottom of this."

Wil turned quickly, grabbed a chair, and pushed it into a wall. He came back toward Luke menacingly with his jaw clenched in anger. "No more surveillance, Luke. Do you understand me, son?" Wil walked over to a phone on the other side of the conference room.

"Yes, Mr. Rivera. No more surveillance." Luke bowed his head in defeat.

"So, Luke, why were you following Jimmy?" Todd asked, shaking his head as if stunned.

"He was attacking kids in school and getting away with it. The principal and nurse are protecting him. I'm not sure why. I wanted to stop him from killing someone."

Todd walked toward Luke and lifted his hand to him calmly. "I understand why you did what you did. You have guts, and I'm impressed with what you unearthed."

Terry walked closer to them as well. "Luke, Wil is not angry with you. The truth is that we've had questions about the LT for some time. You just led us to where we should be focusing our attention."

Wil returned to them. "They did find a bunch of pills in Benji's car. They seized his car, and the County Attorney accepted the charges against your friend. I just checked, and they have a solid case. They are moving forward with the prosecution," Wil said.

Luke slammed his fist against the conference room table. He knew that by confronting Jimmy it had led to this moment. *I should have just backed off*, he thought.

"You know what's odd though? I was on duty that day, and I wasn't called. Jose and Leroy took care of it. They aren't members of the task force," Todd said.

"Well, they do our stops, but yes, the protocol is to call whoever is on duty," David said.

"Freaking LT is a real piece of work, man," Todd said.

"Your friend's alive, at least," Terry said.

"Jimmy broke Benji's hand to send me a message. My friend is a mechanic and plays the drums. Now he will go to prison for something he didn't do." A tear ran down his face. He swiped at it roughly. "Talk with Mrs. Moore, Benji's homeroom teacher. She saw Jimmy messing with Benji's car while in homeroom … watch this." He walked over to the television with the video cassette player and pressed play. They could all see Jimmy delivering the drugs to the patrol car and then the officers smoking the crack in their patrol units. He then showed the corresponding pictures of the events in between, including their meeting with the officers.

Todd held a picture of Leroy smoking crack from a pipe and laughed. "It figures it was something like this."

"I'm not angry with you. I'm just concerned for your safety … to be honest, I'm worried about what your father will do."

"I am, too, but I need to stop Jimmy. I need to face him."

"Luke, we will stop him. There will be no more surveillance unless we ask you to," Wil said assertively.

"The Bully is coming after me next, and I don't know what to do."

"We do, and we will take him down, not you. Stay clear from that piece of shit." Terry stared at him with her arms crossed.

"Luke, take the rest of the day off and visit Benji at the hospital. I'll tell Jorge to go and make sure you get to speak with him. We will come to you if we need anything else," Wil said, pointing to the door.

He drove to the hospital, as pensive as ever, trying to figure out the look on Wil's face. It could have been a disappointment, but it was something else. It was akin to fear. He had seen that look in the mirror before and on Daniel's face when Junior was attacked by Avandeil the year before.

Luke met Jorge in the hospital lobby who escorted Luke to the elevator and then the third floor where Benji was being held. A police officer guarded the doorway. Jorge walked up to the officer, who shook his head up and down. Jorge motioned for him to come over.

"You have ten minutes," Jorge said, opening the door and pointing into the room.

Luke entered the room and froze at the door when he saw his friend handcuffed to the hospital bed with his right hand in a cast. He shook out of it and walked toward the gurney. Benji tried to reach his cuffed hand upward, seeking Luke's touch, and turned his head away. Luke grabbed his friend's hand … *I fell backward and stood before myself, playing a guitar on a stage. The instrumental was a Guns and Roses song called November Rain. I was at the bridge of the song. The sound of the drums startled me. I turned, and Benji slammed his sticks on his kit like a pro* … he moved forward and leaned on the hospital bed rail. Benji turned back toward him with tears flowing freely down his face. Luke shook his head up and down while tears now poured down his face. He was unable to talk, but the message was received. Benji placed his hand on his face and sobbed and laughed simultaneously.

"Are you going to get me out of this jam?" Benji asked.

"Yes, buddy … I cannot see how it will turn out exactly, but I set a path forward to counter Jimmy."

"From where I'm lying, it seems like all is lost. Jimmy and I used to get along. I never thought he could be this evil," Benji covered his face, which appeared contorted in pain.

"Justice must prevail, Benji. Something divine will come forward and stop him."

"Divine justice … maybe I should start attending church with you."

"You're welcome, of course. I'll ask Robert to come pray over you." Luke looked out of the window toward the church, which was visible from Benji's window. "Divine justice, I like that."

"For what, Luke?"

"The *Grand National*, I will name her Divine Justice."

"I'm glad I could contribute something … do you still need to get your car checked out?"

Luke shook his head back and forth. "That can wait until you get released and heal up, Benji."

"God willing, I'll be out of here soon, and I can work on it myself. If not, I will talk to my dad. Please, I want to get this done for you so I can feel normal somehow."

"Of course, Benji," Luke said.

Luke parked at the house and found it challenging to find a spot. He overlooked Wil and Jorge's car. He did not remember that his parents were having friends over for a Friday night barbecue.

He walked over to the table where his father had set up a beverage service. He served some scotch over some ice and downed it in one pull. He poured himself a double, or more like a triple, before sitting on an outdoor sofa near his mom and Kamila, who was over visiting.

"Go ahead, son, drink your father's scotch." His mother and Kamila stared at him worriedly. "What's wrong, Luke?" His mother sat near him on the sofa, trying to soothe him.

"It's been quite a week … a bully at school put Benji in the hospital and now he's in the hospital handcuffed to a bed." He could not look at his mother, embarrassed. He drank the rest of the scotch before trying to bury himself into the sofa with a bowed head.

His father approached them with Wil and Jorge behind him. "Wil filled me in about the Bully Cladhair and his father."

"I'm sorry, Dad. I thought I was doing what you would have done."

"Well, a drug dealer at the school attacked Benji and planted drugs in his car. Benji had cardiac surgery and has a hand in a cast. You did some surveillance and uncovered some corrupt cops. Is that about right?"

"Cardiac arrest? I didn't know that," Luke said, biting into his fist.

"Oh my God, Luke. I'm so sorry this is happening," Kamila said, sitting beside him. Emily joined them as well.

"Thanks, Titi."

His father grabbed the glass from his hand and tossed the melted ice over the deck railing. He returned to the bar, dropped some ice, and poured two fingers of scotch. He handed the glass to his son. "We'll talk about the other stuff later. Once you finish that, go start the barbecue." His father motioned for Wil and Jorge to follow him.

"We'll give you some space, honey," his mother said, standing. Kamila and Emily followed her. She turned back and pointed at the drink. "Last one … I'm serious."

He shook his head, indicating he understood. He took a sip, realizing it was his last one. He was feeling better already. Emily smiled at him and waved as she walked away. *My parents put up with my impulsiveness with taking a drink, but I cannot do this each time I am troubled,* he mused.

CHAPTER NINETEEN

The Locker

Junior walked down the hallway, trying to hit the restroom before his third-period English class on the fourth floor. He turned a corner and saw a large dog led by a police officer. He jumped back against the opposite side of the wall while the team headed in the opposite direction. Seeing a dog in the hallway was concerning, but there were always officers around the school now. Mostly because of the Bully Cladhair. He took a quick piss and washed his hands before heading out toward his classroom. As he rounded the following corner, he saw officers had taped off the hallway heading to his class. Another officer stood next to the Vice-Principal, John Shipmen. *How am I supposed to get to class now*, he thought. He would need to walk around the hallway to the opposite side to get to his next class. He was going to be late.

"Angel, aren't you Luke's brother?" Mr. Shipmen asked.

"I go by Junior, Mr. Shipmen. Yes, I'm Luke's brother."

The officer ducked under the police tape and approached Junior.

Junior stared at the officer's name tag in capital letters— VELASQUEZ. This was one of the officers Luke told him to avoid. He peered past the officer's shoulders and saw that the officers had Luke's locker open and his belongings on the floor.

"Where's your brother, son?" Officer Velasquez asked.

"Ask Shipmen. He has it right there on his clipboard, along with my picture. Are these jokers here for my brother?" Junior asked.

"Son, I'm asking the questions here, and you need to answer them now."

Junior laughed at the absurdity of it all. "It's more like the exact opposite of that. Like I have the right to remain silent. Read the constitution."

"A moment, officer. We need to speak with your brother. I cannot reach your parents on the telephone," Mr. Shipmen said, pretending to be a cordial, respectful counselor.

"My father flew out of the country this morning for an emergency. I don't know where my mother is. Are you all trying to set up my brother for something? Luke is right, you're all pieces of shit." He didn't feel these people deserved respect, let alone deference, as they demanded.

"That's uncalled for. Nobody is setting anybody up, Angel," Shipmen said, looking at his clipboard again. Shuffle off to class now." The man raised his hand toward the officer, who appeared to want to interject.

"Sure thing, Mr. Shipmen." Junior walked calmly, but when he was around the corner, he ran off toward the stairs, aiming for the third floor. While Shipmen spoke, he recalled that Luke would be talking with Alyssa at the doorway near her class on the third floor. He bumped into Luke on the stairs and thought he would knock his brother down. Instead, his brother grabbed and steadied him to keep him from falling. Junior told Luke what he witnessed.

"Freaking *galahs* are trying to take me off the chessboard, aren't they?" Luke asked.

"They sure are. That Velasquez guy is there foaming at the mouth. I'm pretty sure the other one is there, too. You better go home and talk to Mr. Rivera."

"You're right ... let's switch cars." I handed Junior the keys to the *Grand National.*

Junior was mesmerized by the keys in his hand. "Cool … remember the *Taurus* is parked in the lower lot."

"Yes, I know. If you see the police near the car, take the bus home."

"Yes." Junior kept looking at the keys."

"I'm serious Junes. They planned this, but I think they'll only sit on the car until they find me."

"I understand. Good luck, brother."

Luke clenched his teeth and lowered his head. "Don't believe anything they say about me."

"Never … get going, bro," Junior said.

✝ ✝ ✝

Hermoso

Wil sat at his computer, staring at a glowing green screen. He was in the process of approving reports on the government database. Typically, he didn't mind reading reports because they let him know which agents had strengths and weaknesses with case development and what was happening in the field. Today, he was not feeling it. The report he was reading was long and drawn out, and he felt like he was falling into a well.

Terry walked into the room and sat down without speaking.

This startled him slightly, and he was unaware of where he was for a minute. "Go ahead and take a seat," Wil said.

"You're not going to believe this."

"I'll believe almost anything but go ahead."

"I got a call from a K9 handler I know who knew I was the duty agent today. It looks like they got a pretty good drug seizure out of a locker at Lansburg Center High. Do you know whose locker?" Terry asked.

"Jimmy Cladhaire?"

Terry stood up and slammed her fist on Wil's desk. "No, it's

Luke's locker. When the officer recognized the name, he called me. He said that Velasquez and Washington were acting weird."

"Did they call you for the seizure?"

"Juan just called me. He's on his way over to report a seizure involving public corruption and needs to speak with you."

Wil pressed control, alt, and delete on the computer and locked it. "Call Todd and David and get them over to the school. Tell Alan too and have them wait in the school parking lot. Put your acting hat on for when Juan comes over."

Terry smiled before running off toward her desk.

He grabbed his phone and dialed a number.

"Hello, *Hermoso*. Are we still meeting tonight?" Kamila asked with her sexy voice.

"Not now, Kamila ... can you put Helen on please?" Wil asked.

"Okay, hold your horses, *Guapito*. She's with me ... it's Wil. His panties are in a bunch."

"Is it Angel, Wil ... what's wrong?"

"No, it's Luke. Those cops we spoke about are trying to pull a fast one. They planted drugs in his locker. I need you to head to the school and have it out with the principal or whoever is there. I'll join you soon after."

"Sure, I'm leaving now," Helen said and quickly hung up the phone.

Wil stood up and paced in his office. *I need to get out of here now*, he thought. He took a drink from his water bottle and then took a deep breath. He grabbed his phone, dialed a number, and called Marge, his mission support specialist. "Marge, please bring Luke to my office if he shows up."

"Wil, he doesn't work for another two hours."

"I have a feeling he will show up early. Just bring him to my office when he gets in. Tell him not to knock." He hung up the phone and sat in his comfortable leather chair, arms crossed.

"Wil, Juan is here, and he wants to talk privately," Terry said at the doorway.

Juan walked into Wil's office and took a seat. He still had trouble walking from that gunshot to the ankle.

"Sorry to bring you bad news, Wil, but we must speak."

"Terry, close the door and take a seat."

Terry did as she was told and stared at Juan, who looked like he had seen a ghost.

"She hears it now or once you leave, Juan. Get on with it."

Juan's typical confidence seemed slightly deflated. He wanted a one-on-one conversation.

"I'm sorry to say that your wonder boy is a drug dealer. We just seized distribution-level drugs from his locker. Looks like he was dealing along with his friend, Benji Laio."

Wil did not say a word and stared at Juan silently.

"Do you know where he is?" Juan asked.

"School, I imagine," Terry said.

"We cannot find him or reach his parents."

"That doesn't surprise me, but I wonder why you are coming here to tell me this. Terry is the duty agent, so why isn't she filling me in on this?"

Juan stared blankly at him and glanced at his watch.

"I spoke with the LT about this just a few weeks ago. Come to think of it, so did the DEA. Isn't that correct?"

Juan nodded his head and looked at his watch again.

"I already told LT that if he fails to observe the duty agent rotation, we may have to leave the task force. It will mess with our stats and make us irrelevant."

The door opened, and Luke took up the door frame, stepping toward Juan menacingly.

"Hey Luke, what are you doing here?" Wil asked.

"I needed to speak with you."

"Not much to talk about. You've disrespected this office and our agency. You were supposed to learn how to fight crime and not become a criminal," Wil said.

"How could you, Luke? You're making this so difficult," Terry said, a tear running down her face.

Wil shook his head back and forth quickly. She acted as if she was in a soap opera instead of a crime drama. "We trusted and trained you. You betrayed that trust and damaged your family name. Terry?"

"Stand up and put your hands behind your back, Luke."

Luke turned around and did as he was told.

Juan stood up and appeared to want to say something. He approached Luke as if to touch him but backed off.

Luke lowered his head and slumped forward. "I'm sorry, Wil."

"Get him out of my face," Wil said, waving him away like a bug.

"I have a meeting to attend. Would you mind staying while Terry processes Luke in our system?" Terry was actually headed to the school, and not to her cubicle.

"Sure, Wil." Juan's frown disappeared as if he had switched gears to plan B.

Wil showed Juan the break room closest to the cells and showed him how to note the cell checks every fifteen minutes.

"Sure, we do the same."

"Your help is much appreciated, Juan. I will be back as soon as I can." He moved quickly to the front door and met Marge at the reception area.

"Where's Luke? Is he going to take over for me soon?"

"Give me a couple of hours. He's in the wet cell. Juan Bello is watching him. Tell Peanut to call me, please," Wil said and went for the exit.

"Yes, Sir … wait, why is Luke in the cell?"

Wil did not bother answering. He jumped into his government vehicle and drove off quickly toward the school as fast as he could. He had already noticed that Terry was gone and hoped the rest of the crew was already at school.

CHAPTER TWENTY

Mother Hen

Helen felt this was a crucial moment in her and her son's life. She must be confident and direct. Once at the school, she rushed into the principal's office without realizing how she got there or where she even parked. This happened to her when she was stressed. She was rarely protective over Luke. Not because she loved one son more than the other. It was because she felt Luke could pick himself up. His sacrifice to save their family from that demon who nearly destroyed them was impressive. She felt this day was a watershed moment, and she had to protect her son.

An affixed sign on the top of the door said *VICE-PRINCIPAL*, and below the name *JOHN SHIPMEN* on a removable nameplate. There was another door opposite Shipmen, a permanent sign that said *PRINCIPAL*, and a sliding nameplate that said *MATIAS DEVRY*. Something about the sliding nameplates increased her confidence level. Two police officers spoke with a man in the vice-principal's office, presumably John Shipmen. They were laughing. A secretary and a reception desk blocked her path into the office.

"May I help you?" the secretary asked.

"I need to see Mr. Devry now," she said in an annoyed tone.

"He's at a doctor's appointment, and you are?"

"Mrs. Sanz, Luke's mother ... no worries, I will speak with Mr. Shipmen."

"Ma'am?"

She walked directly past the swinging door and into the room with the officers. "Mr. Shipmen, I'm Luke's mother. You and these *wallopers* are looking for him?"

"Where's your son?" Officer Velasquez asked in an authoritative voice.

"I came here to speak with Mr. Shipmen. Somebody will speak to you officers shortly." She motioned for them to leave the room like the insects she thought they were.

Officer Velasquez and Officer Washington look perplexed and angry. "Excuse me ..."

"Officers, please give us the room. We'll be right with you." John appeared confident he could handle this housewife.

One officer grabbed the sealed evidence bags from the desk and reluctantly left the room—John motioned to the chair closest to Helen.

She sat in the other seat, smirking as she did so.

"These officers are part of the local drug task force and received a tip from an informant that your son was dealing at the school. They brought a canine team and found drugs in your son's locker. They need to speak with your son, not you. Simple as that."

"I know who they are. I don't need to speak with them. Your name is John, correct?"

He nodded. "Yes, Mrs. Sanz, you may call me John."

"Call me Helen, please." *Now, how do I approach this man so I can get his attention?* She asked herself and paused in thought. "Do you know what my husband does for a living?" She didn't mind intimidating people by mentioning her husband's employment when that person was a terrible human being.

"No, Helen, I don't. I know you're an artist, but what does this have to do with Luke's actions? We cannot have drug dealing at the school. Period." John seemed confident that an artist was likely a pushover.

"Yes, I'm an artist. Mostly movies, media, and newspapers." She noticed John's eyebrows move upward at the last word. "My husband is a federal agent. In truth, he's a Special Agent in Charge with the Department of State. He runs a task force of federal agents from various agencies who have a presence in Latin America. They respond to kidnappings and other actions against embassy employees in that region."

John looked at her with his mouth open. He looked down to the left, clenching his knuckles, which were turning white. His carotid artery was visibly pulsating through his shirt. Something Angel had told her to look out for when speaking to people. It showed they were agitated and nervous with their current interaction. John remained silent. "So, you understand, any claim that a son of somebody in such high authority is a drug dealer will have to be investigated federally!"

Wil stepped behind Helen with the sealed bags as if on cue. She turned, and a young, attractive, yet tough-looking woman was speaking with the officers.

"Hello Helen, is everything okay?" Wil asked.

"I was about to tell John here that Angel's team is overseas trying to rescue a kidnapped DEA agent's son in Central America. John, this is Wil Rivera."

Wil took out his credential case holder, showed his badge, and then his credentials to John. "Hello John, I am Resident Agent in Charge Wil Rivera with the US Customs Service. Outside there, speaking with your officers, is one of my agents, Terry Garcia. She's a Loudon County Metro Drug Task Force member and the duty agent today. She told me that these symbols on the sealed bags match a recent seizure of theirs."

"What would I know of such things?" John asked, leaning back in his chair. Sweat ran down his brow and into his eyes, which were twitching as he tried to wipe the sweat away with his shirt sleeve.

"Funny you should put it that way. You should know

absolutely nothing, correct?"

"Yes, correct …" John answered with obvious concern.

"John, I see you have cameras in the hallway. Where can we view them?" Wil asked.

John had a deep look of concern on his face. "Why do you ask? That's for us and law enforcement to view."

"Exactly. Funded by the taxpayers through federal grants." Wil stepped out of the room briefly but within earshot. "Terry, call Alan and tell him to come inside with the others and to bring his search kit." Wil returned to the room.

John looked at her with anger and contempt, but Helen looked back at John with a look of sweet success.

"John, you were leading the way to the cameras," Wil motioned in a forward circle, telling John to get moving.

John stood up and buttoned his sports coat. "I'm having trouble understanding why the Customs Service would be involved in this."

"John, don't you know your students? Luke's my intern. This little charade you orchestrated inserted us into this." Wil poked his index finger into John's chest.

John stepped out of his office, passed the officers. He looked at the officers as if looking for help. He tried to speak with them.

"John, you can speak with them later at your convenience. We are on my time now." Wil placed his hand on John's back, leading the vice-principal away from the police officers.

John looked like a scared deer and frowned at Helen in anger. She smiled at him and mouthed you're welcome. *Maybe I overplayed this, but that asshole needs to take his medicine.* She doubted herself but realized these *ratbags* were trying to frame her son.

She stood up, and Wil motioned for her to sit back down.

"Terry, walk Alan and Todd up to us, will ya?"

"Sure thing, boss," Terry said.

"Should we go back on patrol?" Leroy asked Jose, and they began to walk out of the office after John as if to get a word.

"I will see you both later tonight," Terry said, waving at the officers.

As the officers walked away, Helen stared at them, but they quickly looked away from her, with their confidence diminished. She smiled, grabbing her purse and then the cross around her neck.

✣ ✣ ✣

The Spartan

Wil followed Shipmen through the hallway lined with lockers past one door. He knew more about the vice-principal than he let on after speaking to his friend Jorge Villanueva. John unlocked the door and motioned to Terry to ensure she knew which room they entered. Wil followed the vice-principal into the room, but John was already sitting at a workstation with many monitors, and his right index finger was hovering over a button on the right side of the keyboard. He walked over to John and slapped him on the back. "Let's wait for my tech guy. We are dealing with evidence, are we not?"

"Yes, Agent Rivera."

"Call me Wil, John. We are the good guys, aren't we?"

"Sure, Wil, we are the good guys."

"Is that the camera right there? 4th Floor-Hallway, camera 4?" he asked.

"Yes, it is, Wil."

John was one keystroke away from commencing the process of wiping the tape. "Press play, please." Wil took a deep breath, trying not to show any frustration. For a vice-principal, this guy sure acted more like he had the guilty conscience of a criminal.

John pressed play. A knock at the door interrupted them. Alan entered the room, followed by Todd Roberts.

"Alan and Todd, thanks for coming, guys. John, this is Alan with Customs and Todd with the DEA." He said, handing Todd the sealed bags. "Does it look familiar?"

"Yes, from the seizure last week."

Wil saw that, once again, John's right hand was lingering near the rewind button. "Sit over there now," he said menacingly to the vice principal.

"Who's going to operate the player?" John appeared insistent on being able to erase any video.

"Do you see this symbol over here and the initials?" The symbol was a Spartan Helmet, and below it, the letters AS. "I built and installed this system. I'll do fine," Alan said. "This is a video 8 system, with weekly optical storage to laser disc—my personal touch."

John stood up; shoulders slumped forward in defeat. He sat down at a seat in the corner.

Alan took control of the terminal. "Hold on. Some of this footage was already being recorded over. Alan stared at John as he pressed stop on the video player and ejected a cassette. He replaced it with a new one. He moved the tape to a different player, switched to another monitor, and pressed play. "Which one is the locker?" John did not answer. "Which one is the locker, John?" Alan asked with a raised voice. John stood up, looked at the screen, and pointed to the locker before he sat back down like a sulking child.

Another knock on the door, and Jorge Villanueva entered the room. "Vice-Principal John Shipmen, meet Detective Sergeant Jorge Villanueva. Loudon County Police Department," Wil said sarcastically. John placed both hands on his face, leaned down on his knees, and began sobbing uncontrollably. "Oh, sorry. I forgot the detective arrested you recently and you promised you would change your ways," Wil said.

"Guys got it," Alan said in triumph. They all hovered over Alan, who pressed play. A figure emerged from the bottom edge of the screen. The person leaned against the lockers on the opposite side of the suspect area. The figure wore a gray hooded sweat jacket, and the face was not visible. "Tall male, athletic looking. Judging by the lockers, I'd say over 6 feet." The man approached the locker and took two items out of his pocket. He placed the items in the keyhole and then moved them around. The man started messing with the lock and opened it in several seconds. Then, he grabbed a bag from a pouch under his shirt and placed it in the locker. The man grabbed what looked like a black sweatshirt or jacket, shut the locker, and replaced the combination lock. "Less than two minutes."

"Who's the kid, John?" Shipmen looked at him and then away but didn't answer. "I know who it is, but I want to hear you say it … well, at least we know who it isn't. Todd, Jorge, take Shipmen away and work on him." Terry joined them in the room.

"Come on, John, let's have a conversation." Jorge and Todd each grabbed one of John's arms and took him out of the room opposite the administration office.

"Wil, take a look at this." Wil looked at the screen and saw Officers Velasquez and Washington walking down the hallway, and one pointed at the locker. They kept walking, and an officer with his canine, a Belgian Malinois, can be seen walking by the opposite lockers. It darted to Luke's locker and began to scratch. "The officers and the dog are at the locker twenty minutes after it was planted, genius. They planted felony weight on the kid. If we didn't have this video, they would have ruined his life without a second thought," Alan said.

"Makes you think, doesn't it?" Wil asked.

"Yes, it does. I will never look at a duty call the same way again." Alan had a look of disgust. "Wait for a second. I found something new." In the new video, John walked into the frame and pointed at the locker before the unknown male began to plant the drugs. The full video played out.

"Pretty damning against Shipmen and the officers."

"Alan, can you go back and zoom in on the target's hoodie?" Terry asked with a surprised look. Alan toggled to the left and then zoomed into the subject. "Right there, this symbol. Can you isolate that as an image?"

"Yes, will do," Alan said.

"The LT has that same Celtic knot on his raid vest," Terry said.

"It's pronounced *keltic*, like with a K," Alan said obnoxiously, having won one over on Terry.

"Thanks, Alan. How often have I told you not to correct me in front of the RAC?" Terry punched Alan's shoulder.

"Ouch, you ruffian."

"Do you recognize this symbol, Terry?"

"Yes, I have seen it on a raid vest. This is what Luke was talking about. Holy shit. Our boy Luke is a better investigator than we thought," Wil said.

"I'm beginning to see that." Terry smiled and stared at the screen.

"Terry, make sure Todd gets the drugs for expedited testing, including fingerprints and have his GS call me," Wil said. "Do not make other phone calls or share with other task force members. Put the word out." Wil looked at them and then his watch.

"Got it, boss," Terry said.

"Alan put a duplicate tape into the recording system and collect the originals. The principal may come back and view the tapes. I want to see if he destroys the video as well."

"Will do boss. I'll try to make it look like nothing happened. I will wipe over our presence, if I can."

"It's 1320 hours. Let's all meet after hours at my office at 1800 hours. There will be no other discussions until we get there. Todd's GS and OIG or FBI will decide who talks about it. Understood?" This must be handled delicately, or the whole thing will unravel and sink them instead of the Cladhaires.

"What about Luke?" Terry asked.

"Tell Juan that the AUSA deferred prosecution because they violated Luke's reasonable expectation of privacy. Get more inventive and please act better than a cheap soap opera actress. Your performance earlier was terrible."

She punched Wil's arm, causing him to flinch. "I'm right on

it."

"I will meet up with Jorge. Move out as quickly as possible before we have students everywhere." Wil grabbed his forehead and sighed. *Helen, I need to speak with Helen,* he remembered.

He walked over to the principal's office and found her standing with a frantic look. She rushed toward him.

"What's going on, Wil? I am pulling my hair out here."

"Go back home and wait for Luke. We have it in hand."

"How about Luke? What's going to happen to Luke? I'm drowning here, Wil." Helen's concerned look was tragic.

"Nothing is going to happen to Luke. He was framed, and we have proof. This is going to get resolved. Not quickly, but it will get resolved. Speak with your son. I'll come over to have dinner with Kamila."

"Thanks, Wil. I will see you tonight." They hugged, and she walked off quickly as the first bell rang. A sea of students quickly flooded the hallways as they rushed to their classrooms.

"Damn bell," Wil said, angry that he was stuck in a crowd of students at the school.

CHAPTER TWENTY-ONE

The Voice from the Flame

Luke sat in the sterile holding cell for at least an hour, but it felt like it was all day. Luckily, the cell had a toilet, and he had already used it twice. His stomach was doing somersaults. At first, he figured it was all the drama caused by Bully Cladhair's antics, but then it dawned on him that he had skipped breakfast and had now skipped lunch. What a day to deprive himself of protein. Wil and Terry's reaction when he opened that door was revealing. Internally, he sought their approval, and hearing what they said caused him almost to believe he was a bad person. It was a fleeting thought, but he thought he deserved the consequences of what he was being accused of. When Terry handcuffed him, he saw that it was all a ruse to convince Juan that the setup Jimmy had started would work. *The longer they kept me in the cell, I thought I was under arrest.*

Regardless, he remained in the cell, and the thought kept recirculating. He stared at the wall and imagined he stared at himself. It was impossible, but he saw himself being garroted from behind by a man dressed all in black. Impulsively, he turned and shoved his hand into the man and yanked out his heart.

The cell door opened, and he stood up with a smile. He thought Terry was coming to rescue him, but it wasn't her.

"Sit the fuck down, you little shit," Juan said, pointing at the metal bench.

His first thought was to tell him to screw off, but he thought it best to sit down and not antagonize the man. As he sat, he let his hair cover his face.

"Get used to being in a cell by yourself, fat ass."

Another remark that made him want to spout off at this corrupt piece of gutter trash. "We both know I'm the good kid and not the piece of shit you're covering for."

"Maybe, maybe not ... but you don't get to decide who's the trash. That's my choice," Juan said, pointing at Luke's chest.

Luke peered down at the prosthetic boot Juan was wearing and realized Juan was shot by either Mickey or Rocky after the overdoses at the school. "Did Rocky shoot you?"

Juan's face went white. "How do you know about that? Who the hell are you, kid?" Juan walked up to Luke and grabbed his jacket ... *I fell backward in time into a large room full of people sitting on the floor. It looked like a run-down lobby of a hotel somewhere in Latin America because a sign on the wall said Hotel Hermosa. I looked around the room and saw a young man in his late teens sitting on the floor. It looked like Juan Bello from twenty years ago. A man holding a rifle slung on his back walked up to Juan and the man next to him and handed him some identity documents.*

"Juan Bello, my ass," the man sitting next to Juan said in Spanish. "To me, you'll always be Juanito Brillo."

*Juan pushed the man and smile*d ... he was back in the present. Juan had let go of him but stared at him as if waiting for a response.

Sebastian appeared beside him and slammed the staff of his spear on the ground. "Tell this man he cannot walk a few feet in your sandals."

Luke laughed and shook his head because he had never worn sandals. "Where have you been?"

"Are you high, kid?" Juan asked, confused.

"I was at the school watching Terry. I wanted to explain what happened," Sebastian said before sitting beside him.

He put his hand up toward Juan. "I wasn't talking to you, Juanito Brillo."

Juan stepped back into the wall of the cell, stunned. A second later, his face seemed to mutate into a rabid animal, and he approached Luke with his fists raised.

"What are you up to, partner?" Peanut asked, walking into the room.

Juan turned and looked at the horror before him. "Nothing, he was being an ass, is all."

"If you stay outside the cell, it doesn't matter how much of an ass he is, does it?" Peanut stared at the man and motioned for him to leave the cell. "Wil told me to come take over so you can get moving … so beat your feet, Juanito."

Juan stared up at Peanut and then at Luke, who sat calmly on the bench. Juan walked out of the cell without another word.

Peanut stared at Luke without speaking. His look was hard to read. It wasn't disappointment; it was more like indifference.

"Do you want out, or will you keep staring at me like the village idiot?" Peanut asked.

Luke stood up and walked out of the cell.

Peanut shut the door and stared at him again. "I don't think I've ever heard of teachers and cops trying to set up a high school kid for a crime. It's pretty messed up." Peanut handed him a can of soda.

He took the can but saw it wasn't diet, so he didn't open it. "Thanks, Peanut."

"Come on, your mother wants you home now."

Peanut led him to the front desk but held up his hand. "Wait here." The man walked into the receptionist area and briefly looked at the monitors. Peanut returned to the front door and motioned for him to stay. He grabbed a pelican case and walked out the front door to the parking lot.

About ten minutes later, Peanut returned to the office. "Your car is clean, but it will have to be screened every so often. Let me know when you are coming tomorrow. For now, go home and keep a low profile."

"What is my car clean of?" Luke asked.

"Tracking devices. The ones I showed you before. Don't worry about it now. We can discuss this later. Go home and calm your mother down before Wil goes nuts on me."

Luke left the office and drove toward his house. He did several heat runs to see if he was being followed and never saw anybody following him. During the drive, he realized it was long overdue. He needed to speak with Father Robert and pray in a safe environment. He approached an intersection and saw that it was free from traffic. Impulsively, he steered sharply to the left, slammed on the brake, and, within seconds, pressed the accelerator and smoked out the Joshua and Main intersection. He proceeded to the church and parked. In truth, he was upset at himself for missing the turn to the church, which sanctuary he initially aimed to reach.

He entered and saw several people walking around, sitting on pews and standing by votive candles. He saw the black clothing of a priest standing in the sacristy with his back facing him. The man had black hair and seemed familiar. He walked toward the priest, still looking for Robert, but did not see him.

"Excuse me, Father, do you know where Father Robert is?"

The priest turned and backed into the wall, distancing himself from Luke. It was Father Lee. He must have dyed his white hair black. Up close the man's hair appeared glued to his head. Father pointed toward the exit doors that led to the clergy house.

"Thanks, Father," he said, walking toward the exit. He faced the vulnerable priest who stood awkwardly against the wall. "Why do you act that way around me? When we needed you to step up, you turned your back on our family. Father D gave up his life to save us."

Father Lee exhaled and stooped forward in defeat. "I was afraid. It wasn't just you. I failed the Bollings, too." The priest made the sign of the cross.

"You don't need to recoil when you see me. Avandeil was defeated, and we are moving on with life."

"I'm sorry I failed you and your family. Please tell your parents I have asked for our Lord's forgiveness."

"I will. Please know that you're forgiven." Luke turned to walk away but turned around again and pointed his hand to the sky. "Don't fail the next family that needs your help, Father." With that, Luke proceeded to the clergy house. He found Robert wearing workout clothes but sitting on the sofa in the common area of the residence.

Robert stood up quickly and walked to him. "To what do I owe the pleasure of this visit?" The priest embraced him ... *I was ripped violently backward within the ether and landed beside Robert, wearing his purple stole over his customary black priest's clothing.*

"Let us pray. All-powerful and merciful God, we commend you, Luke, your servant and our protector. In your mercy and love, blot out the sins he has committed through human weakness. In this world, he has died to be joined with you forever. Through Christ our Lord."

I recognized this prayer. It was a prayer for the dead, his last rite. I walked past Robert and looked at the man on the gurney. It was me. My face was bloody, and I had a hole where my eye should be ... he released Luke from the embrace. The feeling of being brought into the present brought him vertigo, and he practically fell onto the sofa.

"What did you see? I shouldn't have hugged you like that. I'm sorry, Luke."

Luke was stunned, silent. *What did I see?* He was going to die, and it would be soon. "I saw my dead body and you praying over me in a hospital room." He held onto his head and shook uncontrollably.

"That's horrible. What's going on?" Robert asked, concerned. He almost placed his hand on Luke's shoulder but stopped himself.

"Why are you shaking like a coward? You were shown that for a reason," Sebastian said.

He looked up to see his guardian standing before him

confidently. "It was a shocking thing to see."

"Is Sebastian here?"

Luke shook his head in the affirmative and motioned toward his side.

"Sebastian, why did he see that vision? Do you know?" Robert asked.

"Luke you must fight Jimmy. If you don't you will end up like that. Dead to us, your reason for being here dead. All hope gone with you."

Luke stood and faced Sebastian; confidence restored. "I will not fail. I will stop Jimmy, and I will stop the disaster I am here to prevent," he said, almost yelling. A priest walked into the room and looked at Robert.

Robert stood and waved at the priest, who bowed his head slightly before walking on. "You need to fight back and stop this threat, Luke. Kneel before us, and I will pray for you and ask God to provide a hedge of protection surrounding you."

Luke knelt before Sebastian and Father Robert and placed his hands in prayer. He felt an energy building within him.

Father Robert placed his hand on Luke's head. Sebastian walked over and did the same.

"Heavenly Father, grant your soldier the strength to endure this battle ahead with the forces of evil. Give him, our protector and his guardian, the courage to stand strong in the face of his wicked adversaries. Lend them Your divine fortitude as they safeguard peace. Arm them with resilience, unflinching tenacity, and fierce dedication to righteousness. Amen."

Luke felt a burning sensation begin in his chest and expand outward to his whole body and limbs. He then saw a burning sun before him, and when he opened his eyes, a large flame appeared before him. He reached toward it. It was not hot; it was freezing cold and not painful to touch.

"You will see what you must, Luke. Go before this enslaver and tell him to remove his grasp upon the school. If he doesn't, he will be removed from your path by force," a voice said to him firmly from the flame that dissipated.

Luke stood up and felt as if he was taller than he was a moment ago. He was ready for the fight ahead of him.

"Was that God, Sebastian?"

Sebastian shook his head back and forth. "That was Miguel, the sentry guarding the gate that joined me with your path."

Miguel must be an angel. He knew that with certainty and was prepared for the battles to come.

CHAPTER TWENTY-TWO

One-on-One, Sort of

Luke stopped by the hospital to see Benji, who he had spoken to the prior evening over the phone. His friend had some homework assignments he wanted Luke to drop off at school. It had been a week already since Jimmy had placed the drugs into his locker. The school principal was told that the District Attorney accepted the case against Luke but was concerned with the search itself. Luke had not been suspended yet, but it was coming. The charges against Benji were still pending, but the cop that was posted at his door was gone. Neither one had been expelled yet, which was odd because Mr. Devry seemed to be in Jimmy's pocket.

"How did you sleep, Benji?" Luke asked, sitting on the plush chair beside his friend's bed.

"Okay, I guess. I was getting used to being handcuffed to the bed," Benji responded and then laughed.

"If they cannot pin it all on Jimmy, we may get a matching pair of cuffs."

Benji laughed and started smacking his cast on his thigh. He lifted his hand and stared at it oddly. "It doesn't hurt as much ... thanks for bringing my practice pad."

"No problem. We need you with us. The sooner, the better." Luke stood back up after seeing that his five-minute visit had turned into ten, and he needed to head to the school. "I need to get going."

Benji handed him a brown folder. "There's my homework. Take it to the secretary, and she'll make sure each teacher gets what I owe them."

Luke grabbed the folder and brought it to his chest. "Jimmy's not going to win, I promise you, Benji."

"Don't make promises you cannot deliver," Benji said and then appeared regretful. "Sorry. I believe in you, buddy, but Jimmy, he's just next-level nuts, man."

"I understand. He is a piece of work, but I cannot and will not let him win."

"Before I forget, I arranged for my father to change your oil. Drop off the car tonight, and he'll let you borrow my other car."

"I will do that, Benji. Be positive. You'll be home soon, and Jimmy will be dealt with."

Benji failed to show any optimism. Instead, his friend waved at him as he left the room and headed to school.

Luke arrived at school and saw his brother Junior walking from the underclassmen parking lot. He picked him up and drove toward the senior parking lot.

"How's Benji?" Junior asked. "I didn't recognize you in this Ford *Escort*."

"It's Benji's shop car. Thanks for asking, but he's in bad spirits."

"It's a shitty thing to say, but life goes on. Our parent's did not teach us to give up."

They walked together silently into the building and up the stairway. Jimmy Cladhaire walked onto the second-floor hallway from the stairwell. Luke stopped moving up the stairs and stared down the hallway. It couldn't have been, Jimmy.

"What's wrong?" Junior asked.

"I'm not sure. I could have sworn I saw the Bully Cladhair on the second floor."

"It was him, Luke. Watch your back all day." Sebastian said.

"I thought he was expelled," Junior said, surprised.

"Nothing will ever stop that guy. He was suspended, but that doesn't mean anything here. Get to your homeroom. Watch out for him. I'm sure he knows who you are, and he would do anything to make me regret challenging him. Wait, come here." Luke grabbed his brother's hand and saw what he needed to see. "Go, you'll be fine."

"What did you see?" Junior asked, worried.

"Enough, go. Don't worry." Luke walked to the secretary's office and handed her Benji's homework folder. She looked at him in disgust and waved him off. He arrived in the homeroom class and met with Mr. Conway near the entrance to the classroom.

"How are you holding up?" Mr. Conway asked.

"I'm going nuts, to be honest. I think I saw the Bully Cladhair."

"It could have been him. I heard his suspension was over."

"That makes no sense. Benji is still in the hospital," Luke said.

Mr. Conway appeared as if he wanted to say something, but didn't.

Later, when he went to art class, he saw Benji's open seat. He immediately felt alarmed and defeated. Mr. Aames motioned for him to come over to his desk. "Yes, Mr. Aames."

"I spoke to Benji's doctors on my last visit. He should be out soon," Mr. Aames said.

"Great, I was with Benji this morning, and he didn't say that."

"Doctors don't tend to want to tell their patients when they will be released. Luckily, I know the doctor from the last time I was a patient in the cardiac wing."

He did not know that his teacher had a heart condition, and it did take some level of respect for the man to trust him with his privacy. Thanks for letting me know, Mr. Aames."

"Take a seat and get started with your work," Mr. Aames said, pointing at his desk.

Alyssa waved at him when their eyes met. He walked up to her and gave her a firm hug and kiss. Her scent immediately settled him. "I missed you. How are you?"

"It's only been two days, Luke."

"A lifetime," he said and laughed.

Just before lunch, he went to his teacher and asked to use the restroom. Earlier, when he touched Junior, he saw that Jimmy was planning on confronting his brother. He was making it a point to go there before the confrontation. He was on the first floor and sprinted down the hallway toward the school metal and wood shop opposite the music classes. He hid in the nook of the entrance of an unused classroom. He kept an eye on the hallway and the boy's restroom. He watched Jimmy walk in then and seconds later, his brother. Luke stepped outside of the restroom and leaned up against the wall.

A minute later Junior ran out of the bathroom toward his shop class, with Jimmy following quickly behind.

"Where are you going, mister builder boy?" Jimmy taunted Junior.

"Go back to class, Junior … I got this," Luke said, moving off the wall.

Junior turned and looked at his brother. "I'm not leaving you here with this animal."

"Who are you calling an animal? Your brother's the one who's a Sasquatch," Jimmy said, laughing.

Luke motioned for his brother to step away. "I'm going to stop you, Jimmy. You're done at this school and have to move on."

"You're different somehow … aren't you? I can feel the change."

Luke got into a fighting stance, prepared to unleash on Jimmy in a way he had never done before. "I've been sent to give you a message from above. You're to leave the students in peace or else."

"From above what? You're twisted, man." Jimmy got into a fighting stance of his own.

"Maybe, but today is the day you are going to leave the

students at this school alone and disappear down the *yellow brick road*."

Jimmy bowed his head and shook it in disbelief. "Funny. All the time I spent in church, it always felt empty." He moved toward Luke and tried to kick him, but he blocked it. "Confidence, that's what you found. No matter what you need, you don't have." Jimmy rushed toward Luke's feet, trying to take him to the ground.

Luke landed on Jimmy's back with both elbows. He proceeded to punch Jimmy repeatedly in the ribs with both fists. He tried but failed to break the man's ribs with continuous strikes.

Jimmy stood up and kicked Luke's abdomen. "Nice try, Sasquatch."

Luke doubled over in pain; his breath having escaped his lungs. He tried but couldn't breathe in any air.

Jimmy grabbed Luke's head and tried to hit him with his knee, but Luke swept Jimmy's legs out from under him, causing him to flop hard, strike his head to the ground, and turn onto his back.

Jimmy stood quickly, faced Junior, and landed a forward kick at Luke's unsuspecting brother, who folded on the floor. "Old Jimmy knows what you're doing, Luke."

Jimmy moved to stomp on Junior while he was down, but Luke charged at Jimmy like he was playing football and tossed Jimmy into Junior's classroom.

"Run into the bathroom now, Junior." Luke helped his brother into the bathroom. He glanced into the classroom and saw Jimmy crumpling onto the floor unconscious. He thought it was best that he should leave the area instead of sticking around and getting expelled from school. He quickly ran back to his class. He stopped outside the door and tried to straighten up his clothing.

"That seemed to take quite some time, Luke, and you look beaten down," his teacher said.

"Yeah, I kind of tripped." He looked down at his undershirt and saw the outline of a shoe. He buttoned up his exterior shirt to cover the mark. He hoped Junior did not get blamed for the ass-whooping he had given Jimmy. He realized it needed to happen, but Mr. Devry would expel him if he waited for the consequences.

"Oh, I see. Well, take your seat. We are on page 215."

Once he sat down, he buttoned up his shirt and tried to find his page. He didn't smile but felt some pride for having finally faced Jimmy. He hoped his brother, Junior, was fine.

† † †

Beggars Can't be Choosers

Luke headed to the Customs office and again passed the armed services recruiting sign, the glowing sign guided him into the parking lot like a beacon. It was smaller than he had envisioned. A Marine recruiter sat with a young man at a desk. A Navy recruiter was on the phone. As Luke parked steps away from the recruiting office, he hesitated to get out of his car, taking a deep breath. As Luke walked up to the Army recruiter, who was packing a duffle bag at his desk, he noticed the nameplate on his uniform and rank.

"Hello, Master Sergeant Johnson. I am Luke Sanz, and I want to speak with you about joining the Army."

"I'm on my way out the door. What are you thinking of doing in the Army?"

"Not sure, but I was thinking something in law enforcement. I am an intern with …"

"Law enforcement is a hard occupation to get into." Sergeant Johnson looked him up and down, and it seemed like his mouth had a terrible taste. "The only schools we have ready and available are Culinary, Quartermaster, Mortuary, Water Treatment, and Shower and Laundry." Sergeant Johnson had three tabs on his shoulder: *Airborne, Ranger, and Special Forces.*

"I'm not interested in anything like that."

"That's all I have right now. I don't know what to tell you. Beggars can't be choosers." Sergeant Johnson was not impressed with him at all.

"I'll have to think about it."

"He's a good man, Luke—a warrior. You caught him at the wrong time," Sebastian said, knowing he was angered.

"Leave me your phone number, and I will call you when something opens up," Sergeant Johnson said, grabbing his bag before heading to the door.

Luke did not leave his phone number with Sergeant Johnson. He looked at the empty desk, where a US Air Force sign was affixed to a wall and grabbed a card from that desk.

"I would not bother with him. The Air Force is selective right now."

"Thanks for the advice, Sergeant, but I am selective and not much of a beggar. I need to head to work." Luke left and headed toward his car and unlocked the door.

"Nice car."

Luke did not respond. Instead, he left the parking lot, smoking his tires on his way out. He noticed the sergeant following behind him and then turned with him into the Customs parking lot. The sergeant continued driving toward the fitness place near the other stores and restaurants.

He tossed his backpack on the office chair, knocking it over. He felt terrible during the day and even worse after interacting with that recruiter.

"Easy tiger, that chair is rather comfortable," Terry said.

"I'm just annoyed."

"If you want to eliminate some tension, let me know. We can roll around a little. I may even let you hit me a few times," Terry said with a wink.

"Sure, tell me when."

"Give me an hour. I need to go serve some subpoenas." Terry smiled at him before walking out the front door.

Rolling around on the mat with a firm young woman could calm him immensely. The front door opened an hour into managing the front desk. He was anxiously expecting Terry, but it was Wil. "Hello, Wil."

"Follow me. We need to talk." He followed Wil to his office. Wil walked over to the window, looking outside.

Luke followed and took a seat nervously.

Wil handed him the Robinson security lanyard and identification card that he kept at his desk in his bedroom. "Your father found this in your room. It's my fault for letting you keep it."

"Was he pissed?"

Wil's face became tense, and he walked over to his seat. "No, we spoke about it candidly." Wil appeared to be holding something in.

"What is it? What are you not trying to say?"

Wil appeared to be conflicted about what transpired with his father. "Has your father explained how we met?"

"Yes, sort of. My father said you met overseas in Colombia during one of your investigations." The truth is that he had seen some of what happened to Wil in visions.

"I was working an undercover deal. An informant had arranged a meeting with a cartel boss to get an opening for large cocaine shipments into Florida. I didn't know that it was a ploy to have me kidnapped. It was revenge for a prior seizure of cocaine the informant had arranged. The informant's family had been kidnapped and I was the ransom. The cartel did not know I was an agent, but the informant did and did not seek help from his handler. The cartel boss had me kidnapped because, in their mind, I owed them millions for the loss of the drugs."

"What happened to the informant?" Luke asked.

Wil looked at him and then back into the past. "They killed him and his family. He should have known better ... they took me and tortured me." Wil stood up, opened his shirt, and showed scars on his chest where his nipples should be. "I never admitted that I was an agent. My mind kept trying to delude me by thinking that if I told them I was an agent, they would let me live. I was kept in a small cage in between torture sessions."

"Wil is a courageous man," Sebastian stood beside Wil, shaking his head. "I have been tortured, and it changes you forever."

"My doper persona kept rising. I realized that I needed to get them money, so I set them up in a trap by having them call my bank. It triggered a trace to and they were able to find me in Medellin."

"How long were you being held and tortured?" He was highly interested in this story. It was the most information he had ever heard concerning one of his father's recovery operations.

"Days, a week." Wil stood up, sat in the chair next to him, and grabbed the lanyard from his hand ... *I was thrust backward in time forcibly and landed in the dark dingy room that smelled like a sewer. I'd been in the room before and knew Wil was in his cage. An explosion outside caught my attention. A man sitting in a chair woke up with the explosion outside. The man's head popped into a red mist. The gunfire rang out, along with flashes lighting up the darkness outside. Screams of pain came from outside. A masked man wearing green fatigues entered the room. It was my father.*

"What's your name?" His father stood up and stared out the window. "I'm Special Agent Angel Sanz with diplomatic security. Are you Wildomar Rivera?"

"Yes, I'm Wil."

My father took a knife from his vest, cut open Wil's cage, and released him.

A man ran into the room, and my father shot the man twice in the chest before helping Wil out of his cage. Wil could not stand up, so his father placed Wil on his back.

A soldier walked into the room and looked around. "We seized cocaine, guns, and money. Some men are barricaded in a building and are shooting out of the windows. They killed one of my men," the man explained in Spanish.

"This is a cleaning, not a party," his father answered in Spanish while darting out of the room with Wil on his back. I saw one of the buildings burst into flames while my father drove away with Wil ... he returned to the present, and Wil had the lanyard in hand.

"I'll save this for you for later. We should keep it away from your father," Wil said, placing the item in a drawer.

"Luke, take heed of all you have heard and seen. Your father is a righteous man and was only thinking of others," Sebastian said.

He did not know what to say. Sebastian stood near him and gave him strength. "My father can be distant from us. All he has seen and done must take a toll on him."

"I would do anything for your father, including taking you under my protection to help you grow as a man. You may have a great career in the future, Luke. You must understand that this is not a perfect world, and some of us have been chosen to protect others from the evil that roams the earth."

Sebastian slammed his halberd on the floor. "Even he sees the truth, Luke."

He looked at Sebastian, opened his mouth to say something, and decided not to.

Wil looked throughout the room and said, "I know you have much to worry about. Terry called me to let me know you were upset about something."

"I have a lot on my mind, but it was something else. I feel I need to run away from all of this. I went to the Army recruiter next door, and the sergeant there wanted to make me a cook or laundry guy. It pissed me off."

"You would not be the first person to run away to the Army ... was Sergeant Johnson the recruiter?"

"You know him? He was rude. He called me a beggar and said I should take what he offered."

"He can be a bit of an ass. Johnson is about to retire from the Army. He's a Master Sergeant working his last year as a recruiter before he retires from the Army."

"What do YOU think of me joining the Army instead of attending college?"

"Your father, and especially your mother, will not like it, but truthfully, you are an adult, and I know you don't want to go straight to college. You can always do both. How serious are you about joining the Army?"

"I'm serious, but I don't want to end up doing something I don't want to do." He was extremely comfortable talking with Wil, and it was not lost upon him that he would love to have that type of relationship with his father.

"Get back to me in a few days on this."

They were interrupted by a knock on the door, and it opened. It was Terry dressed in tight workout clothing. "There you are. Get changed. I'm feeling frisky." She walked off.

Luke rose with an open mouth and was more than embarrassed.

"I don't want to know." Wil motioned him away. "Wait, this Army thing could be a mistake. Face your problems now and then decide what to do. Otherwise, you are in denial. You will regret escaping into boot camp." Wil looked pensive. "I would know."

Sebastian stepped out of the doorway and looked at Terry as she walked down the hallway in her tights. "You are one of the chosen, Luke."

He walked past Sebastian. "She only wants to work out."

"Is that what you call it now?" Sebastian stared at Terry's derrière.

He shook his head and walked down the hallway toward the men's locker room. Prepared to get his ass handed to him.

CHAPTER TWENTY-THREE
Roger

As Luke's day at school came to an end, he needed to make a quick stop to the restroom before heading to work. As he was leaving, he felt someone place a hand on his back … *I stood in a restroom watching a kid I knew as Roger speaking with Jimmy. This concerned me because it meant Jimmy had waited for me to leave the restroom. I was about to be attacked and was stuck in a vision.*

"How much flake do you have?" Roger asked quietly.

"You sure are developing a habit. Let me see … I have 5 grams," Jimmy said with his hand in his pouch.

"500?" Roger asked while handing him the case.

"Sold," Jimmy said, laughing.

"Can we make this a regular thing?" Roger asked, sniffling with his nose.

Jimmy looked at the kid and leaned in on him. "Where do you get this money? I smell a rat."

Roger did not seem concerned. "I break into houses … you should come with me sometime. I have some cool toys."

I walked around both of these criminals. Roger was almost a foot shorter than Jimmy but looked wiser somehow.

Jimmy stared at Roger angrily. "I'm not sure I like dealing with thieves. I don't want anybody stealing my shit."

"I don't want to piss you off, Jimmy, but not many high schoolers have access to this much cocaine. I have friends, you know, and we like to party."

"Fair enough, what's your name, again?"

"Roger, Jimmy ... I'm Roger."

"Of course, of course. We can meet here every Friday if you want. What else do you need?"

"Chocolate Thai, some horse, and some uppers and downers."

Jimmy shook his head and smiled. "I may have to close the shop early ...Luke was back in the present. He leaned against the door frame, prepared to push himself into Jimmy and finish their fight.

"Hey, you're Luke. Benji's friend?" Roger asked, out of place somehow, like a fish out of water.

"Yes, to both. How do you know Benji exactly?" Luke stared at the boy. He was leery of this kid. Benji had been out of class for weeks, yet he only started seeing Roger around the school recently.

"From the other kids in school," he said, covering his nostrils and sniffling." If you know what I mean, I'm trying to find some stuff, and both of your names come up. I'm not seeing the other usual suspects around here. Since you are friends with Benji, I figured you could help a brother out."

"Seriously, Roger, Benji's a good kid. The Bully Cladhair set him up. Go find Jimmy. I already know you tapped into him."

Roger tapped his leg nervously and laughed awkwardly. "That's something out of a movie, Luke. Come on, steer me the right way. I'm hurting for a taste!" Roger said, sounding desperate.

"What you need is a day in church and a sauna. If that's all, I'm running late and tired of this conversation." He did not wait for a response; he walked toward the exit. He stepped outside, looked around, and grabbed the back of his head.

"I felt it, too. You're being watched." Sebastian looked around the parking area. "Get to your car, and I will tell you who it is."

He walked down the hallway to the exit closest to the parking lot and got in his car. He drove out of the parking lot and then to the main highway heading out of Lansburg. He caught a glimpse of a red car in the distance.

"It's Cladhaire. Sebastian, is he by himself?"

Sebastian closed his eyes. "Yes, he is. You need to lose him, Luke."

He thought about it, made a left turn down a farm road, and punched the gas. Before he knew it, he drove over 100 miles an hour and quickly approached an intersection. He slammed on the brakes, turned right through a stop sign, and slammed on the accelerator again.

"He can still see you. You need to get into the trees and find a place to stop." Sebastian said. "Wait, let me check," Sebastian said and dissipated.

He headed up a hill, made a left turn, and made a sharp right down a tree-lined road. He stopped the car and stepped out.

"He cannot see you and he's pissed off." Sebastian reappeared, standing beside him.

"I can hear his car but cannot see it," he said, looking through a pair of binoculars he had stashed in the car.

"He passed you and is headed back down the hill on the opposite side. Turn around and head back to the main highway."

Luke jumped back into the car and returned to the main highway. He didn't see Jimmy's red *Firebird*.

"We lost him. It's safe for now," Sebastian said.

"Jimmy must be out for blood, like a shark."

"Yes, I understand completely. I was in a shipwreck once and was on a small *lancha*, or jolly boat, at sea for weeks. A group of sharks followed us most of the time."

Luke cracked a small smile and stared at Sebastian.

"The Bully Cladhair is our current problem. You will succeed in drowning him out of your lives," Sebastian said unaware of the idiom Luke just used.

He drove past the Army Career Center. The sign glowed and appeared to flash repeatedly until he finally passed it. He arrived at work and parked under an awning. He took his seat at the front desk and did not see any other agents or analysts around, so he took out his homework and got started on an assignment. He wasn't interrupted for about an hour.

"Ahem."

Luke peered up from the desk to see Terry looking as beautiful as ever, staring at him.

"Yes, Terry … sorry, was just taking advantage of the lull," he said.

"Follow me. Some of us are in the conference room. Come on," Terry said, leading him from the reception area.

He followed her, catching up to her quickly. He couldn't help but take a peek at her derrière. He knew it was wrong but couldn't help himself. She turned and saw him looking and smiled.

"When do I get to meet, Alyssa?" Terry asked, reminding him immediately why it was wrong to leer at other women.

He snapped his head up quickly. "Like a double date or something?"

"You're funny. I work too much for anybody to want to date me. It's hard to find anybody who would put up with our hours or the travel we do." She stepped into the conference room.

He followed her and saw Todd and David at the podium. Pictures of Jimmy, his father, Juan Bello and images of the school's exterior were affixed to the wall. There were also photos of Jimmy dealing drugs in the bathroom, and one was of Jimmy delivering drugs to the police.

"Luke, take a seat," Wil said.

He followed Wil's direction and sat down, facing the podium on the opposite side of the table. He scanned the room and saw some new faces. Not all of them looked friendly. Peanut was here, which relieved him, and so was Carlos Tirado, the Group Supervisor who had been very helpful since he started at the office.

"Luke, this is Special Agent Robert Curtis with the FBI and

Christian Kelly with the Department of Justice, Office of Inspector General. They are handling the corruption end of this investigation. You know everyone else."

Luke tried to stand up to shake the man's hands, but Agent Curtis waved him off. "Why are you placing so much trust in this kid? I expected better from you, Wil," Curtis said.

"I'm not going to be as pompous as Robert here, but this is a lot of trust to place in someone so young," Agent Kelly said. "No offense, kid."

"None taken. I brought this to their attention because I want Jimmy out of our lives. I wasn't expecting to do it myself."

The door opened, and another young man entered the room. It was Roger from school. He tossed a stack of evidence bags on the conference room table. "I bought all this from Jimmy, five other students who deal, and one gym teacher. They told me not to waste my time with Benji or Luke here because they were good kids and not dealers. Jimmy set them up."

Luke stood up and smiled. "You're a cop? I couldn't tell. You look like you're sixteen, but there was something about you."

Roger laughed and offered him his hand. "Well, that's the point, isn't it."

Luke took Roger's hand … *I stood next to Roger and Todd. They were in what looked like a conference room. They each had a beer in their hands.*

"I liked your presentation on your undercover experience more than all the others," Todd said.

"Thanks. I'm not sure how long I will look young enough to work in high schools and colleges, but I'll have a go at it for as long as possible."

Todd took a long pull from his beer. "I need your help. I have a dealer at a high school who is dealing drugs on behalf of his father, who's the lieutenant of a drug task force. Lots of corruption, and the school is suffering, man."

"Where do you work out of?" Roger asked, taking a drink from his beer.

"Loudon County, Virginia."

"Suburb of DC, right? I'm an East Coaster man who likes to be as far from headquarters as possible."

"I feel you, I get it, but we could use you," Todd pleaded. "There have been some deaths, from overdoses, but also murders to cover the dealing.

Roger took a deep breath and shook his head up and down. "Have your ASAC call my ASAC. They will ask me if I'm interested, and I will insist on working on it."

Todd grabbed two more beers and handed one to Roger. "Thanks, Roger." I appreciate it ... Luke was back in the present, standing before Roger.

"So, what was it about me?" Roger asked.

"You looked a little wise, where most kids ay my school are more like punks, me included," Luke said, all of them laughing together.

"Todd, and now you out your UC to the same kid. You're all in on this kid, man," Agent Curtis said.

"Please all take a seat ... Terry, if you would," Todd said, sitting near her.

"Thanks, Todd, and thanks to all for joining us. Several months ago, Luke, operating in an undercover capacity, led us to a heroin seizure that originated from China. The heroin was moved off a container ship in Portsmouth and then hidden in a modified compartment in a rail car. The buyers of that heroin were part of an Italian mob family in New York, but some of that heroin was also meant for some members of a black gang operating in the DC area. Mainly Mickey, who was killed recently by members of the task force. Both events were widely reported."

"Wil, you didn't tell me that Luke has already worked as an undercover," Agent Curtis said.

"If you had waited, you would have heard," Wil said sharply.

"What was that, 500 pounds?" Agent Curtis asked.

"Almost, it was 480," Luke responded.

"Continue, Terry. I apologize for the interruption."

"We have investigated independently the source-of-supply of the heroin from China, the smuggling method through the seaport, and the bulk distribution by a Chinese gang based out of Centreville." Terry looked at Todd and motioned for him to approach the podium.

"David and I have been investigating the distribution network from the warehouse in Centreville into different areas of Loudon and DC. David and I have found that the network moving the narcotics into the Lansburg area is only one entity. The drug task force itself is the source of supply for the bulk of the drugs in this area, with Lieutenant James Cladhaire, his son Jimmy, Juan Bello, and Morozov as the distributors at the Loudon Center High School. Roger here has purchased drugs from Jimmy and other related dealers including several teachers. From what we can gather, the principal, vice-principal, and even the school nurse is involved. The attacks at the school and all the attempts to set up Benji and Luke have all been investigated, and we are pinning those charges on all the conspirators. We are all here today to discuss when to conduct the takedowns."

"That's very ambitious, Todd. Why not arrest who you want and get them to talk and take the others down one at a time like dominoes," Agent Curtis said.

Terry stood up and stared at Luke. "If we did that, the LT would get wind of it eventually, and he may kill more people. It's a miracle they don't know already. We need to know when to do this to avoid bloodshed and keep the teachers and kids safe."

"The recital, the first week of May. All the students, teachers, and staff will be in the auditorium. Even Jimmy will have to be there," Luke said.

Wil smiled and slammed his fist on the table. "Luke, you will be our guy inside. We need to know which teachers to trust. All of you, start planning. Only trust the people in this room until we are ready to brief the others.

"I'll support that," Curtis said, staring at his watch.

"The AUSA will sign off on everything with the PC we have

thanks to the team in this room," Wil said.

Everything seemed to be in place, yet Luke felt as if something was wrong, and they were doomed. He discarded the feeling as being more akin to his anxious personality than a true vision of what was to come.

CHAPTER TWENTY-FOUR

Confronting Luke

Earlier in the week, Benji told him that the *Grand National* was ready to be picked up. He exchanged the *Escort* for his *Grand National* and could not help touching the fabric on the passenger seat. He drove past Campbell Farms and slowed down when he saw Nancy parked outside the gate. She waved at him, so he parked beside her and stepped out of the car.

"Luke, it is great to see you. How long has it been?"

"A few months at least, Nancy. Since the dinner at Tom's house … how's everything at the farm?"

"Quite well. Lulu has taken over as head of operations. No more real estate for her. She lives in the main house now. Kyle's son lives on the property as well."

"Archie would be proud," Luke said, looking toward the estates, realizing he was running late.

"Yes, he would. Have you joined the Army yet?"

Luke grabbed his long hair and smiled. "I'm not sure I ever will. I have this urge, but I haven't spoken to a recruiter yet. Why do you ask?"

Nancy seemed embarrassed and looked down at the floor. "Now's not the time, but if you ever do, please let me know. It's something Archie had talked to me about the day he passed away."

Luke drove off a bit bewildered and wondered why Nancy would be interested in whether he joined the Army. He was so caught up with finishing high school and dealing with the antics of Jimmy Cladhaire. Very little else mattered.

Once he entered the Mars property, he saw Alyssa waiting impatiently under the portico.

"I'm sorry, I'm late. I saw Nancy at Campbell Farms and wanted to say hello."

Alyssa smiled at him. "I'm just happy you're here now." She grabbed him and pulled him downward within her reach ... *I was once again in the car with Alyssa. We kissed hungrily as I caressed her bare legs. She opened her blouse and pulled my hand toward her stomach* ... she continued kissing him, and his hands ran underneath her shirt and touched her back. "Later, later, my parents are waiting."

She escorted him into the house. "We have a formal dining room, but mostly eat in this room over here." Alyssa's parents were already sitting at the modern-looking table. The room was finely furnished and had a comfortable feel to it. "Sorry we took so long, Mom."

"We only sat down ourselves," Alice said while drinking some iced tea.

They sat on the opposite side of the table, and he nervously took a drink of water. Mary walked into the dining room through a set of double doors, and he saw that it led into a kitchen.

"Would you like a drink, Luke?" Mary asked.

"The water is fine, thanks, Mary." He took a second sip from his water glass nervously.

"Are you sure, Luke? Alyssa has a treasure trove of peach-flavored iced tea." Alice pointed toward Alyssa as if she was telling a secret.

"Grab two, Mary. He'll like it once he tries it," Lee said.

"Sure, thanks." He needed to show some confidence here and just be himself. He took a long breath and prayed for strength. He leaned in toward Alyssa and whispered. "How much iced tea do you have?"

She turned toward him, smiled and responded, "Cases." She then looked toward her father. "What's for dinner, Dad?"

"Chateaubriand steak with a demi-glace and asparagus."

"Mom, what did I tell you guys ... nothing fancy." Alyssa glared at both her parents.

Mary approached the table with a tray of hamburgers, buns, and fries and placed them at the center of the table. She put a bunch of condiments and a tray with toppings, including cheese and bacon, beside the burgers. "We have more, so let us know, Lee. I will be back with the drinks. Sorry, Alyssa, I wanted to get these out while they were hot." Mary walked back into the kitchen.

He let out an uncontrolled laugh but winced when he sensed a disapproving glimpse on Alyssa's face.

Alyssa looked meanly at her father. "Serve yourself, Luke."

"I meant to say we were thinking of Chateaubriand, but we're going to wait for a different day." Lee cracked a smile.

Luke assembled two hamburger patties sans the bread with a stack of cheese and bacon. He considered eating a third with bread but decided against it. The hamburger patties were thin and broad and seasoned perfectly.

"Don't let anything go to waste. We have tons of patties in the kitchen," Mary said after coming back with the tea. "Make some to go as well."

He looked at Alyssa, and she shook her head. After he finished his patties, he put together four double burgers and covered them in foil. Mary brought two brown bags, placed two burgers in each bag, and then added fries.

"Luke, how do you like our house?" Lee asked with his arm around Alice's shoulder.

"It's beautiful. The interior design is so modern. I think my mom would love the house."

"Alice is our interior designer. That is what she does for a living ... you said before that your mom was raised in a large house in Sydney. Are her parents wealthy?"

"My grandfather was a diplomat at a High Commission in the US many years ago. He was the son of wealthy landowners. It's old wealth from cattle and agriculture. I don't know much more than that. My parents had a falling out with them years ago before we moved to Puerto Rico."

"That's terrible. I'm sorry I brought it up." Lee seemed cautious with Luke.

"It's fine. My mom reconnected with them after what happened to Junior last year. They may be coming over to visit."

"How's your friend Benji?" Alice asked with concern.

"He's still in the hospital, but they say his hand will heal well." In truth, what concerned Luke most was Benji's heart. His friend was weakened from cardiac surgery and may never recover fully.

"We hope he improves, Luke."

"Luke, would you like to take a ride in my helicopter? We can fly over all of Lansburg," Lee said with a huge grin.

"Sure, I would like that. I have never been in one. Wait, you fly the helicopter?" Luke was genuinely surprised that a wealthy financial fund manager could find time to learn how to fly.

"Yes, Dad is a pilot. I'll stay behind. You go, Luke. Be back before seven so we can watch the sunset." Lee stood up and stepped into the kitchen. "Mary, we are headed out in the helicopter. Tell Norman, please, and thank Paul for dinner."

Lee walked back into the room. "Are we all ready?" Lee asked while slapping his hands happily. Lee must love to fly his toy helicopter. They walked to the entrance of the house and out to the portico. There was a golf cart that held four people, and they took that to the helicopter pad. "This will be a little different than flying in an airplane. You must wear a headset to talk and hear one another because it can be loud." Lee parked the golf cart in a small parking area and stepped out of the cart. "Luke, get into the left front door, and Alice will sit in the back."

They boarded. It was roomy, but the enclosed area makes him

anxious, primarily because of the unexpected. He grabbed a headset and put it on. He noticed that even Sebastian had joined them and sat in the seat directly behind him.

Lee placed his headset on as Alice got into the helicopter's back seat, which was separated from the cockpit. Lee grabbed a set of laminated papers. "Luke, I will go through the flight checklist, so don't mind me."

"Don't worry, Luke. We will be in the air in a few minutes. Lee always follows the safety checklist," Alice said through the headset.

"Luke this helicopter is a McDonnell Douglas *MD500E*."

"It's distracting, hearing you through a headset and not being able to see you unless I turn around."

"You'll get used to it, Luke," Alice said.

Lee continued to move through the checklist, turning certain switches, moving levers, and turning the handle to his left. "This is the collective, Luke." Lee hit other controls, pointed at gauges, and then began pulling switches on the console. "Clear," Lee said while looking out the window. Lee then grabbed the collective and started moving it around, and the rotor above began to turn the blades. Lee kept going through his checklist and moving the collective. "Luke, we are ready to go. I will take it easy. Once we enter the air, I want to see if you recognize anything from above."

Luke was so anxious that he had difficulty recognizing anything, but he gave Lee the thumbs up. The helicopter began to rise, and the aircraft vibrated a bit. He grabbed onto his legs and felt an adrenalin rush to his chest, making him stare at the door handle with a fleeting thought of jumping out. The helicopter pushed forward and rose simultaneously; within minutes, they were hundreds of feet in the air. They were above large sweeping lawns and mansions beneath and surrounding them sparsely. "This is something else, Lee."

"Oh my, Lord. Tell him to go back down, please. This is worse than when my father sent me to the crow's nest on his ship."

"Seb …" He began to say, caught Sebastian's eyes, and raised his eyebrows.

"Sorry, Luke. I could leave if you want me to … or I will stop talking." Sebastian held his hands up in defeat. "It's my first time in a helicopter."

"It's my first time in a helicopter too!" he said without considering that he was having a private conversation in public.

"Yes, I figured it was Luke," Lee responded, thinking he was nervous.

Luke turned around and leered at Sebastian, who winced.

Alice looked a little worried. "Are you okay, Luke?"

"Sorry Alice, I'm fine … a little nervous being so high up." He inhaled audibly.

"We are at 1,000 feet and will keep it here while we move through the airspace. Do you recognize what is right below us?"

"That's Red Hill Road, and there is the elementary school, and I can see my parent's house."

"You're good at this. Alice cannot see the world from above and recognize it the same way from below."

"Easy tiger, I'm getting better at it," Alice laughed.

"Give me about five minutes of flight time, and we will see if you can figure out where we are," Lee said while he changed direction toward their left.

He could tell they had turned southeast and knew where Lee was headed.

"Luke, did Alyssa tell you she was accepted into the Rhode Island School of Design on a full scholarship?" Alice asked over the headset.

"Ambush, Luke, you are a captive audience," Sebastian thundered through the headset.

He immediately realized Alyssa's parents planned to isolate him from their daughter to have this conversation. "No, she had not mentioned it to me. I know that was number one on her list."

"She's considering going to the local community college here and then transferring to Virginia Commonwealth to be near you. We are concerned she's making a mistake."

He did not answer, mainly because he was taking it all in and knew he had not been honest with Alyssa about his plans for the next four years.

"What's below us, Luke?" Lee asked without joining Alice's ambush.

"My grandparent's house ... Alice, I'm considering joining the Army, but not having much luck. I don't know where I'll be next year, but I'm sure it will not be college."

"We understand, Luke," Alice said, trying to drive Lee into the conversation. "Our daughter loves you and will let her dreams pass by to be with you."

"I will speak with her, Alice. I may not even be in Lansburg for years. I want her to fulfill her dreams, and I don't want her to resent me."

"Thanks, Luke. We only want what's best for our daughter. My wealth could disappear with one bad business deal or financial decision. We want Alyssa to secure her future and not rely on our fortune." Lee was a sincere man who loved his daughter.

"I love your daughter and want her in my life, but I need to solve my problems before we sit and discuss the future. I will tell her that I prefer her to go to Rhode Island. Ultimately, it's her decision, but we are too young to commit to anything. Fair enough?"

"Thanks, Luke, for not being upset about how we did this," Lee said.

"Alyssa is lucky to have such loving parents. On a side note, Lee, could you teach me how to fly one day?"

"Luke, I'm also a flight instructor. I guess I can do that if my fund ever tanks." During the last part of the conversation, Lee turned eastward and flew above Campbell Farms.

"Luke, please be gentle when explaining to Alyssa what happened. She'll be furious, probably a bit vindictive if she thinks we ambushed you." Alice seemed to tiptoe around her daughter's feelings.

"Alice, I'm glad we had this conversation. She's not completely honest about her dreams right now."

"Thanks, Luke. I hope this all works out, and to be honest, we would love to have you as a son-in-law and married to our only child," Alice said.

"Thanks, Alice, but we need a foundation before we consider marrying. Something my parents raised me to believe."

Lee landed the helicopter and quickly began the post-flight checklist. They all removed their headsets and stepped out of the aircraft.

Alice walked up to Luke. "Thanks for being so understanding," Alice said, hugging him ... *I was propelled backward as usual but into the future. I stood near a chair where a young man wearing desert tan camouflage BDUs slept. It was me. Alice stood near Alyssa as she lay in bed being fed ice chips ...* he returned to the present. "You feel like the son I never had." Alice was prophetic in that he would be their son and be on their side for the rest of their lives.

Lee walked up to them. "Break it up. I can see Alyssa waiting for us under the portico," Lee said jokingly. They jumped into the golf cart and headed back to the house.

"How was it?" Alyssa asked with concern while looking at her mother.

"I was anxious at first, but it was a smooth ride, and I got to see what Lansburg looks like from the air."

"Let's go to the dock so we don't miss the sunset."

"Have fun, kids. Don't make us grandparents," Alice says half-jokingly.

"Mom, please stop." A red-faced Alyssa said with genuine embarrassment.

"Come on, Alice, let's get Mary to make us some cocktails, and we can sit near the pool ... see you both later on," Lee said, waving to them. He walked with Alice back up to the entrance of the house.

"Let's go down this path over here. It's a shortcut," Alyssa said while giving her mom an angry look. "Sorry about my parents. They are so protective. I wish they had other children so they could pay attention to someone else, instead of me all the time."

"They mean good, Alyssa. Why didn't they have any other kids?"

"They tried for years after they had me and even went to fertility doctors, but my parents finally gave up when they lost a baby. They almost adopted."

"They are great parents, and you are truly blessed."

"Thanks, Luke. I complain, but I am blessed." They arrived at the deck covered on one end with a block retaining wall. Once on the deck, anybody sitting there would have privacy from any onlookers. There was an ice chest between two chairs. "I brought some tea if you want. Some snacks, too."

"I do. Thanks for thinking ahead." He looked at the position of the sun and the pond. "Looks like we still have a few minutes." They took a seat and held hands.

"What did my parents spring on you?"

"I enjoyed their company, and your father agreed to teach me how to fly the helicopter."

Alyssa squeezed his hand hard. "I know them … they told you about Rhode Island, didn't they?"

"Yes, they did. They want you to go, as I do. I want you to finish college. I may go into government like my father, but I'm just not sure yet."

"Why don't you come with me? You're an Art and Music major like me."

"College, not now, maybe never. I'm probably going into the Army. I need that structure and foundation in my life. I feel the need to serve my country and my God."

"The Army? At least the Gulf War is over. Still, I wouldn't say I like the idea. It scares me to think you could leave and never come back."

The sun began to set. He leaned close to her and got down on one knee. "And if I do join the Army, I want you to go to Rhode Island and fulfill your dream. When I return, I will work on securing a career and want you to be my wife."

"Are you proposing to me?"

"More like mapping out our future, but yes, one of these days, I will propose to you, and if you accept, we will have as many children as God blesses us with."

Happy tears poured down her face. "Yes, yes, let's do that, Luke. I love you so much."

"I love you too, and I thank God that he saw fit to bless me with you in my life."

They embraced and kissed. Alyssa grabbed Luke's hand and pulled him onto her Adirondack chair, which cracked and splintered loudly.

"Sorry about your chair," he said while laughing.

"It's fine. It's old. Let's move to the blanket instead." They moved to the blanket. Alyssa got up and spread it on the deck. They sat on the blanket and hugged while the sun set to the west. It was idyllic because the large pond before them was serene, and the trees on the opposite side of the pond were devoid of other homes.

When Luke embraced Alyssa as they lay on the blanket, he realized that it was the night that Alyssa chose to lose her virginity. She wanted to gift him what she thought was the most she could ever offer any man. He tried to push her back and tell her they needed to wait until marriage. He couldn't stop himself because he wanted her as much as she wanted to give herself to him.

CHAPTER TWENTY-FIVE

The Pin Trick

Luke was ecstatic as if the world belonged to him, and he chose to take it. The evening he spent with Alyssa was unforgettable. He drove his car under the speed limit, which was not typical for him. It was Friday, and after work, he planned to spend as much of the weekend as possible with Alyssa. Red Hot Chili Peppers played loudly in the car as he sang along with the music recklessly. He was on his way to the Customs office and was looking forward to a workout with Terry. She had challenged him to high-intensity workouts and two minutes of sparring together. Suddenly, he saw red and blue lights flashing behind him, quickly followed by a siren. *Pride cometh before the fall*, he thought. He pulled the vehicle over to the curb. It wasn't just one police car; it was at least two, and as soon as he pulled over, the officers jumped out of the vehicle. One blocked the lane while the other was parked directly behind him. Jimmy's *Firebird* was parked facing him on the opposite oncoming lane.

"Driver, turn off the vehicle ... with your left hand, reach and pull the keys from the ignition. Now throw the keys out of the window."

Luke followed the officer's directions.

Sebastian stood outside of his window. "It's the corrupt

officers. Follow their directions because they are planning on killing you."

"Put both hands out of the window now … with your right hand, open the car door from the outside."

He followed each order slowly and opened the door. He pushed the vast door of his *Grand National* open and waited.

"Step out slowly … put your hands up and leave them up. Turn away from the sound of my voice. Stop. Now, lift the top of your collar. Higher!"

A burning sensation ran through his body. He felt like he was watching himself as an actor in a movie. As if he had an out-of-body experience where he could hover above everybody yet still be in control of his body.

"Turn toward us … move toward us slowly."

He couldn't tell before but knew it was the two corrupt officers. These animals must be desperate. It cannot be the drugs; they didn't have custody of that evidence. People on the street stopped and stood close by, watching the event unfold.

"Turn around, place your hands behind your back." Officer Washington said.

When he turned, Luke saw the LT standing on the opposite side of the street. The man's vulture sat on his shoulders, rubbing *its* talons greedily. He complied and placed his hands behind his back. Officer Washington grabbed his hands and put him quickly in handcuffs … *I had never been in handcuffs and immediately felt a sense of defeat and disgust at myself. They had won, and my pride led to my fall. The officer began to pat me down and reached down the outside of my leg to my ankle. Then he started checking the inside of my leg to my crotch. A sharp pain shot through my testicle directly to my chest, causing me to clench both knees together and jump upward. When I came down, I fell on top of the officer.*

"*Stop resisting, stop resisting. He's going for my gun. Jose, he's got my gun.*"

Officer Velasquez ran up to the heap containing both Luke and Washington. "Stop, or I'll shoot."

A shot rang out. Searing pain entered his chest. Blood flowed from his chest and back ... the officer finished searching Luke's ankle and then progressed the search up his leg toward his crotch. Luke clenched his teeth and stood firm, prepared now for the pain. It came and he didn't react. It came again. The second time, he missed the testicle and just hit his scrotum. "Can you please stop stabbing me with that pin, Leroy?" Luke asked rather loudly, hoping one of the lookie-loos standing nearby could hear and see what was happening.

"Hey, officer, we saw that. You need to stop poking that kid in the balls!" the man said, walking closer to them while pointing his finger.

"Washington, just get him in the car. Let's get out of here," Jose said, holstering his firearm.

Washington escorted Luke past the rear of the *Grand National*. Written on the edge of the trunk lid under the spoiler and to the left of the keyhole were the words Divine Justice. *When did Benji do that*, I thought.

The officer tossed Luke roughly into the patrol car. He did not place the shoulder belt on him. "Plan B, asshole." The officer shut the door.

Luke sat and watched as they moved his car. He stared at the trunk lid with the Old English writing, Divine Justice, and prayed. He sat quietly with Sebastian in the patrol car's rigid fiberglass back seat. Fortunately, Officer Washington drove silently into Leesburg. He thought he would be taken to the Lansburg Police Department, but the officer arrived at a gate that said Loudon County Jail. He was taken to a room and told to strip down and remove his underwear. A glob of blood landed on the floor. His scrotum continued to bleed continuously onto the floor. A deputy with a name tag that said JONES kicked the underwear toward a trashcan.

"What did you do to this street trash, Leroy?" Deputy Jones asked.

"This guy stabbed my balls with a pin because he was trying

207

to set me up to take a bullet from his fellow cokehead cop!" Luke stared at Washington in defiantly.

In response, the corrupt cop walked up to Luke and punched him in the face. Luke snarled back at the man but did not fight back.

Deputy Jones pushed the officer toward the booking table and pointed at the cameras. Then Jones whispered into Washington's ear. Whatever he said was enough because he shook his head and left the room.

"That assault on an officer is another charge, young man," Deputy Jones said, establishing his lack of integrity and tarnished badge. The man tossed clothing and tennis shoes to Luke. "Are you an exhibitionist? Get dressed, con."

"I'm not a con or a criminal, man. That piece of work stabbed my groin, and I need to stop the bleeding. At least it's on tape." He looked at the camera and the red light was off.

The man sneered and tossed his clipboard onto the table. He reached for a box at the other end and handed it to Luke. He placed three plastic wrapped packets on the table before Luke. "We keep those around for the feminine types like you. Go ahead, put one on. You can save the rest for later."

Luke grabbed one of the packages and noticed it was a sanitary pad used by women when they were on their period. It wasn't very comfortable, but it would work well. He proceeded to place it on his scrotum in front of the leering deputy.

"Could you please tell me what the charges are?"

"You should know. You did the crime."

Minutes later, he was placed into a large holding cell with dozens of other men, most sleeping, but some were working out. Jones smacked his back … *I stood in front of a line of inmates lined up in a hallway. I saw myself slowly, walking closer to an intersection in the hallway. When the line progressed forward, a man moved in behind me, stabbed my back repeatedly, and then walked away. I tried to reach the wounds in my back, but the handcuffs made it impossible. The blood continued to gush onto the linoleum floor …* he was back in the present. The paperwork fell to the ground around him as the cell door slammed shut behind him, waking half of the men inside. He reached down and grabbed the paperwork. Some of it was wet, which he quickly realized was urine. There were no toilets, but there were drain holes on the floor. The smell was rank and eye-watering. He found a corner and sat on a bench. *I need to take a shower*, he thought.

"Well, are you ready for a whole new adventure?" Sebastian asked, quickly pointing with his halberd to the different threats throughout the room.

"Take it easy, Sebastian. We may be here for longer than we want."

He tried to find something useful in some of the documents, but most were about inmates' rights, and some of them had an X mark near where his signature should have been. He found one piece of paper that mentioned a criminal complaint. Under charge, it said 18.2-58—robbery, resulting in serious bodily injury. "Well, Lord … I might as well take a nap," he whispered, settled on a filthy bench, and closed his eyes.

Grizzly

Luke spent the whole weekend at the jail. In retrospect, on purpose. He sat holding a receiver for a phone, talking to his parents and a lawyer named Rooney Albert, who his mother found in the local telephone directory. They were divided by a glass partition. He could only speak to one at a time. The lawyer just advised him that there was a witness who identified him from a photo line-up as the perpetrator of an armed robbery. They even recovered a jacket with paperwork showing his name.

"Jimmy stole my jacket from my locker. Ask Wil … this is all a setup orchestrated by the LT," Luke said.

"Son, I've known James Cladhaire since junior high. He's a

very by-the-book kind of guy," Rooney said.

"So, what you're saying is that you both are cut from the same cloth."

The lawyer leaned back and stared at the phone receiver before returning it to his ear. "Your arraignment is tomorrow afternoon. I'll ask for bail, and your parents indicated they would pay. We can work out everything else over the next few weeks. If you all excuse me, I need to go file some paperwork on behalf of your son." Rooney handed the receiver to Luke's father and walked away. The man stared meekly at Luke as he left.

"What did you say to him?" his father asked.

"That guy is in on it too, Dad. Do you see the Deputy over there?" Luke pointed at Jones, who seemed to be flirting with one of the female officers.

"Come on, Luke, you are sounding crazy."

"Do Wil, and Terry know what they did to me?"

"Wil and the rest are washing their hands of this, Luke. They think you're too caustic right now. Wil and Terry are sorry, but they think if they insert themselves, the AUSA will drop the case against all of them. They told you to sit tight and man up, son."

"Dad, Officer Washington poked me with a needle or something while he searched me. I saw a vision, and that other officer, Velasquez, killed me right there in the street. It would be best if you got me out of here before court. If you don't, I'm dead."

Luke stood up and showed him the blood leaking into his orange jumpsuit. "It won't stop bleeding. They're going to kill me on the way to court today, I saw it."

"I'm going to kill them all, son," his father said, finally with a fire under his butt.

"Let me speak to Mom, please, Dad."

"You're time is up, kid," Deputy Jones said.

His mother grabbed the phone. Tears were flowing down her face, and she was sobbing. "I'm sorry you're going through this, my love. You don't deserve it."

"Mom, please don't think you failed me. Please tell Alyssa to come visit me."

His mother's face contorted as if he was in pain. She spoke without opening her eyes. "I'll try … I'll try again, but her parents are not allowing it, Luke. They won't let me speak with her again."

He slumped down as the guard tried to lift him, but Luke was not moving.

"They thought they had me with the locker, but Jimmy grabbed my jacket for a reason. I had you to save me from that."

He looked up toward Sebastian, who placed his arm on his shoulder. Energy flowed through him. "I love you, Mom. Don't forget that I love all of you. Take care of Tony." Luke stood and walked off.

He saw his mother start banging on the visitation window, and his father tried calming her. He lost sight of them and hoped it wasn't the last time. He was placed back into the large holding cell and proceeded to lie down and sleep. It was restless and he did not dream.

"Luke Sanz, Sanz, wake up, kid," Jones yelled.

Luke stood up and staggered a bit. His whole body ached in pain. Either the smell in the room or his body odor made his stomach turn. "What's up?"

"Come on, I'm taking you to medical, and they'll let you shower before court."

"Thanks, Deputy."

"Sure, we are all about customer service here. This is medical." Jones opened the door. The man motioned him in.

Luke hesitated, looked around the door, and saw the room was called *Holding Cell 2*. "This is just another holding cell," he said, confused.

"It's a jail. You must enter the holding area before they see you in medical."

At least that made sense. He proceeded into the room and saw a huge man sitting on a bench facing away from him. He tried to turn, but Jones shut the door into him, pushing him into the room and knocking the air out of him.

The large man stood up and walked up to the door's window. Jones lifted the window covering.

"That ones for Juan, you are a damn little punk. This big guy here is from the LT. Go on, Grizzly, give him his lesson."

"I'm supposed to beat your ass before raping you," Grizzly yelled loudly.

I changed something when I spoke to the lawyer, he thought. Luke stood up and tried to move his hands upward but couldn't. He could barely spread his legs apart. "You're wrong, Grizzly. I'm going to put you in the hospital," Luke screamed out, banging his handcuffs on a pipe running from the floor to the ceiling.

"Grizzly, keep it down … shut that punk up now."

Grizzly charged at Luke like a bull and struck Luke, sending him backward to the hard concrete floor.

Luke tried to roll out of the fall, but the hand and leg cuffs tore into his wrists and ankles painfully. He let out another scream.

"Hey, what's that ruckus down there?" somebody yelled outside the holding cell.

"Grizzly, stop playing around," Jones said before closing the window covering.

Luke tried to stand, but Grizzly picked him up instead and placed him in a bear hug. He felt a warm liquid run across his forehead and face. Red poured into his eyes before the man shoved something into his mouth. The man pushed Luke onto the floor like a rag doll. The man started throwing kicks, but Luke felt nothing. He didn't know what the man put in his mouth, but he started losing consciousness.

The cell door opened. "Get out, my boss is coming!"

"I cut him real nice … he'll die soon enough."

"Fine, let's get out of here."

The door closed, and with it, hope that he would be found. He thought it was fine. He thought he was saved, but he wasn't. He drifted into a dark funnel cloud. Sebastian stood beside him, talking, but it was too late. They both failed …

CHAPTER TWENTY-SIX

Revelations

I was in my crib and could not reach for my sippy cup on the kitchen table. My parents were nowhere around and would not come to help me even when I screamed. I cried and raised my hands, trying to reach my cup, but nothing helped. My father then walked into the kitchen with a woman who was not my mother. I cried out and pointed at my cup, but my father pushed the woman over the table and took off her shorts. The woman's bare leg hit my cup, and it fell off the table and rolled toward my crib. It was now close to me. I stared at it and tried to reach through the fabric but could not get the cup. I cried out in anger, with my lips fluttering. I sat down in my soiled diaper and cried more, but nobody comforted me.

"Let's go to the bedroom. I can't get into this with him crying like that," the strange woman said.

"He needs to learn somehow," his father said, raising the woman's leg on his shoulder.

"No, James … at least change his diaper. He stinks." The woman struggled away from his father. She grabbed her shorts off the floor and left the kitchen.

My father walked toward the fridge, opened it, grabbed a bottle of Daddy juice, and closed it.

I saw my apple juice in the bottle before my father shut the fridge.

I pointed at the fridge and my sippy cup on the floor. My father came closer to me and made an odd face.

"You smell just like what you are, Jimmy. A little smelly turd." My father left without grabbing my juice.

My sister snuck into the kitchen, grabbed my cup, and handed it to me.

I grabbed it and tried to drink the whole thing at once.

"What are you doing in there, Karen? Get out, now," my mother yelled at me.

"Mom, let me change him. He's got a poopy diaper and will get a rash."

"Let him rot in it, the foul beast."

A strange man walked into the kitchen. The man was smoking a smelly cigarette and knelt next to me. He blew smoke into my face. "That will help with the smell."

"Leave him alone. He's my baby," Karen said, pushing the man.

"Sure, kid." The man stood up and approached my mom. "Come on, Maeve, let's go for another one." The man pulled at my mother's arm.

"Let him stew in it, Karen," my mother yelled as she was yanked away.

My sister Karen stood up and grabbed me. I dropped my empty cup. My poop was dripping down my legs, yet my sister did not complain or try to wipe it away. She took me to the bathroom, placed me in the bathtub, and began singing a song. I recognized the song as James Taylor's You've Got a Friend. She removed my diaper and washed me with warm water … Jimmy woke drenched with water. That was his mother's favorite way of waking him.

"Wake up, waste of space. You have a phone call," his mother said before walking off with her empty cup.

Jimmy took off his wet shirt and walked to the telephone on the wall in the kitchen. He grabbed the receiver that was hanging carelessly down. "Yeah, who is this?"

"It's done. Tell your father and Juan that I did good," Deputy Jones said.

"Why are you calling me? It was supposed to happen on his

way to court this afternoon," Jimmy said, confused.

"It must have been the lawyer visit yesterday, but Juan said you wanted Luke taken out. He was moved to the hospital yesterday, and we just heard that he passed away. It's over."

Jimmy stared at the phone oddly. *I didn't want him dead*, he thought. Jones was still mumbling about helping him when he hung up the phone. He slammed his fist against the wall.

"Easy, loser, you don't pay the bills around here," his mother yelled from the living room, the television blaring unintelligibly. Walking down the hallway, he heard the song from his dream playing in his sister's room. He pushed open the door and saw his sister sitting near her record player. She held the album cover and motioned him over.

"Jimmy is a good boy," she said, pointing at the album cover. He walked over to her and took the cover. She pointed at the list of songs and some messy handwriting. He read the writing: *I love my baby, Jimmy*.

"I love you too, sis. You've got a friend with me, too."

Karen grabbed his hand and tried to stand up from her wheelchair but couldn't. She motioned for him to come closer to her. Jimmy leaned into his sister. "Don't be bad like Daddy, be a good boy."

Jimmy backed up, and a tear rolled down his face, and he raised his head up and down. He tried to speak but couldn't assure his sister that he would behave. He had just caused the death of a rival, and in retrospect, Luke didn't do anything to deserve to die so young. He was ashamed and dropped the album cover as he ran out of her room. He got dressed and left in his *Firebird* without thinking about where he would go. He was still suspended from school and didn't care to return. He drove into town and thought he saw Alyssa's car passing him. He turned quickly, cutting off some vehicles and burning rubber in the street. He caught up to her car but slowed down because he didn't want to spook her. He followed her to the school and the senior parking lot. He parked behind her and blocked her car. He stepped out of the car and rushed toward Alyssa as she seemed to run toward the school.

"Where are you going so fast, Alyssa?" Jimmy asked as he caught up and grabbed her arm.

"Let go of me, you animal," Alyssa said, trying to shake him off.

"Let's talk, Alyssa. Luke brought a lot of this on himself."

Alyssa stopped trying to get away and stared at Jimmy angrily. "Why are you doing all of this? Luke is a good kid. He should not be in jail."

After his dream and conversation with his sister, he indeed felt regret for getting Luke incarcerated and now dead. "I'm sorry for what happened to Luke. He was in my way, and I had to get him to stop."

"You've always been an animal, Jimmy. I don't know what Todd ever saw in you."

Jimmy let go of Alyssa's arm. "You're right … I've had my moments, but sometimes I cannot help myself. It's almost as if somebody else is at the wheel."

Alyssa stared at him and took a step back as if to run. "We got along as kids, but you turned into a straight-up thug."

"I never meant for it to go this far … I didn't want Luke to die. My father has this hold over me," Jimmy said.

"Luke's not dead, he's not dead. He is going to get bailed out this afternoon, and we're going to prove you, and your corrupt father set him up." Alyssa stood defiantly, pointing at Jimmy as if she would hit him.

Jimmy sensed that Alyssa wanted to scratch his eyes out, but more than that, he felt that she did not know that Luke was gone. "I'm sorry, I thought you knew. He was hurt in jail last night and died at the hospital."

Alyssa held onto her mouth, stifling the scream that tried to erupt. "You took away my future." She darted toward the school, but then returned back to her car.

He followed her and jumped into his car. He narrowly

avoided her car as she reversed quickly and then drove off. He didn't know how to react. His impediments were gone, but the burden on him was not removed. Instead, a feeling of regret crept into him, almost as if he was on his way to being born into something awful, and Luke was the only thing good keeping him from a metamorphosis in the chrysalis he was stuck in. What he would form into was foreign, but it would not have been good if his father was an indication.

✝ ✝ ✝

Subjugated

I followed an aged androgynous guide who pointed instead of talking during a long journey with my brothers. We walked parallel to a broad, turbulent, rapidly moving river until we arrived at some train tracks. The sky was the color of rust, as if the air had burned. I knew we had to cross the bridge, but I needed to find a way across.

The ground was ashen, almost like a fire had devastated a forest and burned the dirt. The asphalt road we traveled appeared long and unending, but we finally approached a raised drawbridge. If the bridge were down, I could finally cross with my brothers to the other side of the river. The guide pointed at the drawbridge. I turned to look at the bridge and saw my brothers climbing the raised bridge. I shook my head, refusing to climb the bridge; it was impossibly steep, and at that angle, a fall back down would result in my death. The guide pointed at the bridge and opened its mouth, releasing an eerie gurgling sound. My brothers had completed the climb successfully and completed their journey, but they vanished. I thought they must have fallen into the rapids. I ran to the road's edge and looked at the foamy water but did not see my brothers. I focused on the bridge and not the scarily steep drop to the angry water. There was a guardrail on either side of the tracks. I grabbed onto the rail and commenced my uphill climb. Digging deep into my strength, I completed the climb, pushed over my legs, and jumped toward the other side without a chance to reach the other end, yet somehow, I landed on the other side. My brothers had walked on ahead of me.

The guide grabbed my arm and said, "prohibere dominus servorum."

"I don't understand," I said and shook my head, confused.

The guide grabbed both my arms now, yelling, "desine servum."

I didn't understand the message and shook my head from side to side again. The guide moved forward and tossed me into a chasm. I grasped for the nonexistent walls. I fell on the rocks instead ... Luke awoke staring at a white, sanitized ceiling. He looked at his wrists, expecting to see handcuffs, but there were none. His body ached after the scuffle he had, but otherwise, he was just groggy. He propped himself up and then brought his feet over the side of the bed. He looked for a pen and paper to write down the Latin words, but there were none.

The door to the hospital room opened, and a nurse in a white uniform walked in, followed by a man wearing a suit. It was FBI Special Agent Curtis.

He stood up and approached the nurse. "Can I borrow your pen, please?"

"Sit back down, Robert, and I'll write down whatever you want. I need to check your vitals," the nurse, whose name tag said *KATIE,* offered.

He was confused but startled at Curtis, who raised his hand as if to silence his inquiries. He sat back down quickly and placed his hand out, expecting her to hand her pen over. "Can I have the pen?"

"Just tell me, I'll write it down for you," Katie responded quickly.

"Okay, it's in Latin, *prohibere dominus servorum and desine servum.* Translate this."

Katie wrote down what Luke had said and did not bat an eye. She went through her assessment of him and checked the bandages on his forehead and scalp. She then left the room and left him alone with Curtis.

"Cease being a slave. Stop the slaveholder. You wake from a dream with Latin words. You certainly are a weird kid."

"Weird, what's weird is why Peanut attacked me like that until I realized it was a ploy to get me out of the jail."

"It was a plan that Terry, and the others devised after your father caused a scene. It worked, and everyone thinks you're dead." Curtis walked toward a small cabinet and retrieved a duffle bag. "Take a shower and get dressed. We are going to move you to a safe house for now."

"Does Alyssa know I'm alive?" he asked, concerned for the pain she must be enduring.

"Nobody knows, for now, not even your parents. We'll talk on the way to the …"

Luke did not wait for Curtis to finish. He walked toward the door and tried to open it, but it was locked.

Curtis approached him and placed his hand on Luke's shoulder … *the motion backward was intense. I stood in an unfamiliar room with Alyssa in my arms.*

"Don't ever leave me again. I felt like I was alone on this earth."

I embraced Alyssa in a room with my brothers, my parents, Kamila, Wil, Terry, and Peanut … he released the doorknob.

Curtis was going to reunite Alyssa and me somehow, he thought. "Fine, let's do it your way, Curtis."

Curtis took a step back and stared at Luke. The man had a curious look on his face. "You're an odd kid. I thought I was going to have to square off with you, and when I touched you … it was like a switch." The agent stared at his hand in disbelief.

"Maybe you'll understand one day, but I like your plan, believe in you, and know it will work." In the vision, Luke saw Curtis' master plans and thought it had a good chance of working if everything fell into place.

CHAPTER TWENTY-SEVEN

The Great Escape

Luke sat and watched television all day long in the large bedroom where he spent most of his time. Viewing tape after tape, was getting old. He asked for a home gym and a treadmill but was only given a jump rope. He threatened to run, so they brought him a cheap treadmill. He tried to force his way through the front door after they refused to provide him with free weights. One of the agents tried to stop him, but Luke picked the man up by his suit coat and almost threw him. Now, he had a rack of free weights in the living room, an Olympic bar, and a weight bench. He worked out twice daily but still felt like he was gaining weight. Possibly because all he did was work out in front of the television and eat constantly. At least he had enough food to feed a family of four, which included lots of pizza, but he stuck with his high protein and fat diet.

He was watching *Escape from Alcatraz* with Clint Eastwood, but it was his third movie of the day, and he felt numb. Then, he started nodding off to the point where he was lost in the film.

I was hiding underneath a commercial trailer. I was wet and not alone. A man was beside me, holding my arm. I motioned for the man to stay low and to be quiet. I crawled in the warm muck. It must have been nighttime because everything was dark. I smelled something new—an unwashed man ... reeking of body odor. I stopped, studied my surroundings, and saw a bearded man holding an AK-47 standing in my path. I crept toward him and grabbed my Ka-Bar knife, ready to use it. I sensed the man was scared, wanted to go home, and unwilling to fight. I put my knife away, not wanting to kill him. I motioned for the priest to follow me and crawled to the opposite side. I pulled a sturdy twig below the trailer and grabbed my Boonie hat from the small ruck on my back. I crept and placed the twig with the hat on the trunk of an abandoned car in the lot. I crawled back to the priest and whispered in his ear. "Prepare to move there," I said, pointing to an area behind another car.

I grabbed a slingshot from my ruck and a rock from the dirt. I aimed at the car window for the car that held my hat. I released it, and the rock shattered the window. The man turned and ran toward the broken glass and started yelling in Somali. I motioned for the priest to move, and I followed behind him. Once we passed the car, we kept moving out of the lot and made it across the yard to my goal ... Luke woke and immediately stood up. He walked to the bathroom and splashed water on his face.

Luke watched a movie about escaping from prison, and then he dreamt about something that may happen in the future when he tried to save a priest. Curtis told him he would remain in protective custody until after the takedown, which would happen in a week. Nobody was to be made aware that he was alive. They even considered holding a funeral for Luke. He realized the forces against him were too great, and the Feds were too worried that operational security would be compromised. It was May 1st, and the recital would take place on May 4th. Mr. Waters was supposed to be preparing for the concert, but instead, he was most likely scrambling to fill Benji and Luke's positions. For all he knew, they had canceled the recital altogether. *I need to see Alyssa and Mr. Waters,* he mused.

Luke walked back into the living room and began to think. The house itself looked like it needed to be secured. One agent was out in the car watching the front door, and another was watching the cameras surrounding the house from one of the bedrooms. They had twelve-hour shifts where they rotated at 0600 hours. He slept in the master bedroom, which had a bathroom. He shared the kitchen, living room, and laundry room with whatever agent was on duty. The backyard had a small area he was allowed to access. He could see the sky, but his view was obscured for those trying to look in.

He walked back to the bedroom, wanting to scream, but didn't want the attention from the agent on duty, who seemed to resent Luke for some reason. He walked into the master closet and grabbed his clothes from the floor, thinking of washing a load of laundry. Underneath the clothes was an access panel on the carpet. He tossed his clothes on the bedroom floor and opened the panel. A small set of stairs led underneath the house into an unfinished basement of sorts. It appeared to be a void used to access the pipes and electrical system. He walked down and found a light switch. The voids ran underneath the complete home. The floor was dirt and, in most parts, was only less than four feet tall. He saw light coming from ahead of him. There was a small door with a latch, which he removed and then propped open. It seemed like an addition that one of the prior owners made to the home. He crawled out of the door and found himself on the side of the house. He peered up and saw a camera pointing toward the street. He could leave and return as he wanted.

Luke took a shower and changed into shorts and a T-shirt. He knocked on the agent's door, who opened it with a book in his hand.

"What do you want, kid?" the agent asked, perturbed. Matt was his name.

"I'm sick, Matt, and think I have a fever," Luke said, coughing.

Matt laughed and shook his head. "What do you want me to do about it?"

"I'm going to try and sleep it off," he responded.

The man pointed the book toward the master bedroom.

"Then, go to sleep. If I cannot be with my kids, I don't have to be a concerned parent."

Luke smiled, returned to the bedroom, changed clothes, and grabbed a black pullover hoodie. He placed bundles of clean sheets and a duvet under the covers and made the shape of a person. He covered it with a comforter and took a step back. It looked like a person. He walked into the utility access and left the house. He used some bushes and trees and was confused instantly with the layout of the housing. It appeared as if houses were built behind one another, staggered somehow. He closed his eyes and listened to the surrounding sounds. Off to his right the sound of cars from the road. He crawled toward the road and saw a bicycle leaning up against a fence. He reluctantly borrowed the bicycle and walked it toward the road, where he saw a street sign that said Rockbridge Drive SE and a sign that said Silver Oaks. There was no way for him to figure out the full address of the house. He jumped on the bicycle and rode over a bridge. The running trail was under the bridge. He needed to find access to the trail. He arrived at a red brick building. A school. *Frederick Douglass Elementary School.* He found access to the trail and rode off. With optimism, he thought he could make it to the school in ten minutes with the trails and streets. Half an hour later, he knew his window was closing. He knew he had a chance to meet with Alyssa during her study room time after one. It was 1:30 p.m., but he was very close now.

He placed the bicycle against the wall near the exterior entrance to the music classrooms and hall adjacent to the auditorium, where the practice instruments were kept. Luke made sure his head was well covered with his hoodie as he entered the music hall doors attached to one side of the auditorium and heard the piano keys. He walked silently toward her from behind, listening to her play the piano. Her eyes were closed as she played.

"Luke, why did you leave without saying goodbye?" she asked, wiping away her tears.

He slowly placed his hand on her back. Sebastian walked behind him and placed a hand on Luke's head. Luke focused and tried to project his thoughts and visions of their future. She winced slightly at his touch and stopped playing.

"I don't understand why you are showing me this … it's cruel to show me a future that could have been." She turned slowly and smiled.

He sat beside her on the piano bench, and she placed her head on his chest and sobbed. "Let it out, I'm here. I'm still here."

"What happened?" Alyssa asked, crumpled into his arms.

"Jimmy and his father set me up along with Juan Bello. They were going to have me killed, but my father convinced Wil and his people to save me."

"Why not tell me? I died inside. I had to find out from Jimmy himself that you were dead."

"I've been in witness protection for days. I found a way to get out of the house and had to tell you I was still here. I need to get back, though."

"Where were you? How long can you stay?

Luke considered her question and thought it out clearly. "Leesburg … I think. I found the trail near a school."

She released her clench from him and looked at him. "You found me. I was trying to get some practice in before class."

"I wanted to see if you were playing the piano or painting one on a canvas." He pressed the keys on the piano. "Do you want to practice for a bit?"

"I would love to."

"Let me grab my guitar from the corner." He took his 1990 Fender *American Telecaster* out of its case and plugged it into the school's 100-amp amplifier. He strummed the guitar strings, then played an excerpt from *Another Brick in the Wall, Part 2.*

She moved behind the piano and shuffled some of the sheets before selecting one. She looked so vulnerable and nervous behind the large piano. "I'll start with *Piano Concerto Number 5.*"

He waited for the right moment and then began playing his

guitar. They had practiced this duet before, which was supposed to end with the class joining in, but it wouldn't happen now.

She launched into the second Movement, Adagio un, Poco Mosso. He always loved that part of the concerto and the Rondo because it reminded him of her personality.

He removed his guitar and placed it in its case before sitting next to her again. I should leave soon. *If Mr. Waters comes in or I'm seen leaving by someone, I am ruined.*

She hugged him. "Don't leave me ever again."

"I'm not planning on it, but we must be careful until they arrest everyone. If it ever happens. I have my doubts about whether this can be resolved."

"You're going to miss the recital. You can't take that back. We've been working on this all year. You're going to regret it."

Luke stood and bowed his head in defeat. "I'm not in the driver's seat, Alyssa. I have no control of what I can and cannot do."

"Why wait a week? Why can't they resolve it on the day of the recital? It's on May 4th. All the students and teachers will be in the auditorium."

I tried that already, but it could still work, he thought. They could just bring up the date and do the takedowns on Monday instead of Thursday. Then, he shook his head, realizing that the managers for DEA, Customs, and FBI were in the driver's seat and that he had no authority to make any demands. A class recital was nothing when it came down to the power of the bureaucratic mind. He gave one final kiss to Alyssa and made it count. He realized that this could be the last time he saw her for a while. He had an impulsive thought and whispered it in her ear. "I love you." She smiled and shook her head yes. "You cannot tell anybody you saw me. Do you understand?"

Alyssa shook her head up and down quickly. "What about Benji? I went to see him, and he was heartbroken. He doesn't think he has a future.

Luke bowed his head painfully, knowing he needed to

respond. "I want him to know, but we're losing here. If Jimmy and his father's people know I'm alive, they will keep attacking. They still may try to hurt people I care for. He threatened to plant drugs on my parents."

"Now, hear me out, cause it sounds ridiculous," Alyssa held her hand on his chest, trying to get him to give her time to get her thoughts out. "When he approached me a few days ago, he seemed regretful. He said that somebody else was driving him like he was not controlling his own behavior."

"I don't know if that's good news or bad. It just makes him even more erratic. Stay clear from him, please."

"I will, Luke," she said and gave him one last hug.

"Can you go to the Customs office please? Tell Terry to come see me at the house tonight."

"Yes, of course."

With that, Luke left the room quickly. Aiming to ride straight back to the house.

CHAPTER TWENTY-EIGHT

Mr. Conway

Luke stepped out of the building and looked around. This area of the school was not well-traveled at any time of day. He was happy to know that Alyssa knew that he was still alive. He realized Benji, Mr. Conway, and others thought he was gone. It was almost two, which meant Mr. Conway was probably in the teacher's lounge opposite the hall. He tightened up the hoodie and re-entered the school. He walked toward the lounge and saw Mr. Conway at the round table. However, there was another teacher there, but she was packing her belongings and left the lounge within a few minutes. He quickly moved into the room and sat next to Mr. Conway.

"Young man, you are not allowed in here," Mr. Conway stared at him perplexed. "It can't be … Luke, is that you?" His teacher and mentor reached and grabbed him … *I was moved into his kitchen. Mr. Conway sat alone at his table with a full, uneaten plate of food before him. He also had a half bottle of bourbon and an empty rocks glass before him. His teacher was sobbing and holding onto himself.*

"I failed you, Luke. I should have stopped Jimmy. I could have stopped Devry or Shipmen." Mr. Conway drained the whole glass of *whiskey* … he was back in the present. Mr. Conway stared at him,

grabbing his chest.

"Easy, Mr. Conway. I'm fine. They had to pretend I was killed. Jimmy and his father were closing the books on me and were ready to do the same on anybody I care for."

Mr. Conway looked alarmed and stared at his watch. The last bell would alert everyone in a few minutes that school was over, and after-school activities were starting. "Go, now. Meet me by the convenience store on the corner. Do you know the one?"

"Yes, I do," he stood and began walking out the door.

"Go now, class is going to end, and hundreds of people will see the ghost of Luke Sanz … go now."

Luke ran and jumped out of the double doors, grabbed the bike, and peddled toward the stairs that led to the lower football fields. The store his teacher described was just past the tree line in the soccer fields. He peddled just as the three bells rang onto the empty fields that would soon be full of students running around them. This would be one of the last times he had touched these fields, as he was due to graduate in about a month. He arrived at the convenience store and saw Mr. Conway's station wagon. He rode up to the door. "I need to get back to Leesburg quickly, but I wanted to tell you what's happening."

"Put the bicycle in the back, and I'll drive you. We'll talk on the way."

"That's okay, Mr. Conway. I can ride back." Luke said.

"That wasn't a suggestion, son. Come on, time is money."

He placed the bicycle in the back of the car and jumped into the passenger seat.

"Where are we going?"

"They have me in a safe house near the Frederick Douglas Elementary School in Leesburg near the old trails. Do you know how to get there?"

"Yes, well sort of, it's been a while. I was a substitute teacher there twenty years ago. Tell me what's going on. I don't need to know everything."

Where to start? The arrest, maybe. I explained everything to my teacher in detail.

"Wait, how would you know that they were planning on killing you, Luke? I love you, kiddo, but you're sounding crazy right now. Maybe you need to go to the hospital for an assessment," Mr. Conway said, parking in the school's parking lot.

Luke took a deep breath and closed his eyes. "The same way I know that when you heard I had died, you sat in your kitchen drinking bourbon with an uneaten plate of food."

"Excuse me, son. What are you telling me now?" Mr. Conway looked stunned.

"The same way I know that I saw how Stitch was shot in that jungle in the Donai Province, and your bible saved you from dying. You stared at the woods stunned and told yourself that when you returned to the US, you would become a teacher and never hurt anybody again." Luke stared at Sebastian, who stood proudly out of his window before him. "When I touch somebody, I get visions at times. Not always, but it happens when God wants me to see something to save somebody who needs saving or just a detail that could overcome evil."

Mr. Conway made the sign of the cross. "How much I hoped over the years that somebody like you would exist in my lifetime. Somebody who God bestowed powers to protect us from evil." Mr. Conway began to laugh and then cry.

"I need to go, Mr. Conway. I need your help with something. I don't want to impose but I could use your help."

"Anything, Luke. How can I help?"

"Be ready to help the agents at the school and elsewhere. You'll know who they are. I need to play at the recital. Can you make that happen?"

"How can you play at the recital? Everyone thinks you're dead."

Luke grabbed onto his hair. "I'll be wearing a disguise. I'll give your information to the agents, and they'll contact you."

"I'll be waiting and willing to help. Do you remember how to get to the house?"

"Yes, we're close. I better hurry before they figure out, I'm gone." Luke left the car and retrieved the bicycle. He walked back to the car door. Mr. Conway looked at him like a prideful father. "Thanks, Mr. Conway. I need you to do one more thing. Go to the Customs office on Market Street and Loudon ask to speak with Special Agent Terry Garcia." He wrote down the address for his teacher. With that, Luke pedaled back toward the trail and quickly found his way. He left the bicycle leaning on the same fence and returned to the house.

Luke washed up in the bathroom and changed into the shorts he had worn earlier. He hesitated at the door but finally opened it and stepped into the living room. It was now 3:30 p.m., but he had skipped lunch. He cooked himself a rib-eye steak he had marinating in a tray in the fridge. He had used the barbecue in the backyard a few times. It was a better grill than the one at his parents' house but not quite as lovely as the one at his grandparents' place. He walked outside and turned on the burners. Thirty minutes later, he sat outside eating the steak and drinking an iced tea. He was waiting for the consequences of his little escape earlier. He expected visitors at any moment and knew they would not be happy.

† † †

Family Reunion

Both FBI agents in charge of his security detail walked out to the backyard, holding onto their portable radios. They looked more than angry, but he anticipated this and was content that the show was commencing.

"Code 4, Curtis, we have the primary." The agent motioned for the other one to leave. "I got this. Go ahead, wait outside until they show up, and then escort them in." Matt walked down to

Luke and sat in front of him. "How did you get out?"

Luke smiled but didn't respond promptly. He may have to leave again. "The truth is that I need to be part of this operation, Matt. I cannot be left on the sidelines. Curtis, Terry, and Todd need me to help close some holes."

"Maybe so. My job was ensuring you stayed safe, and now I'm about to get censured and transferred to Alaska." Matt stood up, walked toward Luke, and sat next to him. "I just got out of a nasty divorce and wanted to get out of town. "I was told if I messed up again to be ready for a move. A paid move to Alaska may just be what I need."

Luke reached out to Matt and offered his hand ... *I was pulled backward and stood near a man, a woman, and three small children dressed in cold-weather clothing. I walked closer to the man and could tell it was Matt, but he had a long beard.*

"Hey Kim, I cannot wait to get into a warm room tonight," Matt said, grabbing his petite wife from behind.

"Not in front of the kids, Mattie," Kim said.

"Here they come, Luke."

"Shoulders, Dad, pick me up."

Matt picked up his tallest son and placed him on his shoulders. The first of the Iditarod racers passed them quickly ... he let go of Matt's hand.

"It looks cold, but you have a little bunny named Kim that will warm you up," Luke said.

"What are you talking about? Curtis warned me you were a bit on the weird side."

"You name your first son Luke." He used both thumbs to point back at himself. "You're going to make Alaska a home. I counted three more kids, Mattie."

"My father's name is Lucas." Movement at the door caught their attention. The exterior FBI agent was there with Agent Curtis, who pointed at Matt and motioned for him to come.

He stood up when he saw Terry Garcia, Wil sporting a black eye, and Peanut followed behind them. Terry reached out and embraced him … *I stood at a doorway, and Terry was dressed in a very sexy lingerie outfit. Her body was as fit as he imagined* … she let him go and motioned to Peanut.

"I would like to take credit for the plan, but most of it was good old Peanut here. He offered to go in and pretend to kick your ass."

"Pretend? I'm STILL sore," Luke said.

Wil approached him, looking concerned. "I need to be honest with you. Your father came to us for help. Initially, we declined because the FBI wanted to keep it separate considering the charges, but your dad was insistent." Wil approached him and placed a hand on Luke's shoulder … *my father stood staring at Wil in his office. Wil looked scared shitless.*

"I saved your life once, Mijo, I never demanded payback, but I am now. Don't let these animals kill my son, or I promise I'll take every one of them out."

"Angel, please be reasonable. The FBI has me by the balls. If we get involved, they threatened to lock us up, too. The AUSA already warned us to stay clear of this."

My father approached Wil, grabbed him, and threw him on his desk. My father raised his hand and was about to punch Wil.

"Am I interrupting something? I thought you two were friends," *Peanut said, walking into the room followed by Terry.*

My father let Wil go and helped him stand back up. Wil still had a frightened look on his face.

"Boss, let me run something by you, okay?"

Wil stood up, flattened out the wrinkles in his suit, and motioned for his agents to sit down. He then motioned for Peanut to continue speaking.

"FBI has authority over deprivation of rights under 18USC242. We can convince them to get involved. So, it's another statute they can throw at everyone, including the judge, jailers, and all those corrupt cops. On top of everything else we have."

"Let's brief FBI, and then Peanut can tell you the second part of his plan."

Wil motioned them out of the office. "Go, we'll drive over together."
Wil turned toward my father. "We good?"

"Save my son, or else?"

Wil shook his head and left the office quickly ... he returned to the present.

"Luke, we need to talk."

"What's wrong?" Luke asked, looking at the entry.

"We haven't told your parents or brothers yet. With you out of the picture, the LT thinks he's won. Don't ask how we know. We just do. Your little stunt caused our timeline to accelerate."

"I figured ... which is why I needed you all over here," Luke said.

"Can someone please tell me what we are doing here?" his mother asked. She walked toward the backyard, where she must have seen Wil and the others standing. His mother took a step into the backyard and stopped. "My boy, oh my God, it's my son." She came running and grabbed onto him tightly.

His father walked up behind her and grabbed him. He quickly realized that his father had punched Wil when he thought Luke had died. Wil, Terry, and Peanut gave them some space. Just then, he saw Junior and Daniel run into the backyard and latched on to them. Next came Joyce with Tristan and finally, Alyssa with Mr. Conway. The cluster of visions he saw at that very moment made his knees buckle. The strength of the friends and family holding onto him kept him upright. He had never felt love so intensely. It did not escape him that Benji was missing.

Luke failed to realize that the very reason Jimmy hated him was this reunion that had just taken place. He made it a point to make sure he asked about his friend but wanted them to absorb the fact that he was still alive. It would be a long night because he would take this opportunity seriously and insert himself into whatever Curtis and the others had planned.

CHAPTER TWENTY-NINE

Command Briefing

Luke and Mr. Conway were in the back seat of Wil's car, which he drove with Terry in the passenger seat. They were headed to the briefing location at the courthouse. He had convinced everyone that he needed to participate in the planning of the operation. He would not be included in the arrests or enforcement aspects, but in at least one critical phase. He wanted to be at the school and not hidden in a house, utterly oblivious to law enforcement's response to counter everything the Cladhaire's did to press their agenda forward. They arrived inside a warehouse near a parking garage, and they all exited the car. They were here to help set up a multi-agency processing center where all the arrestees would be processed before being immediately moved to the Federal courthouse for their initial appearance. They walked through some double doors and were greeted by numerous government employees setting up tables, workstations, and holding areas. Mr. Conway walked in one direction with Wil and Terry. Luke found Peanut and, for the next hour, helped him move the equipment and set it up for the operation.

Wil came to get him and escorted him to a large room with a podium and chairs that were facing the podium. A few dozen people wearing suits, except Luke and Peanut, sat in the front rows. He saw Mr. Conway sitting a couple of rows behind the other suits. "Sit by your teacher. I'm going to the front with Terry."

"Is everything okay, Mr. Conway?" Luke asked.

"Yes, Luke. They were quite professional. They walked me through everything they expected from me. You?"

"I don't have much to do with this. I help them set up the command center, and I get to play guitar at the recital. Everything should be done by the time I finish."

"A ship cannot stay afloat without an intact hull."

Luke let that statement sink in. *I gave them the foundation of the case,* he thought.

"All welcome to this briefing for managers and team leaders for Operation Railcar. My name is Ruth Chambers, and I'm the Criminal Chief for the US Attorney's office for the Eastern District of Virginia. I've been asked to introduce the case agents who have diligently put this case together for the past six months ..."

Peanut sat beside Luke, taking up almost two chairs. "I hope this ends soon. I need to finish setting up the surveillance van back at the office."

"If this is the briefing, then where are the agents?"

"This is just the higher-up type stroking session ... sorry that was negative. These are all the team leaders from the FBI, DEA, and Customs." Peanut pointed in front of where they sat. "Near the podium is the Assistant US Attorney for the case. Wil is talking to other RACs and ASAC types. Terry and Todd, with DEA, are behind them. That Curtis guy with the FBI is with them. They will brief the overall case, and then each team leader will go out and set the parameters for their piece of the pie. Understood?"

"Yes, Peanut. Since they were wearing suits and closer to DC, I figured it would all be bosses."

Peanut shook his head back and forth, almost shaking the other seats around him. "No bosses, that happens when there is a successful operation, and they want to take credit. If this breaks bad, there will be no press conference."

"Oh … ahh, I didn't think about that," Luke said.

"Peanut, is that your name?" Mr. Conway asked.

Peanut shook his head in the affirmative.

"Luke is eighteen and has a bright future ahead of him. Please give him the positive with the negative," Mr. Conway said.

"Sure thing, Teach. Luke, if you want to hear the positive. This would not have taken place without all your efforts. That's positive in my book. Focus on your role in this and do it well."

Luke took in all that Peanut said and did not take it negatively. Peanut was a bit pessimistic, but he'd also been shot at and seen some *gnarly* stuff in his career. He wasn't prepared for everything to fall apart anyway. After Peanut interrupted, he failed to hear what any of the case agents had even said. In his mind, it was all going to work out fine. After this, he wanted to focus on his music and see what happened. It would be a while before he needed to find a career, and after meeting that Army recruiter and being arrested, he was leaning more toward traveling across the country or even back to Australia. Just him and his guitar.

"All, once again, thanks for coming. Once again, timing is key. No matter where we are, we start at 10:00 a.m. One other thing: If you would please indulge me, due to the nature of the case, I asked a priest I know to provide us a benediction … Father?" Terry walked away from the podium, and Father Robert walked from behind Wil and up to the podium.

"You may stay seated or kneel, please." Father Robert seemed to stare directly at him.

Luke moved to his knees, felt a hand on his shoulder, and turned. Father D stood behind him and to his right was Sebastian who placed his hand on Luke's left shoulder. *I will be more of a part of this than I thought.*

"Lord, Your strength enables these agents to protect others while your providence keeps us safe. Help us turn our hearts towards you daily. For these agents and officers actively working in your favor, please give them the strength to go the next mile to fulfill their current goals. Lord, wherever they serve, bless and protect them and return them safely to their families and loved ones when their shifts are done. In your Holy name, we pray. AMEN."

Terry walked back up to the podium. "Thank you, Father Robert, for coming … remember, simultaneous hit starts at …"

"Ten o'clock," the multiple team leaders and supervisors said simultaneously.

Mr. Waters

Typical search warrants take place early in the morning. Luke had convinced everyone to conduct the operations in Lansburg at 10:00 a.m. when the recital would start. Luke was to show up, dressed in disguise, and entered through the music door. Luke drove to the church, seeking time with Father Robert. He found his friend reading a book on a bench outside. Luke joined him and stared at the leaves of the trees blowing in the strong wind.

"What's on your mind, Luke?" Robert asked, closing his book.

"Today is the day."

"Are you troubled by it? Seems like something the agents must worry about more than you."

Luke paused and reflected, and his valid concerns were with the unknowns and those issues that the bureaucratic actions of federal law enforcement officers or the federal judicial system could not resolve. "There's an element of the supernatural here that cannot be fixed by what will happen today. Jimmy's father has a demon attached to him in the shape of a vulture. They can lock him up, but I imagine that demon can go wherever *it* wants."

Robert placed his book on the bench. "I want to pray over you and bring you the protection of our LORD. Not just to keep you and the law enforcement officers safe but also for the power of foresight to what the evil one has in store."

Luke shook his head up and down and then got on his knees, prostrated before Robert and the Lord under the sky.

Father Robert placed his hand on Luke's bowed head and the other hand reached outward. "Sebastian, take my hand."

Sebastian knelt beside Luke and grabbed onto the priest's hand.

"God of power and mercy, maker and love of peace, to know you is to live, and to serve you is to reign. Through the intercession of St. Michael, the archangel, be our protection in battle against all evil. Help Luke and Sebastian overcome war and violence and establish your law of love and justice. Give your warriors the power of sight to see what the evil one has blinded them from seeing. Grant this through Christ our Lord. Amen." Robert stood up and pointed toward the parking lot with his book. "Now go to school, finish that recital, and pray that the arrests are fruitful, and nobody is injured, including Jimmy."

Luke rose and took a deep breath. "Thank you, Father." He turned quickly and ran to his car with renewed vigor. When he saw the lettering for *Divine Justice* on the trunk lid, he tapped it.

He parked in the teacher's lot when he arrived at the school. He grabbed his guitar from the trunk with renewed purpose. Tracing the lettering on the trunk with his fingers brought him peace. He missed his friend and wished they could play together on stage. He wore his Australian riding boots with dark gray pants tucked into them. Underneath his black pullover hoodie, he wore a maroon long-sleeve T-shirt under a gray vest. The rest of his costume was in his backpack. He carried a realistic looking Spanish Morion he found at a costume store in Alexandria.

Cautiously, he opened the exterior door and entered the music wing. Mr. Conway stood there with Mr. Waters, who looked stunned. His teacher walked toward him, smiling.

"Mr. Conway told me you were alive, but my God. You're alive!" Mr. Waters thrust himself at Luke and hugged him ... *I was pushed physically backward in motion but forward to the not-too-distant future. I was in a music studio with my teacher standing at a microphone.*

"Everyone take ten, please," a man behind a pane of glass said.

Some of the people in the room appeared familiar. One was dressed somewhat grungy, but I could not see his face. Mr. Waters sat at a piano and took notes on some music sheets. A man with brown messed-up hair and an untrimmed beard entered the room.

"Are you Romie?" the man asked. "Danny over there says, your Waters."

"Yes, I'm Romeo Waters, but I go by Romie. How can I help you?"

"Well, I've been hearing you sing, and I saw that you wrote them two songs, which I love, by the way."

Mr. Waters looked stunned and unable to speak. "Why, you're Brendan ..."

"It's not about me, man. I see you working on a song. Do me a favor and sing for me, will you?"

Mr. Waters stood up and walked back to the microphone. "It's not ready quite, and there's no music."

"Fair enough. I've been speaking to Danny there, and you're on salary, without a contract, except for those two songs. Why don't the two of us go for a coffee and settle on your future?"

Mr. Waters shook his head up and down and looked at Danny on the other side of the glass, who was giving him a thumbs-up ... Luke couldn't help but be uplifted by the vision of his teacher's future. He was gifted.

"I'm sorry I couldn't tell you I was still alive. I'm ready to play if you'll have me."

"Yes, of course. I spoke with Mr. Conway, and he told me you would be in disguise."

"Yes, I just need to get dressed."

"Nobody is here yet, so come back to this door when you're ready. I'll tell the class you're one of my former students." With that, Mr. Waters entered the music room.

"Thanks, Mr. Conway ... I hope this works out."

"It will, Luke. Have faith. All the stars are aligned, and the correct people are in place for this confrontation."

Luke absorbed Mr. Conway's words. "I believe that God expects us to confront evil when we are presented it." His intensity may have puzzled others but not Mr. Conway. Evil was what had damaged the school and his life.

"Now, it's my turn to agree with you. The school board has asked me to pull aside some students as they pour into the auditorium. It's part of the plan. I was told to be fluid and be prepared to react to what I was confronted with."

"You were chosen to bring the light of day upon the wicked," Luke said, beginning to sound a lot like Sebastian.

Mr. Conway looked at his watch. "You better get going, and you can explain what you mean later."

He walked off but turned around. "I want you to know that I could not have made it in this town without you. You mean a lot to me as a teacher and mentor, and I will never forget you."

"I don't know what to say other than you're welcome, and I may have to retire after this year is up. Remember, I will be a little late, so start as late as possible for my sake?"

"You bet, Mr. Conway." He turned and walked through the door.

The whole music class stood in a circle on the auditorium's stage. All of Luke's peers were present except for Benji. He was dressed in costume and wore a gray balaclava underneath the Spanish Morion helmet. He appeared a bit like Sebastian, who stood beside him, but Luke carried a guitar instead of a halberd. In contrast, everyone else was dressed in black clothing, including Alyssa, who kept smiling at him several times, walking up to him and grabbing his hand.

"Lord, almighty, give us the strength to accomplish this recital without hiccups. Two of our own are not present on this important day. Each of us has a special soul and energy that has moved all of us. Our goal this past year is to be here at this moment. Without the guidance of a higher power, we would truly be alone on this earth. Thanks to Alyssa for putting the stuffed animal of *Benji*, the dog, on the seat for the drums, but we would prefer that our Benji was here." The band members laughed at Mr. Waters' moment of levity. "All of you get into position. We are five minutes out." He motioned for Luke over to him. "Go check the auditorium."

He walked over to the curtain and looked out to the crowd. The front rows were filled, but students were still entering and taking seats. Some teachers were near the other emergency exit doors. All the students entered through one door, which slowed down the seating. He walked back to Mr. Waters. "They are still looking for their seats. It looks like they are only using one entrance."

"Randy. Kevin, please do me a favor. Do the duet you were practicing last week. You know the one," Mr. Waters said.

"Sure, Mr. Waters. Let's get to it, Kevin." Randy motioned to Kevin to get started.

At about 9:55 a.m., Mr. Devry came in from the side of the stage and stumbled up to Mr. Waters. "We are still running on time, just bottlenecked at the door. I will announce you, and then you all take over?" Mr. Devry asked, stuttering.

"Yes, Mr. Devry, that's the plan." Mr. Waters shook his head in disbelief at the principal's lack of sobriety in front of the students.

CHAPTER THIRTY

Getting Rid of the Trash

Mr. Conway manned the auditorium's front door with Todd from DEA, who pretended to be a substitute teacher. They had spent the last fifteen minutes or so looking at each student as they entered through one entryway. All the other doors were locked with no access from outside, but anybody who wanted to leave could do so unimpeded. Their list had ten students with pictures, Jimmy Cladhaire topping it. It was almost ten o'clock, and they located nine of the ten students on the list. Todd could only pick off one on the list, Roger Conners, who happened to be wearing a white hoodie and sunglasses over his head. They took the last student to a classroom near the end of the hall by the first-floor nurse's office used during sporting events.

"Mr. Conway, you certainly know your students," Todd said.

"Well, I see them daily in some of the same clothes as they cycle through them," Mr. Conway said.

"You should have gone into law enforcement," Todd said.

"I was in the Army in Vietnam, and what I did and saw there made me promise myself I would never carry a gun again or take another life. It was a promise I made during a battle, and I meant to keep it."

"Well, I'm sure Luke is happy you became a teacher."

"I hope so. I better go. He will not start until he sees me go in."

"Go ahead, I got this. There are teachers in there anyway. Well, they *were* teachers," Todd said, emphasizing the were.

"What's going to happen to the students?" Mr. Conway asked.

"Most will get probation, but either way, they will not be coming back. Jimmy is a different story," Todd said, staring at the blue taped X on the classroom door ahead of them.

"How about the teachers? I think I saw Vice-Principal Shipmen. What's going to happen with them?"

Todd lowered his clipboard and walked to Mr. Conway. "In all honesty, you never know with the criminal courts. One of your gym teachers should never be around students ever again. He was dealing steroids and other stuff to the students. We have indictments on all of them but haven't even done the searches yet. Some will be fighting charges for months or even years."

"To fall so far and yet not grab onto one branch to break the fall." Mr. Conway seemed distraught.

Marie Radner, the school nurse, walked up to them. "Mr. Conway, I received a notice from Mr. Shipmen to report to Utility Classroom 1."

"This is it, Marie, the one with the blue X on the door. He's waiting for you inside." He smiled at the nurse, but when she walked into the room, the smile turned into a frown. He walked up to Todd and shook his hand. "You're doing God's work. Luke is a brilliant young man and my favorite over all my years." The system seemed to work, and those in charge were finally held accountable for their actions. "I better get going so you can get the party started."

"Take care, Mr. Conway," Todd said. He walked to the blue door and looked inside. The students sat in the room silently. The three agents, pretending to be teachers, were waiting for his signal. He gave the team lead a thumbs up, and the agents rose and took their sports coats off, revealing they were armed. They then put their DEA badges over their heads and tossed on their windbreakers with DEA emblazoned on the back. The only one who noticed was the gym teacher, who stood up and began to walk toward the door. Todd stopped the teacher and sat him down on a chair. The agents commenced to take them all into custody.

Todd exited the room when he heard a door close behind him, so he turned around. Matias Devry walked toward the nurse's office from one of the far exits from the auditorium. The man wore a mismatched suit. Todd heard the man yelling the name Marie repeatedly. Seconds later, the man came out of the nurse's office holding a sheet of paper. Matias Devry staggered a bit, walking toward Todd.

"Who the hell are you, and what's up with this blue tape on this door?" Mr. Devry walked up to the tape and began to tear it off.

Technically, he needed the tape up so the transport officers would know which door held the bodies that needed to be moved.

"Mr. Devry, I am one of your substitute teachers, Todd Roberts. Mr. Shipmen wants that tape on the door," he responded.

Matias let go of the tape and instead tore two packets of acetaminophen open and tossed the pills into his mouth. He then walked over to a water fountain and took a drink, all the while staring at Todd oddly.

"I drank a little too much last night and need to get rid of this infernal headache." Mr. Devry grabbed his head as if it was going to pop. "The question stands. Why are you standing out here? Why aren't you in the auditorium with everyone else?"

"Vice-Principal Shipmen asked me to wait while he watches some discipline cases he separated."

"Without my approval ... where's Shipmen?"

"He's inside, Mr. Devry," Todd said, motioning toward the door.

Matias lunged toward the door, pushing Todd aside. "What's that simpleton up to?" He opened the door and rushed into the room. Several students were being handcuffed by men in DEA raid jackets. Marie was sitting in a chair in handcuffs. So was Shipmen. "What's this?" Matias was astonished and placed his hand in his pocket.

Todd walked into the room behind Matias and grabbed his left arm, placing him in a hold. "I have a warrant for your arrest for conspiracy to violate drug laws," Todd said while pushing Matias up against the wall and grabbing at the hand Matias had in his pocket. He felt the man's hand wrapped around the butt of a revolver.

"Why do you have a gun, Matias?" Todd yelled out so the other agents knew. He yanked it from the man's hand. Todd placed Matias in handcuffs and discovered a sealed bag containing white powder in his shirt pocket.

"What conspiracy? I don't sell drugs."

"Must be close to a hundred grams of cocaine in that bag, which is not personal use," Todd said with a snort. "Drugs and a gun on the high school principal! Who would have *thunk*."

"We have a little more than that." Agent David Narvaez walked into the room with another handcuffed teacher. "We have the transport vans outside. Put the two principals in the front van." More agents poured into the room and began moving the students and teachers.

"Do we have all of them?" David asked.

"All except Cladhaire," Todd said. "I'm curious. Any luck with the search warrants?"

"Yes, positive on all the target lockers. Including cash and some guns. Positive with the nurse's car when they did an inventory before the tow." David walked toward Shipmen. "This dumb ass had a stack of cash with a ledger showing payoffs from all the pushers at the school and bank accounts. He's toast!"

Shipmen lowered his head in disgrace as agents grabbed him and took him out of the room. Both principals were placed in the same custody van, separated from the students and other teachers. The agents put the nurse in a separate cage in the back of the truck.

All the people to be transported were placed in all the vans without any problems, except for Jimmy, who was neither on the run nor still sleeping in his bed at home. Todd jumped into the front seat of the transport van.

"Hey Todd, we have a problem with one of the transport vans. Can you come over to us?" David asked over the radio. Something they had preplanned as a ruse.

"Yeah, copy that." Todd left the van and walked to the teacher's parking lot, where a conversion van was parked. He stepped into the van and met with Alan and David. He closed the door behind him.

"They are just getting started, Todd," Alan said, raising the volume.

"Why did you leave the ledger in your office?" Matias asked in desperation.

"Where was I supposed to put it?" John asked.

"You could have put the cash in the bank account we opened. You could have hidden the ledger. Why your desk? You're such a disappointment."

"You are as screwed as I am. Why would you keep all our cocaine in your pocket?"

"Jimmy gave it to me outside the school. I wanted to give you and the other teachers their piece," Matias said.

"A gun, Matias? Why a gun at the school?" Shipmen asked.

"I wanted protection in case, I don't know, in case somebody tried to take what belonged to us."

"Matias, why did you get me into this? You ruined my life." Marie said weakly from the back of the cage.

"You are the one with the pill habit, honey."

"Jimmy beat all those kids. He almost killed more than a handful, and you supported him until you couldn't get anymore," Marie said with tears streaming down her face.

"What choice did I have? His father had me by the balls. He caught me buying drugs and held it over my head for years."

"Yes, Matias, but the heroin, the overdoses. That is on us," Shipmen said in defeat.

"It's all on us. We knew Jimmy and the others were dealing with it and we hid that other overdose. James Cladhaire promised his son would not sell more heroin at school—those overdoses even scared him," Matias said, sealing his involvement in the night of overdoses.

Todd and David left the surveillance van that contained audio and visual monitoring equipment. "Did it all record?"

"Sure thing. We got some stuff you did not hear as you left the van." Alan raised the volume of his equipment. "They're still talking."

Todd waved at Alan and shut the door. "That takes care of that." Shipmen's cooperation was vital. Still, the audio in that van was solid in obtaining convictions for all the federal charges the agents had lined up for Devry and the others.

"Good job. I know it's not like getting a huge load, but we cleaned out the school," David said, slapping Todd on the shoulder.

"This means more to me than some of my other cases. The cancer at this school ran deep and had to be removed. Parents don't understand that a few crappy human beings teaching their kids can damage the community. I will always be proud of doing this." Todd said, looking into the distance.

"What wonders a system can bring forth when Godly men and women run it. If the wicked were to take over a system, it would have no value." David watched the vans driving away with some of the wicked.

"Sounds biblical. Where did you get that line from?"

"From my priest when I started in law enforcement. Something I needed to hear. When evil is allowed to gain power in a governing system, the system loses its worth to those it was meant to protect or benefit."

"Maybe I should start going back to church," Todd said, placing his hand on his friend and partner's shoulder.

"Did you get to speak with Mr. Conway at all today?" David asked.

"Sure, did. Good man."

"Look, most teachers here only mean good, but when the managers became corrupt, evil descended on the school," David said.

"Jimmy is still outstanding. We haven't finished here," Todd said. "Put it out on our comms and ask Alan to put it out on the Customs net."

David grabbed his portable radio. "All available agents that are not associated with transport, and processing, we have one outstanding subject. Be on the lookout for Jimmy Cladhaire and his red *Firebird*. Let's brief up at the church on Main and Joshua in twenty minutes."

CHAPTER THIRTY-ONE

The Recital — Minutes Earlier

Luke watched as Mr. Conway entered the auditorium and raised his arm high, a prearranged signal that everyone was inside, and the recital could start. He walked over to Mr. Waters and whispered to him, "We are good to go, Romie." Mr. Conway returned to his seat near the entrance to the auditorium.

Mr. Devry approached the podium and looked at Mr. Waters, who gave him the thumbs-up signal. Mr. Devry pointed at the stage manager, who opened the curtains to the auditorium. A spotlight turned on, and Mr. Waters almost fell while covering his eyes with the bright light.

"Everyone, please all settle down and prepare for a treat that Mr. Waters' Music Theory and Practice class has for you. The horns you have been hearing are part of the recital you will watch. I want to introduce Mr. Waters, who will move us forward. Behave yourselves." Mr. Devry walked off the stage but almost lost his balance stepping off the platform as he went in search of nurse Radner to cure his headache.

"Thanks, Mr. Devry, for that eloquent introduction," Mr. Waters said sarcastically. He pointed at Kevin and Randy, who began playing a version of Pink Floyd's *Us and Them*, heavy on the saxophone. "We have a few songs in store for you. Most of them you will recognize, but all these tunes have our class personality incorporated. Relax and enjoy."

Kevin played the synthesizer with his trumpet hanging from his neck. Mr. Waters walked to his lectern and pointed toward the drums with one hand and Luke with another; he was so nervous that he closed his eyes and played. When he reopened his eyes, he saw Mr. Waters motioning at Alyssa on piano and Ace on bass guitar. Next, he pointed toward Randy on the saxophone.

"For Luke," said a voice that sounded dramatically like Benji. George was no longer at the drum kit; Benji sat there playing the drums.

Luke almost stopped playing the guitar and nearly missed his mark. Mr. Waters pointed at Luke, and he began to sing into the microphone in front of him. He tried to disguise his voice, but how could he? Luke couldn't help but notice the rest of the band staring at him, surprised but not as much as he was that Benji could play at the recital. However, it pained him that Benji still thought he had died.

Benji stood and gawked in shock at Luke, but he kept turning away shyly, not wanting to cause a scene.

The students began to clap and cheer, but Mr. Waters raised his baton to the band and they launched into Luke and Alyssa's modified version of *Beethoven's Piano Concerto No. 5 — Adagio Un Poco Mosso in B major*.

Greta played her violin solo and was then joined by Juana on clarinet. Next, Alyssa played the movement on the piano. Randy and Kevin joined in with horns for a short segment. Benji began to play his drums lightly as the music intensified, and then Luke joined in with his electric guitar paired with the violins. They modernized it and gave it a different feel to attract the crowd's attention. They even began the Rondo early, where the piano played loudly as they all began to play together. He moved in closer to Alyssa; it brought him comfort.

Benji kept staring at him, dressed like a Spanish soldier but kept playing the drums without missing a note.

The band finished playing the modified *Piano Concerto No.5*. Some of the audience stood, but all seemed to applaud at the number. Even the teachers in the audience were clapping. "Thanks, everyone. We still prefer the original, but as a class, we had lots of fun putting it together and playing it for you today. We hope you'll love the next song by Fleetwood Mac," Mr. Waters said. Mr. Waters motioned toward Alyssa and began playing *Hold Me* on the piano. Alyssa, Sally, and Benji started singing at the same time.

They were a minute into the song, and Benji again stared at Luke. He lost his place and stood up. George took his place immediately. Benji walked cautiously to the young man playing the guitar who was in disguise. The song is less than four minutes long, but it seems like an eternity with Benji closing in and staring at him. Mr. Waters had told everyone they had an eccentric boy playing the guitar, but it wasn't enough. Before the song finished, Benji grabbed Luke over his guitar. Luke leaned into his friend. "I love you, buddy."

Benji cried in his arms. "Am I dreaming? I thought you left me."

Luke took off his helmet and then balaclava. His bandmates stopped playing, began to gasp, and then stood. Luckily, the song was over.

"People stay in place, one more song. We'll explain later. Use this, and let's put all our emotion into our last song," Mr. Waters yelled at them away from the microphone.

"Take your place on your throne, Benji!" Luke remarked while placing his helmet back on. Sebastian stood beside him, halberd in hand, pointing toward the crowd.

The audience stood up and clapped. "One of my favorite songs, and now my favorite rendition. Our last song, *November Rain* by Guns and Roses, was chosen by our very own Benji Laio, who will be on lead vocals," Mr. Waters said with pride. He raised his hands, motioning toward Kevin on the synthesizer, and the winds section began playing. Mr. Waters gestured toward Alyssa, who started to play the piano. Next, Greta played her violin. Mr. Waters looked at Benji, motioning for him to start playing his drums. A minute into the music, Benji began to sing.

Mr. Waters motioned toward Luke with his baton, who began playing his electric guitar while walking toward Benji and playing behind him. A spotlight formed on him. Luke slowly walked to the side of the stage, where he climbed on a lowered scissor jack scaffolding, which then began to rise upward while he played. The spotlight followed him as he played his guitar solo. Sebastian stood at the bottom of the scissor jack, standing guard. Luke stood at the top of the raised stage with the spotlight's brilliance forcing his eyes shut. The platform began lowering as the end of the song approached. As it lowered, Luke felt dread as to what came next. After all that had happened, he wanted to perform more than he had realized at the recital with his class. The Cladhaires wanted him dead, and many thought he was still dead. The deep feeling of numbness that he felt was loss; his of his childhood and loss at knowing what will come next. As he stood with Sebastian, he realized his future was perilous, and he knew he was ready for it.

Noncompliance

FBI Special Agent Robert Curtis sat in the passenger seat of DOJ OIG Special Agent Christian Kelly's government vehicle. A black Mercury *Grand Marquis*. They were the case agents for the corruption cases against all the law enforcement officers relating to the Loudon County Metropolitan Drug Task Force. Their first targets were Lansburg Police Officers Jose Velasquez and Leroy Washington. The arrest team comprised FBI Special Weapons and Tactics Teams or FBI SWAT. The team commander was named Rick Smith.

The plan was simple: Christian had planned for a group of auditors to meet with the LT, Juan Bello, and Alexei Morozov. The support staff should all be in a conference room of the task force in Leesburg, waiting for a team of auditors from Christian's office. One of the auditors was an armed OIG agent but had borrowed the credentials of a different auditor.

Members of the FBI Special Surveillance Group, or SSG, were surveilling Velasquez and Washington. FBI SWAT operated in two four-man teams driving large Chevrolet *Suburban's*. Their first target was Officer Jose Velasquez. The SSG was behind and surrounding Velasquez. A few civilians were nearby. They were at a fresh red light.

"Green light, target one. Light them up." The Suburban's emergency lights activate simultaneously. SSG units driving in front of Velasquez stopped, pinning the officer from trying to evade them. Teams 1 and 2 pinned their targets and poured out of the rear of their vehicles.

Officer Velasquez pulled over immediately, began to follow all the commands of the lead contact officer, and threw his keys out the window with his gun belt. SRT Team 2 brought Velasquez out of the vehicle and took him into custody without any further use of force.

"One in custody, code 4," Smith called out.

Christian immediately drove toward the last known location of Washington. SRT stated he was parked at the mall after going through a fast-food drive-through. "This one should be easier if he's just sitting in his car eating."

"You never know with cops, Chris. It's fight or flight," Curtis said.

"All, SSG has pretty good box set around Washington. We cannot pin him in because of the way he's parked. SSG will back a car into the spot in front of the target, and then we'll approach. Standby.

"Get us closer, Chris, over there, where we can get a good view of this."

Christian drove to the other area and saw Washington's patrol car and the empty spaces around him. A white Ford *F150* truck went into the parking lot and backed into the spot in front of Washington.

"Seriously, I said a sedan ... why did he back it in," the SRT commander said.

"We can have the pick-up moved and replaced," an SSG agent responded.

The driver stepped out of the pickup, began to walk away, turned to walk back to the vehicle, turned again, and walked off. It looked like he was dancing.

"What was that about?" Curtis asked. "Get ready to move. Washington just turned on his car."

"Approach, execute, execute," the SWAT commander ordered.

Washington sped backward out of the parking spot and struck the SRT vehicle as it tried to pin him into the spot. The agents left the car and started to issue orders to Washington as the second SWAT team drove in and pinned the pick-up in place. The patrol car shot forward, the rear tires spinning, struck the *F-150*, and bent the rear bumper downward, which blew out the left rear tire. The pick-up was forced into the second Suburban, jarring the team members as they left the vehicle. Several of them fell to the concrete.

"I'm not giving up without a fight," Officer Washington yelled through his PA speaker. He placed his vehicle in reverse and slammed into the SUV behind him again.

Agents scrambled to escape and make way by moving behind the Suburban.

Washington drove forward again, striking the pickup, and went underneath it, striking the vehicle's gas tank. The tank ruptured, and fuel spilled on top of the patrol car.

"Washington, stop resisting, or we will be forced to shoot! Let's talk this out," yelled Agent Smith. "Get me a negotiator, now! We have a situation at the Washington arrest site." Smith said over the radio.

Curtis, a negotiator and member of the Hostage Rescue Team or HRT, grabbed the radio. "I'm on site." He released the radio, jumped out of the vehicle, put on his FBI raid jacket, and sprinted toward the scene.

"Curtis, get out of there … come behind the car!" Agent Smith yelled.

Curtis moved across the vehicle with his arms up in the air. "Leroy, my name is Robert Curtis. I'm with the FBI. Let's talk this out, my man." The look in Leroy's eyes was new to Curtis. Leroy must have just done drugs because the adrenalin pumping through his system, coupled with this high-stress situation, looked as if it turned the man's eyes red." *I'm either very brave or foolish*, he thought.

Officer Washington pulled his gun from his holster and shot Curtis right in the chest. He then aimed at the SWAT members and kept shooting.

Several of the agents returned fire. Washington was hit as well as his windshield and door. One of the rounds ricocheted, hitting the exposed gasoline tank of the pickup now located on the squad car's hood. The fuel was sprayed into the vehicle's cab.

"Cease fire, cease fire. Smith yelled out.

Officer Washington fired again, igniting the fuel and the humbled police officer. Leroy pulled himself out of the front window, consumed by the fire.

"Extinguisher. Somebody grab a fire extinguisher!" Yelled out agent Smith, before running toward Curtis, stretched out on his back, staring at the officer squirming within the flames. The smell of gasoline and burning meat made him nauseous.

"I know what you are thinking—you were being foolish," Smith said, helping him up.

"I need to get over to the task force office."

"You need to go to the hospital, Rob … I'll take care of the LT," Christian said.

The pain emanating throughout his chest was horrible, but his vest and the trauma plate he had over it made sure he was at least alive. "I'll go later, bring the car around, and let's get this over with."

It was too late for Officer Washington. He collapsed on the ground, dying on the asphalt in a heap of steaming and charred flesh.

CHAPTER THIRTY-TWO

The Task Force

Agent Kelly parked at a business adjacent to the task force office building. Curtis exited the car and took off his raid jacket and dress shirt. He had a hole in his shirt and a hole in his vest. He removed his undershirt and looked at his chest. He had a purple welt on his right pectoral muscle. When he touched the welt, he winced with the pain.

"What were you thinking, Rob? Nobody will ever say that you are an expert at assessing a situation," Christian said.

"Maybe it's time for me to move to OIG ha?"

Christian laughed, straightened, and placed his suit coat on. "We don't need crazy guys like you over with us."

Curtis put his dress shirt back on and then his tie. He reached into his work pouch and grabbed a shoulder holster with a short H&K *MP5* attached. He placed it over his dress shirt and ran his belt through the loops. He was no longer wearing a vest, but he gambled that he would not get shot twice in one day.

Another vehicle arrived, and four agents dressed in suits exited their cars. Under their suit coats, each wore an *MP5* as well. One of them was Matt, who was part of Luke's protection team. He had not yet been transferred to Alaska.

The six of them stood together and waited for him to speak.

The first auditors arrived at ten in the morning as previously arranged. "They are expecting a second set of auditors and some laboratory inspectors. I don't expect them to be on the alert at their shop, but you never know."

"We heard you took a shot from Washington. You seem fine, though," Matt said.

Curtis frowned and looked toward the task force a few hundred yards down. "I'm not sure I'm fine. Let's get this over with. We go in, and we divide the room. Get a drop on all the armed guys, as we discussed. Copy?"

They all shook their heads and headed towards their target, with Curtis leading. They arrived at the building and pressed the button at the front door. Nothing happened. Several minutes later, they pushed the button again.

"Hello, can I help you?" a woman asked.

"Yes, Ma'am, we are here from the lab for the inspection and the audit."

The door buzzed. Curtis pulled the door open, and they entered the building. He tapped on his shoulder rig, expecting to have to come up shooting, but they were only in the interior reception and had not yet entered the actual facility. He took his hand away from his side and wiped the sweat off his brow. The adrenaline rush was getting the best of him. He took a deep breath, and the door opened.

The woman stepped out and looked at all of them. You don't look like lab-type guys or accountants, for that matter."

"The little guy behind me is the chemist." He walked closer to the door.

She shook her head and looked back into the office space. "I better talk to LT, wait here, please." She was about to turn and most likely warn the LT, which would place the auditors inside in a terrible situation.

He nodded at Matt, who lunged for the door just as he grabbed the woman and covered her mouth. She tried to scream. "FBI, don't scream. Do you understand?" She nodded yes, her eyes darting back and forth. "Are you Monica?" Curtis asked in a whisper. She nodded her head up and down. Monica, are any of them armed inside?" She shook her head quickly up and down. "This agent is going to escort you outside until it's safe. Don't scream because we don't want a shooting." One of the youngsters grabbed Monica and escorted her outside. The five remaining agents entered the office and closed the door.

"Monica, bring them over here," the LT yelled.

Curtis motioned for the agents to follow him. They moved straight down the hallway to the sound of the voices.

"Monica … can't you get anything right?" The LT walked out the door of the conference room.

Agent Curtis shoved the barrel of his submachine gun into the LT's chest. "FBI, you are under arrest, Cladhaire. Put your hands up, don't go for your piece, or I will unload into you." Agent Curtis's look was menacing enough to stop anybody from fighting back, as he blocked the doorway. He grabbed the LT's belt and handed the man over to Matt. When he entered the room, Detective Morozov stood up, but the agent in the room placed his handgun on the corrupt seized property officer's head. "Raise your hands, Juan." The remaining auditors knew to stand and leave the room when it was safe. Juan complied quickly, and an agent placed him in handcuffs and took away his gun. Several support staff members cowered at the table. The City of Lansburg accountant, the paralegal, the mission support staff, and the analyst were present. They were all accounted for.

"We have arrest warrants for each of you and a search warrant for the whole facility and every one of your cars."

"What the hell is this about? This is a federally funded drug task force," Morozov said defiantly as he was being handcuffed.

"You're correct, Morozov. That's why the FBI is arresting you, not internal affairs."

"I would appreciate it if you called me by my title. I earned my Detective badge."

"Thanks for the reminder." Curtis tossed an envelope at

Morozov. "Courtesy of your Chief. Your services are no longer required."

"Morry, shut up," the LT said while being led back inside handcuffed.

"Search them well. Pretty sure they each have more than one gun," Curtis said to the other agents on the arrest team.

The agent that was outside with Monica brought her back inside in handcuffs and sat her down. He leaned in and whispered to him. "Jimmy Cladhaire is on the run."

He walked over to the LT. "Oh, LT, where's little Jimmy?"

"Fuck off! Get my lawyer." The LT stared at him with his chin raised in pride.

"This isn't going to end pleasantly for your son. We have an armed and dangerous BOLO for him," he said, trying to reason with the LT.

The LT moved his shoulders and shook his head in disbelief. "Not my problem. A lawyer now or those last two statements will come up at a motion hearing as coercion."

"Cladhaire, your son was fucked from the start to have you as a father. They can put that in your motion hearing," Matt said. "Luke was right about you."

The LT began to shake in his chair and foam at the mouth. Suddenly, the LT levitated, and the fabric from the top of his shirt tore off from the man. He dropped back into the chair, apparently unconscious.

"What the hell was that?" Matt asked, staring at the LT. He walked cautiously over and tried to check the man for a pulse.

The LT shot up and looked around the room. "Where am I?" He began to squirm in his chair again. "Why am I handcuffed?"

"We just arrested you, LT. We are with the FBI," Curtis said.

"Arrested, I'm a cop. Why would you arrest me? Take these off, and I'll show you my ID."

"What's wrong with him?" Matt asked.

Curtis sat next to the LT and massaged his aching chest. "Okay, I'll go with this. What year is it, Lieutenant?"

"Who are you calling, lieutenant? Year, what are you crazy? It's 1972. Now, get me out of these cuffs. I don't like being confined."

"Where's little Jimmy?"

"Jimmy? I have a daughter." The LT started squirming and ended up passing out again.

"Matt, get him an ambulance. They might as well check me out, too. Get the rest transported to Alexandria."

† † †

Red Shirt

Terry Garcia sat patiently in her SUV in Centreville, waiting for the operation to commence. Most of the Customs agents were at this location, including a Customs SRT team from the Washington, DC, SAC office. Her team was ready for the search, but it would have to be secured by the SRT team first. This warehouse was used by all the members of the Chinese gang affiliated with the smuggling ring using the seaport. She identified it after interviewing one of the warehouse employees who worked here for several months before being asked to secure the drugs coming in through the rail yard. Some DEA agents were present, but Todd and David wanted to work together to make sure they adequately secured evidence to support charges at the school. The large warehouse was used to drop off the large importations that were then distributed to New York City and Chicago, IL. Most of the workers at the warehouse were members of a Chinese criminal street gang but at times they brought in associates from New York City. The Italians arrested were representatives of the New York mob, and the Hispanic guys were members of a street gang in Chicago that the Chinese trusted.

The warehouse had an exterior fence surrounded by an

interior fence. The property had a loading dock with one garage entry behind the building and one tractor/trailer in the lot. The view of the dock was impeded from every direction. Terry mentioned that the warehouse was hidden in plain sight and screamed for people to stay away. Three cars were in the parking lot on the front part of the compound. Nobody was visible on the property. Surveillance over the past few days led agents to believe that there were at least four people in the warehouse.

Terry Garcia and her search team were waiting in the parking lot of a pharmacy. "All, as soon as the clock strikes ten, SRT will breach the warehouse, and we will roll in behind them four to a car. Don't forget your search kits."

Terry was anxious. Mostly because she had this need to be known as a significant case producer, and after the euphoria of the large heroin seizure dissipated, she yearned to build that seizure into a more considerable conspiracy case. She had done that, but she doubted herself and her work enough to be worried it would be a complete bust. So far, they have had no other seizures associated with the warehouse and have failed to corroborate her source's information. She took a deep breath with closed eyes and focused on what mattered trying to remove the inner critic that told her she was wrong. It was truly important that her whole team and the SRT team hitting the warehouse accomplished their goals and everyone left this warehouse safe and sound. Terry looked at her watch. "Let's head out now." They drove toward the warehouse slowly in a convoy of four cars.

Terry parked her vehicle with a view of the front entry of the warehouse. She raised her binoculars and looked at the gate.

During the Customs briefing, Terry learned from the SRT commander, Mark Johnson, that they would have a team of four SRT members, including Johnson, in an armored personnel carrier (APV). It would have a battering ram equipped to the front end. An armored SUV moved behind the APV. Two other SUVs pulled forward and blocked the roads on the corners of the warehouse perimeter. The passenger doors opened, and three agents ran from each of them to the back of the stack.

The APV struck the gate, launching it violently into the air. Then, it hit the second gate, which bowed and popped open. The side hatch opened, and a rifle came out of the hatch. The SRT team moved flawlessly out of both SUVs and into the stack toward the business's front door. SA Johnson joined the pile, and two breachers came out with different equipment. The exterior perimeter team was posted in the garage at the rear of the business. They placed ballistic shields covering two windows on either side of the structure as the stack moved up to the front door. The breachers began to tear down a security gate on the door. "Police, Police with a search warrant."

The first breacher managed to pop open the security door, and the second breacher took a battering ram and slammed the doorknob, which shot forward into the building, but the door did not open. The breacher reared backward with the ram and hit gain, and the door did not give.

"Garage door is opening. The garage door is opening in the rear," Alan called over the radio from the surveillance van.

"Alternate breach, alternate breach. To the rear of the business now," SA Johnson yelled out. They all turned, running in the stack toward the rear of the business.

"What's going on, Terry?" asked one of the agents.

"It must be a fortified door. We need to cover the front entry." Terry reached for her tactical Motorola radio. She couldn't drive up to the entrance because of the blocked street. "Everyone, I'm moving up. Stay here." She dropped the binos on her seat and ran past one of the SUVs blocking the street. She noticed the drivers had exited the vehicles and pointed their rifles at the front of the warehouse. She had an eye on the front door and could see an SRT agent was already covering it. The two other SRT agents moved forward and covered the lone agent covering the door.

"We took down three trying to rush out the back!" yelled an agent over the radio.

The front door of the warehouse opened. A man wearing a red shirt left the building and was immediately confronted by the perimeter SRT agent covering the front door. He pinned *Red Shirt* with the shield. Suddenly, the agent took a shotgun blast to the side of his torso from another man who left through the same door. The man shot again and hit the two agents behind the injured agent. Terry moved out of cover and shot at *Shotgun Man*, who returned fire toward her, striking the SUV. An agent behind her cried out in pain. The agent behind him took some of the pellets to his face and moved back and away from the gunshots. She fired her pistol at the man while trying to get behind a wall. She tried to perform a tactical reload with a fresh magazine when she reached cover, but *Red Shirt* must have followed her and tackled her down to the ground hard. She was stunned, and her firearm flew out of her hand.

She noticed that *Shotgun Man* was aiming at her, so she moved Red Shirt into the fatal funnel of fire. One of the injured SRT agents shot *Shotgun Man*, which caused him to crumple onto himself, firing the shotgun as he fell dead onto the ground.

Red Shirt tried to mount Terry, but she put her hand on his thigh, pushing him back as she kicked him in the ribs. The sound of bones crackling emanated into the air. *Red Shirt* must be on some drug because he threw himself back onto her, landing between her legs in a position of advantage, so he thought, as he tried to grab her neck. She placed her forearm over his elbow and held her hand, twisting away from him. She pushed on the man with her right leg, fulfilling a shoulder lock, and the man's shoulder popped. Other agents arrived, taking *Red Shirt* to the ground while he screamed for help.

The SRT team medic rushed to the front along with a cover team. The emergency medic performed first aid on three of his teammates, who took a close shot with the shotgun.

Peanut left the surveillance van and ran toward Terry. He looked like a charging brown bear. Terry winced in pain as he arrived by her side. "What's up, Terry? Are you hurt?"

"That asshole broke my ribs when he tackled me," she said, turning on her side while getting on a knee. "What are you doing, Terry? You're worrying me. I was about to call for an ambulance," Peanut said.

"Fuck that dice, Peanut. The medic can tape me up." She stood up and walked toward the man who tackled her. "Look at my face. Look at me."

Red Shirt looked at her. "Damn bitch? Where did you learn how to do that?"

Terry grabbed at *Red Shirt's* collar and looked at his face. "You're Tao Chin. You're under arrest. I will add assaulting a federal officer to your list of charges, bitch."

A new car arrived on the scene. Carlos Tirado, her group supervisor, stepped out. "Terry, you're coming with me to the hospital first."

"No, I'm fine, Carlos." Terry insisted while holding her side.

"No choice, Terry. That was an order."

Terry stared at Carlos menacingly but then smiled. "Okay, Carlos, but you're driving." Her adrenalin was wearing off as she slid down to the ground and doubled over on her side. She had trouble breathing but lying on her back and to her left side seemed to reduce the pain and allow her to breathe. Suddenly, she felt nauseous and vomited. *I'm not going to let that little shit take me out of the fight, stand up.*

CHAPTER THIRTY-THREE

The School Administrator

Luke stepped off the scissor jack and walked toward Alyssa and Benji, and they all embraced. If they were not caught up in the moment, they would have heard cheers from the teachers and students in the audience. The rest of the band members joined and wrapped around the trio, who had recently rejoined one another after Jimmy and his actions forced them apart.

"Come on, everyone, let's acknowledge our audience's applause. Step up to the front of the stage."

The group separated, and as they prepared to stand up on the stage, they came across Mr. Conway, who had joined them. They stood before one another for several seconds before their teacher grabbed them.

"I am so happy you could perform together after such horrible adversity." Their teacher and mentor released them. "As soon as we are done here, you must leave, Luke." Mr. Conway appeared defeated.

"What happened? What's wrong?" Luke asked.

"Jimmy never showed up at the school. I don't know if he's in custody yet. Just leave as soon as we finish here. I hope he's in hiding."

While they spoke, a podium and a microphone were relocated

to the front of the stage. The lights in the auditorium illuminated as they all stood on one side of the microphone on the stage and bowed.

Luke imagined that Jimmy could be going after his parents or brothers. Then, he saw Tristan in his mind and knew that Jimmy had to be focused on hurting his nephew somehow.

Mr. Conway walked up to the microphone. "All, please remain seated. We hope you are all pleased with the final performance of the Music Theory and Practice class. We have a few weeks left for the Class of 1992 before graduation, and I believe this was a great way to start winding the school year down. If you bear with us longer, our school board administrator has an announcement."

An older woman ambled to the microphone. "Good morning, Lansburg Center High School. My name is Ruth Green. I am the superintendent of the Lansburg School District. I want to thank Mr. Waters, including his class, for a wonderful performance and his dedication to his students, which was reflected in the performance we all watched," Mrs. Green said with a shaky voice. She looked around the auditorium, grabbed the microphone from the stand, and took several steps to her right, getting closer to Luke, who still wore his helmet. "I have bad news, and it pains me to say this after such a positive morning." She stopped and stared silently at the students and teachers in the auditorium. "During the performance, a group of federal and state law enforcement officers conducted an enforcement operation at the school. Several teachers and staff members, including Principal Devry, Vice-Principal Shipmen, and your school nurse, have been placed into custody. The specifics are unimportant, and there will be much speculation about what happened in the news tonight." Mrs. Green walked back up to the stand to replace the microphone. She motioned to somebody from the side of the auditorium.

Mrs. Moore joined Mr. Conway, and Mrs. Green at the podium. "I'm sure most, if not all of you, recognize Mr. Conway and Mrs. Moore. Mr. Conway will be your acting principal, and Mrs.

Moore will be your acting vice principal. Mr. Conway, would you please?" Mrs. Green stepped aside and motioned to the microphone.

Mr. Conway stood in front of the podium. "This is a sad time. We must be resilient and focused. We will pick up the pieces together to finish this year with our heads held high. Ten of our students have been placed into custody and expelled from this school. If you have seen Jimmy Cladhaire, you should come to our office immediately or call the police. Do not go anywhere near Jimmy. Law enforcement officers are actively looking for him. Over the next few days and weeks, you will hear many negative stories, including rumors about your school. A few rotten apples cannot be allowed to spoil the bin. I promise you all that Mrs. Moore and I, with the support of Mrs. Green, will never allow the rot to consume the whole."

Several students, including Steve Rustova, Stanley Johnson, and a dozen others, walked toward the front of the stage.

"All, please return to your seats until you are released properly."

"Mr. Conway, with all due respect, is that Luke Sanz in that costume?" Stan asked.

"I knew that was you, Luke! What gives?" Steve yelled.

Other students stood up, moved to the front of the class, and started yelling questions. The voices grew, and it was hard to comprehend anything being said.

Luke met eyes with Mr. Conway and shrugged his shoulders, not knowing the best way forward.

Mr. Conway latched onto the lectern and motioned with his hands downward. "Settle down, people. Let me explain." His teacher motioned him over to the lectern.

It didn't work because more students left their seats and walked forward. The crowd of students did not settle down.

Luke approached Mr. Conway, who stepped away from the podium and the microphone.

Mrs. Green walked up to them.

"Talk to them. They want to hear from you what happened," Mr. Conway said.

Luke shook his head back and forth. He wasn't ready or willing to speak to all the assembled students and teachers. He needed to leave and get to his parents. His mind raced with what Jimmy could be up to.

Mrs. Green leaned in toward Luke and grabbed his hand ... *I was forced backward with a jarring motion and was placed in a room with an oval conference table. Mrs. Green sat with Mr. Conway and Mrs. Moore. Wil, Terry, Todd, David, and even Curtis sat with her.*

"From what you're describing, it sounds as if young Mr. Sanz has tried to save our school all while the principal and vice-principal were benefiting from him selling drugs at the school."

"Yes, Ma'am. Everything you've been told about Luke is wrong," Terry said ... he was back in the present on stage with a spotlight upon him.

"Thank you for all you did to get to this point. Please speak to the students and let them know who we know you are," Mr. Conway said.

Luke bowed his head and removed his helmet. He shook his head up and down, and confidence entered him. He walked up to the podium and raised his hands upward and downward. "Please listen up, and I'll explain."

The crowd before him stood still, and slowly stopped talking. "Jimmy Cladhaire has been terrorizing this school for months and has turned everything upside down." As he spoke, the crowd was silent. "He has been selling drugs and beating on our underclassmen. He tried to kill Benji and almost killed Weirdo. Last week, Jimmy set me up by putting drugs in my locker, and then he tried to have me killed by some corrupt cops that work for his father." The crowd began to return to their seats as he spoke. "They tried to have me killed in jail. Some good cops helped me, and now we hope everything has been righted. That's the whole point of this. Teachers like Mr. Conway and Mrs. Moore tried to steer the school toward the light, and Mr. Devry brought us into darkness." He took a deep breath and let go of the podium. "I hope this is over … if you see Jimmy, tell him to turn himself in. Tell him to do it for his sister Karen." He stepped away from the podium, looked at Alyssa and Benji, and waved at them.

Mr. Conway approached him and shook his hand … *I stood beside a coffin. My family sat in front of many people. All dressed in black, including Alyssa, who looked ten years older. Mr. Conway threw dirt onto my coffin* … he let go of Mr. Conway's hand and stared at it. There was dirt cupped in his teacher's hand.

"Get going, and don't let Jimmy win."

Luke ran up to Alyssa and embraced her, and they kissed.

"What's wrong? What did you see?" Alyssa asked.

When he touched Alyssa, he saw the same scene. "Nothing I can't change." He motioned for Sebastian to follow him. "We're going to have to kill Jimmy."

CHAPTER THIRTY-FOUR

Awakening

Luke ran out toward his car, which he parked in the teacher's lot. A strange sensation caused him to start walking on the tarmac. He looked around but did not see anything concerning. He felt like he was being preyed upon by a hunter.

"It's Jimmy. He's watching you, but I don't know from where," Sebastian said while walking alongside him. "Get in your car, and I will look out for him."

As he approached the car, he saw a note fluttering in the wind underneath his passenger-side windshield wiper. He grabbed the paper and opened it up.

I know what you did to my family, Luke.
I will take Joyce and your nephew, Tristan, from you. I owe you for what you did, but now I will take away your family's future.
Yours truly, the Bully Cladhair.

Luke lost the strength in his legs, and his knees buckled. He fell to his knees and crumpled onto himself. He recalled a vision from last year. Joyce ran through the hallway on the second floor of the house on Red Hill Road. Back then he thought the vision was form the past. He was wrong. She was in danger, now.

Joyce was at their home with his mother. His father flew that morning to somewhere in Central America. Jimmy had settled into his evil alter ego. He shook his head in disbelief. *I may die today, but not Joyce or Tristan*, he thought. He stood up and pounded his chest.

Sebastian slammed his halberd into the ground and repeatedly hit his Cuirass with a gloved fist. "Let's take the battle to this coward!"

Luke jumped into Divine Justice and grabbed his analog work phone, which he did not turn in. He smoked up the parking lot as he propelled himself toward his home on Red Hill Road. He called Wil as he drove.

"Hey, Luke, what's shaking?" Wil asked, sounding content with how the day had progressed.

"Wil, Jimmy took my sister-in-law Joyce and Tristan from our house."

"Are you serious? I heard that FBI surveillance teams lost Jimmy, but why would he take Joyce and Tristan?" Wil asked.

"He thinks if he destroys my family's future, it would be worse than killing me."

"Well, DEA and our SRT are out hunting for him. Where are you headed?"

"Home, I need to check on my mom."

Wil was silent for a few seconds. "Do you think he would … be positive. I'll ask Jorge to send some of his guys over. Come back to the warehouse in Alexandria when you can."

"Right-o Wil. If I bump into Jimmy, I'm going to kill him," Luke said, hoping that Jimmy would show himself.

"Luke, check on your mom and then come back here. We'll draw out Jimmy and have SRT deal with him. Do you understand?" Wil asked the last part in Spanish.

"I understand," Luke responded in Spanish. He pressed the end button as he entered the driveway. His mother's van, Joyce's car, and his father's Monte Carlo were parked in the driveway.

He was sure that Jimmy was not there. He parked the car and approached the broken and splintered door. Tony was waiting at the doorway. Blood dripped from his dog's mouth and was drenched on his fur. "What happened, Tony?"

Tony whimpered and looked upstairs.

He placed Tony on the floor. The dog promptly ran upstairs into his parents' room. He reluctantly followed his dog up the stairs and into the room. The double doors were in pieces throughout the floor. He walked toward the end of the room, following his dog's licking sound. His mother lay crumpled on the floor with the phone lying on top of her. Her face was battered, and her eyes were swollen shut. Her arms were tied behind her back. Luke dropped to his knees and held onto his face as he turned red with anger and sorrow. He screamed for what seemed like minutes.

"What's with all the yelling?" Kamila came running up the stairs holding shopping bags, which she dropped to the floor.

His mother moaned weakly and tried to move her arms. He reached for her and grabbed her arm ... *I was thrust backward in a neck-jarring motion and flowed down to the front door of my house. Jimmy Cladhaire stood in front of the door. He tackled the door like a bull throwing himself into it with such force that it appeared like somebody was thrown into the room instead of forcing his way in.*

Joyce walked down the stairs and saw Jimmy standing up in the foyer. She ran up the stairs into Daniel's room, returned with Tristan, and ran up to the attic screaming wildly. I had seen a glimpse of this some time ago.

I followed Joyce up to the attic and saw my mother trying to comfort Joyce.

"It's the Bully Cladhair. I think he's going to kill us," Joyce yelled.

"Not if I can help it." She appeared to be looking for something. "My gun's in my purse downstairs." She tried to run down the stairs, but Jimmy was at the bottom blocking her way.

Jimmy's eyes glowed red. When he walked up the stairs slowly, I saw that Jimmy had his father's vulture sitting on his shoulders. The demon had found a temporary host, but the demon was not embedded in Jimmy like he was with his father.

My mother blocked the stairs and tried to keep Jimmy from moving into the room.

"I'm not going to let you hurt her or my baby, you animal."

Jimmy proceeded to punch my mother. She refused to back off as he pummeled her face repeatedly. She kicked at him and refused to give up. Joyce screamed and ran off toward one of the bedrooms.

"Why are you doing this?" my mother asked, her eyes swelling shut, her jaw appeared broken.

I tried to kick Jimmy, but I was just an observer.

"It's simple. He doesn't deserve what he has. You, his father, his brothers." He looked around the room. "This very house. Why couldn't I have this rather than my life? Instead of what happened to my sister." With that, Jimmy kicked my mother, and she fell to the ground.

He walked past her to one of the windows and grabbed some of the material at the curtain. He walked back to my mother and tied her hands behind her back … he returned forcibly to the present and doubled over in front of his mother. The nausea was horrible.

"Comadre, what happened to you?" Kamila asked, moving closer to his mother.

"It was the Bully Cladhair, Titi. Help me get her on the bed." They moved her gently to the bed, and then he took off her bindings. He could not look directly at his mother. He was embarrassed. He insisted on being at the recital and did not protect his family. His father had abandoned them again in their time of need in favor of another family in a foreign country. Her face was a mess, and she would never look the same again.

"Can you talk, Helen?"

Luke heard some commotion downstairs.

"This door was busted open. Police, is anybody home?"

"Up here, officers. You need to call an ambulance now," he thundered.

His mother was trying to talk and grabbed his arm. He saw bright red as if hit with a spotlight. He knelt on the floor and leaned into her.

"Baby … save the baby."

"I will, Mom." He tried to stand, but she pulled at him forcibly, and he lowered his head back to her battered mouth.

"Kill *it!*"

He rose, and he stared at his mother. He saw the determination in her eyes, and he knew what he must do.

"Kill *it*," she repeated and passed out.

"Are you the Customs guy? What happened here?" the officer asked.

"It was Jimmy Cladhaire. He kidnapped my sister-in-law, Joyce Sanz, and my nephew Tristan." Luke started to walk out of the room but turned back to Kamila. "Stay with her, Titi."

"Son, I need to know more than that. It would be best if you stuck around."

He approached the officer, who he towered over by at least a foot. "You have your job, and I have mine. Somebody needs to pay for what happened today." Luke ran downstairs, jumped back into his car, and headed toward the courthouse, where he realized his destiny beckoned him to finish this mess.

Phoenix

Luke headed east on the parkway. He removed the memory of what happened to his mother out of his thoughts. He wanted to keep emotion out of his decision-making process.

Sebastian formed on the passenger seat of his car. "I found him. Jimmy is parked in his car, looking at a screen with a map and a red blip. He drove off in his car when he saw something move. I don't understand, Luke."

"Alan and Peanut explained it to me. Jimmy must have placed a tracking device on my car. He knows where I am or at least the probable direction. I was wondering why Jimmy didn't slash my tires. He has something else planned. Where's Joyce and Tristan?"

"They aren't in the car, Luke ... I'll try to find them." Sebastian vanished.

He had driven for about thirty minutes and was approaching Tysons Corner. He had not heard anything from Sebastian. He was startled by the ringtone on the phone. "Hello?"

"Where are you?"

"I am near Great Falls."

"I have an SRT team in two black SUVs waiting on the parkway. One will follow you, and the other will look for Jimmy."

"Wil, I think he put a tracker on my car."

"What? I doubt that, Luke. How would Jimmy get one or know how to use it?"

"His father, Wil. Trust me. He knows my direction of travel. I think he wants me to take him to where his father is being held."

"That's wild, but it has been a crazy week. We have air available, and I will send them to look for Jimmy's car. Let me know if you see him."

"I will ..." he said.

He caught some traffic in the Tysons area before he saw two black SUVs parked on the side of the roadway. One of them accelerated quickly, its headlights flashing along with red and blue lights on the grill and upper part of the windshield. Within minutes, the SRT teams were behind him, and all the emergency lights shut off.

His phone rang, and he answered. "SRT guys are behind me."

"I know. Leave the phone on."

"I'm not too far from Alexandria. Maybe he gave up."

"Maybe he has, Luke. The helicopter is still looking for him."

"I'm sorry. Maybe I'm being paranoid."

"Jimmy is close behind you and has a firearm. He's driving fast trying to catch up to you," Sebastian said, dissipating quickly into smoke.

"Gun!" Luke gasped.

"What was that, Luke, about a gun?"

"I was thinking out loud that he may have a gun."

"That would not surprise me … wait a moment."

He heard radio chatter in the background, but it needed to be evident through his phone.

"The helicopter has eyes on Jimmy. The team is going to try and get behind him."

The vehicles behind him began to slow down, and he did as well.

"Don't slow down. Gun it and give us time to stop Jimmy."

He stomped on his pedal, causing the car to launch to over a hundred in seconds. The vehicle was a testament to the American work ethic coupled with ingenuity.

Luke drove silently for several minutes and did his best not to hit cars. Traffic was building.

Sebastian reappeared. "It would help if you saw what just happened." Sebastian removed his glove and made the sign of the cross, then placed his bare hand on Luke's head … *I was yanked backward through my seat and landed in the vehicle with the SRT team directly behind Jimmy. They had activated all their emergency lights, including their siren, and civilians were yielding to the right. Jimmy was not stopping. All the team members wore balaclavas.*

"He's up ahead driving on the shoulder, the moron," the agent in the front passenger seat said. They made their way directly behind the red car again.

"Mark, he's not going to yield," the agent driving said.

"We cannot PIT him at this speed. We would both roll for a mile." Mark opened the glove box and switched his radio to the public address setting. "Jimmy, it's over. Pull over now."

Jimmy began weaving his car to keep them from overtaking him.

The SRT driver hit his brakes and slowed down. "Boss, we are too heavy in this beast. We are going to end up rolling."

He grabbed the vehicle's transmitter. "SRT 2, this is SRT1. Pull ahead and prepare for a rolling roadblock."

"Copy that."

"Okay, get ready to pin him in," Mark said.

SRT 2 pulled forward and got in front of Jimmy who was trying to get past them.

"We're going to have to do this quickly, or he's going to pull ahead of us."

"Now, pull forward," he yelled into the transmitter.

Within seconds, the two SUVs were in front and behind Jimmy. The rest happened rapidly. SRT 2 began to slow down fast. I stared at the speedometer, which was at fifty and slowing quickly. The driver of the vehicle slammed into Jimmy, pushing him into the SUV in front. Smoke shot out from the tires of three cars as they came to a stop.

Jimmy shot his gun into the rear of the SUV, causing several holes in the rear door and shattering the rear glass. The front driver pulled forward, probably trying but failing to avoid the bullets. Jimmy's engine roared as the car launched under the SRT 2's vehicle and slammed into the tire. Jimmy shot forward, leaving both SRT teams stopped in the highway's center, blocking traffic.

"Are both cars out of the chase, or just one?" Luke yelled at Sebastian, who vanished again. He heard Wil speaking again.

"Jimmy took one of the SRT teams out of the fight! He shot two of our agents. You need to get off the highway, park your car, and walk off," Wil said.

"I'll get off on Franconia Road, exit 169," he said.

"What are you doing? Go to a shopping plaza and drop the car." Wil sounded insistent.

In his rearview mirror, he saw a smoky red blob approaching him. "It's too late. Jimmy caught up with me. I can see a lake in the distance, but I'm unsure how to get there. Let SRT know he got off Franconia and is following me." He could hear Wil speaking on the radio. "Where's the helicopter... I'm on Backlick, Wil. There are some stores here, but he's right behind me." His voice cracked, and his desperation seeped through. He was not willing to risk his or others' lives like Jimmy.

"What's that, Luke?"

"Right turn on Backlick. He's catching up. I think his car is on fire. I see smoke."

"No sense parking the car now. I don't know the area, kiddo. I'm not sure where to direct you."

He made a left-hand turn on Highland St and then a right on Accotink Park Road. The thought of failure began to creep into him. He felt that Jimmy had already won. "I'm headed to Accotink Park. It's a lake, Wil. Can you let the SRT guys know?" The speed limit sign says 25 MPH, but Luke accelerated to 100 quickly and did not see the smoke from Jimmy's *Firebird*. He pushed down on the brake pedal when he saw the sign coming up ahead on his left, made a quick turn to the left, and then moved to the right. He arrived at the park and stopped in a roundabout.

"Why did you come this way, Luke? The only way out is where you came from." Sebastian seemed defeated.

"It's okay. I think I lost him for now with that turn into the park trail." He pulled in behind a building, hoping the vehicle was concealed. He waited for a few minutes, although it felt like eons. "I can see smoke from his car. He's on his way to the roundabout. I will pull past him and back the way we came when he passes." He saw the smoke heading away and placed the car in reverse to leave his concealment. He slammed the gas pedal and accelerated past Jimmy. He heard a gunshot, and his rear window shattered. A hole appeared in the passenger seat, and another was on the door near Sebastian. He jerked the wheel, causing the phone to fly from his grasp to the floorboard on the passenger side.

Sebastian looked at him and laughed. "He missed."

He was distracted and drove down a walking trail, hitting his brakes, which caused the vehicle to skid. He almost hit a retaining wall that was part of the reservoir. He turned left and went underneath a bridge. With all its lights flashing, he saw the SRT vehicle flying toward Jimmy and Luke head-on and racing toward him head-on. Jimmy was right behind Luke when the SRT vehicle passed. Jimmy shot at the agent's car, and the agents returned fire with a submachine gun on full auto into his windshield.

"Tell them to stop shooting. Joyce and the baby could be in the car!" Luke yelled, hoping Wil or somebody else would hear him.

Luke turned right, back into the parking lot, and toward the roundabout. He passed the agent's SUV and hoped that Jimmy would follow him. The *Firebird's* engine was screaming as it passed the agents. The SRT agent hanging out of the passenger side window shot his rifle nonstop at Jimmy's oncoming car. The car flew straight toward a hill leading to a berm of the reservoir. The *Firebird* launched into the air, soaring skyward like a phoenix. The vehicle's momentum slowed down, and the car dropped like a lead weight into the water.

He jumped out of his car and tried to climb up the hill. The Customs helicopter descended from its surveillance altitude and hovered over the reservoir. It was challenging, but he refused to give up and arrived at the top of the crest. The water forty feet or more into the reservoir was churning and bubbling angrily in the bright sun from the downdraft of the helicopter blades and the car that plunged into the water. The helicopter's shadow formed the shape of a cross in the water. He waited, but nobody breached the surface.

"I hope this sacred water will wash away Jimmy's sins." Sebastian pointed at the shadow of the cross in the water.

"Luke, get down from there. He has a gun!" One of the SRT agents yelled at him.

"He's going to drown. I need to try and save him!" He removed the shoes from his feet in reverence to the shadow of the cross and the possibility of being on sacred ground.

"Look at the size of the hill you're on. This is a deep part of the reservoir. Get down from there now." The same SRT agent yelled.

He looked down at his muddy socks, then at the churning water. *I need to find my nephew*, he thought. He made the sign of the cross, looking directly into the bright, all-consuming sun without blinking. It gave him power.

He motioned as if to jump into the water, but Sebastian blocked his path. "Your nephew is not in the car. I will search and find them." Sebastian vanished again.

Luke lowered his head and waited several minutes, but Jimmy did not surface. "I'm sorry it ended this way, Jimmy, but you let evil consume you. You were a worthy adversary." He took his socks off one at a time as he put his shoes back on. He walked down the hill confidently. The four agents stared at him with their hands blocking the sun from their eyes. The divine, glorious sun blocked their view of him walking bravely down the steep embankment. "Are you all okay?"

"Yes, one agent took a shot to his arm and another to the vest. Get out of here and meet up with Wil. We'll wait for police and fire," one masked agent said.

"Thanks for your help," he said, hoping to find out who had saved him.

"Go. I want you out of here before the uniforms arrive."

Luke walked away and returned to his vehicle. Jimmy died horribly, but in the end, he was a horrible person. His only concern now was finding Joyce and his nephew, Tristan. If they were dead, Jimmy would have won in the end.

CHAPTER THIRTY-FIVE
The Board

Luke made it to the warehouse. It was closer to the courthouse than he remembered. Tristan consumed his thoughts. He knew that he needed to wait for Sebastian, and then he would return to speak with his mother at the hospital. He approached the courthouse, aiming to park in the nearby parking structure, but it was blocked off. He parked near an ambulance in front of a building. He assessed the damage to the car and shook his head in disbelief. His recent experience had been something out of a crime novel.

A police officer approached him. "Can I help you, young man? Something is happening here, and the feds want it cleared out."

"Yes, I'm looking for Wil Rivera with Customs."

"Your name?"

"Luke Sanz."

"Yes, they're waiting for you. Follow me, please."

He took a deep breath, realizing it may be over. He followed the officer to the entrance of the garage and saw a line of white vans. Beyond the vans were many cages: one with adult men, another with adult women, and yet another with what he could tell were students from his high school. Dozens of agents were moving from different stations, processing their arrests. It was trippy to see the room he helped set up full of law enforcement officers. It seemed productive.

The officer walked him to the back area, where he could see some agents arguing about something. "Agent Rivera, here is Luke Sanz."

"Thanks, officer." Wil walked over to him. "Before you say anything, your mother is at the hospital, and she is stable. How about you? I heard your car took some hits."

"Jimmy shot out my rear window and my passenger side door. Do you know if he's alive?"

"Jimmy's car is submerged in water. They need to set up a diving team. From what I hear, they shot the car at least thirty times."

"Why did they shoot so much, Wil? My nephew, and Joyce, could have been in the car."

"They didn't know. They took some hits and did what they were trained to do. Come over here and look at the board," Wil said, walking toward a large whiteboard.

It appeared as a scoreboard with all the above agencies, arrests, and seizures. At this time, Luke was not interested in the statistics of the whole event and ignored the board altogether. "Where's Terry?"

"She took a hit to the midsection and is at the hospital. Looks like broken ribs."

Luke rubbed his chest sympathetically where last year he broke a rib. He stared at the board again, found Jimmy's name and pictures, and saw that his image was crossed out in red. Jimmy was being chalked up as dead, and they were tallying all the wins up here. All the other targets appeared to be captured. The seizures seemed to be countless.

"Wait a second." Wil grabbed his phone, searched for a number, and made a call. A group of three Customs SRT agents wearing balaclavas walked into the area.

"Did you get hit with any shrapnel, Luke?" one of the agents asked.

"No, it took out my car windows and passenger side door ... how about Jimmy? Is he alive?"

"He could not have lived through that. We stayed there long enough, still waiting for something to surface. We may know more later this afternoon or evening."

"It's sad, the way he went down. It did not have to be that way."

"It was his choice, Luke ... why are you looking at me like that? Not sure who I am?"

"Take off your balaclava," Wil said before hanging up the phone.

Johnson took off his balaclava. "Remember me now?"

"Yes, the recruiter at the career center. Are you in the Army or Customs?"

"Both. I'm a month away from retiring from the Army — great job on this. Come back next week. I have an intelligence school for you."

"Thanks, Master Sergeant, I appreciate that."

"It's agent today ... you earned it kid, so have more of a ballsy attitude. Agents tend to be alpha male gorillas," Johnson said while pounding his chest.

"Not this one, Johnson. He's a humble kid with his head on straight," Wil said.

"We will work on your swagger, Luke. Not today. I have four guys in the hospital, three of them because of your friend, Jimmy." Johnson said, walking away, motioning for the other team members to follow.

"I think many of us will rest easier once they find his body," he said truthfully.

"You're getting there, Luke. Jimmy needed a dirt nap," Johnson said.

"I did not mean it that way ... he was an ass, of course, but he had a literal monkey on his back and a horrible father." He may never be able to speak that way about another person, even

Jimmy Cladhaire.

"Don't worry about him. Johnson is a firm believer in developing a thick skin using humor." The phone rang again, and Jimmy picked it up quickly.

The SRT team guys started walking away. "Luke, come see me next week, and we'll get you in uniform lickety-split."

Luke bowed his head and shook it up and down, knowing that he wanted to take up the sergeant on his offer, but it was so far from his mind that it may be outside of his plans.

"Luke, your mother told me Jimmy was mouthing something about Birdy. Do you know where she lives?" Wil asked.

"I do," Luke responded, ready to leave.

"Go and call me and let me know if they are there. I'll let Jorge know so he can check over there." Wil grabbed his phone and started making more calls.

Luke walked through the processing area and saw a group of men. One was his principal, Matias Devry, and another was Detective Juan Bello. Matias met eyes with Luke and motioned for him to come over with his handcuffed hands.

"Yes, Mr. Devry," he said respectfully.

"Are you an undercover agent?" Matias asked in a low tone.

"No, Mr. Devry. I'm one of your students. You served me up to a wolf. This student happens to be a sheepdog and not another sheep."

"I never meant for it to go this far. I'm sorry for what I did and will take the consequences," Matias said honestly.

"Matias don't bow down to this little shit. He's a rat and taking you for a fool." Juan said, speaking out of his ass.

"You're the rat, Juan. I know you and Jimmy tried to have me killed in the jail. Have fun getting gang raped in prison. I can only imagine you have some friends waiting for you." He saw Vice-Principal Shipmen hiding behind the men. He decided not to tell the man what he thought.

The Shop

Luke had been heading west for the past forty minutes. Sebastian appeared in his passenger seat.

"Luke, it's not good news," Sebastian said.

"Just tell me, I'm headed to Birdy's house to see if they are there."

"They are not. They were. Jimmy went to her house after hurting your mother. He took Birdy and Benji."

"Where are they? Sebastian, what happened?" Luke did not realize it, but he had been driving over one hundred miles an hour.

"They are at Benji's shop. I cannot enter, though. Something is warding me off."

Luke recalled the vision early when he touched his mother. The demon was on Jimmy's shoulder. It must have kept Sebastian from entering. "It's the demon I saw on the LT. It was attached to Jimmy and now must be in that shop."

"What will you do?"

"I need to call for help. I need Robert and Kamila. They are the only ones that can help now." He looked at his watch and the intersection. He was fifteen minutes away from Benji's house. He called both Kamila and Robert and asked them to meet him at the shop. He asked Robert to be prepared to complete another exorcism.

He arrived at the shop and parked near Kamila and Robert's cars. Robert was dressed for the battle ahead, stole included.

Luke walked up to Kamila.

"How's Mom?"

"She's recovering, Luke. It will be a while before she can eat well again."

"I went to see your mother in the hospital and prayed over her, Luke. She's a strong woman ... one other thing, though, she reminded me to tell you that you must do as she says. Do you know what she wants?"

"I think so, Father," Luke said.

"I prayed around the building and sprayed blessed salt on the doorways and windows."

Luke motioned to Sebastian. "Anything yet?"

"Yes, they are inside. They are safe, but there's still something blocking me from entering. We must be cautious."

Luke nodded his head in affirmation. He motioned for them all to follow him. He knocked on the shop's front door, which was not open. He tried the door now, which was unlocked, but when he pushed it, it did not give in. *I know, the side door Benji showed me*, he thought. He walked to the shop garage doors and then off to the side, where there was another door. Robert had already salted the doorway. It was locked, but he knew there was a key inside a hubcap hooked to the wall. He retrieved the key and unlocked the door. He entered the shop with Robert swinging his thurible. He expected the whole place to stink of grave dirt or feel dark like his house did the year before. He checked the garage and waiting room and heard something. "Did you all hear the baby?"

Kamila and Robert both shook their heads.

"Joyce, Benji, it's Luke. Where are you?" he called out. The response was a screaming baby. He ran into the office. Tristan was in his carrier, and aside from the screams and a pooped diaper, he looked fine. Benji and Birdy were tied together with gags in their mouths. He pulled the gag from his friend's mouth. Benji's face was swollen and bloody.

"Where is that freaking, Jimmy?" Benji asked.

"He's dead. He crashed and drowned ... where's Joyce?"

"Check behind the desk." He took Benji's bindings off. "Father, can you check, please?

Birdy started crying as Benji took off her gag and untied her.

"Luke, come here," Robert said.

Luke walked over to Joyce. The sight before him forced the air from his lungs. She lay face down with her hands bound behind her back. The back of her shirt was full of blood and obvious puncture holes were visible. He leaned over and touched her back … *I stood over Jimmy as he sat beside Joyce.*

"Jimmy, please don't kill me."

"Shut up… stop talking. Let me think, shut up. I'm not going to kill her. Shut up." Jimmy took the knife in his hand and stabbed Joyce. Jimmy did not appear to thrust the knife into Joyce with much force. "Stop talking already. I'll do it again." Jimmy stabbed Joyce one more time and screamed. He stood up and threw the knife. Shut up … leave me alone. Stop, I did it. I'm going to kill Luke now. Shut up." Jimmy left the room … Joyce screamed from his touch.

He lifted her and brought her face to him. "Joyce, it's me. It's Luke."

The look of fear on her face drained from her. She started sobbing. "The … the baby … where's my baby?"

"He's fine. I'll take you to him." Luke lifted her and sat her down next to the baby.

She started squirming violently. "Untie me."

Luke removed her bindings, and she grabbed for Tristan. He reached for the phone he thought was in his pocket, but it was gone.

"Kamila, can you call Wil?"

"I left my phone in the car. I can go get it."

Luke motioned for her to stay. "I'll go. Please calm them down, Father."

"Go ahead, Luke. I'll help," Robert said, kneeling next to Joyce and checking the wounds on her back.

Luke headed toward the front door and saw that all the furniture was stacked in front of the door and could not be opened. He entered the garage and hit the button to open the first bay. He left the garage to grab his phone and get help.

"Luke, watch out!" Sebastian yelled loudly.

He saw motion coming in from his right side before a man tackled him at his thigh, causing him to flip in the air and fall on the asphalt on the side of his head. His thigh was on fire; the pain was so intense that his body wanted to shut down. Everything was going dark; he was passing out. He felt at peace and was gladly falling into a slumber. Something slammed against his chest, and a punch to his face woke him.

"Get off him now, asshole," Kamila screamed while hitting the man with her handbag.

He laughed at the sight of his Godmother as she struck the man with a purse until he realized it was the Bully Cladhair, whose face was a gory mess.

Jimmy tossed Kamila inside the garage. She tripped over a floor jack and landed oddly on the ground. She fell to the ground with an unnaturally bent arm and stayed still.

Luke stood up and grabbed onto Jimmy. He intended to control Jimmy while he regained his senses, but Jimmy turned and kicked roughly at his injured thigh. He fell to the ground and screamed in pain while holding onto his thigh. This reminded him of the pain of being thrown into a wall last year during his fight with Avandeil.

"You're such a meddling bastard who will never learn." Jimmy was missing a left eye, and everything else on his face was a purple mangled mess. A hole in the side of his temple was bubbling a frothy white substance. The vulture demon on his shoulders was screaming at Luke and trying to grab him.

"What happened to you, Jimmy?"

"Your friends shot my eye out." Jimmy showed him where the bullet exited his temple. A gory mess remained where his eye once was. "I have not looked at a mirror yet. How does it look?"

"Like you should be in a hospital or buried in a grave."

Sebastian, a sedulous spirit, tried to strike Jimmy with his halberd, but he was unsuccessful, so he dropped the halberd and grabbed Luke's shoulders. "Get up, Luke. Don't let this spawn of the devil best you."

He rose, a different person. He didn't feel empathy for Jimmy; he felt fury. "It figures a headshot didn't kill somebody with no brains!"

"You are such a pussy, Sasquatch. Stand still so I can finish you off once and for all."

Jimmy charged at him and began to throw punches. Luke blocked each attempt before kicking Jimmy in the solar plexus. As Jimmy doubled over, he kneed the Bully on the bridge of his nose and then kicked him in the chest. "That was the old me, Jimmy, and you deserve the new me." He grabbed one of Jimmy's hands, placed a foot on his neck, and began pushing and pulling. The sound of broken bones resonated in the air.

Father Robert sprayed holy water on Jimmy and the vulture, who began to screech loudly. Then he grabbed a purple bag from his jacket and poured the contents over the demon's carcass, causing it to burn like a phosphorous grenade. "Oh God, Creator and Savior of all flesh, who in mercy has rescued your beloved servant Jimmy, safeguard him by your providence and keep him in the freedom your Son has given him. Grant O Lord, the spirit of iniquity may no longer have power over him."

Luke released Jimmy's hands, grabbed the abomination, pulled it off of Jimmy, and tossed the burning mess onto the garage's concrete floor. Jimmy fell to the floor like he was made of jelly with all his broken bones. Luke shook his head to Father Robert, then ran to the car, grabbed his phone, and called the police. He came back, and the slimy decomposing vulture formed into the shape of the LT. It was trying to grab at Father Robert.

"Out, get out and away from him, by Your command." Father D materialized beside Luke.

The demon vanished into a black mist that dissipated into the ground.

Luke fell to his knees and looked up at the spirit of his mentor. "Thanks, Father. I was kinda getting a little tired."

"Don't be too tired. You're only getting started." Father D winked at him and dissipated into the ether.

He walked to the garage and checked on Kamila. Her arm was broken. He looked at Jimmy, whose breathing was getting more shallow.

"Serves him right. He broke my freaking arm. I've never had a broken anything before," Kamila said.

"Sasquatch, come here," Jimmy said.

Luke peered down at Jimmy who was trying to reach out to him with a broken bloody hand. He shook his head back and forth at the broken man.

"Luke, grab my hand. Please, Luke."

Luke knelt beside Jimmy and grabbed his hand … *I was on the bridge waiting for the two men to approach me. They were sent by my father to kill me so he would collect the life insurance policy he had made on me. I sensed that the second man was going to hold me down so the first man stabbed me. They wanted to throw me over the bridge so that I would drown* … he let go of Jimmy's hand. He sensed that Jimmy never hated him per se but was enviousness of what he had. He knew at that moment that the demon attached to the LT drove Jimmy to violence. "What did you do to me Jimmy?" he asked, because he felt different.

"I gave you what was good inside of me. It's a better gift in your hands than it ever was in mine." Jimmy coughed up blood through his mouth and whatever healing he had with his eye erupted with fluid as well. Jimmy slumped over, unconscious or worse.

"Father, please pray for him," Luke said. He stood up and walked toward Benji who sat with Birdy against a wall of his shop. He sensed that Benji and Birdy felt safer as he approached. *I think Jimmy was a type of empath,* he thought.

"I will administer last rites, Luke," Robert said, standing before the mangled Jimmy.

Luke did not think that Jimmy would die. The man was a tyrant, but he was never a weakling. He thought he would live, but he would never be the same.

Jimmy's face was covered in blood, and pieces of bone from his clavicles were protruding through his skin. He was never terrified of the Bully Cladhair. He was worried that the violent man inside of him would be released, uncontrolled. That didn't happen. At least not entirely. He was a violent man, but he was in control. The shy, peaceful boy was gone, and left behind was a man whose courage was the size of where it came from, the sky above.

Jimmy had to be stopped, and he was, but the shadow of the old Luke remained enough to bring clarity. Jimmy wanted him dead and kidnapped Joyce, Tristan and then Birdy and Benji. Maybe Jimmy was meant to die for all that he had done, but sparing his life was not altruistic. It was because Jimmy was not meant to be the first life he took. It was as simple as that.

The Chariot

Luke sat on a metal folding chair in the middle of the football field. He stared directly at a stage where all the graduating seniors were taking their turn to grab their graduation certificate from Mr. Conway. Luke's name was called, and he stood up.

Cheers rang out from the sitting graduates as he walked down the aisle of empty chairs from the other graduating peers. The newly minted permanent Principal Conway handed him his certificate. They shook hands ... *I stood in the hallway of the LC staring at a display case of items from the past. The janitor opened the case for me, and I reached for the Lansburg Center High School identification card of Principal J. Lucious Conway. The year of the ID was 2010. A nearby plaque said, in loving memory of our longest serving principal — 1992 until 2010. I made the sign of the cross and put the identification card back.*

"Thanks, Mr. Wilson."

"Sure thing, Agent Sanz."

The janitor locked up the display case and left. I noticed a young man standing nearby waiting and listening. He had seen me identify myself to Mr. Wilson by showing my badge and credentials. He appeared interested in what I was doing. I moved down the lengthy display case and found a section with older memorabilia. A small index card said, Class of 1992. Nearby was a group photo of my music class that was taken before we graduated. A nameplate read, Grammy Winner, Romey Waters Music Theory and Practice Class. Next to that photo was another of me on a scissor lift jacked high into the air playing my guitar during our recital. The nameplate read, The Second Savior of Lansburg.

"Who is that guy dressed up in that costume?" the interested boy asked.

I looked at the kid and was going to tell him something sarcastic. "It's me at eighteen when I had no idea where life would take me."

"What's your name?"

"Luke Sanz."

"Like Daniel Sanz, the first basemen."

"Yes, I'm his younger brother. Have you heard of Daniel before?"

"He plays for the Yankees, now." The boy pointed to the shelf above my picture. A school photo of Daniel at first base.

Seeing my brother so young brought a tear to my eye. "What's your name, kid?"

"William. Will Buchanan. I'm running for class president," Will said and offered me his hand. I reached for it ... he returned to 1992 and the shock of seeing Mr. Conway in front of him caused him to embrace his teacher, and friend. "Thanks, Mr. Conway. I'll always rely on what I have learned from you."

"Go out there and make your mark on this world."

Luke walked off the stage and noticed that everyone was standing and looking toward him silently. Alyssa was waiting for him below the steps, and they embraced. Benji stood next to Birdy. Linette and Sandy were there as well. "Why is everyone standing and staring at us?"

Alyssa pulled him away from the field toward the exit. "They are just showing their appreciation for getting rid of the oppressors in their lives. Come with me."

He walked down the field past the seniors, who began clapping slowly. They walked down the track toward the exit gate. Numerous students stood by the exit. Stanley and Ron Johnson were the most noticeable because of their height. The front of the crowd was comprised of the Bully Cladhair victims. He noticed David Villa was standing with his brother Junior. They both approached him.

"Luke, thanks for keeping that animal off my back," David said.

Luke bowed his head to his brother's friend. "Any time, David.

Junior walked up to Luke and gave him a firm hug ... *I stood in a hospital room. My grandfather, Julio, lay on the bed. A man stood next to my grandfather who looked old and fragile. I walked toward the opposite side and saw that it was my brother Junior who looked much older. Like forties old!*

"Junior, your brothers are all going to receive something when I die, but I'm leaving you, my business."

"I'll sell it Grandpa and divide it amongst the family."

"No," my grandfather used all his strength to prop himself up. "I left everyone something, but you will continue where I finished." My grandfather collapsed back into the bed looking even weaker.

Junior began to cry and sob. "All I ever wanted from you was your love, and you taught me how to live. I don't need anything ..."

My grandfather waved off Junior. "I live through you ... tell your brother, Daniel that he must be the man his father raised." My grandfather closed his eyes, and his breath became faint.

"Luke, do you want me to tell Luke anything?"

My grandfather's breathing became shallow, and he did not reopen his eyes again. "Stop it ... prevent the calamity." With that my grandfather took his last breath ... Luke released from his brother's embrace and looked intently at him.

Tim "Weirdo" Hall approached them and tapped Luke's shoulder ... *Tim sat in a college class with a pen in his mouth. He had short hair and stared intently at a chalkboard with all sorts of equations and problems* … Luke took a step back, trying to run from the visions and the physical contact. "Thanks for what you did, Luke. That took balls."

"Thanks, Tim. Good luck with college," Luke said and walked toward the countless other underclassmen. Possibly hundreds of the students stood in the path leading to the underclassmen parking lot.

Stan approached him. "Well done, Luke. Thanks for delivering us from that tyrant."

"You're welcome, Stan." Luke walked toward the path and hundreds of underclassmen parted to either side to allow him entry. They grabbed or tapped his shoulder as he passed them. Numerous visions built within his mind causing him to get vertigo. Everything was distorted as if the atmosphere was on fire. A cacophony of voices thanking Luke added to the overload of sensory information. "This is surreal, Benji. Who arranged this?"

Benji leaned into Luke. "Stan, but Alyssa and Mr. Conway did the heavy lifting." It was so loud Benji had to yell.

He looked down the path to the parking lot and saw Divine Justice waiting for him. He heard thunderous yells and the sound of a horse stampede. He turned around and saw a golden chariot rushing toward him in between the line of students parted on the path to where his *Grand National* waited for him. The vulture demon rode atop the chariot. He stood his ground when he sensed that the chariot rider was not a threat. As the it approached the students walked into the path and the chariot rider vanished.

Luke turned and continued his walk toward his car. He grabbed Alyssa's hand firmly and pulled her toward the car. He opened the passenger door and let her take a seat. She brought her bare leg into the car and smiled. *Do all girls want you to notice their legs?* He smiled back.

Benji walked up to him and handed him a set of keys. "Your

chariot awaits … Tom forgot to give you the second set of keys."

"Thanks, Benji. Let them know this all meant a lot to me."

Benji gave him a hug and patted his back.

Luke saw a vision, but it would have to wait for another time.

"When do you leave for basic?" Benji asked.

"Next week, buddy."

"What's the rush, Luke? Take some time off, let's go hang out in Australia or something."

"I have a schedule to keep, Benji. I have somewhere to be in September, next year." Luke took a step back and saw that the underclassmen were staring at the two of them speaking.

"Where?"

"Somewhere sandy, dusty, and not at all friendly." Luke jumped into the car driver's seat and leaned toward Alyssa trying to steal a kiss.

"I almost forgot. I wanted to take a picture," Benji said, grabbing a disposable camera from his pocket. He leaned into the car as Luke and Alyssa lips separated, as their friend took the photograph without allowing them to pose. A cherished image for decades to come by the Sanz clan. Luke's dance with the Bully had to happen. It was his destiny and infused in him a power he would use for good.

Epilogue

I ran down a dirt road, blowing dust made it difficult to see. I had a man on my shoulders but tried to shake it from my thoughts. Each subsequent breath built onto the layer of dust caked in my mouth and throat. Other soldiers ran near me. We all wore desert camouflage battle dress uniforms, body armor, and helmets. We fired our rifles as we moved. Numerous run-down buildings surrounded us. The sounds of gunshots and the smell of burning tires added to the filthy air. I was accustomed to running, but the dust and smoke made breathing almost impossible and caused me to wretch uncontrollably. Yet I kept running. The man over my shoulder had been quiet for some time. The bullet, or shrapnel, I took to my left shoulder and chest added to the burden of carrying the man. I shot several people after joining the other soldiers running to safety. I was bothered by the lives I had taken, but that would have to wait until another day.

"We're coming up on the convoy, Rangers! Dig deep and push," yelled one of the sergeants.

I continued my run alongside the bloodied soldiers and arrived at the convoy moments later. I was breathless. I placed the man on my back inside an armored transport before leaning against the vehicle.

"What the hell are you doing out here? You're Intel, son, get into the transport, or I will leave your ass behind!"

I tried to respond but couldn't catch my breath. "I ... I ... I'm a Ranger," he screamed before adding, *"Sir ..."* Everything blacked out ... he woke with a start.

"Why do you keep dreaming of that same day? It's over. You survived." Sebastian would seem unusual to onlookers. The soldier sat in my vehicle's passenger seat, comfortably in his armor.

"Not my choice, Sebastian. It pops up whenever it wants to,"

Luke responded.

"Get ready. Your team is heading to the hit."

Even though it was almost 0600 hours, it was not dark; everything was lightly illuminated by the soon-to-rise sun. The sound of crickets, other critters, and the light drone of commuter traffic from the Interstate 19 Freeway probably put him to sleep. Now, there was the sound of many footfalls of agents as they stepped on gravel with purpose.

The agents all wore dark blue, including their body armor. They lined up silently near the entrance of the residence. He grabbed his breaching tools, placed a sledgehammer on his back, and held onto his favorite battering ram, prepared for the knock and announcement from his team leader. Whoever was in the house would soon discover the feeling of being startled during their sleep. Hopefully, he had an early day and could return to Alyssa before she left the house. One never knew when battling the evil that lurked on Earth under His sky.

Author's Note

In the first draft of Under the Sky, Book 1 of the Luke Sanz series, the Avandeil plot was intertwined with the Jimmy Cladhaire subplot. My editors from the Story Ninja, Randy Surles and Laura Graves pointed out that I should pick one plot and stick to that and then they advised me to remove the music subplot altogether. My first draft, after cutting out the Bully Cladhair plot, included removing all mention of Luke's playing guitar. My wife was angry and told me that now Luke was missing that part of himself that meant something to him. His music. I added it back.

I wanted Luke to play at the recital, because he wanted one more moment as a teenager in high school. After almost dying, I thought that if Jimmy prevailed, Luke would have only the vanishing of Avandeil as an accomplishment toward his true calling.

The *Getting Rid of the Trash* and *Recital* scene occur within minutes of one another. I tried to wrap into it the brokenness of the school that had been perpetrated by Jimmy and the adults that should have been protecting the students from the influence of the Cladhaires that were being led by the whims of a demon. I modeled the book itself as a version of the story of Exodus where God's hand was used to lead his people (students) out of enslavement of the overseers (corrupted adults).

Luke will be back in 2025 in Cardinal Down where the Vatican will task him to save a kidnapped priest in Somalia on October 3, 1993.

About the Author

Sig. Alexander is a retired law enforcement officer who lives in the Matanuska Valley of Alaska. He spends his mornings and evening placing his thoughts on Scrivener. Sig has ten Luke Sanz novels planned leading to the calamity Luke Sanz is meant to stop with the help of his guardian, Sebastian.

Instagram: www.instagram.com/Sig. Alexander/

https://sigalexander-lansburg.com/ - Join Sig. Alexander's mailing list to receive a signature plate.

https://www.amazon.com/author/sig.alexander.lansburg

https://www.kirkusreviews.com/author/sig-alexander-1//

Upcoming Books:

Anchorage Box Racer – Early 2025
Cardinal Down, A Luke Sanz Novel: Book 3 – Late 2025

www.ingramcontent.com/pod-product-compliance
Lightning Source LLC
Chambersburg PA
CBHW020914200626
46814CB00001BA/328